Charles Hallé, Marie Hallé

Life and Letters of Sir Charles Hallé

Being an Autobiography (1819-1860) with Correspondence and Diaries

Charles Hallé, Marie Hallé

Life and Letters of Sir Charles Hallé
Being an Autobiography (1819-1860) with Correspondence and Diaries

ISBN/EAN: 9783744716543

Printed in Europe, USA, Canada, Australia, Japan

Cover: Foto ©Raphael Reischuk / pixelio.de

More available books at **www.hansebooks.com**

LIFE AND LETTERS

OF

SIR CHARLES HALLÉ

BEING AN AUTOBIOGRAPHY (1819-1860) WITH
CORRESPONDENCE AND DIARIES

EDITED BY

HIS SON, C. E. HALLÉ

AND

HIS DAUGHTER, MARIE HALLÉ

WITH TWO PORTRAITS

LONDON
SMITH, ELDER, & CO., 15 WATERLOO PLACE
1896

NOTE

In the task of preparing this autobiography of my Father for publication, and in the selection, arrangement, and revision of the letters and diaries which form the remainder of the volume, my Sister and I are greatly indebted to the valuable and sympathetic assistance of Mr. CHARLES L. GRAVES.

C. E. HALLÉ.

CONTENTS

ILLUSTRATIONS

LIFE AND LETTERS

OF

SIR CHARLES HALLÉ

———+———

CHAPTER I

1819 1838

I WAS born on April 11, 1819, at the moment
when the church bells began to ring in Easter Morn,
as my dear mother often told me in after years.
Curiously enough, Easter Sunday fell every eleven

B

years on April 11 until I was fifty-five years old, but will not do so again during my lifetime. Hagen, in Westphalia, where I saw the light, was then a little town with from 4,000 to 5,000 inhabitants. My father, Frederick Hallé, originally from Arolsen, in the principality of Waldeck, was organist of the principal church, and ' musik director,' which means that he conducted the concerts, for, although the town was so small, there were concert societies there of no little importance. My father, besides, gave innumerable lessons in singing, as well as on almost every instrument. He had a charming tenor voice, and was a first-rate performer on the piano, the organ, the violin, and the flute. His activity was not restricted to Hagen alone, for when concerts were given in neighbouring towns, such as Iserlohn, Limburg, Dortmund, Schwelm, and others, he was generally invited to conduct them; and was known far and wide as a remarkable wit, many of his clever sayings being quoted for years. He was handsome, most winning in appearance, and nothing could equal the enthusiasm with which he cultivated his art, to which I owe the love, the adoration of music which has never left me during my long life. My dear mother, Caroline Hallé, née Brenschedt, came of an old Westphalian family. She was, when I could begin to appreciate her, one of the sweetest of God's children, and continued to be beloved by all who knew her until her death at the ripe age of eighty-eight years. She also was a good musician, though not a professional one, and sang most charmingly with a sweet soprano voice. Often was I lulled to sleep, when a baby, by the duet-singing of my parents, but many years must have passed before I could understand the merit and beauty of it. I remained for upwards of eight years their only child, and feel sure that it has been given to few men or women to recollect so happy a childhood as mine was.

But this childhood had its troubles, although they were little felt by me. I have only learned in later years that my babyhood was most precarious—that I was a miserably weak child, and nobody, not even the doctor, thought I could live long. Although not actually ailing, I had to be brought up like a hot-house plant, was seldom taken into the open air, which at the period I speak of was mostly considered dangerous, and hardly ever admitted into a sick-room; and if I have outgrown that weakness, and falsified the prognostics of the doctor, I owe it probably to the tender care of a most loving mother. Through being kept constantly indoors, my life became different from that of other children; there was no romping for me in the playground or the garden, and my mother had to find occupation for me in the house. She first taught me to read when I was but three years old, and at the age of four I read as fluently as ever since. Together with the alphabet she taught me my notes, to amuse me, and as a natural consequence of the musical atmosphere in which we lived. Well do I remember a square book, bound in red morocco and containing music paper, in which she had written the notes

with their names, and which altogether bore testi-
mony to my progress, for all the little exercises
and small pieces which I had to learn were
written in this book, first by her, then by my father,
when she handed me over to him. At that time
it was most unusual to teach from a printed 'Pianoforte School'; the music master was expected in the
case of beginners to compose exercises and short
pieces during the lesson, and write them down in a
book kept for that purpose by the pupil. Such
was my book, which I treasured for forty years,
until it was lost with my other luggage on a railway
journey through Belgium. I have been told many a
time by my parent teachers that I took to music with
extraordinary eagerness, that it became my only joy,
and that my progress was remarkably rapid. It
must have been so, for the above-mentioned red book
testified that at four years of age I played a little
sonata, composed for me by my father, at one of the
subscription concerts of the 'Concordia' Society.

About that time my constitution had become a
little stronger, and my parents had hopes that I
might live a few years longer. I was, therefore, less
confined to the house, and now and then taken to a
concert, which explains my appearance there as a
most precocious soloist. To be taken to a concert,
to listen to a symphony or an overture, was at that
early age my greatest joy, and I may say that I grew
up in music, and thought and dreamt of nothing else.
And well was the life in Hagen calculated to foster
this taste, for music seemed to be its chief occupation,

just as it was in all the surrounding small towns with which I became acquainted in my boyhood. The number of good amateurs on various instruments was great; every house resounded with music; about ten subscription concerts were given every winter by the 'Concordia' Society, the orchestra of which consisted of professionals and amateurs, about forty in number, and was conducted by my father. There was also a 'Gesang-Verein,' which met once a week the whole year through, with the exception of two summer months, and of which my father had also the direction. With the help of this society a few concerts were given in the summer for the performance of some oratorios, a kind of small festival to which the public flocked from all the neighbouring towns. To these societies I owe my earliest acquaintance with most of the works of the greatest composers; for my progress upon the piano had been so rapid that when I was still a child my father made me accompany at the meetings of the 'Gesang-Verein' instead of doing it himself. Thus I became thoroughly familiar with 'The Creation,' 'The Seasons,' 'The Mount of Olives,' some of Handel's and of Spohr's oratorios, with numerous other works, at an age when they generally are but names to other children. My functions at the subscription concerts were of a different nature. I had taught myself the violin up to a certain degree, in the hope of being enrolled as an amateur second violin, but it so happened that the gentleman who played the kettle-drums left the town, and I, although

seven years old, was considered so good a time-
keeper that my father promoted me to that important
and dangerous post. And for eight years did I hold
it, though not altogether to my credit; for although
I found no difficulty in coming in at the right time,
perhaps on the third beat after fifty-seven bars' rest,
I could never accomplish a satisfactory roll, hard as
I laboured at it. The kettle-drum is not exactly an
instrument suited to a drawing-room, so I could get
no practice, and I remember even now how I envied
and admired the drummers of any military band that
passed through our town, recognising them by far
my superiors.

My efforts at these concerts were, however, not
confined to the drums. Having once played a little
solo on the piano at the age of four, my kind friends,
—and I believe the whole town consisted of them—
wanted to judge every year of my progress, and I
had, therefore, to play at least once every season
gradually more and more important pieces. One of
these appearances has left a lasting impression upon
my mind. I was then eight years old, and played
the variations by Ferdinand Ries on 'Am Rhein, am
Rhein, da wachsen uns're Reben,' a stock piece at
that time of a very brilliant character. Before the
end of the piece, which I did not play from memory,
I had to stop and tell my father that I could not see
any more; there was a veil before my eyes. Our
own doctor, who was one of the audience, came at
once to look at me, and pronounced that I had the
measles, a malady much dreaded at that time. So,

instead of finishing the variations, I was carefully
wrapped up, and carried home in my father's arms.
I was long ill and confined to a room, the temperature
of which was kept at summer heat, the fire never
being allowed to go out. I was watched every night
alternately by my father and my mother, and it so
happened that one night when it was my father's
turn, he had been overcome with fatigue and fallen
asleep, and lo! when he awoke, the fire had burnt
out. In his anxiety to light it again, there being no
real firewood at hand, and the servant sleeping in
another storey, he broke up his beloved flute, a yellow
one, I remember—upon which I had heard him play
many a solo by Tulou and other great flautists. The
fire was relit, and he never regretted, or even alluded
to, the sacrifice which his paternal love had induced
him to make; but I cried bitterly over it when it
came to my knowledge.

In course of time I was cured of the measles, but
they left a very serious inflammation of the eyes, in
consequence of which I was shut up for weeks in a dark
room. There was a piano in it, and as soon as I felt
strong enough I began to practise all my pieces from
memory in the dark, having to feel for the keyboard,
for there was not the slightest glimmer of light. I
still remember how amused I was with certain variations by Abbé Gelinck (a very popular composer
then, but now totally forgotten), in which there were
many rapid crossings of the hands, and how delighted
I was when at last I could judge of the distances so
as to hit the right notes. Illness forced me to try

this experiment, but I should recommend it to many young players in good health, for it certainly improves the knowledge of the keyboard. After this temporary but severe illness music became again the all-absorbing interest of my young life, and by accident I gave evidence of having a good ear. Returning one day from a visit to a great-uncle who lived in the same town, and touching our piano, I said to my father that the pitch of my uncle's piano was a quarter of a tone lower than that of ours, and verification proved me to be correct, to the evident satisfaction of my parents. At the same time it became an amusement to them and to their friends to put me in a corner of the room, strike several notes together, sometimes the most incongruous and discordant ones, and make me name them, from the lowest upwards, which I invariably accomplished. This faculty has proved to have one drawback—viz. that the pitch of that period, a good half-tone lower than the present one, has remained so impressed on my brain, that when I now hear a piece of music for the first time, it seems to me in a higher key than it really is written in ; I hear it in C when it is in B, and have to translate it, so to say. My friend Joachim shares this peculiarity with me, and it is now and then very perplexing.

At that time, when I was eight years old, school life had necessarily begun for me—for though far from robust, I was then in perfect health—and continued till the year 1835, when I had worked myself up to the second place in the highest class. But all my free hours were devoted to music, sometimes even those that ought not to have been free. The weekly meetings of the 'Gesang-Verein' made me familiar with all the best choral works; the practice for the subscription concerts, with orchestral works, while my father had many quartet parties at our house, when I was allowed to turn the leaves, and made my first acquaintance with Haydn's quartets. Then my father often played with me pianoforte duets, the sonatas of Mozart, and arrangements of the symphonies by the great masters; also duets for piano and violin, as he was an excellent violinist, and my love for Mozart and Beethoven's violin sonatas dates from that early time. We also played trios with a friend of our family, Herr Elbers, a wealthy iron-merchant, a remarkable bass singer and good violoncellist, and how I enjoyed Beethoven's wonderful trio in B flat I cannot find words to express, nor can I describe the enthusiasm with which my father exclaimed: 'The whole of Beethoven is to be found in the Scherzo!' I must have played this trio before the year 1827, although I was only seven years old, for when I heard of Beethoven's death it seemed to me as if a god had departed, and I shed bitter tears. In addition to these musical experiences Herr Elbers invited me to spend one evening each week at his house for the sake of playing violoncello duets with him, and for many years these meetings were continued. They were a great pleasure to me, not the least part of the enjoyment consisting in the excellent supper which followed our musical exertions. He was an enthusiastic amateur, and I fully believe that we played every piano and violoncello duet, good, bad, or indifferent, composed up to that time. The five sonatas by Beethoven were repeated innumerable times and always with the same zest, but those by Hummel, Ferdinand Ries, even Reissiger and others were not neglected.

In this manner my store of knowledge increased constantly. Music, heard by my inner ear, accompanied me at all times and during all my walks, and I created for myself a singular test by which to know if a piece of music was beautiful or not. There was a spot, a bench under a tree by the side of a very small water-fall, where I loved to sit and 'think music.' Then, going in my mind through a piece of music such as Beethoven's 'Adelaide,' or the Cavatina from 'Der Freyschütz,' I could imagine that I heard it in the air surrounding me, that the whole of nature sang it, and then I knew that it was beautiful. Many pieces would not stand that test, however hard I tried, and those I rejected as indifferent.

During my childhood my father took his family every summer to his native town, Arolsen, on a visit to his elder brother, who inhabited the house in which he had been born. These visits were a delight to me, fond as I already was of travelling, and I looked forward to them for many months previous. The mode of travelling differed greatly from our present one, but was all the more enjoyable, especially to a young and impressionable mind. The journey would nowadays occupy about four hours, but at that time a sort of 'Vetturino,' called *Handerer* in German, was sent from Arolsen to fetch us, and the two amiable horses. driven by a coachman bearing the poetical, almost Wagnerian name of Friedewald, accomplished the distance in two days. On one of these visits, in August 1828, my father took me to Cassel, a drive of about four hours, in order to pay his respects to Spohr, who was then 'Kapellmeister' there, and at the same time to get his opinion as to my musical abilities. Spohr was at that time at the height of his reputation, not only as a violinist but as a composer. From our weekly practices at Hagen I knew his oratorios by heart, knew his concertos by having heard my father play them, and had been fascinated by his luscious melodies and wonderfully sweet harmonies and modulations. He was therefore one of my demi-gods, only a few degrees lower in my estimation than Beethoven, Mozart, and Haydn, with which revered names I always associated his. My excitement during the few minutes we had to wait for his appearance in his drawing-room was intense, and when his huge figure, looking twice its size through wearing a loose dressing-gown reaching to his feet, entered, I was awe-struck. He received us most kindly, and when I had quite recovered my breath he made me play to him, the result of which was that he insisted upon my giving a concert in Cassel, he himself undertaking all the arrangements, enrolling vocalists from the operatic troupe, actually two of the most celebrated singers of the time, the

soprano, Mlle. Heinefetter, and the tenor, Wild. The
concert took place in the first days of September,
and created much interest, musical prodigies (I was
nine years old) being then not so plentiful as they
have since become. Of the programme, or rather
my part in it, I ought to feel ashamed, for, in accordance with the fashion of the hour, it consisted of
variations by Henri Herz and by Ries, but also, I am
glad to add, of a rondo by Hummel, which, I hope,
was more to my taste. As an executive display by
a child it was much commended in the papers, some
of which are still in my possession, and Spohr himself
was pleased, so much so that, when I met him again
after a lapse of more than twenty years, he began
at once to speak of this concert, which I thought
long forgotten.

I have dwelt upon this, my really first appearance
before the public (for the concerts at Hagen were
family affairs), at some length, because it was my
only one during my childhood; my fond father,
jubilant as he was at my success, saying to me on
returning from the concert, 'My dear boy, once, and
never again!' a resolve which he kept, and for which
in later years I have felt profoundly grateful. The
temptation to exploit me must have been very great,
for we were not in affluent circumstances; but,
although healthy then, I was far from strong, and it
is doubtful if I could have stood the wear and tear
of the life of a musical prodigy, which consideration
must have weighed heavily with him; and it is
certain that my studies would have been arrested,

my knowledge of music, instead of progressing, would have remained stationary for years, and my youthful enthusiasm for music might have been jeopardised.

After our return to Hagen from this momentous excursion, I plunged with renewed zest into my daily musical studies, and in addition to the piano and the violin began to play the organ. My father was organist at the principal church, and I had long been accustomed to accompany him every Sunday, and sit with him in the organ loft, watching his manipulation of the pedals and listening with delight to his improvisations. I now asked him, timidly at first, to allow me to replace him when simple chorales had to be accompanied. He granted this, sitting by my side to guard against any blunders which might have disturbed the congregation. I soon gained confidence, and after a few months I could often go alone to the church, and with the consent of the clergy replace him altogether. It was the custom then, and still may be, to accompany the Holy Communion by soft and appropriate music, always improvised, for, according to the varied number of communicants, it had to be of longer or shorter duration, and I well remember those minutes, and how hard I tried to make my improvisation impressive. It was a new branch of music that opened itself to me, to which I took most eagerly, and which gave me many new joys. At the same time my father presented me with Gottfried Weber's treatise of harmony and composition, one of the very best

books on the subject ever written, which I devoured
with eagerness.   For years I studied it diligently,
and derived from it, not only great benefit, but also
an inestimable amount of the purest pleasure.

There remains nothing to tell of my childhood
except one incident, characteristic of the unconscious
daring of a boy who does not appreciate the difficulties with which he has to contend.   Hagen was
visited every season by a travelling troupe of singers
and actors, who during two months gave performances
of operas, dramas, and comedies in the large ball-
room of the principal hotel, where a stage was
erected, there being no regular theatre in the town.
About a month previous to their visit the director,
Herr Conradi, came to form the orchestra by inviting
all the best amateurs to take part in it along with a
few professional players, and asking my father to
conduct the performances, without any remuneration
of course.   The love of music was so great that he
never met with a refusal, and my own progress upon
the violin having been declared sufficient, I was enrolled as a second violin.   Those were *fête* days for
me, and I became intimately acquainted with many
of the best operas by taking an active part in them.
On one of these visits, when I was eleven years old, it
chanced that after the first few weeks my father fell
ill, thus threatening to bring the performances to a
premature end.   Herr Conradi was in despair, seeing
which I, with a boy's confidence, offered to replace
my father, was entrusted with the bâton, and remained
at the conductor's desk to the end of the season.

Among the operas which I conducted were 'Die Zauberflöte,' 'Der Freyschütz,' 'Die Schweitzer Familie' (by Weigl, forgotten now), 'Preciosa,' 'Zampa,' 'Fra Diavolo,' 'Die Stumme von Portici' ('Masaniello'), 'Maurer und Schlosser' (by Auber), and others, and it will easily be believed that I felt my importance, and was not a little proud of it. Nervousness I never felt, but sometimes I cried whilst conducting, when the scenes were very affecting, or when I was deeply moved by the beauty of the music. My acquaintance with an orchestra at so early an age and under such circumstances has not been without advantages to me in later years. The remembrance of these performances, the first I ever witnessed, is still very vivid: I enjoyed them thoroughly, and admired even the *mise-en-scène*, which, of course, was of the most simple and primitive kind. Once the performance of 'Don Giovanni' was enlivened by an amusing incident. In the first act, when the Commendatore steps out of his house to chastise Don Giovanni, and gets killed for his pains, instead of being accompanied by servants with torches, he only carried a candle which he let fall when drawing his sword. This unfortunate candle kept burning on the ground in dangerous proximity to the side scenes, but nobody perceived it except the dead Commendatore who, being the director of the company and proprietor of all the scenery, &c., tried in his anxiety by grunts and whispers to draw the attention of somebody to the impending danger, and not succeeding, deliberately sat up, put the candle out with a wetted finger, and lay down again, dead as before. I did not conduct that night, fortunately, for I am afraid I should never have recovered my gravity sufficiently to bring that act to its conclusion.

Few concert-givers visited our town, which offered but small inducements to them; my opportunities for getting acquainted with the outside musical world were therefore very restricted. I remember, however, the visits of two talented French children of little more than my own age, Louis Lacombe and his sister, both pupils of the Conservatoire, and very clever pianists. The remarkable finish of their execution impressed me greatly, and never did I practise so diligently as after hearing them. Louis Lacombe in after years made his mark in France both as a pianist and composer, but I never met him again, although as boys we were very intimate. The neighbourhood of Hagen, especially Elberfeld, a flourishing town, was more favoured, and my father went there on one occasion to hear Paganini, about whom he raved for many months afterwards. Madame Catalani, the most celebrated singer of the time, also gave a concert there, which I remember from a description of her powers given to us by a non-musical friend who had made the journey from curiosity to hear her, and on his return, full of the most extraordinary enthusiasm, told my father: ' in one air she sang higher and higher, and when she could not get any higher, she still sang a little higher, and there *she did a roll* !' (meaning she made a shake).

So, until the age of fifteen, I continued this most

happy life at home, steeped in music, my all-absorbing passion. Many happy hours I spent in putting the quartets by Haydn and Mozart, and some of the latter's concertos, into scores (full scores being then seldom attainable), gaining thus an insight into the working of the great masters I could not otherwise have obtained. My public appearances at the 'Concordia' concerts continued annually, and became gradually more important. The A minor and A flat concertos by Hummel, the E flat and C sharp minor concertos by Ferdinand Ries, the D minor concerto by Kalkbrenner, the C minor concerto by John Field, are some of those which I recollect having performed, as well as hosts of smaller pieces. Now and then I was allowed to play in one of the neighbouring small towns, but on the whole my father was against these exhibitions, for which, with great justice, he did not consider me ripe. He felt that it was now time to send me to some great masters for further study in harmony and the piano, and after long debate it was decided that I should first go to Darmstadt to study counterpoint with Rinck, the celebrated organist, and then to Paris in order to take lessons from Kalkbrenner.

So the chapter of my childhood was closed; a childhood so happy that even now it stands vividly before my eyes, and the recollection of its manifold enjoyments is one of my greatest pleasures. It was made still brighter by one of those friendships which, contracted in earliest youth, endure through life. The son of a schoolmaster, our nearest neighbour, one day older than myself, was my constant companion, and never can there have been a greater similarity of character, of taste, than between Cornelius Flüss and myself. We shared every joy, every grief, and, I may say, every dream. For we were dreamers both, as was manifested in many ways. Thus, when we were eleven years old, and got hold of Fenimore Cooper's exciting novel, ' The Last of the Mohicans,' our imaginations were at once filled with a longing for wood-life, for wild adventure, and we plunged into a dense wood which crowned one of the hills near Hagen, sought out the most retired spot, forcing our way through brushwood, and there determined to build us a hut where we could play at Indians and think ourselves far away from any human beings. By cutting saplings and clearing a small piece of ground, we managed to construct a tiny hut, just large enough to creep into, covered it with branches and leaves, and there we often lay for hours, dreaming all kinds of dreams. It had been the work of weeks, for only spare hours could be devoted to it, but when completed we were not satisfied but must needs make a little ditch all around it with what implements we could stealthily bring to the spot, and then raise a tiny wall round our dwelling, which assumed the aspect of a miniature fortress, into which we retired with a most delicious feeling of isolation and safety from intruders, even though they were ever so many wild Indians. For two summers our hut was our joy and our secret, until one day we found it destroyed and an angry note put up by the proprietor of the wood to the effect that trespassers would be prosecuted and dealt with according to the utmost rigour of the law. So the stern reality shattered our dreams and taught us that God's nature was not free for boys to use, as we had fondly believed.

Another of our pleasures was to go out in the evening with a lantern to study the stars and the constellations; we did not, however, look at the skies by means of the lantern, but it enabled us to read the map, and in time we became great astronomers. Music was a further bond between us; his appreciation of the art being most keen, and his knowledge of its literature extensive. Cornelius in later years became one of the teachers at the 'Hoch-Schule' in Hagen, and remained my trusted friend till his death a few years ago, which seemed to deprive me anew of part of my beloved childhood. The world has changed so entirely during the last seventy years that children of the present day are no longer like the children of that past time. Where is the child to be found now that up to the age of eight or nine years will hold the firm belief that the gifts on Christmas morn are brought by an angel from heaven—'Christ-kindchen' in our homely German? Such was my belief, and that of all the children of my age. On Christmas Eve there stood the large empty table decked with white linen, in the drawing-room, ready to receive the gifts, and who could describe the feelings of confiding awe with which I knelt before the open window, praying the good angel to bring me nice gifts, and looking up to the stars wonderingly,

and half afraid of seeing him descend? Then came
the night, full of expectation, retarding sleep until
very late, from which I was aroused at seven o'clock
by my mother with the joyful words: 'Christ-
kindchen ist hier gewesen' (Christ-child has been
here). And lo! there stood the Christmas-tree, with
its hundred tiny wax lights, its golden nuts and
apples, in the middle of the table, covered now with
toys and other small gifts, amongst which I always
found a new piece of music, generally coveted long
before. It was a happy day, and so deep and lasting
has been its impression upon me, that wherever, and
under whatever circumstances, I have spent Christmas
Day, even when alone in Paris, I have had my
Christmas-tree, got up by myself in the old fashion,
sometimes under considerable difficulties. I was
eight years old, I believe, when another boy, a little
older than myself, told me that we owed the Christmas
gifts to our parents, that they did not come from
heaven. This gave me such a shock that I fell with
both my fists upon the boy, pommelling him with all
my might; but I got the worst of the battle, almost
the only one I fought in my life, and came home crying to ask for confirmation of the dreadful tale. My
dear mother had to give it, but did it in such a
delicate way that, although I felt the mysterious
poetry of that night was gone, my love for my
parents was increased.

The summer in Hagen brought other delights
when I was a little older. Placed in a lovely narrow
valley on both sides of a small, clear river—the

Volme—Hagen was surrounded by gardens, rich
with fruit trees, strawberries, and other dainties.
Through the narrow lanes formed by these gardens,
and with the smell of the rich vegetation in our
noses, my father walked every summer evening with
me by his side, telling me stories of the great composers and anecdotes from his own musical life, thus
filling me more and more with love for music.
Great was my joy when now and then he took me
on a fine afternoon as far as Limburg, a small town
with a beautifully situated castle on the top of a hill,
the residence of the Prince of Hohen-Limburg. This
was a walk of about an hour, mostly through a forest
of pine- and beech-wood covering two hills we had
to pass. The goal of our promenade was an inn,
Herr Polcher's, very primitive, but with a beautiful
garden, a good assembly room, which generally,
when my father's visit was expected, saw many of his
friends assembled around a long table, the *réunions*
being often graced by the presence of the good old
prince himself, who was a great lover of music and
the other fine arts, and fond of genial society. In
spite of the large star that decked his breast, his
princely dignity was soon forgotten in the banter of
wit in which he good-humouredly joined. I remember one amusing incident, the thought of which pro-
vokes my mirth even now. The whole company,
prince included, sang in chorus a simple German
ditty, 'Der La-la-la-la-Laudon rückt an' (Laudon advances), repeated innumerably; the fun consisting in
the manner in which the leader (my father) started

each repeat, which the whole company had to
imitate, now giving it out in full stentorian voice,
then in a whisper, now in sentimental adagio fashion,
then in humorous dance rhythm, now standing, now
sitting and turning their faces to the wall, every
change being totally unexpected. In one variation
my father jumped upon the chair, set one foot upon
the table covered with bottles and glasses, a feat
which the fat little prince had no slight trouble in
imitating, and then the song had to be gone through
without an audible sound, with motion of the lips
only, the uplifted right hands marking the rhythm.
At this moment one of the waiters entered with a
fresh supply of bottles and glasses, and was so overcome by the extraordinary spectacle of so many
guests having apparently gone suddenly mad that he
let the bottles slip, and their crash and the stare on
his astonished face changed the mute scene into one
of boisterous laughter. After these good-natured
follies came the enjoyable walk home through the
still moonlight, the metallic notes of the innumerable
frogs ('Unke') forming a concert, which often made
our steps linger, and harmonised with my father's
talk about music and musicians. Passing through
the dark wood I crept close to him, my imagination
peopling it with highway robbers, and found a sense
of protection and comfort in the touch of his hand
and the glow of his long pipe.

At that time the public force in Hagen consisted
of one policeman and one night-watchman; it was
fortunate, therefore, that robbers were not to be

found in flesh and blood. The night-watchman, with his horn and long staff, was an object of mysterious interest to me, a shadowy form, only to be seen once every year, in the night from December 31st to January 1st, as I shall relate presently. But every evening I heard the sounds of his horn, blowing once at 10 o'clock, twice at 11, three times at midnight. What he did after that hour, if he added one blow at every hour or went to bed, I have never learnt. I was always happy to feel that some one was watching over me, and felt more comfortable in bed when I heard the horn and the simple ditty which the watchman sang every hour :

> Hört, ihr Leut, und lasst euch sagen,
> Die Glocke hat zehn [elf, zwölf] geschlagen :
> Bewahrt das Feuer und das Licht,
> Damit euch kein Schaden gebricht.[1]

Once in the year, on New Year's night, this performance was varied at 12 o'clock midnight. A chorus, principally of children, accompanied the watchman through the streets, and after the three notes of the horn, sang with him this verse :

> Das alte Jahr vergangen ist;
> Wir danken dir, Herr Jesu Christ,
> Dass du uns in so mancher Gefahr
> So gnädiglich behütet dies Jahr.[2]

The tune was one of the fine Lutheran chorales, but

---

[1] 'Listen, people, and take heed. The clock has struck ten [eleven, twelve]. Look well to your fire and light that no harm may come to you.'

[2] 'The old year is passed away. We thank thee, Lord Jesus Christ, for so mercifully preserving us in so many perils this year.'

much embroidered. The first line in the original standing—

was sung—

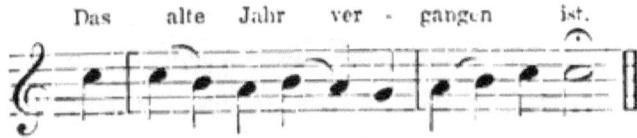

The effect of the clear children's voices through the stillness of the night being heard faintly in the distance at first and gradually drawing nearer and nearer was overpowering to me, and made all my nerves tingle. I always insisted upon being led to the open window when the small singing crowd passed our house, and then I could admire the watchman with his lantern, look at him with deep-felt gratitude, and envy the children who were allowed to accompany and sing with him. Strange to say my recollection of those emotional nights is always associated with a clear starry sky, and pure white snow covering streets and houses, so that I sometimes wonder if the weather never was bad on December 31 in my early youth. It may have been so, but certainly very seldom, not often enough to tarnish their bright image. It was the custom of my father to sit up with his family into the New Year, drinking our health at the stroke of midnight in a glass of self-brewed punch (a custom which I have religiously preserved up to this day). It was the one exception to our early bed-going, and it was thus that I got a glimpse of the night-watchman, only to see him again after another year had elapsed.

As there was but one policeman and one night-watchman in Hagen, so there was also but one letter-carrier, a man beloved by all children on account of his great kindness to them. It was only in much later years, but when I was still a young man, that I heard the singular story of this man, and tried even, but unsuccessfully, to unravel the mystery connected with it. He was born at Aix-la-Chapelle in 1792, his parents being French emigrants; he was christened there, and his name entered in the register as Louis Chabot. He was confided to a nurse, his parents having to continue their flight, and for years he was amply provided for, until suddenly the supplies were stopped, and no further tidings were received from his family. He had no means of tracing them, and a life of misery began for him, through which he fought bravely, being at last stranded as the solitary postman at Hagen. The universal belief of all who knew him and his story, a belief fully warranted by the refinement of his manners and the dignity of his aristocratic bearing, was that he belonged to the great French family of the Duc de Chabot-Latour. He himself believed it, and in his humble circumstances lived so that a sudden call to fortune and to an eminent position would have found him quite fit for the change. The family of Chabot-Latour was approached on his behalf, and on one occasion a gentleman came from Paris to Hagen to inquire into the circumstances, but apparently some link in the chain of proof of his identity was missing, and Chabot—perhaps Duke Chabot —died a postman, respected by the whole community.

One more anecdote about Hagen and I shall leave the dear place. Everybody knows that in Prussia there is a State lottery, and in every town, big or small, there is a collector, appointed to sell the tickets or 'Loose.' To the collector in Hagen came a servant girl (in service in a family of our acquaintance), and asked if she could buy No. 23. He had not got it, but the girl seeming much in earnest, he kindly promised to inquire if any of the collectors in other towns had that particular ticket still to dispose of, and he succeeded. The drawing took place some weeks afterwards, and Hagen got into a state of feverish excitement when it became known that the girl had won one of the big prizes, representing some thousands of pounds sterling. She became of course the one object of interest in the town, was 'interviewed' constantly, and when asked how she could have fixed upon No. 23, she gave this simple and lucid explanation: 'I dreamt one night No. 7, and a second night I dreamt 7, and a third night 7 again, so I thought 3 times 7 makes 23, and I bought that number!' So much for the value of knowledge![1]

In June, 1835, I left my beloved parents, and my dear native town, and travelled up the Rhine to

---

[1] The late Mr. Locker-Lampson relates in his *Confidences* that he heard this story from Mr. Hallé—as he then was—and subsequently told it to the late Dean Stanley, whose ignorance of arithmetic was notorious, and that the Dean, unable to see the joke, observed, not without a shadow of dejection, 'Ah, yes, I see, yes; I suppose three times seven is *not* twenty-three.'

Darmstadt, a two days' journey at that time. Rinck, a somewhat stout and elderly man, with a most benevolent countenance, received me most kindly, and helped me soon over the timidity with which I had approached him at first. Rinck was one of the most learned musicians in Germany, and his organ compositions, most of which I was familiar with, have remained models of their kind. The very next day we arranged for the beginning of my studies, but I was slightly taken aback when he fixed 6 o'clock in the morning as the hour of my lessons, and wondered also at the remark he made when appointing that early time: 'From five to six I compose'; the process of composing seeming to me scarcely compatible with fixed hours. But this habit may perhaps account for a certain dryness attached to most of his works. I worked very diligently during the year I remained with him, and apparently to his satisfaction.

It was, however, fortunate for me that I had studied harmony and counterpoint for years before, otherwise I might have profited little by Rinck's teaching. It was his custom, when correcting exercises, to say, 'I should have done it *so*,' never vouchsafing a reason for his corrections; the pupil, if advanced enough to understand and appreciate the improvement in Rinck's version, learned a great deal; if not, the teaching did not improve his knowledge. Besides working at strict counterpoint with my master, writing canons, fugues, &c., &c., my general musical studies were also largely directed by Gottfried Weber, to whom I had been introduced by

Rinck. Weber, the author of one of the best works on harmony and composition, was not a professional musician, as he held a high position in the law: but there were few professional musicians who had his knowledge, his judgment, and his love for the art. He was no mean composer himself, having written Masses, cantatas, songs, and other works, and nobody could point out the beauties of the great composers' creations better than he did, or make one feel their power. Many were the works I had the privilege of studying with him, and delightful were the hours spent over them. It was he who made me first love and appreciate Cherubini, one of his favourites, with whose compositions I had, until then, been little acquainted. His mature mind also harboured the same enthusiasm for Beethoven which lived in my youthful soul, and nothing could be more interesting, or more instructive than to hear him analyse some of the master's symphonies.

It was in Darmstadt also that I first heard a really fine orchestra—powerful and well trained, to which our homely orchestra in Hagen could not be compared. The then grand duke was a great lover of music, a musician himself, and under his watchful care Hofkapellmeister Mangold had brought together a band equal to any of the best in Germany. To my great joy I was allowed to attend the rehearsals: and these were most numerous, taking place almost daily, and apparently merely for the pleasure of the practice. They seemed to be the only occupation of the members of the orchestra; in fact in quiet Darmstadt nobody appeared to have anything in particular to do, and nothing could exceed the stillness of its vast and regular streets. I remember up to the present day the deep impression which Beethoven's Eroica Symphony made upon me, especially the marvellous Funeral March.[1] Sitting in a dark corner of the half-lighted theatre (the rehearsals took place on the stage), I was rapt in wonderment and trembling all over. There is in particular a long A flat for the oboe, about thirty-four bars before the close of the march, for which I always waited with perfect awe, and which made my flesh creep. The rehearsals of this one symphony were continued a full month, by the end of which I knew it by heart, not having missed a single one. During that month it was the all-absorbing topic of conversation amongst musicians, and the rehearsals, far from being shunned by the members of the orchestra, as is so often the case, were expected with impatience.

The studies with Rinck and Weber, and the equally important study of the works of the best composers, either by hearing them in Darmstadt or in Frankfort or by reading them, made me neglect the piano to a certain extent; nevertheless I had many opportunities of playing in private circles, and if I did not make any progress as a pianist during the year in Darmstadt, I promised myself to work all the harder in Paris, where the study of the piano would not be interfered with by anything, and would be my sole object.

[1] In obedience to his wish, this March was played at my father's funeral.—C. E. H.

I left Darmstadt and my dear old master with sincere regret in the autumn of 1836, travelling by 'diligence' *viâ* Metz and Chalons, sleeping at each place by order of the doctor, for I was even then not very robust, and such a journey was at that time a formidable undertaking. A great disappointment awaited me after having crossed the French frontier and finding myself in the interior of the huge 'diligence' with four Frenchmen. At school I had been considered a very fair French scholar, reading and even speaking the language with a certain amount of fluency; great, therefore, was my astonishment when I did not understand a word of the conversation of my fellow-travellers, although I was all attention, and I arrived in Paris very crestfallen. It took a long time before my ear got accustomed to the unfamiliar sound, but then my former studies proved of great advantage. I may relate here that when two years later I paid a visit to Hagen and met my old teacher of French he addressed me joyfully in what he believed to be that language, but I no longer understood *him*, and he left me fully convinced that I had forgotten all he had taught me.

Arrived in Paris, and settled in a small German hotel in the Rue Vivienne, I began after a few days to deliver the letters of introduction I had brought with me, one of my first visits being to Kalkbrenner. Kalkbrenner and Hummel were at that time considered the greatest pianists, and even Chopin had come to Paris a few years before to learn from Kalkbrenner. I therefore approached him with considerable trepidation, and great was my disappointment when he told me that he no longer took pupils. He, however, kindly invited me to play something, to which he listened carefully, and then made some unpleasant remarks and advised me to take lessons from one of his pupils. As I was about to leave him he offered to play for me, saying that it might prove useful to me to hear him. I accepted eagerly and was full of expectation, when he sat down and played a new piece of his composition, entitled 'Le Fou,' one of the most *reasonable* and dullest pieces ever perpetrated. I admired the elegance and neatness of his scales and legato playing, but was not otherwise struck by his performance, having expected more, and wondering at some wrong notes which I had detected.

I did not at once follow his advice with regard to the teacher he had recommended, and two or three days later I received an invitation to dinner from the banker Mallet, to whom an uncle of mine, Harkort of Leipzig, had recommended me, and found myself sitting beside Chopin. The same evening I heard him play, and was fascinated beyond expression. It seemed to me as if I had got into another world, and all thought of Kalkbrenner was driven out of my mind. I sat entranced, filled with wonderment, and if the room had suddenly been peopled with fairies, I should not have been astonished. The marvellous charm, the poetry and originality, the perfect freedom and absolute lucidity of Chopin's playing at that time cannot be described. It was

perfection in every sense. He seemed to be pleased
with the evident impression he had produced, for I
could only stammer a few broken words of admiration, and he played again and again, each time
revealing new beauties, until I could have dropped
on my knees to worship him. I returned home in a
state of complete bewilderment, and it was only the
next day that I began to realise what was before me
—how much study and hard work, in order to get
that technical command over the keyboard, without
which I knew now that no good result could be
achieved. Strange to say, the idea of taking lessons
did not occur to me then; I felt that what I had to
do could be done without a master; lessons of style
might be more useful later on. I shut myself up and
practised twelve hours and more a day, until one day
my left hand was swollen to about twice its usual
size, causing me considerable anxiety. For some
months I hardly ever left my rooms, and only when
I received invitations to houses where I knew I
should meet, and perhaps hear, Chopin. There
were not many of them in Paris, for Chopin, impelled
by growing weakness, began even then to lead a very
retired life. He used still to visit principally Count
de Perthuis, the banker August Leo, Mallet, and a
few other houses. Fortunately for me I had been
introduced by letters to the above three gentlemen,
and enjoyed the privilege of being invited to their
' réunions intimes,' when Chopin, who avoided large
parties, was to be present. With greater familiarity
my admiration increased, for I learned to appreciate

what before had principally dazzled me. In personal appearance he was also most striking, his clear-cut features, diaphanous complexion, beautiful brown waving hair, the fragility of his frame, his aristocratic bearing, and his princelike manners, singling him out, and making one feel the presence of a superior man. Meeting often, we came into closer contact, and although at that time I never exhibited what small powers I might possess as a pianist, he knew me as an ardent student, and divined that I not merely admired but understood him. With time our acquaintance developed into real friendship, which I am happy to say remained undisturbed until the end of his too short life.

From the year 1836 to 1848, a period during which he created many of his most remarkable works, it was my good fortune to hear him play them successively as they appeared, and each seemed a new revelation. It is impossible at the present day, when Chopin's music has become the property of every schoolgirl, when there is hardly a concert-programme without his name, to realise the impression which these works produced upon musicians when they first appeared, and especially when they were played by himself. I can confidently assert that nobody has ever been able to reproduce them as they sounded under his magical fingers. In listening to him you lost all power of analysis; you did not for a moment think how perfect was his execution of this or that difficulty; you listened, as it were, to the improvisation of a poem and were under the charm as long as

D

it lasted. A remarkable feature of his playing was the entire freedom with which he treated the rhythm, but which appeared so natural that for years it had never struck me. It must have been in 1845 or 1846 that I once ventured to observe to him that most of his mazurkas (those dainty jewels), when played by himself, appeared to be written, not in 3-4, but in 4-4 time, the result of his dwelling so much longer on the first note in the bar. He denied it strenuously, until I made him play one of them and counted audibly four in the bar, which fitted perfectly. Then he laughed and explained that it was the national character of the dance which created the oddity. The more remarkable fact was that you received the impression of a 3-4 rhythm whilst listening to common time. Of course this was not the case with every mazurka, but with many. I understood later how ill-advised I had been to make that observation to him and how well disposed towards me he must have been to have taken it with such good humour, for a similar remark made by Meyerbeer, perhaps in a somewhat supercilious manner, on another occasion, led to a serious quarrel, and I believe Chopin never forgave him. Any deliberate misreading of his compositions he resented sharply. I remember how, on one occasion, in his gentle way he laid his hand upon my shoulder, saying how unhappy he felt, because he had heard his ' Grande Polonaise,' in A flat, *jouée vite !* thereby destroying all the grandeur, the majesty, of this noble inspiration. Poor Chopin must be rolling round and round in his grave nowadays, for this misreading has unfortunately become the fashion.

I may as well continue to speak about Chopin here and take up the thread of my narrative later on, all the more as it will fill little space. His public appearances were few and far between, and consisted in concerts given in the 'Salon Pleyel,' when he produced his newest compositions, the programme opening, I think, invariably with Mozart's Trio in E major, the only work by another composer which I ever heard him play. He was so entirely identified with his own music that it occurred to no one to inquire or even to wish to know how he would play, say, Beethoven's sonatas. If he was well acquainted with them remains a moot point. One day, long after I had emerged from my retirement and achieved some notoriety as a pianist, I played at his request, in his own room, the sonata in E flat, Op. 30, No. 3, and after the finale he said that it was the first time he had liked it, that it had always appeared to him very vulgar. I felt flattered, but was much struck by the oddity of the remark. In another direction, he did not admire Mendelssohn's 'Lieder ohne Worte,' with the exception of the first of the first book, which he called a song of the purest virginal beauty. When one reflects on the wonderful originality of his genius, the striking difference of his works from any written before him, without making comparison as to their respective worth, one feels it natural that he should have lived in his own world, and that other music, even the very greatest, did not touch all his sympathies.

When I first knew him he was still a charming companion, gay and full of life; a few years later his bodily decline began; he grew weaker and weaker, to such a degree, that when we dined together at Leo's or at other friends' houses, he had to be carried upstairs, even to the first floor. His spirits and his mental energy remained, nevertheless, unimpaired, a proof of which he gave one evening, when, after having written his sonata for piano and violoncello, he invited a small circle of friends to hear it played by himself and Franchomme. On our arrival we found him hardly able to move, bent like a half opened pen-knife, and evidently in great pain. We entreated him to postpone the performance, but he would not hear of it; soon he sat down to the piano, and as he warmed to his work, his body gradually resumed its normal position, the spirit having mastered the flesh. In spite of his declining physical strength, the charm of his playing remained as great as ever, some of the new readings he was compelled to adopt having a peculiar interest. Thus at the last public concert he gave in Paris, at the end of the year 1847 or the beginning of 1848, he played the latter part of his 'Barcarolle,' from the point where it demands the utmost energy, in the most opposite style, pianissimo, but with such wonderful *nuances*, that one remained in doubt if this new reading were not preferable to the accustomed one. Nobody but Chopin could have accomplished such a feat. The last time I saw him was in England; he had come to London a few weeks after my arrival there in 1848, and I had the privilege and the happiness to hear him several times at Mrs. Sartoris's and Henry F. Chorley's houses. The admiration which he elicited knew no bounds; there we heard for the first time the beautiful valses, Op. 62, recently composed and published, which since have become the most popular of his smaller pieces. I had the pleasure afterwards to welcome him to Manchester, where he played at one of the concerts of the society called the Gentlemen's Concerts in the month of August. It was then painfully evident that his end was drawing near; a year later he was no more.

To return to my own experiences in 1836, I have to relate that a few days after having made the acquaintance of Chopin, I heard Liszt for the first time at one of his concerts, and went home with a feeling of thorough dejection. Such marvels of executive skill and power I could never have imagined. He was a giant, and Rubinstein spoke the truth when, at the time when his own triumphs were greatest, he said that, in comparison with Liszt, all other pianists were children. Chopin carried you with him into a dreamland, in which you would have liked to dwell for ever; Liszt was all sunshine and dazzling splendour, subjugating his hearers with a power that none could withstand. For him there were no difficulties of execution, the most incredible seeming child's play under his fingers. One of the transcendent merits of his playing was the crystal-like clearness which never failed for a moment even in the most complicated and, to anybody else, impossible passages; it was as if he had photographed them in their minutest detail

upon the ear of his listener. The power he drew
from his instrument was such as I have never heard
since, but never harsh, never suggesting 'thumping.'
His daring was as extraordinary as his talent. At
an orchestral concert given by him and conducted by
Berlioz, the 'March au Supplice,' from the latter's
'Symphonie Fantastique,' that most gorgeously instru-
mented piece, was performed, at the conclusion of
which Liszt sat down and played his own arrangement,
for the piano alone, of the same movement, with an
effect even surpassing that of the full orchestra, and
creating an indescribable *furore*. The feat had been
duly announced in the programme beforehand, a
proof of his indomitable courage.

If, before his marvellous execution, one had only
to bow in admiration, there were some peculiarities
of style, or rather of musicianship, which could not
be approved. I was very young and most impressionable, but still his tacking on the finale of the
C sharp minor sonata (Beethoven's) to the variations
of the one in A flat, Op. 26, gave me a shock, in spite
of the perfection with which both movements were
played. Another example : he was fond at that time
of playing in public his arrangement for piano of the
'Scherzo,' 'The Storm,' and the finale from Beethoven's 'Pastoral Symphony; ' 'The Storm' was simply
magnificent, and no orchestra could produce a more
telling or effective tempest. The peculiarity, the
oddity, of the performance, consisted in his playing
the first eight bars of the 'Scherzo' rather quicker
than they are usually taken, and the following eight

bars, the B major phrase, in a slow andante time; 'ce sont les vieux,' he said to me on one occasion. It may serve to characterise the state of musical knowledge in Paris, at the time I speak of, when I state that at a concert given by Liszt in 1837, in the Salle Érard, the B flat Trio by Beethoven, which stood at the commencement of the programme, and Mayseder's Trio in A flat, which was to begin the second part, were transposed for some reason or other, without the fact being announced to the public. The consequence was that Mayseder's Trio, passing for Beethoven, was received with acclamation, and Beethoven's very coldly, the newspapers also eulogising the first and criticising the length and *dryness* of the other severely. Of the *man* Liszt I shall have now and then something to say when I arrive at the time of our more intimate acquaintance.

With Thalberg there came a new sensation in the same year. Totally unlike in style to either Chopin or Liszt, he was admirable and unimpeachable in his own way. His performances were wonderfully finished and accurate, giving the impression that a wrong note was an impossibility. His tone was round and beautiful, the clearness of his passage-playing crystal-like, and he had brought to the utmost perfection the method, identified with his name, of making a melody stand out distinctly through a maze of brilliant passages. He did not appeal to the emotions, except those of wonder, for his playing was statuesque; cold, but beautiful and so masterly that it was said of him with reason he would play with the same care and finish if roused out of the deepest sleep in the middle of the night. He created a great sensation in Paris, and became the idol of the public, principally, perhaps, because it was felt that he could be imitated, even successfully, which with Chopin and Liszt was out of the question.

The hearing of Liszt and Thalberg put Kalkbrenner's advice still more in the shade. I went on listening to the three mighty heroes as often as I had an opportunity and relentlessly pursuing my studies by myself. By the help of some influential introductions I had brought with me, I made by degrees interesting acquaintances. It was probably on account of my youth, and my great enthusiasm for music, that I was at once treated with great kindness by men at the zenith of their fame and much older than myself. This was the case with Meyerbeer, Halévy, Liszt, and others, to whose nearer acquaintance I was helped through the then all powerful music-publisher, Maurice Schlesinger. The Parisian artistic and literary society, at that time, was so constituted that to know a few men of mark was to know them all, and certainly more by luck than by any merit, I soon found myself at home in circles of which I had read and dreamed, but which I had not hoped to enter. Gradually I had then to throw off my reserve and to play when I was asked, confining myself to excerpts from Beethoven and a few other composers. I met with success and encouragement, but for three years I resisted all attempts to make me appear in public, for which I did not feel myself ripe.

During this time of labour I was visited one day, only
a few months after my arrival, by a gentleman, Monsieur Guibert, a rich 'agent-de-change,' who had
heard of me, and made me the following proposal.
He had two sons, ten and twelve years of age, was
extremely fond of music, his wife and only brother
equally so, and he wished to form the taste of his boys
and make them thoroughly acquainted with the best
compositions, for which purpose he asked me to devote
one evening every week to himself and his family,
and play for them whatever I liked and as much as I
liked. It reminded me of the evenings with Herr
Elbers; and M. Guibert adding a very handsome
pecuniary inducement to his proposal, we soon
agreed, and from that time for years I dined every
Thursday at his table and revelled in music for hours
afterwards. No strangers were admitted, and it was
a delight to me to expound and make them feel the
beauties of the various works we went through. Of
course the sonatas of Beethoven were chiefly and
diligently studied, but Mozart, Haydn, Bach, Weber,
Dussek, Hummel, Clementi, and others were not
neglected. I even played the arrangements of Beethoven's, Mozart's, and Haydn's symphonies; in fact,
there was hardly anything in the whole range of
music capable of being rendered on the piano with
which I did not get familiar by familiarising my friends
with it. These *séances*, repeated so constantly—for
we only allowed a break of a few months in the
summer—were of immense advantage to myself, for
there were many pieces I might have neglected but

for the desire to increase our *répertoire* to the utmost.

I owe them also one great joy which alone would have made them for ever worthy of my remembrance. It was in 1838 that M. Guibert asked if for once I would allow him to admit a friend, a sincere lover of music, to be present on one of our evenings. The request being readily granted, the friend came on the following Thursday, and turned out to be Salvator Cherubini, the eldest son of one of my idols, the great composer. Overjoyed as I was, my rapture became indescribable when a few days later M. Salvator called upon me with a message from his father, to the effect that he wished to make my acquaintance and hoped I would sometimes spend a Sunday evening with him. I felt as if I had received the Grand Cross of the Legion of Honour, and of course the next Sunday evening I presented myself at the ' Conservatoire,' where Cherubini lived, trembling with emotion. The veneration I felt for him must have been strongly depicted on my face, for he received me smiling and endeavoured, by speaking of the pleasure I had given to his son—which pleasure he hoped soon to enjoy also—to encourage and set me at my ease. No easy task, for only in the presence of Beethoven could I have felt the same emotion. His old friend Berton, the once greatly-renowned composer, was with him (' les inséparables ' they were called), and greeted me with equal kindness. Cherubini had a great regard for my former master, Rinck, also for G. Weber. After some conversation, of which they formed the subject, I was requested to play one of Beethoven's sonatas, Cherubini professing to be but little acquainted with them, which I found to be the truth by his asking for certain movements, even for whole sonatas, over again not only on this but on many subsequent occasions, for to my intense satisfaction I was invited to repeat my visit. Most of the sonatas I had then the privilege of playing in the presence of Cherubini and Berton were evidently new to them, somewhat to my astonishment, but there could be no doubt about the interest with which they listened to them—an interest demonstrated solely by their silent attention and the requests for repeats, for not once did Cherubini make a remark on the beauty or the character of the works, or criticise them in any way. His silence reminded me of the story told of his witnessing the first performance of one of Halévy's operas, from the composer's box. He kept silence there, until after the second act Halévy, his pupil, asked, ' Maestro, have you nothing to say to me ? ' when Cherubini snarled back, ' I have been listening to you for two hours and *you* have said nothing to *me.*' But in listening to Beethoven's sonatas his silence could certainly not be attributed to a similar cause ; that I saw clearly, even by the play of his handsome features, and why should he have asked me to repeat my visits, had it not been for the interest he felt in these sonatas, which seemed to grow the more I played of them ?

Sayings of his, like the above to Halévy, were currently quoted at the time and made him the terror of most people who had to deal with him. There seemed to be no actual 'méchanceté' in him, only an inability to calculate the effect of his words, as in the case of the young man who applied for admission into the operatic class of the Conservatoire, but was so ill-favoured by nature that the professors thought it would be a kindness to him to deter him from trying his luck on the stage. But who was to tell him in a delicate way? Cherubini volunteered to do so, sent for the young man, and said, 'Dear sir, the Conservatoire regrets to be unable to accept you as a pupil because—you are too ugly.' That was his manner of softening a rude blow.

My evenings at the Conservatoire were greatly enjoyed by me, and if Cherubini was reticent in expressing an opinion on Beethoven, he could talk enthusiastically about Gluck, Spontini, and music as an art and a science. About Rossini and the whole school of his followers, then in the ascendant, he could become very sarcastic; it was a topic carefully to be avoided. And so was the mention of the name of Berlioz, who had already become one of my friends. But of him later.

POSTSCRIPT

Of the first sixteen years of my father's life, passed almost entirely at home, but one short letter has been preserved; it is a little birthday greeting, written at the age of six or seven to his favourite Uncle Hügel, and only remarkable as bearing the promise of the firm, clear, and beautiful handwriting that he retained all his life.

Two compositions also remain to us; the first, which he called a 'hops' waltz, is dedicated to the same 'dear Uncle Hügel,' by 'Carlchen Hallé,' and thus endorsed by Herr Hügel:—

A token of affection from Carl Hallé. This darling child composed and wrote out the above waltz at the age of five ; the little genius already plays several sonatas by the great masters with great perfection and feeling.

The second composition, also a waltz, was written the following year :—

Waltz for my dear father's birthday, the 15th March, 1826, composed by your son,   CARL HALLÉ.

The page is adorned with a little vignette, representing a winged cupid standing on a footstool, and playing on a pianoforte, the work of his fast friend and ally, Uncle Hügel.

My father has described in his memoirs the visit to Cassel with his father, in 1828, the concert he gave there, and his interview with Spohr. In those days, when advertising had scarcely been invented, almost the only announcement of this concert consisted of the following statement, written entirely in my grandfather's hand, on a large sheet of foolscap paper, now yellow with age :—

On Tuesday, the 16th of this month, my son, Carl Hallé, nine years old, will give a Musical Evening in Herr Oestreich's Hall, and will perform several pieces by Ries, Herz, &c., on the pianoforte. The rare talent of this child induces me to hope that he will afford the amateurs of music an enjoyable evening's entertainment, the more so that Fräulein Heinefetter and Herr Wild have kindly promised their assistance, and will sing several songs.

In order to cover the expenses of the evening I take the liberty respectfully to beg the ladies and gentlemen, who intend to honour the entertainment with their presence, kindly to inscribe their names below.

The Soirée will commence at 7 o'clock, and the entrance will be 15 g. gr.   FR. HALLÉ.

Cassel : September 18, 1828.

Then follows a testimonial written and signed by Spohr :—

I take pleasure in attesting that this boy's talent is quite extraordinary ; and that, for his age, he executes the most difficult modern compositions with inconceivable facility and steadiness.   LOUIS SPOHR.

The signatures of some twenty ladies and gentlemen, presumably the chief musical connoisseurs of Cassel, fill the rest of the sheet.

The programme of this concert, the first of the long series of programmes that was to stretch over nearly seventy years, also lies before me ; its very first words strike one rather curiously to-day : ' *Mit obrigkeitlicher Bewilligung.*' ' *With Magisterial Authority,*' proving the censorship that extended even to the programme of a concert in the year 1828. This is probably the only concert my father ever gave at which he contributed no work by any greater or more classical composer than Ries and Herz.

A little anecdote, which we have reason to know my father would have inserted in the record of his childish years, may here find place. When he was some seven or eight years old, a schoolmaster from a neighbouring town, a great amateur performer on the piano, came to visit Herr Flüss, the Hagen schoolmaster. The gentleman was not only a great virtuoso, but a little inclined to be vain of his accomplishment, and very soon volunteered to play one of Beethoven's sonatas to his host ; when he had finished and looked round for applause, Herr Flüss thanked and praised him very much, but added : ' You see, we are very far advanced in musical matters here at Hagen ; the little boys in the street play Beethoven almost if not quite as well as that,' and in answer to the incredulous smile, and ' Oh indeed !' with which the pianist received this statement, he continued : ' But I will prove it to you.' He thereupon tapped at the window, through which he could see his son Cornelius and my father playing marbles before the door, and said : ' Come in, Carl,' and as soon as he appeared, bade him sit down and play the sonata that lay open on the piano.

The little boy looked at his hands, and asked permission to go and wash them. 'Never mind your dirty hands, sit down and play.' My father obeyed, and the astonished schoolmaster had to confess that the performance was better than his own. It is not known whether Herr Flüss allowed him to go away with the impression that all the little boys of Hagen could leave their marbles to play Beethoven in an equally masterly manner.

The above-mentioned Cornelius Flüss, my father's senior by a single day, was the inseparable comrade of his boyhood, and remained to the day of his death, in 1881, the man the most after his own heart of all his friends. My father always spoke of him as the most gifted man he had ever known, and would sometimes regret the want of energy, or perhaps the philosophy, that made Cornelius Flüss content to fill the place his father had held before him, as schoolmaster of the then small country town of Hagen. It is a matter of deep regret that not one of my father's letters to him has been preserved; during his last illness Cornelius asked for the whole collection, which he had always most carefully preserved; he read them through once more, and then destroyed them. And it is curious that my father, who, as a rule, kept every letter, however insignificant, addressed to him by his family and intimate friends, should have made one exception in the case of Cornelius; only one letter, written in a kind of nonsense-verse, having been found among his papers.

Cornelius had a most chivalrous punctilio on the subject, and always refused to listen to any extract, however interesting, which my grandmother or aunts might offer to read to him from my father's or any other person's letters. As to the suggestion of reading it himself he would regard it in almost the same light as the suggestion to pick a pocket.

Another of my father's correspondents, almost the only one outside his own family, with whom his busy life allowed him to keep up a more or less regular interchange of letters, Stephen Heller, also destroyed his correspondence shortly before his death. His own letters, some of which are given here, indicate very clearly that my father's must have been most interesting, and of great value to the musical history of the long period—1818 to 1887—that they cover.

Before leaving the subject of those early years at Hagen it is worth noticing that some of my father's most striking characteristics were inherited from my grandmother, whose loving, dutiful, and obedient son he proved himself until the last day of her long and honoured life. Such were his great love of order, his invariable sweetness of disposition, and the almost passionate love and admiration for the beauties of nature, which could make him write from Cape Town in 1895, that the view of the Kloof repaid him for the journey there.

It was Frau Hallé's habit, when out walking with her children, to point out all the various beauties of wood and field through which their path might lead, and during their winter rambles among the wooded hills that encircle Hagen, she would make them pick up some little frosted twig or branch, and, laying it on her muff, would describe its delicate traceries and the transformations of the frost, in language so simple and beautiful, that it never faded from their minds.

Her son's love of colour, his strong dislike for black and dingy hues, also date from those early days; he never quite ceased to regret, while most rigidly obeying it himself, the law that ordains the universal blackness of male attire. He would say how much nicer it was when one man wore a brown coat, another a green, and another a blue; that it made the streets and all assemblies so much gayer and more brilliant.

Endless were the stories of his childhood with which he would delight his own children's ears during the evening hour, the only portion of the day we were allowed to spend in his study. I think he told them as graphically and carefully to us as if we had been a most distinguished audience; one or two there were always reserved until after the 'little ones' had gone to bed, for which we often asked, to which we listened with somewhat bated breath, and which made the going along dark passages on our own way to bed rather an uninviting prospect.

One tale he told but seldom, and never without the reverence of tone which he observed towards all well-authenticated manifestations of a supernatural character, though no one could be called less superstitious than he. The event, although it had occurred many years before his birth, and he had only known of it by hearsay, had made a deep and lasting impression upon him.

At the beginning of this century his maternal grandparents lived at Altena, a small Westphalian town some twenty-five miles from Hagen, with their children, the third of whom, Christina Brendschedt, then about ten years old, was the heroine of the tale. She and her younger sister, Caroline, my grandmother, shared the same room, and one night Christina roused her sister in great alarm, saying she saw someone standing at the foot of her bed, holding back the curtain. The two little girls, although Caroline saw nothing unusual in the room, began by hiding their faces under the bed-clothes, and when Christina, venturing to look a second time, saw the figure still, they began to scream, and called their parents, who were in the next room. Their father first contented himself by calling back to them that Christina had been dreaming, and that the figure would go away as soon as she was wide awake, but the child cried again that the figure looked ' so anxious,' and was pointing to the window. This happened two or three times, until their father said he would come and see for himself, upon which the child said to her little sister, ' Now he drops the curtain.' As soon as Herr Brendschedt entered the room he saw to his amazement that a great gap was in the wall, and he had but the time to save the children and give the alarm before the wall gave way. A new well had been recently dug too close to the house, and had weakened the foundations. My great aunt Christina lived to a good old age, and whenever she spoke of this event, which was but seldom, she would say that she had forgotten the faces of all whom she had known at that time of her life, but that if she could draw, she would be able to reproduce the countenance of

E

her 'Guardian Angel,' as she called the vision of that night.

Many years afterwards, as will be seen in one of my father's letters, he took his mother and aunt once again to Altena, and on his return to England he told us how their first visit had been to the old house, now inhabited by strangers, and how they had stood a long while in the garden looking up at the wall, restored and repaired, but plainly showing the marks of the fissure that had so nearly proved fatal.

At the close of the Napoleonic wars a detachment of Prussian troops was riding through Altena amid the joyous acclamations of the people, and a young officer, chancing to look up, caught sight of Christina Brendschedt at a window with her sisters, watching the passage of the troops. The young soldier told a comrade the next day that he had seen the girl he meant to make his wife, if he could find her out and win her. He did both; and soon afterwards Christina Brendschedt married Gustav Harkort, who rose to be one of the most trusted councillors of the King of Saxony, and whose statue now stands in one of the public squares of Leipzig, erected after his death by his grateful fellow-citizens.

When we read or hear of the doings of those by no means remote ancestors, the conviction is forced upon us that there must have been a great vitality and vigour, a great power of enjoyment and of endurance in the youths and maidens of the first twenty years of the nineteenth century. The girls of the Brendschedt family were very fond of dancing, and it was by no means an unusual or remarkable occurrence for them to perform a day's journey *on foot* to attend a ball in a neighbouring town, to dance the whole night through, and return next day in the same manner. It must have been a merry company that would start off from Altena in the early morning, their destination Cologne, a ten hours' march, their path lying across the hills and valleys of the rich and pleasant *rothe-erde* of Westphalia, their escort a stout serving-man when their fathers or brothers were not with them, but in the latter case the journeys would be made less fatiguing for one or two, who could ride on pillions behind the gentlemen. Dress was simpler then, and for a ball, a knot of ribbons, and a few fresh flowers, were considered sufficient adornment of the universal low-necked white muslin gown.

Those low-necked gowns seem to have been worn in winter as in summer, and it is with something like a shiver that one hears of skating parties, where the young ladies disported themselves for hours on the ice with no thicker mantle over their low, short-sleeved dresses than a gauze scarf, worn more for 'coquetterie' than warmth, as my great-aunt Altgelt candidly admitted in talking of the pleasant gatherings of her youth. Top-coats seem to have been unknown, not only to the young men, but also to the elders of those hardy days.

In the evening, the illumination in my great-grandfather's house, when the family were alone, consisted, if tradition speaks truly, of one candle placed on the table, round which the whole family were gathered, and that candle, made of tallow, and often requiring to be snuffed, stood close to Herr Brendschedt's elbow, where he sat at the head of the table reading his book or the gazette. By this dim and distant light his daughters yet managed to do the finest imaginable needlework, those delicate white embroideries, of which the few specimens that remain are now so highly prized.

On one occasion, when she was quite a young girl, my grandmother, the fame of whose sweet singing had spread beyond her native town, was invited to take part in a concert at Iserlohn, at some distance from Altena. At that time there existed no carriage-road nor even a cart-track between the two towns, so one of the members of the committee charged with the arrangements for the concert was deputed to ride to Altena, and bring her back on a pillion behind him by the rough bridle-paths, or, where they failed, across country, 'thorough bush, thorough briar,' and then convey her home again on the day after the concert in the same way.—M. H.

CHAPTER II

1838–1848

IN the winter of 1838–9 Stephen Heller arrived in
Paris, which makes an epoch in my life. A friendship sprang up between us almost at once, which
endured uninterruptedly to the end of his days in
1888, and had a most decided influence upon my
intellectual development. Only those who have
known him as intimately as I have (and I doubt if
there are any) can appreciate the high quality of his

gifts, the superiority of his intelligence, and the sound-
ness of his judgment in all matters musical, artistic,
and literary. He brought few of his compositions
with him, and, in fact, nearly all his works date from
Paris, but these few revealed the real musician, the
original thinker, and had already attracted Schumann's attention, with whom Heller corresponded
frequently. I was happy to meet a man whose whole
soul was wrapped up in music—as my own was—and
the long hours we spent together at the piano playing
duets form some of my most cherished recollections.
It was during these *séances* in my humble lodgings in
the Rue Notre Dame de Lorette that we made acquaintance with and revelled in the beauties of Schubert's
great C major symphony, then recently discovered
and published as a pianoforte duet. It was a revelation to us, and we were never tired of playing it
through. But the same was the case with all the
great compositions for orchestra, or orchestra with
chorus, arranged in a similar form. How often we
must have played Beethoven's symphonies it is impossible to tell, and how we enjoyed them! All the
more as the opportunities of hearing them performed
by the orchestra were then most rare, the Concerts
du Conservatoire only bringing forward two or three
during a season, so that certain of them, for instance,
Nos. 4, 7, and 9, were heard perhaps once in three or
four years. In 1839 neither Heller nor I had ever
heard the Choral Symphony performed, and were
therefore all the more eager to study it closely.
Such a performance was approached with a certain

solemnity. When our means—slender at that time—
permitted, a bottle of champagne was sent for and
drunk during the performance as on a festive
occasion. But here, for once, we felt the inadequacy
of the piano; much as we admired the three first
movements, we could not understand the finale, hard
as we tried; it left on us a disagreeable impression,
somewhat akin to sea-sickness, in spite of which we
renewed again and again our endeavour to fathom it,
but with no better result.

Heller was a remarkable pianist, but shrank from
playing in public, and perhaps he had not the gift to
impress a large audience. There was a singular
modesty and reticence in his playing of his own
works, an indication only of expression and *nuance*,
as if he felt shy of telling all the secrets of his heart.
This shyness, however, left him entirely when he was
improvising, a gift in which he excelled all great
musicians that I have known. The change that came
over him and his execution in such moments, or
hours, was marvellous. As a rule he was not a very
great master of technique, but when improvising all
difficulties seemed to vanish, and it is certain that if
he had been able to place before him in print what he
accomplished in these moments of inspiration he
would have stared, and it would have taken him
weeks of hard study to play what had seemed so
easy. Whether he improvised quite freely, or on
subjects self-chosen or given to him, he was equally
fascinating, dominating his listeners and pouring out
a wealth of ideas of which his published compositions

give no idea. He had an extraordinary faculty of combining the most dissimilar themes, and proved it once—the only time, I believe, he ever improvised in public—where the opening of 'Don Giovanni,' 'Notte e giorno faticar,' Pedrillo's 'Viva Bacco, Bacco viva,' from 'Il Seraglio,' and his own 'Wanderstunden,' were given to him, and after the one and the other had been treated most ingeniously for some time, they were all three, or the semblance of them, heard at the same time, a feat so difficult of execution that it would have required long practice on the part of any pianist to master it, and here it was accomplished spontaneously. The occasion was a visit he paid to England in 1862, of which I may speak here, as it is connected with his talent for improvisation. I had heard from him that he was what is commonly called 'hard up,' and in order to replenish his exhausted exchequer had obtained for him several engagements in England and induced him to give a concert in Manchester. Everywhere we played duets for two pianos, Heller being too nervous to appear alone ; but for the Manchester concert, which I was most anxious should have a good result, I had insisted on his including in the programme an 'Improvisation on subjects given by the audience.' After a hard fight he had submitted, and my expectations of a crowded house were fully realised. I little knew that a catastrophe was impending, from which fortunately I was able to save Heller. On the day previous to the concert a charming young lady, who with her sister took lessons from me, asked me, 'Is it really true that Heller is going to improvise?' 'Yes, it is part of the programme,' was my answer. 'Oh, how droll! and may any one give a subject?' 'Certainly, anybody that can think of one.' 'So, if I said—sponge, would that do?' I cannot imagine what the consequence would have been, but the improvisation would have been 'sponged' out.

I return to my narrative of very happy times, made principally so by my friendship with Heller and by the interest with which I and a few other intimate musical friends watched and enjoyed his productions. By the time Heller came to Paris I had already made a good many friends and could be of some use to him by introducing him to people he wished to know. In my turn I owe him some most interesting acquaintances. My circumstances were gradually improving, thanks to the number of my pupils increasing constantly, so that I was able to move into better quarters, in the Rue d'Amsterdam, where I first began to have a few musical evenings at home, reunions of friends, such as Berlioz, Heller, Ernst, Batta (the accomplished and refined violoncellist), Artôt, known as 'le bel Artôt,' Delsarte, the marvellous tenor without a voice, and several others. On one evening Artôt proposed that we should play the Kreutzer Sonata, and we did so. Now Artôt, most elegant violinist and most successful performer though he was, was entirely out of his element in such music, which was so painfully evident that when he had left us rather early, Ernst sprang up and said, 'Come, Hallé, let us play the *Kreutzer*!' He played it magnificently, and I have never better

understood than on that evening how much depends
upon the power of interpretation; how the want of it
can deprive the finest work of its charm and interest.

From the Rue d'Amsterdam I moved to the Rue
Lafitte, where I had charming, quiet rooms with a view
upon some beautiful gardens, and here it was that
Heller first brought Heinrich Heine to me. They knew
each other from being both contributors to the 'Augsburger Allgemeine Zeitung,' Germany's most important paper then. Heine, then only about forty-two
years of age, of handsome and winning appearance,
strong and healthy, with no indication of the sufferings that were to be his fate later on, was, of course,
a most welcome guest. He came often, always with
Heller—in fact, I cannot remember a single occasion
on which our trio developed into a quartet, and many
were our discussions on music, in which he took great
interest—perhaps without really understanding, as
some of his remarks seemed to show. I had brought
with me, after an excursion to Germany, the book of
songs by Mendelssohn, in which the first is the
setting of Heine's 'Auf Flügeln des Gesanges.' I
spoke of it with enthusiasm to Heine, who came the
same evening with Heller to the Rue Lafitte, most
eager to hear this version of his poem. I had a feeble,
but not altogether disagreeable tenor voice, and sang
the 'Lied' to him with all the expression I was capable
of, and certainly correctly as regards the music. Great
was my astonishment, and Heller's also, when at the
conclusion he said in a disappointed tone, 'There is
no melody in it.' As there is nothing but melody in

it, we long puzzled over the riddle—What sort of melody may satisfy a poet when he hears his own words sung? An insoluble one, I am afraid.

Irresistibly charming was Heine when, the conversation flagging, which often happens when three smokers sit together, he would, after a more or less long silence, suddenly recite one of his shorter poems, clothing it with undreamt-of beauty by his manner of delivery. We sat in mute wonder, and it seemed quite natural that he should add musingly in a half unconscious tone : 'Beautiful!' The oddity of the remark, coming from himself, never once struck us : it was so perfectly true. Our relations remained for years the most friendly ; then suddenly and unexpectedly he showed the cloven hoof. I had already begun to give concerts and had been treated most kindly by him, when one day, after one of them which he had attended, I met him on the Boulevard, went up to him to shake hands, and was cut dead. There was no mistake, and often as we met after that he took no notice of me. At that time he wrote to the 'Augsburger Zeitung' that I was a small prophet whom the whale would have spat out promptly if it had swallowed him. I had reason to believe that a mistake made in the tickets sent him for my concert was the source of his anger, and was extremely sorry for it ; but as he ought to have known that the mistake could not have originated with me, I was too proud to seek an explanation. So we passed each other for many months without so much as a look, until one day, meeting on the same Boulevard, he came up to me, shook my hand warmly in the old friendly manner, and after a few commonplace questions, asked : 'Were you at Doehler's concert yesterday?' and hearing that I had not been there, he added *à brûle-pourpoint*, 'I do not like him. No, no; to hear somebody who plays *really* well, one must come to you!' 'Hallo!' I said, 'and what about the whale?' Upon which he laughed most heartily, shook my hand again, and departed without further explanation. After that we were the same old friends again.

Towards the end of the year 1839 Heller brought one evening to my rooms a young musician, my senior only by six years, whose acquaintance he had made through Maurice Schlesinger, and who, as he told me in a side whisper, stood in great need of kindness and assistance. The name of this young musician was Richard Wagner, a name which at that time meant nothing to us, as we were in absolute ignorance of the talents he might or might not be endowed with. We knew that he was in great straits, had unsuccessfully applied for an appointment as chorus singer in a small theatre, and for his living made all kinds of arrangements for Schlesinger, even to an arrangement of Halévy's 'La Reine de Chypre' for *two flutes*, to which Heller suggested the addition of a big drum. Wagner himself used to laugh at this occupation, the result of dire necessity; and we, never having seen or heard a note of his own compositions, took it almost for granted that he was not fit for much more. He was no pianist or he might have given us some idea of his own work. He rarely spoke of his aspirations, but

when he did so, it was usually in a strain which made
us wonder if, as the phrase goes, he was 'all there.'
We liked him as a most frank, amiable, and lively
companion, modest and full of enthusiasm for all that
is beautiful in art. And he felt evidently at home
with us. He came often to the Rue Lafitte. Heller
improvised, I played, or we played duets, and I
remember that one evening when I had played to
them Schumann's 'Carneval,' then quite new, we three
indited a letter of thanks to the composer, which
letter I saw more than forty years later in the hands
of his widow. In 1876, when I met him at Bayreuth,
his first words alluded to the pleasant evenings with
Heller at my rooms in Paris. What an immense
change had taken place! What a difference there
was between the man of 1839 and the man of 1876!

Schlesinger, the proprietor of the 'Gazette
Musicale,' the most important musical paper in
France, gave to the subscribers annually a few concerts with a view to increasing their number, and in
the spring of 1840 he included in the programme an
overture by his *then protégé*, Richard Wagner. The
overture was called 'Christoph Colomb,' and as it was
the first time we were to hear a specimen of our friend's
works, we were naturally very curious, and attended
the concert with great expectations. The result was
disastrous. Whether it was that the performance,
for want of rehearsals, was most imperfect, or that
the style was what we might now call *ultra-Wagnerian*,
or for both these reasons joined together, the whole
overture struck us as the work of a madman, and we

had no opportunity to reconsider our judgment, as
'Christoph Colomb' has never again seen the light.
It was not many months after this *fiasco* that we heard
with amazement of the great success his opera,
'Rienzi,' had achieved in Dresden, and still greater
was our astonishment when the perusal of the score
showed us that the success was perfectly justified.
Here was a case of unrecognised merit, if ever there
was one—or rather a proof of the difficulties that
confront the musician who is a composer. A painter
shows his picture and the world judges it. But the
composer of an opera may carry the score round with
him for years and nobody will be the wiser for it. In
after years I met Wagner seldom, and each time found
it more difficult to recognise in him the genial, modest
young companion I had known so well. His manner
of speech had become bombastic, often not to be
'understanded of the people.' In 1862 we met by
accident in the ruins of the old castle of Heidelberg.
In the previous winter I had given concert performances of Gluck's 'Iphigenia in Tauris,' in Manchester,
London, and other towns with remarkable success.
This apparently had interested Wagner greatly, and
rather surprised him. He spoke of it at length, and
concluded by saying : 'The English are an extraordinary people—*und dennoch weiss ich nicht ob es je
bei ihnen zu dem Seufzer kommt, ohne den der Blumen-
duft der Kunst nicht in den Aether steigt.*' I have
quoted this wonderful sentence in the original German, but it may be roughly translated : 'Still, I do
not know if ever they arrive at the sigh, without

which the aroma of the art does not ascend into space.' Dr. E. Becker, for so many years librarian to H.M. Queen Victoria, was with me on that occasion, and immediately wrote down the sentence in his pocket-book. We never understood it, but felt it was worth preserving.

At Bayreuth, in 1876, during one of the welcome entr'actes, we met in the open air, he being surrounded by a crowd of admirers. It was then that he alluded to the pleasant evenings in Paris, expressed how gratified he was that I, too, had come all the way from England to hear his works, and ended by saying emphatically, 'You see, my dear Hallé, I shall make Bayreuth the centre of civilisation.' 'A noble aim, my dear master,' was my answer. We never met again.

To return to 1838, a year so rich to me in reminiscences. I must say a few words about a man, in his way the most remarkable of his time, Paganini. He was one of the wonders of the world to me, so much had I read and heard about him, and I deeply deplored that he had given up public playing, and—so I was told—even chose his lodgings so that the sound of his violin could not be heard outside. The striking, awe-inspiring, ghost-like figure of Paganini was to be seen nearly every afternoon in the music shop of Bernard Latte, Passage de l'Opéra, where he sat for an hour, enveloped in a long cloak, taking notice of nobody, and hardly ever raising his piercing black eyes. He was one of the sights of Paris, and I had often gone to stare at him with wonder until a friend introduced me to him, and he invited me to visit him, an invitation I accepted most eagerly. I went often, but it would be difficult to relate a single conversation we had together. He sat there, taciturn, rigid, hardly ever moving a muscle of his face, and I sat spellbound, a shudder running through me whenever his uncanny eyes fell upon me. He made me play to him often, mostly by pointing with his bony hand to the piano without speaking, and I could only guess from his repeating the ceremony that he did not dislike it, for never a word of encouragement fell from his lips. How I longed to hear him play it is impossible to describe, perhaps even to imagine. From my earliest childhood I had heard of Paganini and his art as of something supernatural, and there I actually sat opposite to the man himself, but only looking at the hands that had created such wonders. On one never-to-be-forgotten occasion, after I had played and we had enjoyed a long silence, Paganini rose and approached his violin-case. What then passed in me can hardly be imagined; I was all in a tremble, and my heart thumped as if it would burst my chest; in fact, no young swain going to the first rendezvous with his beloved could possibly feel more violent emotions. Paganini opened the case, took the violin out, and began to tune it carefully with his fingers without using the bow; my agitation became almost intolerable. When he was satisfied, and I said to myself, with a lump in my throat, 'Now, now, he'll take the bow!' he carefully put the violin back and shut the case. And that is how I heard Paganini.

The most important friendship I formed at that time (or it may have been at the end of 1837) was that with Hector Berlioz—'le vaillant Hector,' as he was often called—whose powerful dominating personality I was glad to recognise. How I made his acquaintance is now a mystery to me—it seems as if I had always known him—I also wonder often how it was he showed such interest in an artist of so little importance as I then was; he was so kind to me, and, in fact, became my friend. Perhaps it was because we could both speak with the same enthusiasm of Beethoven, Gluck, Weber, even Spontini, and, perhaps, not less because he felt that I had a genuine admiration for his own works. There never lived a musician who adored his art more than did Berlioz; he was, indeed, 'enthusiasm personified.' To hear him speak of, or rave about, a real *chef d'œuvre*, such as 'Armida,' 'Iphigenia,' or the C Minor Symphony, the pitch of his voice rising higher and higher as he talked, was worth any performance of the same. And what a picture he was at the head of his orchestra, with his eagle face, his bushy hair, his air of command, and glowing with enthusiasm. He was the most perfect conductor that I ever set eyes upon, one who held absolute sway over his troops, and played upon them as a pianist upon the keyboard. But discussion about his genius and his works is superfluous at the present time; even his life is so thoroughly known that I need only relate of him what has come under my personal knowledge.

He also came often to my humble lodgings, and I must say that his visits to me were more frequent than mine to him; for even at that time Madame Berlioz, the once charming and poetic Ophelia, had become somewhat repellent, and it was impossible to imagine her acting or anybody falling in love with her. To her honour it must, however, be said that she upheld Berlioz in his hardest struggles, always ready to endure the greatest privations when it was a question for him to save money enough for the organisation of a concert on a large scale, concerts which seldom left any profit. I had the pleasure of introducing him to Stephen Heller, who soon won his esteem, and remained on friendly terms with him until his death. Berlioz was no executant upon any instrument (for being able to strum a few chords on the guitar does not count), and he was painfully aware how much this was a hindrance to him, and to his knowledge of musical literature, which, indeed, was limited. I was often astonished to find that works, familiar to every pianist, were unknown to him; not merely works written for the piano, such as Beethoven's sonatas, of which he knew but few, but also orchestral works, oratorios, &c., known to the pianist through arrangements, but of which he had not chanced to see a score. Perhaps many undoubted crudities in his works would have been eliminated had he been able to hear them before committing them to paper, for I had several proofs that the eye alone was not sufficient to give him a clear idea of the effect of his musical combinations.

F

Thus at the time when he scored Weber's 'Invitation à la Valse' for the orchestra, he made me play it to him, and when I had come to the point where, after the digression into C major, the theme is resumed in the original key, D flat, he interrupted me with the words, 'Après tout, cela va,' confessing that from the perusal of the piece he had thought the modulation too harsh, and almost impossible. On another occasion, much later, he arrived at my house and eagerly told me he had found a new cadence to end a movement with. 'The last chord,' he said, 'is the chord of G major, and I precede it by the one in B minor.' When I told him there were hundreds of examples of such an ending, he would not believe me, and was greatly astonished when we searched for and found them.

In some of the most interesting moments of Berlioz's musical career in Paris I had the privilege of being with him. Thus on December 5, 1837, I went with him to the Hôtel des Invalides to witness the first performance of his 'Requiem,' and was, therefore, an eye-witness of what took place on that occasion. Habeneck, after Berlioz the most accomplished *chef d'orchestre* in Paris, conducted by rights, and Berlioz sat in a chair near him. Habeneck, who conducted not only the Grand Opera but also the 'Concerts du Conservatoire,' had the habit of now and then putting his conducting stick down and listening complacently to the performance of his orchestra. It was, therefore, perhaps force of habit that made him discard the bâton at the commencement of the

'Tuba mirum,' this time not to listen, but leisurely
to take a pinch of snuff! To my amazement I suddenly saw Berlioz standing in Habeneck's place and
wielding the bâton to the end of the movement. The
moment had been a most critical one, four groups of
brass instruments, stationed at the four corners of
the large orchestra, which with the chorus was placed
under the dome in the centre of the building, having
to enter successively, and, without Berlioz's determination, disaster must have ensued, thanks to the unfortunate pinch of snuff. Habeneck, after the performance, thanked Berlioz profusely for his timely
aid, and admitted that his own thoughtlessness might
have caused a break-down, but Berlioz remained
persuaded that there had been no thoughtlessness,
and that the break-down was intended. I could not
believe this, for the simple reason that when such a
thing occurs it is always the conductor on whose
shoulders the blame of the break-down is laid, and
most deservedly so ; it is, therefore, most unlikely
that he should himself try to provoke one. The
effect of the 'Requiem,' and especially of the 'Tuba
mirum,' was so overpowering that I have never dared
to produce it in England, where it has been my joy
to conduct so many of Berlioz's works ; the placing of
four orchestras at the corners of the principal one is
impossible in our concert rooms, and I consider it indispensable for the due effect of the movement and
the carrying out of the composer's intention.

Of his perfect command over the orchestra,
Berlioz gave an extraordinary proof on the occasion

of a grand concert given by him a few years later in the 'Cirque Franconi.' There had been a very long rehearsal in the morning, at which I was present, as I had to play Beethoven's G major concerto, then very seldom performed. After some hours' hard work Berlioz dismissed the orchestra; I remained with him, and hardly had the last member of the band vanished when Berlioz struck his forehead, exclaiming: 'I have forgotten the overture!' He stood speechless for a few minutes, then said with determination: 'It *shall* go nevertheless.' Now this overture was the one to 'Le Carneval Romain,' to be performed that evening *for the first time*, and never rehearsed. Musicians who know the work, with its complicated rhythm and all its intricacies, will easily understand how bold the venture was, and will wonder that it could be successful. But to see Berlioz during that performance was a sight never to be forgotten. He watched over every single member of the huge band; his beat was so decisive, his indication of all the *nuances* so clear and so unmistakable, that the overture went smoothly, and no uninitiated person could guess at the absence of a rehearsal. This absolute command over the orchestra I had already admired during the preparations for the first production of his 'Romeo and Juliet' in 1839, which took a long time, but resulted in a magnificent performance, stirring the public to enthusiasm. His own public I mean; totally distinct from the general one, which did not appreciate or understand his music. Berlioz had at all times a not inconsiderable

number of devoted followers, who made up in zeal
and admiration for their want of numbers, and to
whom he was warmly and somewhat gratefully
attached. The indifference shown by the crowd, and
even by many musicians, towards his works he felt
deeply, although he tried to make light of it, and
any real success, however temporary, was eagerly
welcomed, and brightened up his life for a while.
So the well-known Paganini incident of the previous
year had strengthened his courage for a long time,
and from a morose made him a most cheerful companion. But thereby hangs a tale which, as all the
actors in it are gone to their rest, may be divulged
without inconvenience. Armand Bertin, the wealthy
and distinguished proprietor of the 'Journal des
Débats,' had a high regard for Berlioz and knew of
all his struggles, which he, Bertin, was anxious to
lighten. He resolved therefore to make him a
present of 20,000 fr., and in order to enhance the
moral effect of this gift he persuaded Paganini to
appear as the donor of the money. How well Bertin
had judged was proved immediately; what would
have been a simple *gracieuseté* from a rich and
powerful editor towards one of his staff became a
significant tribute from one genius to another, and
had a colossal *retentissement*. The secret was well
kept and never divulged to Berlioz. It was known,
I believe, to but two of Bertin's friends besides myself, one of whom is Mottez, the celebrated painter;
I learned it about seven years later when I had
become an intimate friend of the house, and Madame

Armand Bertin had been for years one of my best pupils.

It was in the year 1840 that I overcame my scruples, and, emerging from my long retirement, gave my first public concert in the 'Salle Erard.' Alard and Franchomme assisted me, and the programme opened with Beethoven's trio in B flat. I had hardly played a few bars when I noticed that the pedals had been unhinged and would not act. There was no help for it, and I had to play to the end of the trio without them, after which a few minutes sufficed to set matters right. The consequence of this untoward accident was that all the critics praised me for my judicious and sparing use of the loud pedal, and this reputation clung to me in Paris ever afterwards, although undeservedly so. I was much flattered to see Liszt, Chopin, and Meyerbeer amongst the audience, and felt deeply grateful to them for thus encouraging a young artist on his *début*. The concert was successful, and from that moment my public appearances multiplied, my name became known, and the number of my pupils increased constantly, so that in 1841 I felt justified in marrying, and once more the number 11 became of significance in my life; for I was twice 11 years old, and married on the 11th of the 11th month of the year. My wife, *née* Desirée Smith de Rilieu, was born at New Orleans, and had been residing for some years in Paris with her mother, a widow. Madame Smith had a negro servant, formerly one of her slaves, who had followed her to France, and was much attached to her.   It was customary in Paris to give a party, a ball generally, to the friends of the bride and bridegroom on the eve of the wedding, a custom which we followed.   Madame Smith's confidential servant had been instructed to engage a number of day-waiters for the occasion, and great was my consternation when at the proper moment the ices were brought in by ten waiters—all grinning niggers !

In the summer of 1842 I made a short concert tour through Germany, playing at Wiesbaden, Mayence, Frankfort, Darmstadt, and other towns. At Frankfort I had the happiness to meet Mendelssohn, and to spend a few weeks closely associated with him and rich in musical delight.   At the con cert I gave, he and Hiller played with me Bach's triple concerto in D minor, and at Hiller's house, where we usually met, I became acquainted with the Scotch symphony, then unpublished, of which he had just finished the admirable arrangement as a pianoforte duet, which we played over and over again from the manuscript.   There I heard also for the first time his 'Variations Sérieuses,' and some of the then unpublished 'Lieder ohne Worte,' amongst them the now so popular 'Frühlingslied.'   Mendelssohn's playing was not exactly that of a 'virtuoso,' not to be compared with that of Liszt or Thalberg (he himself called it 'en gros spielen'), but it was remarkably perfect, and one felt the great musician, the great composer, in every bar he played.   He was also a great organist, and I had the privilege of

hearing him improvise, and also play two of his fine
organ sonatas. The greatest treat, however, was to
sit with him at the piano and listen to innumerable
fragments from half-forgotten beautiful works by
Cherubini, Gluck, Bach, Palestrina, Marcello, 'tutti
quanti.' It was only enough to mention one of them,
whether it was a Gloria from one of Cherubini's
Masses or a psalm by Marcello, to hear it played to
perfection, until I came to the conclusion that he
knew every bar of music ever written, and, what was
more, could reproduce it immediately. One morning
Hiller and I were playing together one of Bach's
organ pieces on the piano, one of no particular
interest, but which we wished to know better. When
we were in the middle of it, a part hardly to be distinguished from many other similar ones, the door
opened, Mendelssohn entered, and, without inter-
rupting us, rose on tip-toes, and with his up-lifted
finger pointed significantly at the next bar which
was coming and contained an unexpected and striking modulation. So from hearing through the door
a bar or two of a—for Bach—somewhat commonplace piece, he not only recognised it at once, but
knew the exact place we had arrived at, and what
was to follow in the next bar, a most surprising proof
of intimate knowledge. His memory was indeed prodigious. It is well known that when he revived
Bach's 'Passion Music,' and conducted the first performance of that immortal work after it had been
dormant for about a century, he found, stepping to
the conductor's desk, that a score similar in binding

and thickness, but of another work, had been brought by mistake. He conducted this amazingly complicated work by heart, turning leaf after leaf of the book he had before him, in order not to create any feeling of uneasiness on the part of the executants.

Mendelssohn, and certainly Berlioz, would have been amazed if they had witnessed the modern craze for conducting without the score ; *they* never did so, even with their own works, which certainly they must have known better than anybody else. There can be no possible advantage in dispensing with the score, a glance at which shows to the conductor the whole instrumentation, and enables him to watch over every detail of the execution, and over the entries of the most secondary instruments. No conductor could write by heart twenty pages of the full score of a symphony, or other work, exactly with the instrumentation of the composer (perhaps the composer himself could not do it); he must therefore remain ignorant whilst conducting, of what the minor instruments, say the second clarinet, second bassoon, second flute, and many others, have to do—a serious disadvantage. The public who go into ecstasies over ' conducting by heart' do not know how very easy it is, how much easier, for instance, than playing a concerto or a sonata by heart, at which nobody wonders. Without the score the conductor has only to be acquainted with the general outline of the composition and its salient features ; then, the better the band the easier the task of its chief.

But to return to Frankfort. The few weeks spent

there in the intimacy of Mendelssohn and Hiller are
amongst the most precious, the most interesting, I
have ever lived, and are engraved in my memory
with a point of gold. I never met Mendelssohn again.
On a renewed visit to Frankfort in the autumn of
1843 I received an invitation to play at Darmstadt
before the Grand Duke of Hesse, and I was delighted
to see my dear old master, Rinck, again on the same
occasion. Coming to the castle on the appointed
evening I was ushered into the still untenanted music-
room, where after a time I was joined by a gentleman in simple evening dress who entertained me
most politely, telling me that the Grand Ducal party,
which included the Grand Duke of Saxe-Weimar,
would soon appear. I took my informant for one of
the gentlemen of the Court, and as he was so very
amiable I asked him to be kind enough to point out
to me the different distinguished personages, who, I
said, would probably be familiar to him by sight, but
were not so to me. He promised most willingly to
do so, and it gave me rather a start when I found
half-an-hour later that my kind *cicerone* was the
celebrated Prince Alexander of Hesse. The party
was a small one, and listened to my performance
with a willing ear. What has impressed the evening
upon my memory is the circumstance that while I
was playing, a despatch was brought in announcing
the birth of a son to the Crown Princess of Russia (a
Princess of Hesse Darmstadt), which caused such
joy that the two Grand Dukes not only embraced,
but in spite of their bulky persons, which hardly

permitted their short arms to reach each other, waltzed together through the long and almost empty room. It was a touching but curious spectacle. After half an hour's interruption I was allowed to continue my performance. The next day I had the honour of being received by Prince Alexander at his own villa, and could explain my *bévue* of the previous evening.

During the few months my wife and I spent in Germany, having before our departure given notice to quit the rooms in the Rue de l'Arcade, in Paris, with which we were dissatisfied, a cousin of my wife's, the Comtesse de Rochefort, proposed we should take the rooms which she occupied in the Rue Blanche, as she was leaving for the south of France. I had been often at her evening parties, knew the rooms perfectly, which were most convenient, and we struck the bargain at once. Great was my consternation when, on arriving in September at these much coveted rooms, I found that the building opposite was the Gymnase Musical Militaire, from which nearly all the regimental bands were recruited, and in which hundreds of young men practised the whole day long with open windows, weather permitting, all the wind instruments ever invented, all at the same time, every man in his own key, and doing his own exercises. No more infernal noise can be imagined and I was in despair, but I had signed a short lease and we were obliged to remain where we were; and such is the force of habit, that after a few months I was no longer disturbed by the abominable neighbourhood, and could even give my lessons in peace.

There was one thing, however, which was impossible, viz., to have musical afternoons on Sundays. Our friends could not have enjoyed them, for Sunday was no day of rest for the poor 'piou-pious' opposite; they had to practise till six in the evening as on week-days. I therefore ventured to call upon the director of the Gymnase, the whilom celebrated Italian composer, Carafa, stated my case to him, and induced him, not without trouble, on a certain number of Sundays during the season to stop all practice from three o'clock in the afternoon, much to the relief of the overworked pupils, who were always anxious to give me proofs of their gratitude. Indeed, once, when a fire had broken out in our kitchen, they swarmed into the house, extinguished it, and in their zeal did much more mischief than the fire could have done. These musical afternoons became gradually more and more important, and it was there that, timidly at first, I tried to win acceptance for some of Beethoven's pianoforte works; for, with the exception of two trios, the Kreutzer and the so-called 'Moonlight' sonata, none were known to other than a few earnest students. A great attraction was the exquisite singing, or rather declaiming, of Delsarte, a most extraordinary artist whose dramatic power I have never heard equalled. His voice was far from fine, being rather disagreeable, but it was immediately forgotten after the first few notes, and he held his hearers spellbound. I shall never forget the impression he created when singing Gluck's beautiful air : 'Cruelle, non, jamais ton cœur ne fut touché par mes alarmes.'

It was indescribable. Every syllable told, and the accents of despair were irresistible and inimitable. He sang at nearly every one of my matinées, for which I owe him a debt of gratitude. Lamartine, Odillon Barrot, Ledru Rollin, and Salvandy, who heard him at my house, each one complimented him in the same words: 'Monsieur, vous êtes un grand orateur,' of which he complained to me with perhaps pardonable pride by saying, 'These gentlemen think there is nothing above an orator.' Delsarte died in a monastery, for which, at the time I knew him intimately, he certainly seemed to have no vocation.

My life at this time became one of uninterrupted intellectual enjoyment, which will be easily understood by my readers when I enumerate a few of the names of distinguished men, in the most various walks of life, whom I could call personal friends: Ary Scheffer, Lamartine, Salvandy, Ledru Rollin, Alexandre Dumas *père*, Ingres, Meyerbeer, Halévy, Delacroix, Louis Blanc, Guizot, 'Maitre' Marie, not to forget Berlioz, Heller, Heine, Ernst, Jules Janin, Liszt, Chopin, and a host of others equally remarkable. Paris was then in reality what Wagner wished to make Bayreuth, the centre of civilisation; and such a galaxy of celebrities as it contained has, I believe, never been assembled again. The charm of Parisian life at that period was that in certain 'salons,' on fixed evenings in the week, most of these 'mighty ones' were to be met.

Such a 'salon' was that of Armand Bertin,

made delightful as much by the charm of his wife as by his own intellectual power. It was there that I often met M. Ingres, and had the honour of playing some of Mozart's violin sonatas with him. Great artist as he was, with an immense reputation, he thought less of his painting than of his violin playing, which, to say the least of it, was vile. He generally was so moved by any Andante we played together, that he shed copious tears, and he drew them also from the eyes of his listeners, but they were not tears of delight. His immense superiority as an artist made this little weakness very interesting. An amusing incident occurred when, after his return from Rome, where he had been for years the director of the French 'Académie,' a grand dinner was given him, as a welcome, in the Salle Ventadour, at which every notability in Paris was present. After the speech in his honour, pronounced by whom I cannot remember, and received with uproarious enthusiasm, Ingres rose and returned thanks, and after wiping his spectacles, wet with tears as usual, he drew a paper from his pocket, adjusted it to the light, and the first words he read were: 'Les acclamations que je viens d'entendre.' It seemed odd and 'naïf' that the words should have been written before the cheers were heard.

Ingres was passionately fond of music—a passion shared by nearly all the great painters with whom I have come in contact—while amongst poets and literary men the devotees to music seem to form an exception. Ary Scheffer, the noble painter whose fame was at its zenith in the forties, was never happier than when listening to music; hence his friendship with Chopin, Liszt, and a select number of musicians amongst whom I was happy to hold a place. To play to him in his studio, whilst he was engaged upon one of his great canvases, was to me one of my greatest delights. The well-known picture of 'Christ tempted by Satan' (Liszt sitting as a model for Satan) was commenced and finished with the accompaniment of my music. Scheffer's works no longer hold the position in the world of art which they held at that time—a time when they were sought for, in England especially, with avidity; he knew this, and on one occasion, speaking of this popularity, he added musingly, after a moment's silence, 'Cela me donne à penser.'

In 1843 I made my first acquaintance with England, a very unsatisfactory one as it proved. Unannounced, I came over in the middle of the season on the invitation, principally, of one English friend, Mr. Fitzherbert, whom I had known for years in Paris. My name was not sufficiently known to open the doors of the big institutions to me at once; still, I received an invitation from the directors of the Philharmonic Society to play at their last concert, but coupled with the condition that I should perform a concerto by Griffin, one of the directors. This I declined, and consequently did not play at all. I took part in a concert given by Sivori, and gave a concert in the Hanover Square rooms, at which Clara Novello and Balfe sang, and Sivori played, but the success of which was indifferent. So, after a sojourn of about eight weeks I returned to Paris, firmly resolved to shun England for ever! The short season had, however, not been altogether uninteresting to me, enlivened as it was by a dispute between Ernst and Sivori on the subject of the authorship of 'Le Carneval de Venise.' I was charmed to meet Sivori in London, having made his acquaintance in the previous year, and fully recognised his claims to distinction, in spite of the pompous title 'only pupil of Paganini,' which he assumed. I was often with him and glad of his society, when a few weeks later Ernst arrived. He was fresh from a triumphant tour through Holland and Belgium, and his coming was expected with much curiosity. Ernst was an older friend of mine than Sivori, as a musician he was far his superior, our tastes were more similar, and I naturally continued those friendly relations with him which had so long been my wont. I did not mean to neglect Sivori, but found to my surprise and sorrow that he looked upon my conduct with regard to Ernst as upon the worst of all betrayals. He had fully expected that I should *cut* Ernst, whom he considered his rival, and could not understand how I could dream of being friends with both sides. I had indeed dreamed of bringing them together, which would have been a pleasure to Ernst; but when I hinted at this, the ire of Sivori knew no bounds, and I had to make a selection between the two, much against my will, but of course in favour of my old friend. Ernst achieved a great success and a well deserved one, for his talent was at its very height and his passionate playing most impressive. I rejoiced at his triumph all the more, as for a short time I had harboured serious doubts on the subject, prompted by a curious and somewhat ludicrous scene which I had witnessed a few days after his arrival.

The directors of the Philharmonic Society had decided upon fêting Ernst on his arrival and arranged a party at Richmond in his honour, which took the shape of an early dinner. The day was very fine, the company, including the principal critics, very numerous, and the dinner sumptuous. Ernst had to respond to many civilities, to empty his glass at the separate request of each of the 'convives,' so often that at last I saw that he was overcome, and feared that he might roll under the table. It was at that critical moment that somebody proposed Ernst should play something. The proposal was cheered vociferously, and as Ernst's violin did not dine out, some one was despatched into the village to try and find one. He soon returned with a violin, the price of which, with the bow, was marked fifteen shillings. This was handed to Ernst, and he gave the very first proof of his talent to a select English audience by playing his arrangement of Schubert's 'Erl King,' for violin alone, an impossible piece, which in his best days he could not play satisfactorily. Upon this wretched instrument and in a more than half-tipsy condition, it was excruciating, and I gave him up for lost; but, whether it was that his listeners were in the same state as he, or that the extraordinary sounds they heard bewildered them,

his triumph was complete ! What is more, after his
great and legitimate success, at a concert given on
July 18 in aid of the German Hospital, his first public
appearance in London, I heard it said with conviction, 'Ah, but his playing at Richmond was even
finer!' The party was further enlivened by poor
half-blind George Macfarren running straight into
the Thames and having to be fished out, fortunately
without any hurt to him.

I had brought a few letters of introduction with
me, one of which was to a most amiable man, a member of Parliament, who a few years later rose to a
high position in the Government. I had left the
letter at his house with my card, and he called upon
me the very next day, was charming, most kind, and
to my great satisfaction spoke French most fluently.
He knew from the letter it was my wish to be heard,
and as it so happened that he had a large evening
party two days later, he proposed that I should play
a few pieces during the evening, saying that I should
meet many influential people, with whom I would
certainly be glad to make acquaintance. I accepted
readily. When he withdrew he turned back at the
door and said, 'Might I ask you in what style you
play?' I was puzzled and could not give a clear
answer. He next asked, 'Do you know Mr.
Alexander Dreyschock?' 'Yes,' I said, 'he is an
admirable and powerful pianist.' 'Do you play in
his style?' 'No, I can conscientiously say that my
style differs from his.' 'Oh, I am so glad,' said my
friend, 'for he plays so loud, *et cela empêche les dames*

de causer.' I meekly suggested that no music at all might perhaps be more to the purpose, but he would not hear of that, insisted upon my coming, and I did go, played two pieces, and can give myself credit for not having *empêché les dames de causer*, nor the gentlemen either. This shows in what estimation music was held in 1843 in the most fashionable society; the change that has taken place since then is astounding.

Another of my letters of introduction was to Count d'Orsay, the brilliant and eccentric *roi des modes.* I drove to Kensington Gore, where he lived, and after ringing the bell at the gate, a small side door opened to give passage to the head of the porter who inquired my business. I told him I had a letter to deliver to Count d'Orsay, and at his request gave it to him, together with my card. He then shut the door, leaving me wondering in the street. About ten minutes later the door opened again, I was admitted and conducted through a long avenue to the luxurious house, in which the Count received me with the utmost politeness and grace. When after half an hour I took my departure, he begged me to renew my visit and to excuse him if he did not return my call, as for various reasons he did not go out much. It then dawned upon me that if he ventured out he might possibly not re-enter the house for a long time, and that for this reason such precautions were used in admitting unknown visitors. I was afterwards invited to several small evening parties at Gore House, made delightful by Lady Blessington's grace and d'Orsay's wit. Prince Napoleon was generally one of the guests, but at that time only interested me by his historical name, and I cannot recollect anything characteristic connected with him. In July I returned to Paris with Ernst, little satisfied with England, and much less anticipating that it would eventually become my home, my cherished home.

Nothing of importance happened during the rest of the year, and the circle of my acquaintance extended further and further, the number of my pupils increased steadily, and I had every reason to be satisfied with my lot. My ambition, however, was not entirely satisfied, for, although successful at my own and many other concerts, I had not been invited to play at the 'Concerts du Conservatoire,' which then, even more than at present, was the highest distinction to which an artist could aspire. I did not venture to claim the honour for fear of a refusal, which would have pained me. One evening, returning on foot from a late party, as I was passing Rue Taitbout I sang tolerably loud, there being no one very near, the theme of the Finale of Beethoven's Choral Symphony, which I had heard on the previous Sunday at the Conservatoire. I had not noticed a gentleman who was walking about five yards before me in the same direction, and who, hearing me sing, stopped when I came up to him, when I recognised the redoubtable conductor of the 'Concerts du Conservatoire,' M. Habeneck, whose personal acquaintance I had not made. He addressed me with, 'Ah, vous chantez la neuvième?' and on my replying with a few enthusiastic expressions, he asked brusquely: 'Who are you?' I gave my name, upon which he shook hands with me, said he had heard often of my doings, and to my surprise and delight ended with the question: 'Why don't you play at our concerts?' I explained frankly that I had not dared to apply for such an honour; and 'Call to-morrow and we will arrange that,' was his welcome answer. And so I played at the Conservatoire most unexpectedly in 1844, and had every reason to be satisfied with the reception that was accorded to me. I had chosen Beethoven's E flat concerto, my interpretation of which met with almost general approval. I say 'almost' because after the performance a much respected member of the orchestra, Urhan, the principal viola, apostrophised me with: 'Why do you change Beethoven?' I had not really *changed* anything in the text, but, misled by the example of Liszt, I used then for the sake of effect to play some passages in octaves instead of in single notes, and otherwise amplify certain passages. This Urhan did not like, and his rebuke was well merited. I think Liszt must have felt equal scruples, for when, on the occasion of the unveiling of Beethoven's statue at Bonn in August, 1845, he played the same concerto, he adhered scrupulously to the text, and a finer and grander reading of the work could not be imagined. Urhan was a remarkable viola player, the best I ever heard, and a singular character, very outspoken, as his remark to me proves, and one of the most upright men that ever lived. He was of an extremely religious turn of mind, and accepted the position of principal viola at the Grand Opera, which he held for a long term of years, only on the condition that his seat was to be so arranged that he might turn his back upon the stage and avoid witnessing the abominations of the ballet. The Beethoven festival at Bonn, mentioned incidentally just now, to which Berlioz and I journeyed together from Paris, drew together a large number of the most notable musicians from all countries, all anxious to do homage to the memory of that incomparable genius. It was graced by the presence of the King of Prussia and his guests, Queen Victoria and the Prince Consort, who witnessed from a royal box built purposely in the square the unveiling of the statue, which, to the astonishment of the multitude that surrounded it, was found when the veil fell to turn its back upon the Royalties.

Liszt was the hero of the fête, and justly so, for without his colossal exertions it would never have taken place. He was seldom to be approached by us, so great was the crowd of his admirers that besieged him constantly; but the occasional half hours that he could spare to Berlioz and myself were made memorable by the flashes of his eloquence and his wit. His speech was indeed golden. At the first concert he played us, however, an unpardonable trick. For the opening of the programme he had composed a cantata of considerable length, devoid of interest, as the rehearsals had shown us, but which we had resigned ourselves to listen to patiently, and so we did. Hardly was it concluded, and we were

preparing ourselves to enjoy Beethoven's music, when
the Royalties, who had been detained until then,
entered their box, and Liszt, to our dismay, began
the whole cantata over again, inflicting it a second
time on the immense audience, who, out of respect
for the crowned heads, had to endure it, though probably not without inward grumbling. One morning,
during this week of festivities, I found him alone, and
the conversation turning upon events and anecdotes
which had made the years from 1838 to 1846
memorable to both of us, he suddenly exclaimed,
' Ah l'heureux temps! où l'on pouvait être si bête!'
He spoke feelingly, and I think rendered himself justice, for the things he could say and do during that
period when he was the best fêted artist that perhaps
had ever lived bordered really on the ludicrous.
Thus, after his great triumphs in Germany, especially
in Berlin, where the ladies had fought for his gloves,
I heard him say at one of his receptions in Paris, the
name of the King of Prussia being mentioned : ' Le
roi a été très _convenable_!' To be different from the
rest of mankind, to know nothing of the usual modes
of living, or rather to appear ignorant of them, seemed
his one aim. Once, having accidentally met me on
the Boulevards, he asked me to dine with him at the
Café de Paris. We enjoyed a good but simple dinner,
and when the waiter brought him the bill, which could
hardly have amounted to 30 frs., he asked me quite
seriously if I thought 40 frs. for the waiter would be
sufficient! ' Je ne sais jamais ces choses,' he said,
and without my remonstrances he would have given

to the waiter more than the whole dinner had cost. Calling upon him one day I found him engaged with his tailor, and busy looking at patterns for waist-coats. 'I have at least sixty,' said he to me, 'but never find one to my liking when I want it.' 'What do you say to this pattern?' he asked presently, and on my approving of it he came out with 'Voulez-vous que je vous en fasse faire un?'—a kind offer which was declined with thanks.

One scene I witnessed characterises another side of his behaviour at that time. The programme of one of his concerts given in the 'Salle du Conservatoire' contained the 'Kreutzer' sonata to be played by Liszt and Massart, a celebrated and much esteemed violinist, professor at the Conservatoire. Massart was just commencing the first bar of the introduction when a voice from the audience called out 'Robert le Diable!' At that time Liszt had composed a very brilliant fantasia on themes from that opera, and played it always with immense success. The call was taken up by other voices, and in a moment the cries 'Robert le Diable!' 'Robert le Diable!' drowned the tones of the violin. Liszt rose, bowed, and said: 'Je suis toujours l'humble serviteur du public, mais est-ce qu'on désire la fantaisie avant ou après la sonate?' Renewed cries of 'Robert, Robert!' were the answer, upon which Liszt turned half round to poor Massart and dismissed him with a wave of the hand, without a syllable of excuse or regret. He did play the fantasia magnificently, rousing the public to a frenzy of enthusiasm, then

called Massart out of his retreat, and we had the
'Kreutzer,' which somehow no longer seemed in its
right place. On another occasion, at a concert given
for the benefit of the Polish refugees at the house of
Princess Czartoriska, he did me the honour to ask
me to play a duet for two pianos with him, and chose
Thalberg's well-known 'Fantasia' on 'Norma.' We
had no rehearsal, but he said to me: 'Let us take the
theme of the variations at a moderate pace, the effect
will be better.' Now the first part of this theme is
accompanied on the second piano (which Liszt had
chosen) by octaves for both hands, which octaves in
the second part fall to the lot of the first piano.
What was my horror when, in spite of the caution
he had given me, Liszt started his octaves at such a
pace that I did not conceive the possibility of getting
through my portion of them alive. Somehow I
managed it, badly enough, but if I ever understood
the French saying 'suer sang et eau' it was then. I
had my revenge, however. In the second variation,
where the pianos successively accompany the theme
with chromatic scales, Liszt, instead of confining himself to the scales, altered them by introducing double
and additional notes, a feat of amazing difficulty,
which made my hair stand on end, but which I did
not feel compelled to try and imitate, simple chromatic scales neatly and rapidly played being, on the
whole, more effective ; so when my turn came I confined myself to them, and earned a round of applause
in which Liszt most generously joined.

Of his ready wit the following little anecdote,

hardly known I believe, may serve as an example. A choral society of amateurs had been formed in Paris under his direction, most of the members belonging to the highest aristocracy. At the rehearsals Princess Belgiojoso, an accomplished musician, accompanied on the piano. As an accompanist she had, however, serious faults, for she took great liberties with the time, treating what she had to play as if it had been a 'Nocturne' or 'Ballade' by Chopin, her admired master. During one of these rehearsals, at which I was present by invitation, a young German tenor, not perfectly at home in the French tongue, complained of these liberties by muttering in a low voice at first, but which grew louder and louder: 'Il n'y a pas de *tact*, il n'y a pas de *tact*,' evidently under the impression that the German word 'takt' had the same meaning in French. After a while Liszt corrected him by saying: 'Monsieur, Madame la Princesse manque de *mesure*, mais *vous* manquez de *tact*.'

Of the years between 1843 and 1847 it only remains to relate that in 1843 I had the honour of being commanded to play at the Château d'Eu on the occasion of the visit of H.M. Queen Victoria and Prince Albert to Louis Philippe. The orchestra and chorus of the Conservatoire had also been summoned, and Auber was director of the music in general. On the entrance, on Louis Philippe's arm, of Queen Victoria into the music-room, she was most appropriately greeted with the beautiful chorus from Gluck's 'Iphigénie en Aulide,' commencing ' Que de grâce, que de majesté.' Those were brilliant days, favoured by the most beautiful weather. One incident connected with my trip to Eu was very original. I learnt, one day before the concert at which I was to play, that there was no piano at the château fit to be used on such an occasion, and I had to send one from Paris. But how to send it? That was the question. There was not time for the usual mode of conveyance, so I went to the office of the diligence, where the mention of a grand piano by Erard as part of my luggage was at first received with derisive laughter. But the magical words ' Par ordre du roi ' overcame the difficulty, and the piano was stowed on the top of the huge diligence, the only instance on record, I believe, of a pianist travelling in the same carriage with his instrument.

The year 1847 forms an epoch in my musical life. I had then long been prominently before the public, and felt strong enough to venture upon the institution of a series of ' concerts de musique de chambre,' never before tried in Paris. In Alard and Franchomme, the two foremost performers on the violin and violoncello, admirable artists both, I found willing, even enthusiastic, colleagues. The ' Salle du Conservatoire ' was granted us, and in February 1847 we gave our first concert, before an audience which included the very *élite* of Parisian artistic and literary society. Lamartine, George Sand, Horace Vernet, Ary Scheffer, Guizot, Salvandy, Ledru Rollin, Marie, Alexandre

Dumas, and many others equally celebrated, filled the boxes as subscribers. I was well aware of the progress the taste for good music had made during the last decade. Still, the success of these concerts, purely instrumental ones, surpassed my most sanguine expectations. Soon it became almost as difficult to obtain tickets for them as for the great concerts of the Conservatoire; in fact, we scored a great success. The programmes consisted exclusively of *ensemble* music, from duets to quintets, Armingand holding the post of second violin, and Casimir Nery that of viola. The preparation for the concerts was a labour of love for us all, and rehearsals took place every day while the series lasted. It seems strange to me now, writing in 1895, that so many universally-known works like Mendelssohn's trios, Schumann's quintet and quartet, had then the charm of absolute novelty. This first season having been so eminently successful, the announcement of the second in 1848 drew together a still greater number of subscribers, so that every place was disposed of before the first concert, which took place at the commencement of February.

Two concerts had been given when the Revolution broke out, and to me everything was changed as by magic. In Paris by far the greatest part of a musician's income was invariably derived from teaching; so it was with Chopin, Heller, many others, and myself; but from the day after the Revolution the pupils disappeared, and at the end of a week I could only boast of one (he was an old Englishman), and my friends Alard and Franchomme had none left. The

audience at our third concert did not number fifty
people, although every place was subscribed for. The
outlook was most gloomy and I realised soon that a
serious crisis had arrived in my life, and that an immediate determination had to be taken for the sake of
my family, which consisted then of my wife and two
small children. What determination it was to be I
could not at once decide, but I felt that I must be
free, and resolved therefore to abandon the remaining
five concerts of the series, my colleagues concurring
readily. We announced that the money would be
returned, and on the very day that the announcement
appeared my house was literally besieged from morning to evening by eager applicants, money being for
a while so scarce that daily processions of people were
seen going to the mint to exchange their silver valu-
ables for ready cash.

Of the Revolution itself I can only relate what I
saw with my own eyes, and that is very little, although
at one moment my life was in danger, viz. on the eve
of the Revolution, when nothing serious was expected.
I had gone with a friend (M. Guibert) to look at the
crowds on the Boulevards, and found that the Foreign
Office on the Boulevard des Capucines was guarded
by a *carré* of military, which obliged us to pass through
the Rue Basse des Remparts, having the soldiers some
10 or 12 feet above our heads. This street was
densely crowded and we advanced very slowly, when
suddenly, without any warning, we were fired into
with terrible effect, a woman close by my side and a
child within my reach being both shot dead. The

surprise was dreadful, and Boulevard and street were cleared in an instant. I reached my house without accident, meeting only flying people, and intensely enjoyed the feeling of safety. We lived then at the corner of the Place St. Georges, a circular place into which four streets lead. The next morning, between five and six o'clock, I was awakened by a singular noise under our windows, and, stepping upon the balcony, I saw that the four streets had been barricaded and that all communication between the Place St. Georges and the rest of the world had been cut off. The barricades were manned by a set of ill-looking, hirsute people, armed with antediluvian weapons. The construction of the barricades not being finished yet, the mob paid small attention to the inhabitants of the houses that surrounded the Place. A little later, however, when stepping a second time on to the balcony, I saw Madame Thiers come out of her house in a loose dressing-gown, carrying several guns and handing them to the insurgents, with whom M. Thiers, as leader of the Opposition and credited with Republican tendencies, stood in high favour. As I had the advantage of a slight acquaintance with M. and Mme. Thiers, whose house was the second from the one in which I lived with my family, I descended quickly and approached her, to compare notes, not a little pleased to put myself apparently under her protection and thereby to gain some respect from our ruffian captors. But there was little to fear from them, as it proved. They asked for arms, of which I had none to give, and for wine, which they drank 'on the premises,' but without excess. The flags on the barricades bore on the first day the inscription, 'Vive la Réforme,' which was changed the next day into 'Vive la République.' Being pretty far from the centre of Paris, we heard no news, everything seemed quiet, and only twice during the day did we see a regiment of soldiers pass through the Rue St. Lazare, at the end of our street, with their guns reversed, from which we concluded that at all events part of the army had fraternised with the people. Our friends of the barricades cheered them most vociferously, but had no more news of what was going on than we.

On the evening of the second day this imprisonment became intolerable to me, and I ventured to ask the sentinels if I might go to inquire after my friends. Permission being given, I passed through and found a second barricade at the end of the street, which also proved no obstacle. Fortunately, I found my friends, of whom Heller was the first I visited, all well, heard for the first time of the flight of Louis Philippe, the formation of a 'Gouvernement provisoire,' and after an hour's absence returned home with this weighty news. Approaching the lower barricade of our street, I was challenged by a most ferocious-looking individual in the gruffest of voices with 'Qui vive?' I drew as near to him as I could and said that I really did not know under the circumstances what was the proper answer to give, but that I only wanted to return to my family in the Place St. Georges, which I had left but an hour before. Apparently satisfied, he screamed out, looking more grim than before, 'Eh bien, passez! mais prenez garde là-bas!' Alarmed and thinking of possible ambuscades, I asked him what danger threatened me 'là-bas.' 'C'est qu'il y a de l'eau,' was the answer. It had been raining, and the pavement having been partially taken up, there were pools of water here and there, and my formidable-looking challenger was anxious that I should not wet my feet! A rose-coloured revolution, indeed! One, however, which completely destroyed my prospects in Paris and forced me to consider very seriously what to do next. I could not remain in Paris, and my thoughts began to travel towards London, when one day M. de Soligny, formerly French Chargé d'Affaires in Mexico, called with a message from M. de Lamartine, the chief of the 'Gouvernement provisoire.' The message was nothing less than the offer of the secretaryship at the French Embassy to the German Diet in Frankfort, Soligny being the chosen ambassador. I believe, however, that he never occupied the post. Twenty-four hours were given me for my decision, and those were most anxious hours, but at the end of them I felt that musician I was and musician I must remain. I declined the tempting offer, and went direct to Lamartine to express my thanks and to explain my reasons for refusing it. A fortnight more was spent in consultation with my best friends, the result of which was that I decided upon going to London, there to seek a new existence for my family.

I left Paris in March 1848 with a very heavy

heart indeed; not only had I to leave my family behind me at first, but the separation from so many friends, from a society which I had good reason to think unequalled in the world, was a hard wrench. Often during my twelve years of residence there had I said to myself that it would be impossible for me to live anywhere else, and now I had to say 'adieu' most unexpectedly; for, one short month before, I thought myself secure in Paris for the rest of my lifetime. A new life was to begin for me in England; but before I narrate what befell me here, I must throw a few retrospective glances upon people I met in Paris and who have not yet been mentioned in these memoirs.

'*Place aux dames.*' In my earliest recollection dwells one evening in 1839, when a friend took me to one of the receptions of Mademoiselle Taglioni, the celebrated dancer, the admired of the admired, whose every attitude, every motion, was an embodiment of grace, a study for the sculptor and painter. My admiration for her knew no bounds, and to be in her own salon was great happiness to me. There were crowds of people there, and the best names of France were represented: my excitement was intense when she kindly asked me to play something. I did so, and then behind my back I heard her say to a friend, 'mais il joue comme un ange;' words that thrilled my every nerve. I could not approach her again during the evening, and the next time I met her was about forty years later, when at a dinner-party in London I found myself seated by her side. Then I told her of that, to me, memorable evening, repeated to her the very words she had spoken, never forgotten by me, and added: 'Ah, Madame Taglioni, if you knew how deeply in love I was with you at that time!' 'Et vous me dites cela maintenant!' was her prompt reply.

Another remarkable lady, very different from Mademoiselle Taglioni, for she was a confirmed invalid, was Mademoiselle Louisa Bertin, sister of Armand Bertin, spoken of in Parisian society invariably as Mademoiselle Louisa, just as if she had been some royalty. She was a most distinguished lady, and a very clever and serious musician, accomplishing even the composition of an opera, 'Esmeralda,' which, through the influence of the 'Journal des Débats,' was actually performed at the Grand Opéra, called then 'L'Académie Royale de Musique.' The work had no success, and was withdrawn after a few performances. What I remember best was the general rehearsal, when the stalls were crowded with celebrities of all kinds: friends of the autocrat Armand, and also of the very amiable lady whose work they were invited to judge. Rossini was placed on the stage in an easy chair close to the scenery on the left side, and was, of course, the observed of all observers. He gave no sign during the first act, but in the middle of the second, when a momentary pause had occurred, he rose and advanced slowly towards the conductor. Immediately a whisper ran through the whole house—'Rossini va parler'—everybody was all ears, and this was what he said: 'Monsieur Habeneck, vous ne voyez donc pas? Il y a un quinquet qui fume;' and he returned to his seat. A somewhat similar scene, of which, however, I was not an eye-witness, had occurred at one of the rehearsals of his own 'Guillaume Tell.' There, also, during a pause, he had crossed the stage up to a spot from which he could speak to M. Brod, the celebrated oboe player, professor of the Conservatoire, whom he addressed with, 'M Brod, have you your snuffbox with you?' 'Yes, maestro.' 'Then give me a pinch.' The pinch duly taken, he continued: 'M. Brod, in the introduction to such and such an air there occurs an F which you play sharp; I should prefer it natural, if you please. With regard to the F sharp, *ne vous en tourmentez pas ; nous trouverons moyen de la placer ailleurs.*' I had occasion to relate this little anecdote to Berlioz, who jumped up from his chair, exclaiming, 'C'est foudroyant d'esprit!'

A remarkable man I met now and then at the house of M. Mallet in 1840 and 1841 was Donizetti, a most distinguished, amiable, and fashionable gentleman, as elegant as most of his music. He was young still, but such a prolific composer that at that time he had already written upwards of forty operas. I remember talking with him about Rossini, and asking if Rossini had really composed the 'Barbiere' in a fortnight. 'Oh, I quite believe it,' said he, 'he has always been such a lazy fellow!' I confess that I looked with wonder and admiration at a man who considered that to spend a whole fortnight over the composition of an opera was a waste of time. Another and much more remarkable man, whom I saw several times at my friend Leo's house, was Alexander von Humboldt, certainly the most celebrated man of his time.   When the invitation bore the words 'To meet Humboldt,' the rooms were naturally crowded, and he was the cynosure of all eyes.   Wherever he stood a crowd of eager listeners assembled around him, all mute and full of reverence, and intent on every word that fell from his lips.   He never attempted to lead or originate a conversation in the true sense of the word ; he always spoke alone, delivering a lecture on one subject or another, and was never anxious to hear anybody else's opinion.   I was once asked to play for him, and looked upon this invitation as an event in my life.   There had been a momentary silence in the rooms, but the moment I began to play von Humboldt began to hold forth on a new and evidently most interesting topic, his voice rising with every one of my *crescendos*, dominating my most powerful *fortes*, and resuming its normal level only with my most delicate phrases.   It was a duet which I did not sustain long—' je pliais bagage,' and left the ' champ de bataille ' to him, undoubtedly much to the advantage of those whom he addressed.

CHAPTER III

1848–1866

WITH my arrival in March 1848 begins a new epoch
in my life, by far the most important and active one,
which in many respects has been full of surprises to

me. Very far indeed was I then from anticipating that I should one day feel thoroughly at home in England, be proud to become one of her citizens, and play a humble but not altogether unimportant part in the development of her musical taste. My first call was upon my friend Berlioz, who was in trouble through the bankruptcy of Monsieur Jullien, by whom he had been engaged to conduct the opera at Drury Lane. I did not meet him, but returning home from a long round of calls I found the following characteristic note :

Mon cher Hallé,—Je suis bien *fâché* d'avoir le plaisir de vous voir, je vous remercie néanmoins d'être venu à la maison aussitôt après votre naufrage sur les côtes d'Angleterre. Si vous y êtes ce soir, nous nous désolerons ensemble en *fumant*. Je reviendrai chez vous vers les dix heures. Tout à vous,
HECTOR BERLIOZ.[1]

And we did 'désoler' ourselves together, the future looking very black indeed. The five years which had elapsed since I left London in '43 had, however, brought some change in my position as an artist, and, instead of having to solicit engagements, the opportunity of playing in public was offered to me spontaneously. Some grand orchestral concerts were given at Covent Garden under the direction of Signor Costa, and I soon received an invitation to play Beethoven's E flat concerto at one of them. This

---

[1] Dear Hallé,—I am very *sorry* to have the pleasure of seeing you, nevertheless I thank you for having come to this house so soon after your shipwreck on the coast of England. If you are at home to-night we shall lament together while *smoking*. I shall come to you about ten o'clock. Ever yours,   HECTOR BERLIOZ.

I may consider my first public appearance in England, and it was favourably received and criticised. An invitation to play at the Musical Union followed immediately, and was renewed several times during the season. The Musical Union, the predecessor of the Popular Concerts, was originated and directed by Mr. John Ella, and, at the time I speak of, was very flourishing, and the most important concert institution (for chamber music) in London. The Duke of Cambridge was president, and there was a committee composed of members of the highest aristocracy, who, however, did not interfere with the management of the concerts. That was entirely in the hands of Mr. Ella.

Before relating what passed between Mr. Ella and me on the occasion of my first performance at the Musical Union, I must remind my readers that I speak of the year 1848, since which time such a revolution in musical matters has taken place, that what happened then may seem incredible now. When Mr. Ella asked me what I wished to play, and heard that it was one of Beethoven's pianoforte sonatas, he exclaimed, 'Impossible!' and endeavoured to demonstrate that they were not works to be played in public; that, as far as he knew, no solo sonata had ever before been included in any concert programme, and that he could not venture upon offering one to his subscribers. I had to battle for several days before he gave way. He consented at last, and was then much surprised to find that the sonata I had chosen (Op. 31, No. 3 in E flat) pleased so much that several ladies who heard it arranged afternoon parties in order to hear it once more. I have searched the columns of the 'Musical World' for at least fifteen years previous to 1848, but have not found one instance of a sonata being included in a concert programme ; Ella therefore may have been right in considering my venture a bold one. Subsequently he made no difficulty about admitting other sonatas ; he only recommended me to be careful in their selection, and to choose those that could more easily be appreciated. I advanced therefore very cautiously, the second sonata I played being the one in D, Op. 28, commonly known as the 'Pastorale.' What a contrast 1848 offers to 1895 ! *Then* the question was : Can this or that sonata be understood by the audience ? Nowadays the difficulty lies in finding one not too hackneyed.

These few public appearances did more for me to keep starvation from my door than the host of letters of introduction I had brought from Paris, some of them to very interesting people. One was to Lord Brougham, who received me very kindly in his mansion in Grafton Street, but candidly told me that music was not at all in his line ; another was to Mr. Richard Cobden, who said with equal candour that he had never been able to distinguish 'God Save the Queen' from any other tune ; a third was for Chevalier de Bunsen, the Prussian Ambassador, a most distinguished and amiable man and a great lover of music. In his family circle I have spent many a pleasant hour, although my first ap-

pearance in his 'salon' had been far from agreeable
to me. I had received a very kind invitation from
him to play at one of his receptions, and had set
great hopes upon it, for necessarily there would be
many people there who could favour my views if I
succeeded in gaining their approbation. The rooms
were densely crowded, everybody standing, as nearly
all the seats had been removed, and a frightful babel
of tongues was going on. When I was asked to
play, I thought in my innocence that silence would
be established and sat down to the piano; but after a
few minutes I rose again with the conviction that
not a note of what I had played could have been
heard. The thanks of the chevalier seemed a cruel
mockery; still, when later in the evening he asked
me to play again, he was so amiable, that out of
deference to him I did so; but unable at the moment
to recollect a shorter piece than the one I had played
half an hour before, I repeated it, and neither the
chevalier nor anybody else detected the identity!

To another introduction, that to Mrs. Sartoris
(*née* Adelaide Kemble), I owe some of the greatest
pleasures I have enjoyed in London. She was indeed
a rare woman, and her somewhat taciturn husband a
man of vast intelligence. Both were musicians to
the core, intensely enthusiastic, and of sound judgment. Their house reminded me strongly of the
'salon' of Armand Bertin in Paris, for it was the
rendezvous of most of the remarkable people in
London: poets, painters, musicians, all feeling equally
at home, and all finding something to interest them.

It is to Mrs. Sartoris that I owe my first acquaintance
with Browning, Thackeray, Dickens, Leighton, Watts,
Wilkie Collins, and a host of other celebrities; and
it will always be my pride to have enjoyed their
affectionate and intimate friendship till death removed
them both.   Another house, the tiniest in London
perhaps, but a real gem, to which I repaired often with
great pleasure, was that of Henry F. Chorley, the
musical critic and contributor to the 'Athenæum.'   I
was always sure to find interesting men there, and met
Cockburn and Coleridge, who both rose to be Lord
Chief Justices of England, for the first time under his
roof.   He was a man of strong views, fearless in his
criticism, perfectly honest, although often and uncon-
sciously swayed by personal antipathies or sympathies.
Of his oddities I shall have to speak now and then.

Slowly I laid the foundations for a new existence;
pupils came to me, some of them being former pupils
who had fled from Paris like myself and continued
their lessons in London.   Amongst them there was
the daughter of M. Guizot, who, fallen from his high
estate, was living in a modest house in Pelham
Crescent, Brompton.   After the sanguinary June
days in Paris, during which I was tortured with
anxiety for my family, I sent for them and had no
rest till I saw them safe in London.   Soon after a
hard blow fell upon me, crushing for a time all my
energies—the death of my beloved father.   My grief
was beyond all expression, and under the weight of
memories that crowded upon me I felt as weak as a
child.   Stern necessity roused me at last out of my
stupor; the London season was drawing to a close;

a musical autumn and winter season did not then exist, and all I could hope for was to find some stray pupils and to derive from them an uncertain income.

At this crisis I received an important communication from Manchester, through a brother of my Parisian friend Leo, who was residing there. Mr. H. Leo had several times visited his brother in Paris; I had made his acquaintance and found him not only a very amiable man, but a most enthusiastic amateur of music and a great connoisseur. He held a good position in Manchester, and, as far as music was concerned, he was looked upon as an authority and deservedly so. At the end of June he came to London purposely to propose that I should take up my residence in Manchester, and he assured me, on behalf of many devoted lovers of music, that Manchester was quite ripe *to be taken in hand*, and that they thought me the fittest man to stir the dormant taste for the art. We had several interviews, and in the end, although I knew absolutely nothing of Manchester beyond that it was a large and rich town, I determined to give it a trial; on the condition, however, that a fixed number of pupils (not a small one) should be enrolled to begin work from the day of my arrival, and the further condition that I should always be allowed to spend the summer season in London, where I had been too successful already, and had made too many friends to harbour the thought of abandoning it altogether. Not a week had elapsed when I received the news that the pupils I had stipulated for were found and awaiting me, and I was summoned to keep my promise. Reassured as to the financial prospects of the future, and attracted powerfully by the hope of fostering the taste for music in so large a community, I proceeded to change my residence for a second time in the course of three months.

I left many friends behind, amongst whom I must name dear old Moscheles, in his younger days the most brilliant of pianists, many of whose compositions, especially his studies, will remain as standard works for all time. Moscheles had often been at my house in Paris, even daily during the few months which he spent there, occupied with the composition of his second pianoforte sonata for four hands. I have indeed reason to remember that sonata, for whenever he had added twenty or twenty-four bars to the unfinished work, he came to me with the beautifully written manuscript to try them over. And in order to give them their due effect, as he said, we had always to begin from the introduction and to go through the whole sonata until the new portion was reached, so that for every twenty new bars in the finale, we played the introduction, the allegro, the andante, the scherzo, and the finale, so far as it was ready. Often I was fetched from my house even as late as midnight by the amiable and charming Madame Moscheles, because ' they had a few friends with them who were anxious to hear the sonata.' I must have played it a few hundred times in this mutilated way before, on its completion, Moscheles gave a grand evening party at Kalkbrenner's house to produce it before the artistic and literary world. It

met with success, but has never eclipsed the first
sonata, which remains superior to it in freshness of
ideas. I am still glad that I never showed any signs of
impatience during this long trial; ever since I battled
as a boy with Moscheles's ' Variations sur la Marche
d'Alexandre,' and his G minor concerto, I had
venerated his name and felt happy and proud to be
chosen by and associated with him on this occasion.
His good feeling towards me remained the same when
I came to London, of which he gave me a proof by
sending his eldest daughter to me as a pupil; at
which I felt elated and which was not without a
certain influence on public opinion. Benedict, Sterndale Bennett, Davison, Henry Broadwood, that prince
of pianoforte makers, were amongst the other friends
that I quitted unwillingly, but with the hope of seeing
soon again.

In Manchester I was most kindly received, especially by the German colony, which was prosperous
and important. Preceding my small family by a few
weeks in order better to prepare for their installation,
I was introduced in a short time to most of the
notabilities of the town, went through a succession of
dinner parties, and, in short, was ' made much of ' as
the phrase goes. My pupils were ladies of the most
various ages, many of them having evidently joined
the ranks merely for the sake of making up the
requisite number. Their accomplishments were as
various as their ages, but I found goodwill and
perseverance amongst all of them. One pupil gave
me a great surprise. She belonged to a family con-

sidered the most musical in the neighbourhood, and brought as a test of her powers a sonata for piano and violin. When I suggested that a piece for the piano alone would be more to the purpose, she said *this* was a piece of which all at home were very fond, and she hoped I would allow her to play it for me. In answer to my question if her father or a brother played the violin part, she said, 'Oh, no, I always play it alone.' Now the copy she had did not contain the violin part, and I began to feel some curiosity as to how she would deal with certain parts of the composition principally allotted to the absent instrument. The sonata was a simple one by Mozart, and the lady began to play it most correctly. Soon she came to a series of eight bars in which the absent violin had all the melody and the piano nothing but an old-fashioned accompaniment in broken chords. She played them attentively, and after four bars of this unmeaning twaddle, I heard her say to herself with deep emotion, 'Beautiful!' Shortly after she omitted about twenty bars, without apparent reason, and when I asked, 'Why don't you play this part?' she gave a never-to-be-forgotten answer, 'Oh, that is in a minor key, and papa does not like minor.' How musical must have been the family capable of expunging from every piece of music all the modulations into a minor key! I did not try to convert the papa, but the daughter had to put up with pieces in minor and soon grew fond of them.

Not long after my arrival in Manchester I had occasion to hear one of the concerts of the oldest and most important musical society of the town, called 'The Gentlemen's Concerts,' from the fact that it was originally founded in 1774, I believe, by amateurs, twenty-six in number, who constituted what may be called the orchestra, but who all and every one of them played the flute! In course of time other instruments were added, and in 1848 the modern orchestra had been completed for more than a score or two of years. The society was wealthy, would-be subscribers having generally to wait three years before room could be made for them; in consequence every artist of renown who had visited England had been engaged, and the older programmes of the concerts are remarkably rich in celebrated names. At the concert which I attended, Grisi, Mario, and Lablache sang; but the orchestra! oh, the orchestra! I was fresh from the 'Concerts du Conservatoire,' from Hector Berlioz's orchestra, and I seriously thought of packing up and leaving Manchester, so that I might not have to endure a second of these wretched performances. But when I hinted at this my friends gave me to understand that I was expected to change all this—to accomplish a revolution, in fact, and begged me to have a little patience. At the next concert I was engaged to play the E flat concerto by Beethoven, and Mr. Zeugher Herrmann was invited to come over from Liverpool to conduct it, which he did with great skill, accomplishing all that could be accomplished with the unsatisfactory material he had to deal with. During the same month of August Chopin came, played, but was little understood. He

remained a few days only, then went to Scotland on
a visit to Miss Stirling, a pupil to whom he dedicated
several of his works. The Scotch climate tried his
weak constitution severely and hastened his death.

In the winter of 1848–49 I ventured upon a
series of six chamber-music concerts, assisted by two
modest local artists; but in spite of the efforts of my
friends, who canvassed most energetically for subscribers, their total number reached only sixty-seven;
the sale of single tickets for the first concert amounted
to three, and to a few more for each one of the succeeding concerts. These were small beginnings indeed, but did not dishearten me. Every item in the
programme was new to the small audience and received
with appreciation. I felt that there was a whole
musical education to make, and devoted all my energies to the task. When I began a second series in
November 1849 the subscribers numbered 193, and
by general desire I had to add a short series of four
concerts in February and March 1850. During that
winter Ernst and Piatti made their first appearance
in Manchester at these concerts, and from that time
remained identified with them. The summer season
of '49 I spent in London, where I was engaged to
play at the whole series of the concerts given by the
Musical Union. My choice of pieces was then un-
fettered, and it was a pleasure to me to introduce
many works unknown to the audience until then.
Among these was Schubert's trio in E flat, the performance of which was connected with an amusing
incident. Mr. Ella had written an analysis of this

work, to be inserted in the programme, in which he had dismissed the 'Menuetto' with the short sentence, 'This movement is not very interesting.' When he showed me the proof on the day previous to the concert, I remonstrated and said he would probably find that this 'Menuetto' was the gem of the whole trio. He replied that he had carefully read it through, and that it had not struck him as particularly remarkable. We had a short discussion about it, but I felt I could not convince him. The conversation turned upon other things for some time, when just before taking leave he referred once more to the 'Menuetto,' and said: 'Well, I do not mind making a slight change in the paragraph you object to.' He showed me the proof again, and I read to my surprise: 'This movement is . . . very interesting.' The change was indeed slight—only one word omitted—but it could hardly have been greater.

On my return to Manchester after the summer season of 1849 I found the town in a state of excitement, caused by the announcement that Jenny Lind would give a concert for the benefit of the infirmary. She was then at the height of her popularity, had never sung in Manchester before, and it was natural, therefore, that every ticket should be sold long before her arrival. The hall was consequently crowded, and I was accommodated with a seat on the platform. I had never heard her before and my curiosity was at the highest pitch, but the reality surpassed all my expectations. Never had I been moved by any singer as by her, and never again shall be, I feel certain.

I

Her first air was the grand scena from 'Der Frey-schütz,' and never shall I forget the impression it made upon me. Her singing in the first recitative of the long high note with the descent which follows, upon the words 'Welch' stille Nacht' nearly suffocated me. I was sobbing audibly, and yet this extraordinary effect was produced by the simplest means. It was indeed true art coupled with enthusiasm and uncon-scious inspiration. Added to this there was a per-fection of execution which was itself a marvel, and I can say without fear of contradiction that we shall never hear her like again. Shortly after this concert she gave two more on her own account, which were equally crowded. Since then I have heard her often and often, and my admiration always remained un-altered. The concerts in Manchester were followed by a short tour through the provinces, during which I was engaged as pianist, and had occasion therefore not only to revel in her singing, but also to witness the enthusiasm with which she was received every-where, and which sometimes led to great incon-venience. Crowds of people were always waiting at the door of her hotel to get a glimpse of her, and the police had often to be called for her protection. At Worcester, on one occasion, I had entered a carriage with her and the horses had drawn us about two yards when the pressure of the crowd suddenly broke both the windows, the splinters of the glass flying about to our consternation. I got a nasty cut. She remained fortunately uninjured, but we had to return to the hotel, and after that I was shy of the honour of driving out with her. Whether her judgment in music kept pace with her marvellous genius as a singer I have not been able to decide, for I have seen her cry when hearing a beautiful masterpiece well sung by a good chorus, and seen her cry also when some very commonplace ditty was given by the same chorus.

At the end of the year 1849 the conductorship of the 'Gentlemen's Concerts' was offered to me, and I accepted it on the condition that the band should be dismissed and its reorganisation left entirely in my hands. This was the first step towards the position which Manchester now holds in the domain of orchestral music. I had then to be satisfied, however, with attracting to Manchester a certain number of first-rate instrumentalists, mostly from London, with displacing others, changing the position of the instruments which had been absurd—the double basses, for instance, standing in front—and recruiting in the neighbourhood the best talent available. The result was a good one, much approved of by the subscribers, and from that time the cultivation of orchestral music in Manchester has been my chief delight and remains so still. That the taste for chamber music began to grow and that Ernst and Piatti were often seen and heard at my concerts I have already related. During the winter of 1849–50 I proposed to Ernst that we should give a similar concert in Liverpool. He readily assented, and, relying upon his great reputation and my rising one, we promised ourselves great success, engaged a good violoncellist, made an excellent programme and gave the concert. The audience consisted of eleven people, four of whom were reporters! Such was the beginning of my acquaintance with that flourishing town, with the musical life of which I have since become so intimately associated.

The circle of my acquaintances in Manchester had by this time become so extended, and I had come across so many amateurs with fair voices and an ear for music, that in 1850 I was able to found the 'St. Cecilia Society,' in imitation of the German 'Gesang-Verein,' which dwelt in my memory from the days of my childhood. It consisted of ladies and gentlemen of the best society, at first about fifty in number, who met weekly for the study of choral works under my direction, and found such pleasure in it, and worked so well, that soon these meetings became a source of great pleasure to them and to me. The society grew from year to year, and contributed not a little to spread that intelligent love of the art which distinguished Manchester. I conducted it for many years, till my engagements became too numerous, and I had reluctantly to hand it over to my friend Edward Hecht, an excellent and thoroughly reliable musician, who later on became my chorus-master, and rendered me most valuable services. Death snatched him away in the prime of life, but he is most affectionately remembered by all who knew him.

Pupils came to me in increasing numbers, many giving me extreme satisfaction by their real disposi-

Charles Hallé
1850

tion and love for music; others there were who, like the young lady with the father who hated minor keys, offered me much food for amusement. Of these I will give only one specimen, which will stand for many.

A clergyman of middle age appeared one day at my house with the request that I should give him some lessons. He had brought a friend—a total stranger to me—in order that the friend might introduce him. This seemed odd, but did not prepare me for all the oddities that were to follow. Day and hour having been duly fixed, he came at the appointed time, armed with a music book, entered my study, and without any greeting stood before me smiling. After a few moments, seeing my astonishment, he pointed with his finger to his throat, which I took for an indication that he had lost his voice. I expressed my regret at this, when he said, 'No, no; I have only taken off the badge.' I then understood that on coming for a music lesson he had judged proper not to appear in the character of a clergyman, and had exchanged the customary white necktie for a black one. I accordingly invited him to play something in order that I might know how far he had already progressed. 'Yes, yes, immediately,' he said; 'but before I do so I wish you to look at the list of my deficiencies, which I have prepared in order that you might know at once how to deal with me.' He handed me a sheet of paper, the margins of which he had ornamented with arabesques, evidently whilst musing on what he would have to write down, which paper I have carefully preserved up to the present day, and which runs as follows :—

List of Deficiencies.

1. Deficient in the shake.
2. Deficient in general execution.
3. Very deficient in the performance of scales, both diatonic and chromatic.
4. Deficient in rapidity of fingers.
5. Deficient in equality of touch.
6. Third finger very weak.
7. Extreme nervousness when playing before company.

Questions.

1. How many hours (a day) ought I to practise?
2. What style of music ought I to study?

Having pocketed this remarkable document, I renewed my request for the performance of some piece or other, and he proposed to play Beethoven's Sonata with the Funeral March, contained in the book he had brought with him. Sitting down to the piano, he looked attentively at the music and then put his fingers down upon two wrong notes—two E naturals. 'E flat,' I said. He held fast to the wrong notes, looked at the music, at his fingers, up and down several times, then turned his head towards me with a smile, said, 'To be sure,' and then removed his fingers from the wrong to the right notes. In the very next bar a similar mistake occurred. I corrected it; then came the same operation of looking up and down, the same smile, and the same 'To be sure.' This having been repeated four or five times in as many bars, I remained silent afterwards, thinking only of how to get rid of so unpropitious a pupil without giving him offence. He struggled on through about half the first page, which took a considerable time, then suddenly closed the book, held it before my eyes, and said, with another smile, ' Is not that nicely bound ? ' I assented ; and ' I got it bound when I was at Cambridge,' was the information he gave me. Re-opening the book, he began again at the identical note in the middle of a bar at which he had left off, and after another ten minutes' stumbling he reached at last the end of the first page. By that time I had made up my mind, and told him politely that he was not advanced enough to become one of my pupils, and advised him to go to some other teacher. He was sorry, but submitted. Before leaving he said there was one piece he was most anxious to learn, and ' did I think he could master it ? ' ' Which piece ? ' I inquired ; and ' A Fantasia on the Prophet, by Liszt,' was the answer ; to which I could only reply : ' Not in this world ! ' During this last colloquy he had been putting on his gloves, which gave rise to the following little dialogue. Holding them up to my eyes, he said : ' They are very bad.' I : ' They seem to have been of service.' ' Yes,' said he. ' I am a poor clergyman, and I paid for them 3 fr. 75 c., so I must wear them a little longer.' To get away from this somewhat painful topic, I asked if he had been in France lately. ' Oh, no,' was the reply ; ' I never was in France.' ' In Belgium, then ? ' ' Oh, no, never.' ' Well, you told me just now you had paid

3 fr. 75 c. for the gloves; where did you get them?'
'Oh, I bought them in Market Street; but,' with
another good-natured smile, 'you are a Frenchman.'
After which kind remark he looked at his watch and
said: 'I must go quickly, I have to preach.'   I
resisted the temptation to follow him and hear his
sermon, which in spite of his musical peculiarities
may, I hope, have been a good one.

Another, this time a real pupil of mine, a gentleman of undoubted musical abilities, gave me a shock
of another kind on one occasion.   He played very
well and was extremely fond of Chopin's music,
playing many of his pieces, even some of the very
difficult ones.   I brought him the sad tidings of
Chopin's death.   'Capital!' he exclaimed: 'now I
can have his complete works bound!'

My life now became a very busy one ; added to my
duties at the 'Gentlemen's Concerts,' many London
engagements, and hosts of pupils, there came in the
winter of 1855 the offer to conduct a series of operas
at the Theatre Royal, Manchester.   A very excellent
troupe had been engaged, comprising Mme. Rudersdorff, Mme. Caradori, Mlle. Agnes Bury, Herr
Reichardt, Carl Formes, and other remarkable
vocalists.   Most of the operas were given in German,
and it was happiness to me to conduct really first-
rate performances of 'Fidelio,' 'Don Giovanni,' 'Der
Freyschütz,' 'Die Entführung aus dem Serail,' alternately with more modern works such as 'Robert le
Diable,' 'Les Huguenots,' 'La Favorita,' and others.
Madame Rudersdorff was one of the most dramatic

and accomplished singers I have ever listened to, and achieved a real triumph as Leonora in 'Fidelio.' Formes was at the zenith of his powers and equally admirable as Leporello or as Don Giovanni. Reichardt was a charming tenor who sang Belmonte in 'Die Entführung' to perfection, and all were musicians to the core, having their heart in their work.

The public appreciated our efforts, but nevertheless the pecuniary success of the season was not complete, the expenses being too great, and daily performances during several months being more than a town like Manchester could digest. The obstinacy of the *entrepreneur* and proprietor of the theatre, John Knowles, who never listened to a counsel however well-meant or useful, was also a drawback. His peculiarities were many and sometimes amusing; thus, when Formes, then one of the foremost singers in any country, sang the part of Don Giovanni and insisted upon having a bottle of real champagne in the finale, we could never bring Knowles to consent to give it; he would rather have dispensed with the performance altogether. The consequence was that on such evenings I came to the theatre with a bottle under my cloak, and was probably called a fool for my pains by the excellent Knowles. On one occasion 'Lucrezia Borgia' was to be performed, the numerous minor parts in which were distributed amongst the best of the chorus singers. Coming to the last rehearsal on the morning of the performance I was met by the stage-manager, who told me with a long

face that, by order of Mr. Knowles, the doors of the
theatre would be closed that evening, and no
'Lucrezia Borgia' performed. On my inquiring for
the reason of this totally unexpected step he answered, 'All the *nobles* want half-a-crown apiece.' The
nobles meant the minor parts, and there were about
eight of them. I satisfied them out of my own purse
and the performance took place, much to the satisfaction of Mr. Knowles, who, however, never alluded
to my interference. During this same performance a
perplexing accident occurred, nearly causing a break-
down. Formes at the last rehearsal had earnestly
asked me to make a cut of eight bars in one of his
airs, to which I had assented. The cut was duly
marked in all the orchestral parts and observed in
the evening; but, lo! Formes had forgotten all about
it, made no cut, and sang the eight bars to which
there was no accompaniment. To jump back with a
whole band was an impossibility; all its members
were however immediately aware that something was
wrong and had their eyes upon me. For a moment
I wondered what was to be done; but soon there
occurred a chord upon which I seized, made the
band hold it out pianissimo and allowed Formes to
sing to it what remained of the eight bars, as a kind
of cadenza, until he had rejoined us, when we jogged
on together again. The best of the joke was that he
was not aware of the trick he had played us, or that
there had been anything unusual; such a thing would,
however, not be possible with any but Italian music
of the Bellini and Donizetti school.

From the year 1850 I had commenced to give pianoforte recitals, until then unknown in England. In London I gave them for several years at my own house, until I transferred them to St. James's Hall. In other towns I chose the most suitable concert-rooms, and found willing ears nearly everywhere. The programmes comprised every kind of pianoforte music, and if at first I avoided the more abstruse works, such as the later sonatas of Beethoven, I soon discarded this precaution and played whatever I wished to make known. Beethoven, Mozart, Haydn, Bach, Weber, Hummel, Dussek, Scarlatti, Rameau, Mendelssohn, Schubert, Schumann, Chopin, Heller, and others were put under contribution, and all the pleasure which the evenings at the Guiberts' house in Paris had given me was renewed on a larger and more public scale. Of the towns besides London and Manchester which I have thus visited and visit still, there is none to which I have gone more constantly and with more pleasure than Edinburgh, or where I have found a more intelligent and music-loving public. Friendships formed there have still further endeared the town to me, and amongst these friends stands out conspicuously Georg Lichtenstein, who, after being aide-de-camp to Kossuth, was exiled from Austria, and after months of trouble had settled down in Edinburgh as music-master. He is no more, and I am therefore at liberty to say that it would be diffi-cult to find a more accomplished, versatile, genial, and, above all, upright and kind-hearted man than he was. His conversation, always full of charm, and touching often upon the political events in Hungary at the time of the insurrection, in which he had been an actor, has made many an hour delightful and memorable to me. To his kindness in correcting the proofs of my local programmes I owe it that they were free from blunders, which was often not the case in other towns, where I had not an opportunity of revising them myself. Thus on one occasion when I had sent a programme to Scarborough, which included a 'Caprice brillant sur la Truite (Schubert), by Heller,' I found it printed to my horror as 'Caprice brillant sur *La Trinité*'!

In the winter 1852–53 the number of subscribers to my 'Chamber-Music Concerts' in Manchester had largely increased. I therefore constituted them into a 'Chamber-Music Society,' with an influential committee, keeping the entire management in my own hands. The room in the old town hall, very favourable for music of the kind, was not very large, holding about 450 seats. These were all subscribed for, and there was a list of from 80 to 100 would-be subscribers who had to wait for vacancies. Such gigantic strides had the love of music made in three years. The visits of Ernst, Molique, Sainton, Vieuxtemps, became now regular, and Piatti was the violoncellist at all the concerts. The intimacy with these men, great artists all, forms one of my happiest recollections. They were always guests in my own house, and we revelled in music. Good old Molique with his broken English, the meaning of which had often to be guessed at, was a subject of constant,

harmless amusement. As we were taking a drive together one day, Molique, thinking the driver had lost
his way, leaned out of the cab and shouted : 'Coachman, *who* are we ?' translating the German ' wo'
(where) by 'who.' He got the immediate reply :
' Well, sir, if you don't know who you are I cannot
tell you.'

Molique had a horror of cats, but, strange to say,
our cat was attracted by his playing and was generally
found sitting before the door of his room when he
practised, which greatly disturbed him when he
opened it, and could not muster courage to pass out
or to drive it away. Piatti, who occupied an adjoin-
ing room, never failed before retiring to bed to catch
the cat and hide it under Molique's bed. When
Molique discovered the intruder a most ludicrous
chase began, lasting sometimes an hour and more, as
he did not dare to approach the cat, but tried to
drive it away by merely hissing at it.

Molique was a great executant, knowing absolutely
no difficulties, finding easy what gave great trouble
to all other violinists ; but his style was polished and
cold, and he never carried his public away with him.
Ernst was all passion and fire, regulated by his
reverence for, and clear understanding of, the masterpieces he had to interpret. Sainton was extremely
elegant and finished in his phrasing, but vastly inferior to the others I have named. Vieuxtemps,
whose appearances were more rare, was an admirable
violinist and a great musician, whose compositions
deserve a much higher place than it is the fashion

now to accord to them.   Of Piatti, the incomparable,
I need not say a word beyond this, that during an
intimate friendship, extending over forty-six years,
my admiration of the artist and my love of the man
have gone on constantly increasing.   He is the only
one remaining to us of the above-named quintet; the
others are now listening to the harmony of the
spheres.

The Chamber-Music Society was dissolved in
1858, when the institution of my orchestral concerts
no longer left me time to devote the attention to it
which it imperatively required.   The five years from
1852 to '57 were uneventful; the summer seasons
were spent in London with my family, which had
rapidly increased, the autumns and winters in Manchester, leaving time, however, for my peregrinations
to provincial towns, both in England and Scotland.
During my annual sojourns in London I made the
acquaintance of Robert Browning and his gifted
wife, who were both passionate lovers of music, and
especially of Beethoven's sonatas, which I had often
the privilege of playing to them at my own house in
Mansfield Street.   Browning formed an exception to
the rule that poets and literary men care less for
music than painters, in whom the love of our art
seems almost invariably to be inborn.   Thackeray
and Dickens had a certain liking for music, but
Tennyson listened to it with great indifference, and
his loud talk whilst I was playing some superlatively
fine work has now and then 'agacé' my nerves.
Browning knew the whole literature of music, had

an unfailing judgment, and sometimes drew my
attention to pieces by older masters which had escaped
my notice and which I have always found worth
knowing. He must have been a good pianist himself,
but I could never prevail upon him to give me a
proof of his powers as such. I enjoyed his friendship
to the end of his days, and he endeared himself to me
especially through the kindness with which he forgave my incapacity to understand his poetry—an
incapacity which I frankly confessed to him more
than once.

Meyerbeer I had the pleasure of meeting again in
London, admiring, as before in Paris, his high-bred
manners, his cultured *esprit*, invariable tact, and great
savoir-faire. One day my friend Chorley had a small
dinner party, composed of the then Lady Hastings,
two other ladies, Meyerbeer, Costa, and myself. The
conversation fell on Mozart's 'Zauberflöte,' which had
been given at Covent Garden a few days before.
Lady Hastings had not enjoyed the performance and
abused the work in unmeasured terms. Especially
was she angry with the recitatives; 'those intermi-
nable, monotonous, unmeaning recitatives,' she called
them. Meyerbeer looked puzzled, Mozart's opera
containing no recitatives, and asked quietly : 'Quels
sont donc les récitatifs dont Lady Hastings parle ? '
'Ils sont de moi, monsieur,' said Costa, and Lady
Hastings began to talk of something else.

Spohr also visited London during one of the
seasons I spent there, and I was happy to be able to
speak with him once more of my childhood, and to

express my gratitude for the kindness he had shown to me when I was a boy. He attended one of the concerts of the Musical Union at which I played one of his pianoforte trios and also a sonata by Beethoven, the one in D major, Op. 10, No. 3. After the concert he came into the artists' room, said some flattering things to me about my performance of the latter, and added, ' a fine sonata ; ' then, with a tone of astonishment, ' und gar nicht veraltet ' (not antiquated); a remark with which I totally agreed, but which struck me as very superfluous.

In 1856 Manchester began to prepare for the ' Art Treasures Exhibition,' which was to be held in the following year, the musical part of which was entrusted to me. The committee—Sir Thomas Fairbairn (then Mr. Fairbairn) was chairman—acted with unparalleled energy, and succeeded in bringing together a marvellous collection of masterpieces of the different arts, such as I believe has never been equalled since. Her Majesty the Queen visited the exhibition, and how successful its whole career was, what hosts of distinguished visitors it drew to Manchester until its close, is too well known to dilate upon here. I was most anxious that music should hold its own, and not suffer by comparison with the other arts. To this end a first-rate orchestra was absolutely necessary, an orchestra better than the one of the ' Gentlemen's Concerts,' which, though a vast improvement upon what it had been before, left still much to desire. Fortunately the committee agreed with my views, placed ample means at my disposal, and I succeeded, not without considerable trouble, in bringing together a thoroughly satisfactory band by engaging competent performers from London, Paris, Germany, Holland, Belgium, and Italy, in addition to the best of our local players. Concerts took place every afternoon, but I conducted only on Thursdays. They were much enjoyed by crowds of visitors, and soon became one of the chief attractions of the exhibition. Thousands and thousands of people from the northern counties there heard a symphony for the first time, and it was interesting to watch how the appreciation of such works grew keener and keener almost with every week. The whole exhibition was like a beautiful dream, justifying its motto, ' A thing of beauty is a joy for ever!' and its elevating and refining influence cannot be overestimated. As usual, the Catalogue had its humorous points by accidental interchanges of numbers: thus a picture of King Lear on his death-bed was described as ' There is life in the old dog yet,' and you could daily hear the remark ' How true!' when passing it. Another, representing a madman sitting stark naked on the bare ground with his arms clenched round his knees, was called ' Portrait of Lord John Russell.' An old man was heard to remark, ' Probably when he was out of office!'

To this exhibition I owe my intimate friendship with Richard Doyle—Dicky Doyle, as he was called familiarly—the genial, gifted humorist and delightful companion. My acquaintance with him had been slight, but sufficient to warrant my inviting him to

K

be our guest for a few days, and so to see the
exhibition. He came, promised to stay three days,
and remained two months, to our intense delight.
Daily we studied the marvellous pictures together,
and he opened my eyes to many beauties which I
might have passed by. He was no less quick in
seizing upon any comical figure that presented itself
in the motley crowd, and many were the pen-and-ink
drawings which in remembrance of them he put on
paper during our quiet evenings at home, and which
I preserve carefully. An oddity in the railway
arrangements during that time I cannot leave un-
noticed : a single ticket from London to Manchester
cost then 33s., but a return ticket (from London to
Manchester and back) cost only 21s., and several
times have I seen people, who in ignorance had taken
single tickets, exchange them, when enlightened, for
return tickets, and receive 12s. into the bargain. The
ways of railway directors are mysterious sometimes.

When the exhibition closed its doors in October,
1857, the orchestra which I had taken so much
trouble to form, and which had given such satisfaction, was on the point of being dispersed to the four
points of the compass, never to be heard again in
Manchester. This was excessively painful to me,
and to prevent it I determined to give weekly
concerts during the autumn and winter season at my
own risk and peril, and to engage the whole band,
trusting to the now awakened taste for music for
success and perhaps remuneration. The necessary
preparations retarded the execution of this project

until January 30, 1858, when the first concert took place before a scanty audience. I was not disheartened, for I remembered how the Chamber Music Society had grown from small beginnings, and judged rightly that the crowds who had thronged the exhibition did not specially come for the music, and that concerts offering nothing but music, and at necessarily higher prices of admission, stood upon another footing. I felt that the whole musical education of the public had to be undertaken, and to the dismay of my friends I resolved to give thirty concerts, and either to win over a public or to fail ignominiously. The 'Gentlemen's Concerts' were an exclusive society; none but subscribers were admitted and no tickets sold. Before my advent they had never even published the programmes of their concerts, and the directors had only done so since 1850 at my earnest request, because I objected to conducting concerts of this clandestine sort. To the public at large symphonies and overtures were therefore *terra incognita*, and it was not to be expected that they would flock to them at once.

Beethoven's symphony in C major headed the first programme and was vehemently applauded by the meagre audience. The loss upon the concert was a heavy one, and was followed by similar losses week after week, until my friends were debating whether for the sake of my family I ought not to be locked up, and I myself began to feel rather uneasy. It was not before nearly half the series of thirty concerts had been given that things took another aspect; the audience gradually became more numerous and more appreciative; at last full houses succeeded each other, and the day after the thirtieth concert my managers and dear friends, Messrs. Forsyth Brothers, brought me, with the statement of receipts and expenses, ten brand-new threepenny bits, the profits on the whole series—a penny per concert! Perfectly satisfied with this result, which I considered most encouraging, I at once made arrangements for a second series to be given during the winter season 1858–59. It consisted of twenty-seven concerts, but for the third series I reduced the number to twenty, and opened a subscription list, which soon was adequately filled, showing that high-class orchestral music had taken hold of the public and that my ventures of the previous years had borne fruit. Since then those concerts have continued to prosper and have now reached their thirty-eighth season. The orchestra, at first only sixty strong, has gradually been increased, until for the last ten years it has numbered upwards of one hundred performers, and added to it is a chorus of three hundred singers of uncommon excellence, for the performance of oratorios and secular choral works. It is not my intention to write a history of these concerts, I shall only allude now and then to some of their more salient features, such as the production of new or neglected works; but I can look with a certain pride at the catalogue of works performed up to the present time (summer 1895), which comprises 32 oratorios, 71 other choral works, 110 symphonies, 214 overtures, 205 miscellaneous orchestral pieces, 183 concertos with orchestral accompaniments, and minor pieces without number. In 1860–61 the concerts had to suffer an interruption, as I was called upon to conduct a season of English opera (organised by Mr. E. T. Smith) at Her Majesty's Theatre in London, which counted Mmes. Sherrington and Parepa, Messrs. Sims Reeves and Santley, among its artists.

The most remarkable feature of the season was the production of two new English operas, the 'Amber Witch,' by Wallace, and 'Robin Hood,' by Macfarren, neither of which however took hold of the public in spite of some very clever and some charming pieces admirably sung. Both operas are forgotten now. Other works such as the 'Bohemian Girl,' 'Fra Diavolo,' in English dress, and 'La Reine Topaze,' by Massé, also given in English, were more successful and drew larger audiences. All were sung and acted to perfection. One performance of the first-named of these operas I remember still with considerable amusement on account of an odd incident. It had been substituted for another work in which Mr. Sims Reeves had the principal part, this gentleman having sent word in the morning that he was suffering from hoarseness. When in the evening I was crossing the stage to go to the conductor's desk the call-boy ran after me shouting, 'Mr. Hallé, we have forgotten the child!' This very child has to be seen sitting at the window when the curtain goes up, and in ten minutes I had to commence the overture. 'Go, fetch one quick,' was my answer. 'All right,'

said he, disappeared, and before three minutes had
elapsed he came back with a struggling girl, about
five years old, in his arms, and followed by an apple-
woman whose daughter he had unceremoniously
captured in the Haymarket. The child was carried
off to be dressed whilst the mother was pacified by the
stage manager, and I was able to begin the overture at
the appointed time. At its conclusion I rang up the
curtain with some diffidence, but there sat the child,
neatly dressed, at the window with the nurse, and we
proceeded quietly with the opera. In the first scene
where the Polish Count (Santley) takes leave of his
daughter before his departure from home, the little
girl is brought to him and he has to sing a touching
and rather lengthy farewell ballad. So the child
came down on to the stage, but the moment she saw
the foot-lights and the public behind she yelled with
fright, screaming at the top of her voice. Santley,
however, was equal to the occasion. He knelt down,
threw his large cloak round the girl, took her head
under his arm and kept it in chancery, all the time
singing his ballad with the utmost pathos, unmindful
of the kicking feet and struggles going on under the
cloak, hardly perceived by the public. Madame
Parepa, a most excellent vocalist with a splendid
powerful voice, was of a colossal size, which led to an
amusing scene on the occasion of the performance of
' Fra Diavolo,' in which she took the part of Zerlina.
When in the bedroom scene Zerlina undresses and
remains clad in white, Madame Parepa looked simply
enormous. Standing before the looking-glass, admir-

ing herself, she has in the English version the unfortunate words to say :—

> There really is not much amiss
> When you can boast of a figure such as this.

The moment she had uttered them the whole house roared with laughter, renewed again and again. After the performance Mme. Parepa asked me innocently if I knew what had happened to make people laugh so much, being totally unconscious that she was herself the cause of the hilarity.

Another unrehearsed effect enlivened one of the performances of 'Robin Hood.' Mme. Sherrington was Maid Marian, and Mr. Sims Reeves Robin Hood. In the last scene Maid Marian brings the reprieve to Robin Hood, condemned to death, and waving it rushes at him from the farthest end of the stage. On this occasion Mme. Sherrington came down with such impetuosity upon Mr. Sims Reeves that he, unprepared for the onslaught, was toppled over, his head coming close to the footlights, and Maid Marian on his back. Unable to shake her off at once, he raised his head and blew with all his might into the footlights which were nearly singeing him, thereby causing an hilarity amongst the audience sufficient to play havoc with the concluding scene of the opera.

The season being brought to a close, I returned to Manchester with the intention of producing during the following winter some interesting and striking novelty at my concerts. After a good deal of cogitation I fixed upon some of Gluck's operas, banished from the stage, for which therefore the concert room would be the proper place. 'Iphigénie en Tauride' was the one I chose first, remembering how the dramatic power of the music had in my younger days in Paris drawn tears from my eyes when I was simply perusing the score. From this self-same score I had to copy the whole of the orchestral parts, none being printed, and Gluck's scores being so carelessly engraved, with so many and such extraordinary abbreviations that to confide the task to an ordinary copyist was out of the question. Chorley undertook the translation of the libretto, Messrs. Chappell published a neat vocal score, and on January 25, 1860, the work was performed in the Free Trade Hall, Manchester, with an enormous success. Mme. Catharine Hayes, Messrs. Sims Reeves, L. Thomas, and Santley, were the interpreters, and could not well be surpassed in their respective *rôles*. It had to be repeated several times during the season, and Messrs. Chappell undertook a similar performance in London under my direction, and with the same artists, which was equally well received. This led to another private performance, remarkable in many ways. Lord Dudley, that munificent patron of the arts, asked me if I could give the work in his own noble gallery, with a small orchestra and chorus, and on my answering in the affirmative he left me *carte blanche*, stipulating only that the very best vocalists should be engaged, namely, Mme. Titiens, Messrs. Sims Reeves, Belletti, and Santley, and that the band should include Messrs. Sainton, Piatti, Lazarus, and others equally well known. I set to work at once, trained a small but efficient chorus from the Italian Opera, and after a few rehearsals one of the most exquisite performances that I have ever been privileged to listen to, took place. To my surprise Lord Dudley had invited but few friends, about forty, to share his pleasure; but he was thoroughly satisfied; said to me repeatedly that he had never had so fine a concert in his house, and requested me to call the next morning with the bill of costs. When I drew this up the sum total was so enormous that I felt some anxiety as to how it would be received, fearing that his satisfaction of the previous day might be somewhat damped. I handed it to him, and whilst examining it he spoke again of the pleasure the performance had given him, made a few pencil strokes on the document, wrote a cheque and handed it to me, saying, '*I have doubled all the terms*; it is the only way in which I can show my entire satisfaction.' Such princely generosity is rare indeed, and I was amazed; still more so when he added, ' Can you arrange for a second performance soon? But (with a smile) I suppose it will not be necessary to double the terms again.' The second performance did take place about a fortnight later and gave equal satisfaction to all concerned.

Having produced ' Iphigenia ' for the first time in England, I turned my attention to another of Gluck's masterpieces, ' Armida,' the translation of which had in the mean time been completed by Chorley. The printed full score of this opera, dating from 1778, is, if possible, in a worse and more misleading state than

that of 'Iphigenia.' I could not, therefore, confide
the task of copying out the orchestral parts to an
ordinary copyist. Anxious, however, to be spared
such a labour myself a second time, I applied to
Berlioz, whose knowledge of Gluck and all his works
was complete, Gluck being one of his idols, and asked
him if the parts of 'Armida' could be obtained in
Paris, where this opera had been so often given in
former times. I received the following reply, interesting in more than one sense :—

Mon cher Hallé,—Je *nous* félicite du succès éclatant de
votre tentative pour révéler Gluck aux Anglais. Il est donc
vrai que tôt ou tard la flamme finit par briller, si épaisse
que soit la couche d'immondices sous laquelle on la croyait
étouffée. Ce succès est prodigieux, si l'on songe combien
peu l'Iphigénie est appréciable au concert, et combien l'œuvre
de Gluck en général est inhérente à la scène. Tous les amis
de ce qui est éternellement beau vous doivent, à vous et à
Chorley, une vive reconnaissance.

Il n'y a pas d'autres parties séparées d'Armide que celle
de l'Opéra, et certainement on ne vous les prêterait pas. En
outre elles contiennent une foule d'arrangements faits autre-
fois par Gardel et autres, et des instruments ajoutés par je ne
sais qui, dont vous ne voudriez certainement pas faire usage.
Vous avez l'intention de produire Gluck *tel qu'il est*. Force
vous sera donc de faire copier les parties sur la partition, qui,
du reste, est l'une des moins fautives et des moins en désordre que Gluck nous ait laissées. Sans qu'on sache pourquoi, l'auteur n'y a jamais employé les trombones; il en est
de même dans Iphigénie en Aulide. Dans Orphée, Alceste,
et Iphigénie en Tauride, au contraire, cet instrument joue un
rôle très important. Dans Iphigénie en Aulide Gluck a fait
des *changements* pour quelques passages, et des *airs de danse*
qui ne se trouvent que dans la partition manuscrite de
l'Opéra. Vous ne pourrez pas faire votre édition anglaise

bien exacte sans venir à Paris. Mais si ce n'est qu'une
édition pour le piano, le mal sera moins grand. Jamais, je
crois, il n'exista un compositeur plus paresseux que Gluck,
ou plus insoucieux de ses œuvres, dont pourtant il paraissait
très fier. Elles sont toutes dans le désordre et le désarroi
les plus complets.

Je n'ai pas, que je sache, été attaqué par Wagner; il a
seulement répondu à mon article des 'Débats' par une lettre
prétendue explicative à laquelle personne n'a rien compris.
Cette lettre amphigourique et boursoufflée lui a fait plus de
tort que de bien. Je n'ai pas répliqué un mot.

Adieu, mon cher Hallé, veuillez me rappeler au souvenir
de Madame Hallé et faire mille amitiés de ma part à Chorley
quand vous le verrez.

H. BERLIOZ.[1]

[1]   *[Translation]*

My dear Hallé,—I congratulate *us* on the brilliant success of your
attempt to reveal Gluck to the English. So it is true that sooner or later
the flame bursts forth, however thick may be the layers of rubbish under
which one thought it smothered. This success is prodigious, when one
remembers how little the 'Iphigénie' can be appreciated at a concert, and
how closely Gluck's works in general are bound up with the stage. All the
friends of what is eternally beautiful owe you and Chorley a great debt of
gratitude.

There are no other separate parts of 'Armida' except those of the
Paris Opera, and they certainly would not be lent to you. Moreover,
they contain a host of arrangements formerly added by Gardel and others,
and additional instruments inserted by I know not whom, of which you
would certainly not make use. Your intention is to produce Gluck *as he
is.* You will, therefore, be forced to have the parts copied from the score,
which, however, is one of the least faulty and the least untidy which
Gluck has left us. For some unknown reason the composer nowhere
employs the trombones in it; it is the same in 'Iphigénie en Aulide.' In
'Orphée,' 'Alceste,' and 'Iphigénie en Tauride' on the contrary, this instrument plays a very important part. In 'Iphigénie en Aulide' Gluck

The musical phrase which Berlioz quotes at the end of his letter occurs in Iphigenia's grand air in the second act, ' O malheureuse Iphigénie,' and, with its melodious, wonderfully vast sweep, is one of those inspirations which even a great genius finds but seldom, and thoroughly deserves the notes of admiration added by Berlioz.

I had now to give up the hope of getting the coveted parts from anywhere, for they had never been printed, so I sat down and wrote them out myself, as I have done for 'Iphigenia.' Trying as the labour was it was still one of love, and I felt fully recompensed when on September 28, 1860, I conducted a performance which unfolded hitherto unknown beauties to a vast audience. The success of ' Armida,' if somewhat inferior to that of ' Iphigenia,' was still great enough to reward me for my trouble. Many years later I had the additional satisfaction of being able to lend my parts to Mme. Jenny Lind Goldschmidt for a performance at the ' Rhenish Musical Festival,' only made possible by the happy circumstance that I had them in my possession.

.   .   .   .

has made some *changes* for certain passages, and written some *dance-music* which is only to be found in the MS. score belonging to the Opera. You cannot make your English edition very exact without coming to Paris. But if it is only a pianoforte edition the harm would be less great. I think there never existed a lazier composer than Gluck, nor one more careless of his works, of which, however, he seems to have been very proud. They are all in the most complete disorder and disarray.

I have not, to my knowledge, been attacked by Wagner; he merely replied to my article in the *Débats* by a pretended explanatory letter which no one could understand. It was an inflated and bombastic letter that did him more harm than good. I did not answer a single word. Farewell, my dear Hallé, pray remember me to Madame Hallé, and say a thousand kind things to Chorley when you see him.—H. BERLIOZ.

CHAPTER IV

By Charles E. Hallé

1865 1895

IT has been left to me to record the last thirty years of my dear father's life, to take up the pen which dropped from his hand the day before he died, and to conclude the task he left uncompleted.

It will be a labour of love to recall and chronicle those events in his life at which I either personally assisted, or of which he spoke to me in the intimacy of our friendship—a friendship which never from my earliest childhood to the day of his death suffered

the slightest break, or was marred by even the most
transient misunderstanding on either side.

The readers of the preceding chapters will have
formed an estimate of my father's character, of his
indefatigable industry, his entire devotion to his art,
his modesty, and his genial and lovable nature; but
it is only those who lived in daily association with
him who could fathom the depths of his kindness and
of his unselfishness, his sympathy, and the chivalry
which led him not only to forgive, but to conceal the
pain of any hurt he might receive. There never was
a kinder father or a better friend, and the void his
death has made, not only in his family, but in a wide
circle of acquaintances, will be felt for many a year
to come.

It will be in vain for me to attempt to make this
chapter as interesting and amusing as those that
have gone before. Apart from my very inadequate
power as a chronicler, my father repeatedly told me
that what he would have had to say about the last
thirty years, the period from 1865 to 1895, which
has been left to me to record, would be sadly lacking
in interest after the story of his youth and the most
exciting portion of his career.

In undertaking the task I suffer from the extreme
disadvantage of not being a musician myself when
so much of what I have to say is connected with that
beautiful art, of which my father was such an ardent
disciple. A great love for it I do indeed possess; my
childish ears were made familiar with the noblest
creations of Beethoven, Schubert, and Bach before I

left my cradle, and as my childhood and boyhood—
owing to delicate health—were spent at home, music
was the daily accompaniment of my life. In short
I have never ceased to feel that my early familiarity
with all that was most beautiful in the art of music
developed an understanding in me for other forms of
beauty which otherwise I might never have possessed.
And thus my own experience has made me rightly
understand the importance of the work my father
accomplished during the many years he laboured to
bring music to the ears and hearts, not only of the
rich, but of the most humble.

How many a factory hand or office clerk in the
busy towns of Manchester and the North of England
may have owed his only knowledge of what was
beautiful to the music he had an opportunity of
hearing at my father's weekly concerts during the
dreary winter months!

It is impossible to believe that some element of
refinement has not been developed in the large
audiences of working men who, standing and packed
together in great discomfort as I have often seen
them, have yet listened for hours, and evidently with
much appreciation, to most intricate and delicate
music; or that the taste thus formed in one direction
should not have had its effect in others, and possibly
have coloured their whole lives.

Every evidence of such appreciation was very
dear to my father, and the three following letters,
treasured among his papers, were found after his
death, along with many others of the same kind. The

first, from an anonymous correspondent, must have
been written in 1864 :—

How slight and subtle may be, and ofttimes are, the
links of that electric chain whose vibrations arouse in our
hearts memories and thoughts that have long lain buried
there! These and similar thoughts filled my mind at the
sight of a programme—a programme of the eighteenth concert of the seventh season of Charles Hallé's unrivalled
orchestra. Seven years ago he led such an orchestra, and
drew from the keys of his pianoforte such harmonies and
melodies as beforetime were reserved exclusively for the
wealthy. In the glass building prepared for the exhibition
of Art Treasures we first listened to him, and the strains of
that delicious music floating through the building became so
associated with all that is most beautiful in painting and
sculpture, that it is almost impossible to separate them.
And when the first notes of his band peal through the Free
Trade Hall, that noble, but now somewhat dingy, room
becomes transformed into a fairy palace, bathed in summer
sunshine, and instead of a closely packed and (except in the
reserved seats) plainly-dressed audience, we see groups of
gaily-attired ladies, or distinguished-looking men sauntering
through the galleries of paintings or gazing on the glittering
armour, or students intently absorbed in the contemplation
of some remarkable work of long ago. But we will suppose
the day a Thursday, the time 2 P.M., and by one accord the
loungers are drawing towards the orchestra; the discordant
sounds emitted from various instruments being tortured into
tune subside; a slight, fair-haired man bows slightly around,
takes his place, raises his bâton, and the first note of some
lively overture, or it may be of some enchanting symphony,
floats through the nave, enchaining the listener, who perforce almost holds his breath, lest he should lose one note of
that sweet music; while over all glows the brilliant sunshine, and the scent of summer air floats through the building. Under such circumstances we first heard Charles Hallé,

and often as we have attended his concerts, the charm has never failed. Last night—a wet, splashy February evening —every sense of discomfort was dispelled, and all our interest absorbed in the music, as if we heard it for the first time. A very few moments after the time named on the programme Charles Hallé appeared, and the hush of pleased expectation stole over the miscellaneous company assembled at the Free Trade Hall. Glancing over the orchestra, we recognise many familiar faces—Seymour in his accustomed place, though the lapse of years has left unmistakable signs on his face and figure, still discourses sweet music on his violin, which he handles as if he loved it; now he plays seriously, not as in bygone times, when one has seen his gravity disturbed by the frolicsome Jacoby; the latter has now subsided into a grave middle-aged man. De Jong is still there—and Baetens —but Richardson is gone, and some few others we miss. From this reverie we are aroused by the sharp tap of the bâton, and a flood of music flows around. This dies away— a vocalist has the next part—then again the instruments have their turn; all is delicious, but we wait for the treat of the evening. Charles Hallé's solo on the piano; the silence which had previously reigned deepens and becomes intense as we watch his fingers fly over the keys, wooing the music from them. If it did not seem fanciful, I should say the sensation is almost that of playing on one's very heart-strings —we almost forbear to breathe. To those who have not heard him I cannot convey any idea of the power and sweetness of Hallé's playing; while those who have had that pleasure need no words on the subject from me.

This is a long essay to write upon a programme, but so pleasant have been the thoughts and scenes that it conjured up in my own mind that I fancied it might give pleasure to others. The memories of the past seven years, the joys, the sorrows, the perplexities and the anxieties that have marked their course, are to me very much associated with these concerts. I do not know that I have ever seen such vivid pictures of the past as are painted for me by Charles Hallé's orchestra; on these I must not trust myself to write, or I should run on to a wearisome length, but will wind up my prosing by thanking you for the frequent pleasure you have given me by introducing me to these concerts.

The next letter was written on a long narrow sheet of paper such as is found in workshops :—

Nov. 10, 1873.

Dear Sir,—Having had the pleasure of attending your first concert this season, I beg to tender you my best wishes for your future success; and not having had the pleasure of hearing such a display of talent before, I felt most delighted, and beg you will please accept the small token I forward you.

Respectfully yours,
AN OPERATIVE.

The small token consisted of two yards of fine white flannel, which my father carefully preserved for many years.

The following is the second of two letters, the first of which has been lost, from an old member of his Manchester Choir :—

King City, Missouri, U.S.A.:
Nov. 16, 1884.

Dear Sir,—Your kind letter of October 16, enclosing your photograph, came duly to hand, for which please accept my heartfelt thanks.

On looking at your photograph, your features seem so lifelike that you don't seem to have altered since I last saw you, which is over twenty-two years ago. May you long live and look as well!

I enclose you a copy of my photo., taken the day I was sixty years old. I do not know if you will be able to recognise me. I still keep up my interest in choral music. I conduct a small society here, and play the organ at church, and teach the Sunday-school children to sing. This I have

to do in what little time I can spare from business. I have
given it up several times, thinking I was getting too old,
but no one seemed to take it up; and I hated to see the
young folks without any one to lead them. So went at it
again. I guess I shall have to die in harness yet; but the
proverb says, 'It is better to wear bright than rust.' Hoping
we may meet where harmony never ceases,

I remain, dear sir,

Yours very truly,

WM. DICKENS, Senr.

Dealer in lumber, coal, and farm machinery.

My father had always the greatest respect for his
audiences, of whatever sort they might be, and never
gave them anything but the very best at his command, whether it was his own playing or the performance of his orchestra. My mother used to relate
how on one occasion, soon after his arrival in England,
he and Ernst the violinist, with whom he was touring
in the provinces, arrived at a small town where
amateurs of music were so few that scarce a dozen
persons had assembled to hear them. From the
artists' room they could see how small was the
audience, and simultaneously exclaimed: 'Then we
must play as we have never played before!' They
kept their word, and at the close of the concert the
impulsive, highly-strung Ernst threw himself into my
father's arms, saying, 'Hallé, we never played like
that in all our lives!'

To bring his band by training and careful recruiting as near perfection as possible was the hobby of
his life, and to this end he spared neither trouble nor
expense. He never for a moment allowed any ques-

tion of money to stand in his way, and his agents
were often driven to despair by his engagements at
ruinous terms of artists who did not make the difference of a sixpence in the receipts; indeed, to my
certain knowledge, he several times gave cheques to
members of the band, or to singers whom he engaged
for the concerts, on his private banking account, so
that he might escape the 'talking to' he knew he so
well deserved, if Messrs. Forsyth had got wind of his
goings on.

It is not for me to say anything about the excellence of the Manchester orchestra, or of the chorus
which he also formed there. They have been heard
in London, and the orchestra has played in all the
leading provincial towns in England, and at Edinburgh, Glasgow, Dublin, and Belfast, so that they are
both well known. It is obvious, however, that over
a hundred skilled musicians, recruited from the best
talent obtainable in Europe, playing constantly together for years under the direction of an artist who
was on terms of intimate personal friendship with
many of the composers whose works he interpreted,
have formed an orchestra of quite exceptional merit,
which it should be the endeavour of the City of
Manchester to keep together under the bâton of the
best conductor who can be found to take my father's
place.

It seems strange in the early part of these
memoirs to read how little a certain class of music,
which is now so familiar, was known fifty years ago
—to see that even Cherubini did not know the

sonatas of Beethoven until my father played them to him, and that in London until he came here they had never been heard in public. What priceless treasures of sweet sound were locked up until he turned the key!

To give a list of all the works for orchestra and the piano which he introduced for the first time in England would include a large proportion of all the choral works, symphonies, concertos, and chamber music ever produced here; nor was this all he achieved in the cause of music. He edited a complete set of Beethoven's sonatas, besides executing endless other editorial works, and compiled a School for the use of Students of the Pianoforte, which by easy grades should conduct them from the elementary to the most difficult stages of the art. He was largely instrumental in founding the Royal Manchester College of Music, which had been the dream of his life ever since 1852, when he elaborated his scheme in a correspondence, now unfortunately lost, with Mr. Adolf Meyer, but which was only fulfilled in 1893. He was elected first Principal of the college, and took the liveliest interest in his duties and in the progress of the students, but he was snatched away after two brief years of labour in this field, in which he had hoped to accomplish so much.

My father's industry was perfectly astounding, and he must have had a constitution of iron, in spite of his delicate health as a child, to go through the amount of fatigue he did without apparent discomfort. He was incessantly travelling; but railway journeys, however long, never seemed to tire him. Many and many a time he would travel, say from Manchester to Edinburgh, conduct a rehearsal in the afternoon and a concert in the evening, and return to Manchester the same night, reaching home at four or five o'clock in the morning, and yet after a few hours' sleep he would be quite fresh again and ready for his next day's work. Many and various were his adventures on these journeyings, and he was never tired of relating them. On one occasion he was snowed-up in a train in Scotland, and he and his two or three fellow-travellers were nearly starved, when the guard remembered that a fine pig had been placed in the van. This unfortunate animal was promptly converted into pork chops over the engine fire and furnished an excellent supper, in spite of his shrill protests at being immolated for the public good. Another time the train he was in broke down, and as he was to play at a concert that evening he was sent on to his destination in a tender attached to the engine. He dressed for the concert as he went along, and the two good-natured stokers helped him into his clothes; but their valeting left marks on his shirt-front, which caused much amusement among his audience when he at last reached the concert-room.

Another most amusing adventure was also connected with the break-down of a train. On this occasion my father had a band of some fifty members of his orchestra with him, and after a long and tedious delay it occurred to one of them to express

his feelings of strong dissatisfaction at things in
general by an improvised solo on his instrument,
which happened to be a bassoon. This encouraged
others in different parts of the train to join their
lamentations to his, each man on his own instrument,
and soon night was made hideous by the most
lamentable sounds ever suggested by the goddess of
despair. Presently there came a move on the part of
the train of a few yards, when flutes and clarinets
set up the liveliest airs of rejoicing; but again there
was a stop, and fresh wails of anguish smote the
astonished air.

My father was mightily enjoying the *charivari*,
and Mr. Straus, who was with him, was preparing
his fiddle to take part in it, when, happening to look
out of the window, they discovered they were not in
the open country as they had imagined, but in the
suburbs of a town. The inhabitants, awakened out
of their virtuous slumbers by the appalling din, were
leaning out of doors and windows in night attire,
with flat candlesticks in their hands, evidently by
their gestures protesting against the performance of
the Hallé band, but the noise was so great they could
not be heard. Fortunately at this juncture a fresh
engine arrived, and the train escaped wreckage at
the hands of a population goaded to fury.

'I little thought I should ever travel with a life-
boat on either side of the railway carriage,' he once
quietly remarked on his return from a concert in the
Midlands at the time of a great flood. On our
inquiring if he had got wet, 'No,' he said, 'the water

did come in a little, but I put my feet up on the seat, and fortunately the engine fire was not put out.' No difficulties or hindrances ever prevented him from doing all that was humanly possible to keep his engagements. The only time my father was in a bad railway accident was on December 23, 1894, when the terrible collision occurred at Chelford on the L. & N.-W. Railway. He was going to London with his sister and eldest daughter for the Christmas holidays, and they had a miraculous escape, my father's calm presence of mind never for a moment deserting him.

Railway journeys, even unattended by adventure, always gave him a certain amount of pleasure; he liked them, he liked the rapid movement of the train, the certainty of a few hours' respite from his incessant occupations, and, strangest taste of all, he adored Bradshaw. Nothing pleased him better, if any of us were going a journey, than to look out the trains, and the mention of an expedition to the Continent took him away from any other occupation to arrange the whole tour, and present us with a way-bill with the time of departure and arrival of all the trains we should take neatly written out in his beautiful handwriting for our guidance.

The only thing he thoroughly disliked was when the trains did not keep their time. I well remember the first occasion on which he went to Rome, the country was in flood, as Italy usually is in autumn, and the bridges broken, which is also not an uncommon occurrence, and we were taken round by An-

cona instead of taking the usual route. Of course
my father worked it all out in Bradshaw, and timed
our arrival accordingly; but, alas! for the calculations of that trusty book, twelve hours after we were
due in the eternal city we were still slowly crawling
through a romantic but desolate-looking region somewhere in the centre of Italy, where the only food
obtainable was bad coffee, green apples, and unripe
grapes; and it was then my father gave vent to his
sentiments—he did not say much, it was only ' What
would I not give to be in a railway carriage on its way
from London to Manchester,' but it summed up his
opinion of Italy and all things Italian better than
torrents of abuse. It was not till we had been a day
or two in Rome under the excellent care of those
admirable caterers to the wants of their fellow-
creatures—the brothers Genre, of the Hôtel d'Angleterre—that he forgot the impression of that most
lamentable journey.

My father was a most delightful travelling companion; his interest in everything was intense. He
enjoyed his holidays immensely, and the most trivial
incidents afforded him a fund of amusement—his
great love for beautiful scenery and keen appreciation of painting and architecture made it a real
pleasure to go with him where such things were to
be seen. I well remember my first expedition abroad
with him; it was to Hagen, his native town, when I
was about fifteen, and this journey was a very momentous one for me, as after I had duly made the
acquaintance of all my German uncles, aunts, and

cousins, I was taken to Düsseldorff, and afterwards to Paris, and given the choice of the two schools of painting. I elected to remain in Paris, and was put under the care of my dear kind old friend, M. Victor Mottez, and worked in his studio for a year. Mottez was a pupil and great friend of the famous Ingres, so that during the happy months I spent with him I made the acquaintance not only of that great painter but of many others of my father's early friends in Paris, more especially Stephen Heller and Hector Berlioz, whom I used to meet almost every Sunday evening at the house of Madame Damcké, and who always spoke of my father with the greatest affection; *le Bayard sans peur et sans reproche* was Berlioz's description of him. A severe attack of bronchitis having interrupted my studies in France, I was sent to Italy to recover my health, and remained there for several years; but I always look back with keen interest on the time I spent in Paris, as I gained an insight into the artist life my father describes so graphically in the early pages of his memoirs and letters. He evidently intended to say a great deal more about the many interesting people he knew in the twelve years he spent in Paris (between 1836 and 1848), as his MS. shows that he broke off in the middle of an anecdote about one of them, Spontini, to go on with his own tale, evidently intending to go back to that part of his memoirs and greatly augment it.

It must, indeed, have been a wonderful society in which my father spent his time during those years.

He has dwelt more especially on the musicians with whom he had intercourse; but in the long conversations I had with Stephen Heller in 1886, when I painted his portrait, many and many a name occurred of men famous in literature and art who were their daily associates. Victor Hugo, Balzac, Alexandre Dumas and his son, Alfred de Musset, and Scribe, were but a few of the brilliant host who daily met and dined, or took their coffee together on the Boulevards. I asked Heller one day when he was talking of those times and the days he and my father spent together, which of all these men had left the most vivid impression on his mind; without a moment's hesitation he answered, 'Alfred de Musset.' He told me that it did not matter who was present, nor who was talking—Hugo, Balzac, Heine, or Dumas—everybody ceased when Alfred de Musset opened his lips—his individuality and personal fascination were so great. There has never been in the world's history, I suppose, a time when so many remarkable men in literature, music, and art lived together as were found in Paris during the twenty years from 1830 to 1850, and where are they all now? Only two are left that I know of, our dear old friend Manuel Garcia, who is still with us here in London, and bears his ninety years without a sign of discomfort, and my old master, Victor Mottez, who lives in retirement at Bièvres, near Paris. These two have still memories which are green, and many a tale have I heard from them of the sayings and doings of these many merry men of genius; for merry they were, in spite of the struggles and poverty in which so many of them lived. This aspect of their lives was forcibly brought home to me by my father a few years ago. I was going out to dinner, and noticing that my waistcoat was showing marks of age, I went to my father's study to conceal the ravages of time by the application of a little ink to certain white patches which do not usually form portion of an English gentleman's evening dress. My father watched my operations with the keenest interest and delight, and when I asked him what he saw in my threadbare garment to cause him so much happiness, he told me that what he saw reminded him of his early days in Paris, when an ink-bottle was the one essential requisite of his and all his friends' toilettes. It was applied to hats, coats, boots, cravats indiscriminately, and as he added, 'So many of us were poets, there was always plenty of it about.'

Of these men, who were at that time all poor together, some afterwards achieved popularity as well as abundant prosperity; some, equally gifted, failed to obtain recognition, and some, again, fell upon evil days when advanced in life. Stephen Heller, the dreamy composer and sensitive, nervous man, pushed to one side and neglected in the busy Paris of to-day, was one of these; in addition to other misfortunes he became nearly blind in his old age, and with the loss of his sight lost the means of earning the little that sufficed to support his modest existence. My father, who had maintained the closest intimacy with Heller, became aware of his trouble and felt that this could not, should not be, and that some among the thousands who had enjoyed his music must come forward and save the aged musician from want. A 'Heller Testimonial' was started, and soon enough money was subscribed to purchase a small annuity and enable our dear old friend to end his days in peace. Their correspondence shows the infinite trouble my father took in the matter, not the least part of which was the difficulty of persuading Heller to allow his necessity to be made known.

It may surprise those who know how popular Heller's music has become, especially in England, to learn that it did not bring in an adequate return; but the annals of art are full of similar cases. A picture which may some day fetch thousands at Christie's, a book which may run through many editions, and a song which may be sung all over the country will, as often as not, fail to produce anything for the author or the artist but the most paltry sum. Thus, the 'Wanderstunden,' by Heller, which is to be found in the library of every musical amateur, was sold out and out with four other pieces for 15*l.* !

The prompt sympathy which made my father come forward to the relief of his old comrade is not to be wondered at, but his ready willingness to assist those in want who had no real claim upon him was evinced in a hundred directions. His purse was always open, and in many other ways was he ready to give assistance when needed. A touching evidence of this was given to us many years ago in Manchester, when my father, returning to his house in Greenheys, noticed that the old postman who was in the habit of bringing him his letters had evidently been too generously regaled at the houses at which he had already called—it was Christmas time—and was not in a fit condition to deliver the rest of his letters. Knowing that the poor man would be dismissed if his state was discovered or any mistake occurred in the letters entrusted to his care, my father went the rest of his round with him, delivering every letter to its proper address, and, when the bag was quite empty, took the postman home with him and did not let him go until he was quite sober again. It is gratifying to add that the man was exceedingly grateful, never again lapsed from the path of sobriety, and continued on his old beat for some years afterwards.

Cabmen were also great friends of my father's; he got on beautifully with them and they with him, and many an amusing story would he bring home about them, especially after a visit to Dublin. One honest and worthy Jehu evinced his devotion in a very striking manner. At the time of the Franco-Prussian war it was rumoured in Manchester that my father would have to go and serve in the German army, so 'James,' for such was his respected name, came to our house one evening and begged to be allowed to take my father's place and go out as his substitute to the seat of war.

My father was also very fond of children and delighted in playing with them, especially with the little urchins whom he met on his way to and from the

College of Music (about the longest walks he ever took), half a mile each way; but then he hated that form of locomotion, except during his holidays abroad. If he could catch a little boy unawares, he would take off his cap or pull his hair, or have some other game of the sort with him, generally followed by the gift of a penny; but these friendly advances were not always taken in good part. On one occasion, having captured the headgear of a youngster aged about four, the little rascal turned on him, to his great amusement, and kicked him valiantly on the shins until his cap was returned to him with all the honours of war.

A great love of animals was another of my father's characteristics. Every house he was in was sure to contain birds, cats, and dogs, especially dogs. He generally had 'Scot,' a collie, and a little terrier, 'Clootie,' on either side of his chair at meal times, and he did his best to induce them to occupy those positions in his study; but music and the smell of cigars were tastes he had not in common with his four-footed friends, and they generally deserted him when he opened his piano or began to smoke. There were pugs and other varieties of the canine race in favour from time to time, and one day he announced that a member of his band had presented him with a fine Mount St. Bernard pup. At this, however, my sisters rose like one woman and said the huge collie was quite enough for him, and for them. So the St. Bernard pup was returned, though not without many heart-burnings on my father's part, who would gladly have kept him, and, indeed, for that matter, half a dozen like him.

Horses my father knew nothing about. I don't think it ever occurred to him that a horse had a separate and distinct existence from a cab, or that it was ever intended to serve man in any other fashion; nor was he much of a sportsman. On only two occasions did he sally forth with a gun, and on neither did he achieve much glory. His first experience, soon after his arrival in England, was at Burton Constable, in Yorkshire, when, to the dismay of his host, Sir Clifford Constable, who kept a pack of hounds and hunted three or four days a week, my father came home one evening and proudly announced that he had shot—a fox. 'Mr. Hallé, if you know where you have left that fox, pray borrow a spade from a gardener and go and bury it,' was all poor Sir Clifford could say.

His second adventure was at Heaton Park in Cheshire, where Lord Wilton sent him out one afternoon to shoot rabbits, and lent him a dog. A rabbit was soon put up and promptly missed. This happened twice more, when his intelligent companion looked up into my father's face and wagged his tail to show there was no ill-feeling. Evidently considering, however, that as their views of life were so different, further association was undesirable, he trotted back to his kennel. My father accepted the lesson and never again loaded a gun. On the other hand he was very fond of fishing. Given a warm afternoon, a slow stream or a pond, a comfortable chair, a boy to put on the bait, and a plentiful supply of cigars, he would be perfectly happy for hours, especially if now and then an ill-advised carp would allow himself to be hauled out of his native element—to be as likely as not put back into the water after a brief sojourn on the bank by my kind-hearted father.

Nothing, however, took my father away for long from his beloved piano. Wherever he might go for his holidays Messrs. Broadwood would send him one of their big instruments, and much amusement have we had in seeing the whole fisher population of some seaside place turn out to trundle the big case up to the house my father might have taken. Cowes was for many years his favourite holiday resort, at first a cottage at East Cowes, and later Egypt House, West Cowes, a delightful place with a garden down to the sea, at that time a school, but my father was able to take it during the holiday months—August and September. Here the piano, with many 'yo-heave-hos' and other nautical sounds, would be installed, and then how delightful it was on hot summer nights to sit in the garden, or on the low wall overhanging the sea, and hear the 'Moonlight' and other divine sonatas played as only my father could play them.

Our dear friend Richard Doyle once wrote, in refusing an invitation to repeat a visit to us there:—

I dare not run away for a day, because I know that once in sight of the sea I should not be able to move from it. And oh! the Schuberts, Hellers, and the moonlight nights, how I wish my eyes and ears were among them.

M

Many were the friends who would wander in to listen with us, and certainly music heard under those conditions has a charm

> ‘ Ch’ intender non la può
> Chi non la prova.’

I do not know how much real musicians are affected by the conditions under which music is heard —whether to them it is a matter of indifference whether they listen to it in a crowded concert room or among surroundings such as I have described above, but as to an artist a picture conveys quite a different expression when seen in the church for which it was painted, or when forming part of the decoration of a beautiful room, from what it does when hung in an auction room, so to a mere amateur do beautiful surroundings and the sympathy of friends enhance the pleasure derived from music.

A house where all these conditions were enjoyed to perfection was that lovely cottage in Kensington, the home of the Prinseps and of Watts, Little Holland House.

Here on Sunday afternoons in summer, men who were famous and women who were beautiful would assemble ; croquet and bowls, tea and strawberries, would serve as accompaniments to merry, witty talk, and here at dusk and often far into the night, my father and Joachim would take to their instruments, and convey the thoughts of the great masters of their art to the ears of Tennyson and Swinburne, Burne Jones and Rossetti, Watts, Browning, Leighton,

Millais, Fred Walker, Doyle, and many another poet and painter who lingered on to listen to them.[1]

My father always delighted in having such men to play to; with painters, as he has himself said, he was always safe—with *littérateurs* he was occasionally not quite so fortunate. They were fond of talking and found it difficult to sit long and listen, whatever other sounds were being made, and at times matters fared even worse. Some years ago, in 1864, Professor Ruskin asked him to come and play to a school of young girls in whom he was greatly interested. My father readily consented, and as the Professor was there himself, and it was the first time he had played to him, he was careful to select what was most great and beautiful, and played his very best. When it was all over and my father was about to leave, one of the girls told him she had been practising Thalberg's arrangement of 'Home, Sweet Home,' and would very much like to hear my father play it before he went away. He told her it was a pity they should listen to a trivial thing like that after the beautiful music they had just heard, but as she appeared disappointed and some other girls came forward with the same request, he gave way, sat down again, and played it. To his chagrin, Ruskin, who had been politely appreciative, now became enthusiastic and told him *that* was the piece he liked best far and away. Of course my father said nothing at the time, but it got to the ears of the

---

[1] An interesting record of this time is to be found in the portraits Mr. Watts painted of my father and many celebrated men, lately presented by him to the nation.

Professor how disappointed my father had been, so he wrote him the following letter :—

Winnington Hall, Northwich, Cheshire :

Dec. 3, 1864.

Dear Mr. Hallé,—My 'children' tell me you were sorry because I liked that 'Home S. H.' better than Beethoven—having expected better sympathy from me. But how could you—with all your knowledge of your art, and of men's minds? Believe me, you *cannot* have sympathy from any untaught person, respecting the higher noblenesses of composition. If I were with you a year, you could make me feel them—I am quite capable of doing so, were I taught—but the utmost you ought *ever* to hope from a musically-illiterate person is honesty and modesty. I do not—should not—expect you to sympathise with *me* about a bit of Titian, but I know that you would, if I had a year's teaching of you, and I know that you would never tell me you liked it, or *fancy* you liked it, to please me.

But I want to tell you, nevertheless, *why* I liked that H. S. H. I do *not* care about the air of it, I have no doubt it is what you say it is—sickly and shallow. But I did care about hearing a million of low notes in perfect cadence and succession of sweetness. I never recognised before so many notes in a given brevity of moment, all sweet and helpful. I have often heard glorious harmonies and inventive and noble succession of harmonies, but I never in my life heard a variation like that.

Also, I had not before been close enough to see your hands, and the invisible velocity was wonderful to me, quite unspeakably, merely as a human power.

You must not therefore think I only cared for the bad music—but it is quite true that I don't understand Beethoven, and I fear I never shall have time to learn to do so.

Forgive me this scrawl, and let me talk with you again, some day.

Ever with sincere regards to Mrs. and Miss Hallé, gratefully and respectfully yours,   J. RUSKIN.

There was perhaps one further reason for my being so much struck with that. I had heard Thalberg play it after the Prussian Hymn. I had gone early that I might sit close to him, and I was entirely disappointed, it made no impression on me whatever. Your variation therefore took me with greater and singular surprise.

In commenting on this letter my father never would admit that he could not appreciate Titian without instruction, and he had such a genuine love for pictures and such a good eye that I felt with him the Professor had failed to prove his case.

My father never went much into general society; big entertainments and receptions were a dreadful weariness to him, and I can imagine the amazement with which he received the confession from that wonderful and delightful old lady, Mrs. Procter, when sitting beside him at a dinner party, that she would have *one* regret on her death-bed—the thought of the many pleasant parties she had missed! But genial little dinners, especially when he could be sure of meeting his dear friends, Joachim and Piatti, and of discoursing music with them afterwards, he delighted in. He has himself spoken of Mr. and Mrs. Sartoris, of the many days he spent in Park Place, St. James's, and at Warsash in Hampshire with those two friends, for whom he had such a genuine affection and admiration, but there were other houses at which he was often to be found. Sir Alexander Cockburn's was one of these; Lady Revelstoke's, Mrs. Benzon's, Mrs. F. Lehmann's were others, and there was one social gathering which he would never miss if he could possibly help it, and that was Sir Frederick Leighton's annual party in the spring. He dearly liked playing in a studio and among pictures, and one of the dreams of his life was to found an institution where the two arts should work in harmony together.

When the Grosvenor Gallery was started and I was appointed one of the directors he thought his opportunity had come, and for one or two seasons he gave concerts of chamber music in the gallery; but as his recitals had formerly been always held in the afternoon, the change of hour to the evening caused much disappointment among his regular subscribers, many of whom were students at musical colleges; so the Grosvenor concerts had to be abandoned, and the venue changed to the Prince's or St. James's Hall.

Concerts and recitals have become a matter of such every-day occurrence in London nowadays, and so many pianists of amazing skill arrive here each season, that my father no longer saw the necessity of continuing his recitals regularly every summer, and of late years they were somewhat interrupted. It was, however, his intention to give a farewell series of pianoforte recitals during the coming spring (1896), in order to play all the Beethoven sonatas once again in consecutive order, and he had already fixed the dates and taken the St. James's Hall for the purpose. With what devotion he would have accomplished this final act of homage to the genius of the hero in whose service he had spent his life, only those able in some degree to measure the depth of his reverence for him can form any idea.

With the music of a Beethoven concerto he first appealed to English ears more than half a century ago, and in the quiet of his study, the room he loved best, which he always quitted with regret and returned to with eager pleasure, within the twenty-four last hours of his life, he sat playing a Beethoven concerto almost within the shadow of death.

From 1869 onwards my father's recitals had ceased to be concerts for pianoforte alone, concerted chamber music being regularly introduced as well as an occasional vocal piece. The artists most constantly associated with him were Mme. Norman Neruda, Herr Straus, and Signor Piatti, and among the many works introduced by him for the first time in England were trios, quartets, and quintets by Brahms, Dvorák, Saint-Saëns, and other modern composers. A list of all the works performed at his Manchester Orchestral Concerts will be found at the end of the volume.

In 1880 my father brought out a work at his orchestral concerts in Manchester, the production of which gave him the greatest pleasure and interest; this was Berlioz's 'Faust.' The Hungarian March and the 'Ballet des Sylphes' were well known, as they had often been given at previous concerts; but to give the work in its entirety had been my father's ambition for years, and he at last ventured on it in spite of the doubts expressed by many of his friends as to its proving a popular success. The concert excited much interest throughout England, and many well-known musicians repaired to Manchester to hear the first performance of a work which had been so much discussed, and about which so many contrary opinions were held.

The performance, which had been preceded by many careful rehearsals, was at all points magnificent, and reflected the greatest credit upon both band and chorus, whilst the principal vocalists, Miss Mary Davies, Mr. Lloyd, Mr. Hilton, and Mr. Henschel rendered the solos admirably. The work was received with so much enthusiasm that my father gave it a second time during the same season, a very rare proceeding on his part. Indeed, it is worthy of note that during the thirty-eight years' existence of the Manchester concerts, this compliment has only been paid to the following great choral works:— Handel's 'Messiah,' of which a double performance takes place every Christmas; Handel's 'Jephtha,' owing to the remarkable success of Mr. Sims Reeves in 1868; Gluck's 'Iphigenia,' given three times in the course of 1860; and the music to the 'Midsummer Night's Dream,' by Mendelssohn, given twice in the season of 1857–58.

The following year, 1881, my father took his band and chorus to London and gave a performance of 'Faust' at St. James's Hall, the soloists being the same as in Manchester. Again the *chef d'œuvre* of Berlioz was received with acclamation, and both there and in Manchester it has been repeated over and over again with ever increasing popularity, whilst in nearly all the greater towns of England it has been performed with the utmost success.

I went to Manchester for the first performance of
'Faust,' and being anxious to know something about
it before the concert took place in the evening I
attended the rehearsal. A little incident occurred
which revealed to me my father's wonderful accuracy
of ear, and which I may be pardoned for repeating.
In the second part of 'Faust,' when the hero of the
legend meets his doom and is consigned to the
infernal regions, there occurs an interlude for the
orchestra expressive of the exultation felt by the
denizens of hell over their latest victim. When I
first heard this piece I felt inclined to think my father
had given *carte blanche* to every member of his band
to make any noise he liked, provided it was loud and
of a horrible nature.

When it was over, what was my astonishment to
hear my father quietly say : 'The second clarinet
played an E flat instead of an E natural in the eighth
bar. I hope he will take care not to do so at the
concert this evening !'

Musicians may possibly scoff at this anecdote,
and say that it is only what any good conductor
would have done ; but, as I said at the beginning of
this chapter, I have no knowledge of music, only a
great love for it, and an absolute faith that the
manner in which it was presented to me by my
father, whether in his playing on the piano or his
conducting of his orchestra, was the best of all.
Many pianists had greater executive skill, as he was
the first to admit, but none had his absolute forget-
fulness of self, none, I think, so limpid and liquid a

touch when translating into sound the thoughts of the master whose score he had before him.

This quickness of perception and clearness of expression were part of his character as a man, and were as remarkable in his speech as in his rendering of music; no one was ever left for a moment in doubt as to what he meant, and I think it was this gift which made even the most difficult music intelligible to the unlearned when my father was at the piano or in the conductor's chair.

At the end of one of his concerts the remarks overheard were not so often 'How splendidly Hallé played,' or 'How wonderfully he conducted,' as 'How beautiful was that sonata,' or 'How glorious that symphony;' and I think that was the highest tribute that could be paid him, and the one which his modest nature and single-minded devotion to his art most appreciated.

Another gift my father possessed, and which never failed to fill me with astonishment, was his marvellous memory. A piece of music once read or heard seemed to be indelibly imprinted on some portion of his brain, and was there at his command whenever he wanted it. A remarkable instance of this occurred some years ago when Stephen Heller was here on a visit to us. He and my father had been talking about the evening on which the Revolution of 1848 broke out—how they heard the first shots fired as they went for a stroll together before parting for the night, and this naturally led them to recall the stirring events of the next few months, events sufficiently exciting and momentous to them both to obliterate, as one would have thought, all the incidents of the quiet evening they had spent together on that fateful night before they heard the firing. Presently Heller said to my father: 'Do you remember, Hallé, that I had composed a little sonata on that day, and when you came to me in the evening I asked you to play it to me? I wonder if you could play it to me now.' 'Good gracious!' said my father, 'I have never given it a thought from that day to this, but I'll try,' and he sat down at the piano and played it through without the mistake of a single note!

In spite of this unfailing memory he would often play, but would never conduct, without having the score before him. He maintained that to give an exhibition of his memory was not part of the programme of the concert, and that however perfect his recollection of a symphony or other concerted piece might be, he had greater command over his band when he could give all his attention to the proper rendering of the work they were about, without being distracted by any exercise of memory; yet when occasion demanded, his power of playing and conducting by heart never failed him, and very useful at times did it prove. Once, when about to go on the platform to play the Kreutzer Sonata with Lady Hallé, he discovered that the music had been left at home. 'Never mind,' he said; 'let's play it without,' and they went through it without a wrong note.

My father's excellent memory was not confined to music. It combined with a love of accuracy and order, and that power of calculation, so often accompanying the musical gift, which he possessed in a high degree, to make him a splendid man of business.

From the early part of October to the middle of March he had to make, year after year, arrangements for from two to five concerts every week, some in Manchester, others in different parts of England, Scotland, or Ireland. These concerts were either orchestral, when his whole band accompanied him, or recitals of chamber music, where the performers were Lady Hallé and himself. The correspondence, the business arrangements, the selection of programmes for all these different towns, and the care that had to be taken not to give the various audiences the same piece twice over within a given time, involved an enormous amount of work, and yet my father never kept a secretary, and had every detail of this vast business so clearly in his head that he was never at fault, and would often send his agents instructions about financial arrangements, programmes, &c., when he was on a journey away from his letters and note-books.

The quickness with which he despatched his correspondence always filled his family with astonishment. He would sit down to his study-table with a pile of letters before him, yet in an incredibly short time they were all disposed of. His system was to answer, or file for reference, each letter as it came, before he opened the next, and however hurried he might be, he never showed in his handwriting, which was faultlessly clear and beautiful, nor in what he wrote, any sign of haste. His business letters were models of conciseness, with never a word too many or too few, while he seemed to have an equal facility in expressing himself in English, French, or German.

He would probably with his business capacities have been very successful financially as well as artistically in all his undertakings had not his artist's temperament run away with him whenever it became a question of money being weighed in the balance against music. Music was his goddess, who had always to be decked in the richest raiment, and all other considerations vanished in face of the primary aim of making his concerts as good as money could make them. He would calculate the expenses and receipts with the greatest facility, and audit his accounts to the fraction of a penny; but whether the balance was to or against his credit was always a matter of comparative indifference so long as the concert had gone well. This and a large-hearted generosity led him to live up to his income without much thought for the future, though he was singularly simple in his habits and content with very little. He was neither a speculator nor a gambler. A report did once certainly get about that he spent a great deal of time at the card-table, and the rumour became so prevalent that a good-natured friend was at last urged to remonstrate with him about it. My father naturally expressed indignant astonishment that such an unfounded statement should have been circulated, when to his amazement he was told that his first wife, my mother, was the author of the report. It seems my poor mother had once told a friend how distressed she was that my father, after working hard all day, would not go to bed and take his proper rest, but would sit up *playing* till far into the night. She meant playing the piano, but her friend, probably through imperfect knowledge of French, had construed this into playing at cards, and had straightway gone and announced from the housetops that my father was an inveterate gambler!

He was certainly a very good card-player and dearly loved a rubber of whist when he could find time for one, but this was not often of late years, as he could seldom go to his club. His favourite game, so often mentioned in his Australian Diary and in his letters, was one called 'Sixty-six,' at which he had mighty encounters with Joachim, Piatti, and especially with Straus when travelling about the country from one concert to another—the stakes were always sixpence a game, and great was the triumph of the one who could boast, after a journey say from London to Edinburgh, of winning half-a-crown. Another form of card-playing he much indulged in was of a still more innocent nature. He would sit for hours of an evening when he really needed rest, finding relaxation for his mind in trying to work out problems of Patience with two packs of cards. He never cared for them unless they were exceedingly difficult, and many failures only seemed to spur him to further efforts. That this had been for many years a favourite amusement with him is proved by the following charming note addressed to him by Fanny Kemble, the celebrated actress, in 1853 :—

'6 Albany Terrace : Mardi, le 29 Juin.

' Cher M. Hallé,—Si jamais dans le malheur, la maladie ou l'ennui (et Dieu vous garde également des trois fléaux) vous prenez entre vos mains ces petites cartes, puissent-elles vous rendre en " patience " tout le bien que vous m'avez fait—et rappeler à votre souvenir votre très reconnaissante

'FANNY KEMBLE.' [1]

Another favourite game was chess, which my father played very well, and I have in my possession a sketch by Dicky Doyle representing my father and Manuel Garcia absorbed in a game.

My father was a man of so much energy and activity of mind that idleness was irksome to him in the last degree. His form of rest from work was to take up some other pursuit, either, as I have said above, the solution of some difficult problem of chess or cards, or else a book. He was a great reader, and it is astonishing how much he read considering the number of hours he gave each day to his work. Unlike his friend Heller, whose thoughts always dwelt on the past and whose favourite author was Horace, my father with his strong vitality and love of life lived in the present day and with authors who were his contemporaries. Books of travel and adventure, the history of this and of the latter half

[1] ' Dear Mr. Hallé,—If ever in sorrow, in sickness or distress (and God guard you ever from all three scourges) you take these little cards in your hands, may they return to you in " patience " all the good you have done me—and recall to your remembrance your very grateful

'FANNY KEMBLE.'

of the last century, works of fiction by living French
and English writers, the topics of the day and the
latest discoveries in science—all interested him
greatly.

In religion he was a Catholic, the faith of his
first wife, my mother, who died in 1866; of his
second wife, Wilhelmina Norman-Neruda, widow of
L. Norman of Stockholm, whom he married in 1888;
and of the nine children his first wife gave him, eight
of whom are still living.

In politics he was a staunch Conservative, but I
regret to say his interest was never keen enough to
overcome his objection to recording his votes at
election times. He somehow connected polling-
booths with jury-boxes, and thought if he did his
duty as a citizen in the former capacity he might be
called upon to serve in the latter, to which he had a
particular objection. He thought too by remaining
quietly at home when a parliamentary election was
going on, the officer whose business it is to collect
jurymen would forget his existence and leave him
alone, and whatever grounds he had for building up
this theory it certainly is a fact that only once was
he ever called upon to serve on a jury. I shall never
forget his consternation when he received his
summons, but his friend the Lord Chief Justice, Sir
Alexander Cockburn, to whom he at once repaired
in his trouble, arranged matters for him and got him
off, and I think must have asked that his name
should be taken off the list of possible jurymen per-
manently, as he was never called upon to serve again

either in London or in Manchester. Curiously
enough my father had a much greater dread of the
jury-box than of another place connected with it,
generally considered a still more unpleasant abode
—the jail.   He often playfully said that nothing
would please him better than to be locked up as a
first-class misdemeanant for three months with lots of
books, there were so many subjects he would like to
study, and for which he would never find time
whilst he was left at large, and had access to a piano.
I am glad to say that neither Sir Alexander Cockburn nor two other Lord Chief Justices of England,
with whom he was on terms of friendship, Lord
Coleridge and Lord Russell, have indulged this whim,
and that he refrained from courses which would have
brought him within the pale of the law on his own
account.

My father was a great respecter of law and constituted authority and desired to be at peace with all
men ; he had many friends and but few enemies,
except amongst those to whom all success in their
fellow men is a source of dislike and enmity.   He
was slow to anger, but when his wrath was roused
he was, I am bound to say, a very hard hitter.
Criticism on his own account he cared nothing about,
but woe to the luckless wight who threw a stone at
one of his gods in his presence, and who, to glorify
some modern composer, would decry one of the great
masters of the art of music.   My father had a fine
command of words which his great knowledge, unfailing memory, and accuracy, enabled him to use

N

with much effect, and would reduce even the most truculent adversary to silence in a very short time.   I used to love to be present at one of these encounters, but they were rare : 'peace and goodwill to all men' might have been his motto through life, and I am sure even his opponents soon forgot and forgave what was never meant in malice.

Of the many proofs of friendship and esteem, public and private, which my father received, I do not think that any, not even his knighthood, conferred in 1887, gave him so much pleasure as the doctor's degree conferred upon him at Edinburgh. He had the robes made for him, sat to me for his portrait in them, and expressed a wish that he might be buried in them—a wish which, needless to say, was piously observed by us when the sad time came for giving effect to it. H.M. the Queen was always very kind to my father and showed him many marks of her favour ; he was often bidden to Windsor, Balmoral, and Osborne, to play to her and to the late Prince Consort and to give instruction or to play 'à quatre mains' with her daughters. The Princess of Wales was also a pupil of my father's, and one for whom he had the greatest regard, as her talent was considered by him of a very high order. Both Her Royal Highness and the Prince of Wales treated my father with great affection and friendship, and he was often a guest at Sandringham and Marlborough House. The numerous extracts from my father's diaries and letters, translated, collected, and arranged by my sister at the end of this volume, make it unnecessary for me to add much more to these brief notes, and the reader will doubtless be anxious to return and listen to my father himself. His account of his two journeys to Australia and of his visit to Africa last summer will, I think, be read with interest, more especially the latter, as he and Lady Hallé went on their peaceful errand of music to Johannesburg and other places in the Transvaal only a few weeks before they became the scene of so much strife and disorder. It was also my poor father's last journey on earth, but little did we think so when he returned home full of health and spirits and apparently stronger and better than he had been for some time.

He came to a private view at the New Gallery a few days after his return to London, and meeting Manuel Garcia there, said to him: 'Eh bien, nous sommes toujours là, mon vieux,' to which Garcia replied, 'Je crois bien, nous sommes si occupés nous n'avons pas le temps de mourir.' Alas! Death and Time go hand in hand, and both work and play must go down before them. Within a fortnight the younger of these two old friends and valiant workers was snatched away.

I cannot dwell upon my father's death—it was too heavy a blow for us all and too recent, but for him it was in its suddenness the most merciful ending he could have had. My father's love of life, happiness in his work and surroundings, and superabundant energy made the thought of death singularly distasteful to him. He would never talk about it, and, I think, contemplated it as little as possible: when it came he had no knowledge of it at all, and was spared all suffering of mind or body, though I feel that had it been otherwise he would have borne all with the courage, fortitude, and resignation he had shown throughout his life whenever pain or misfortune came upon him.

Music, in which my father may be said to have been born, which was his ruling passion through life and in which he died—as he carried his work on to within a few hours of his death—was to him something more than an art : it was a sacred mission. He believed that music, which from all time has accompanied man in his strongest moments of joy and sorrow, which stirs him to deeds of courage and is his ultimate expression of love and praise, is a force for good, which cannot be gainsaid. He believed, as all lovers of music believe, that it is above the power of words in its influence on the spiritual side of man's nature, and that many a heart has been stirred to a sense of what is good and beautiful through music which otherwise might have gone through life unconscious that such things are. It was this faith that made my father's work of such absorbing interest to him, and which made him choose as the field of his labour those busy manufacturing towns of the north of England, where men's lives are spent in work—too often mere monotonous drudgery, and amid surroundings of dirt and ugliness such as the world has never seen before. To these grimy workers, to these makers of ships and of guns, of engines and of fabrics, whose ears were wearied by the ceaseless noise of machinery, he brought the strains of the most exquisite music ever heard by man, and made them forget, if but for a few minutes, the office and the workshop, and remember that existence has other things to offer. This was my father's life and work for nearly fifty years spent in England. He may have had a mistaken idea of the power of music and overrated the importance of it as a refining influence in men's lives, but he acted from the highest of all motives, and the work he did he did thoroughly and well.

On the morning of Friday, October 25, 1895, after a few hours' illness, he passed peacefully away. *Requiescat in pace.*

LETTERS

—◆◇◆—

TO HIS PARENTS

(Translated from the German)

Darmstadt : June 18, 1836, 10 A.M.

Beloved Parents,—Late last night I arrived here, at last, and already I feel compelled to sit down and have a little chat with you ; I hope it may do me good ; I then can see you standing before me and the hateful distance that separates us disappears. As the ship took me away from you, and as I gradually lost sight of you, then I first fully realised how hard the parting was ; it seemed, and it still seems, like a sad dream that I shall not see you, my dear ones, for such a long time, and it will be long before I get accustomed to the reality. As you stood motionless on the bridge, looking after me, it seemed impossible that I should see you and not be near you. I felt as if I must break away and fly to you, as if I could never separate myself from you ; I should have liked to have waved my hand, but I could not move, and I had to bite my lips not to cry aloud and expose my tenderest feelings to the ridicule of those around me. As you disappeared from my sight, I was obliged to sit down, my knees trembled so ; I saw and heard nothing more. Oh ! if I could only have seen and embraced you once more—only once more ; but I was taken ever further from you . . . A year is short, but far from you it seems an eternity. As soon as I found myself alone I could not keep back my tears, and I wept aloud ; it did me good. You can imagine that the first day of my

journey was quite lost to me; it was impossible to notice my
surroundings, however beautiful they might be.   I thought
only of you, and always of you; all your love, all your care
came back to my remembrance.   Now I clearly feel that the
happiest time of my life is past.   I must break off here or I
shall get too sad.   Later I will, if possible, write of indifferent
things; only, I implore you, show the above lines to nobody,
not even to my aunts, for no one understands what I feel for
you.   I had to give vent to my feelings, and if I could only
say all I feel, you would know how much I love you, but
I cannot put it into words.

June 21.

As you know by the beginning of this letter, I arrived
here on Friday, the 17th, without accident, at half-past
nine, tired and exhausted, but now I am quite well.   The
morning after my arrival, having rested long and taken my
coffee, I went to the Court apothecary; Flashoff, however,
was not there, as he works at a laboratory outside the town.
I got myself directed, and at last found it after a deal of
running about.   Flashoff welcomed me warmly; he is a dear,
kind man, and how glad I am to have him here, you can
imagine.   He was just distilling and could not leave his work,
so I remained with him until it was finished, which lasted an
hour.   By then it was midday, and as I did not care to get
to my lodgings just at meal time, I went back to the 'Grapes'
with Flashoff; we ate together, and after dinner went at once
to my lodging.   The old Hofräthin received me very kindly;
she had sent twice to Flashoff to inquire if I was coming.   I
am pleased with my rooms.   My sitting-room is beautifully
papered, but the furniture is bad and quite unworthy of the
walls.   My bedroom is not very beautiful, but I shall make
the best of it; but how different it was at home, my dear
ones!   I am perfectly satisfied with the food, and that is the
principal thing.   The best proof that it is good lies in the
fact that six young men, who are free to go where they please,
have come here for their meals for years.   Also, the Hofräthin
is highly spoken of by all, and especially, what I most value,

by our old Rinck. To him, now my master, I went on the afternoon of the same day. My heart beat a little; I had imagined an old, dry, and perhaps crabbed pedagogue, but how pleasantly was I surprised! He greeted me with the most unaffected cordiality and a hearty shake of the hand. He is a strong, stately man; no one would say he was sixty-six years of age. I should have said fifty-three or fifty-four. He sent at once for a bottle of wine, but I thanked him and declined on the ground that I had brought a little cough with me from the Rhine, so he drank several glasses alone to your good health and to mine. He inquired after you, and charged me with his greetings, then he talked of music and of my own piano-playing. Through all he said shone the greatest goodness of heart. In this first hour of intercourse he won my affection. When we had deliberated for an hour upon music, and he had spoken of several of his pupils, he said that as the weather was beautiful, he would like to take me to the prettiest spot near Darmstadt, that I might have a good first impression of my present place of sojourn. He took his stick, and led me up a steep hill to the Ludwig's-höhe, a fine open place on the top of it. This man of sixty-six clambered up so quickly it was all I could do to follow him. The view from this height is enchanting; one can see five or six different parts of the Rhine, winding through the enormous plain, and the towns of Mayence, Worms, Trier, Mannheim, and many more. Darmstadt lies at one's feet, on one hand the Bergstrasse and on the other the Taunus range of hills. But of this also I shall write more in my next. Of Rinck only this, that I am to have my first lesson this afternoon and that he will give me four lessons a week.

Now, I have only one piece of work before me which I rather dread—the unpacking of my trunk. The Frau Hofräthin has offered to help me, but I prefer doing it alone, for I know what is before me: that every article I take out will remind me of all the tender love and all the trouble with which you, dear mother, have cared for me; all the work and labour which you have so unweariedly devoted to me will

pass before my eyes. Yes, that will be a sad hour for me.
I had a great deal more to say, but I must soon come to a
stop for want of room. Now, write to me *soon, very soon*. I
shall not feel easy until I have heard from you and have some
of your dear handwriting before my eyes. Tell me if you
returned home the same day that we parted, or if you went
to Bonn—how much I wish the latter for you! You must
really *both* of you write, and the two little ones also. Bernard
will be able to write a word or two himself, and you can
guide Anna's hand; I must have something from each of you,
and you will do it, will you not? But in order that you can
write to me, I will give you my address: bei Frau Hofräthin
Stockhaus, in der Bau Strasse; you must not forget ' in the
Bau Strasse,' as there are many Stockhauses here. Now, I
have one more request, and you must not laugh at me. Tell
me, in your letter, of one day and hour on which you will
think for certain of me. Oh! how happy I should be to be
able to say: ' *Now*, now they are thinking of me at home!'
It will seem as if we were for an hour in our cosy little room
together: on the sofa you are sitting, dear father, with your
pipe; you, dear mother, and I close by; our two dear little
ones are on the sofa near my father, and he plays with
them. Heavens! when this comes so vividly before me, I
cannot keep back the tears, and it seems impossible that I
can bear to be so long separated from you; my only
hope is that when I have a great deal to do it may
distract my thoughts. Now, my dearest parents, and
you, dear children, *lebt alle wohl!* Write to me soon;
write all, and grant the request I made above. Also inform
me how often you will write, and how often I may write to
you; remember me to all my relations, to Mr. and Mrs.
Elbers, and to the whole choral society. I kiss you, dear
parents, and the children, a thousand times. Write and tell
me that you dearly love me; as much as I love you, you
never can! I will certainly be industrious, and do all that
you wish me to do; I know no greater happiness than to
please you. Now be careful to keep well, but if you are

in the slightest degree indisposed be sure you write and tell me. Now good-bye, father, mother, Bernard, Anna, Aunt Lotta, farewell, and think often of your ever loving son and brother, CARL HALLÉ.

II

TO HIS PARENTS

(Translated from the German)

Darmstadt : July 6, 1836.

Beloved Parents,—Your dear letter caused me indescribable pleasure, all the more that I had not expected it nearly so soon; thanks, a thousand thanks, that you granted my request, and all of you wrote. Oh! how often I have read it, and put it by, and then taken it again, thinking I might have overlooked something; but you might have written much smaller and closer together, and made more of the small space which, alas! is all one has for a letter. Take example from me; I could write you a whole ream, and then I should not have put down nearly all I had to say. I am only sorry that Mino [his dog] was too busy to write to me; I should so have liked to see his handwriting. When I first opened your letter I looked at once for the bill of health, and only after having found that, thank God, you are all well, I began to read the letter through, and now will answer all your questions.

I have overcome my depression by dint of hard work, and, in my moments of leisure, by going to Flashoff, whom I like more and more. To guard against falling into it again, which I know would be bad for me, I have resolved not to mention it in my letters, and should I be tempted to do so, then I shall say: 'Ab! fertig! von oben herunter!' and stop writing; therefore, no more of it. Next in your letter come the greetings to Rinck which I delivered at once, and told him that you, dear father, hoped to thank him personally, which pleased him greatly; you were not quite unknown to him, he had read your praises in either the 'Iris' or the 'Eutonia' (two musical papers), neither of

which you will have seen. Rinck promised to send a few
lines for you to be enclosed in this letter, but should I not
get them in time, I shall send them with my next. You
are anxious about my cough, that is quite unnecessary; it is
true I had caught a little specimen on the Rhine, but the
second day after my arrival here I had got rid of it, therefore be quite easy, and rest assured that I have too great a
fear of falling ill not to be very careful. Had you seen me
after my journey, you would not have known me, so dreadfully sunburnt was I, I looked like a peony, and have not
yet recovered my *fine complexion*, for the heat here is terrible;
since my arrival it has only rained once, and in this sandy
desert it ought to rain every other day to be bearable; it is
impossible to go out in the daytime, and nobody does so,
one has to wait for the evening, and even then it is very
warm. I was very glad to hear that you went to Bonn, as
I hear from Louis (Flashoff) that there is much worth
seeing there, so I hope you enjoyed yourselves. I laughed to
read how you had gone astray from Mühlheim: poor Stolle,
[the driver], how many *donnerwetters* he must have heard!
I am still quite content with my lodgings and also with the
food; the latter is really remarkable, as in general in this
country; except the peas, which are far from being as good
as at home, I knew none of the vegetables, and some are
very curious, but I do not appreciate them; for instance,
green turnip-tops; but I eat well, never fear; if shyness
were my greatest fault I should be a very good fellow. I
will describe my sitting-room a bit: first, it has four fine
yellow and green-papered walls; second, three windows with
beautiful long curtains; third, against one of the walls
stands a green, yellow, and black sofa, but I am afraid it is
stuffed with wood; before it a small ugly square table; to
the left a large stove, to the right a big bureau with many
drawers, in which I have put all my chattels, except my coats
and cape, which hang in a wardrobe in my bedroom; between
two of the windows hangs a looking-glass, and under it there
is a small table; four chairs, very bad ones, covered like the

sofa, stand about the room, and opposite the sofa, my piano;
through Rinck's mediation I have been able to hire it from
Klösz, the instrument maker, but it is a very bad one; in
the upper octaves the tone is atrocious, and in the bass I
should say it was hellish; worst of all it does not keep in
tune, and all the same costs me one Prussian thaler a month;
from what I hear (from musicians as well) the piano-maker
(Vierheller) of this town lends very good instruments on the
same terms; if this be true I shall give up the one I have
after one month; how Rinck got hold of this Klösz, who is a
very insignificant maker, I really do not know, but the man
is poor, has many children, and Rinck has a very good heart.
That is all very well, but that I should lose all taste for the
piano out of good-nature would be asking too much. The
Hofräthin is a most kind and worthy woman, who looks after
us all seven with almost motherly care; morning after morning she herself brings me a large plate of beautiful cherries
(the sight of her might almost take away one's appetite, she
is such an ugly old *donnerwetter*). I take my coffee with
sugar in my own room, but dear *Schwarzbrod*, how I miss
thee! instead of that I eat two big rolls of white bread,
which are good also. Dinner takes place punctually at half-
past twelve, we are generally nine at table, and the saying
that in a large company one can eat more than in a small
one is confirmed in my case; supper is punctually at half-
past eight, and after it I generally walk up and down in the
nice garden behind the house; at ten o'clock I go to bed,
and get up precisely at six the next morning, as sometimes I
have my lesson with Rinck at seven, sometimes at eight
o'clock, which I like very much, as it gives me the whole
day without a break. Now we come to an important matter,
the teaching of Rinck; you want to know my opinion of it;
as a whole I cannot yet express an opinion, but can tell you
that, so far, he pleases me very much; I will explain his
method from the beginning, and then you, dear father, can
judge of it yourself. At the beginning of the first lesson he
asked if I had studied any other theoretical works besides

Weber's. I told him I had *studied* no other, but had several times read through Reicha's 'Theory'; this he did not know. Then he began (as you had predicted) by writing the first lines of the Chorale, 'Kommt, lasst euch den Herren lehren,' to which I had to put six, six, I say, different basses, and also six different harmonies, five were simple, and one a florid bass. Two I finished during the lesson, and he was very pleased; of faults, he only found one or two, but he lays a mighty stress upon the flowing movement of all the parts, so here and there he had to make some changes; he made everything so clear to me that those who say Rinck is hard to understand must be wooden-headed; he repeats everything several times, and then always asks if one has understood what he meant. He said he set great value upon these exercises (of simple counterpoint), and said it would be very good for me to work upon five or six chorales in this way. After having worked three, viz. 'Kommt, lasst euch den Herren lehren,' 'Nun danket alle Gott,' and 'Jesus, meine Freude,' in six different four-part settings (which was sometimes a head-splitting business; try it for once and put to the notes —d, f, e, c, d—six *different* basses) he said I had the four-part harmony so well at command that we need no longer devote our time to it. We had given four lessons to it, viz. one week. Then he gave me four-part modulations, in four-bar phrases, to be done, like the chorales in the strictest style, from C major by progressive fifths to C sharp major, therefore from C to G, G to D, D to A, and so on, and then from C sharp major back to C major; then from F major in the same way to G flat major, viz. from F to B, B to E flat major, and so on, and back again; then through all the minor keys, on the understanding that all must be different from each other. That was also a difficult task, it was as if I had to make thirty-two *different* modulations from C major to G major, or from A minor to E minor (by ascending fifths), and just as many *different* ones from F major to B major, or from D minor to G minor (by descending fifths); all hte same, I

finished all those sixty-four modulations so quickly that they
only occupied two lessons (which means I did them at home,
and only showed them at the lessons). This exercise has
given me great facility in four-part writing as well as in the
modulations, for I had to modulate in every possible fashion
in order to be always different. He was very pleased, and
assured me he had not believed me to be so well advanced;
he found little to alter, and that of an unimportant nature.
Then we went on to imitations; after giving me a very clear
and intelligible explanation of what was meant by the term
(which I knew already), he wrote a little example of five or
six bars in further elucidation, spoke, but only for the
moment, in passing, of ' stretto,' inversion and double counterpoint; then, at the end of the lesson, set me, as a task to do
at home, to invent, even if only five or six bars, in which I
should introduce an imitation in the octave. I sat down at
home, took the following two bars

as a proposition, and made a composition of two and a half
pages, in which, at my own instigation, I employed everything
he had mentioned in passing, but of which I knew something
before—viz. the ' stretto,' an inversion, and the double counterpoint in the octave—he was immensely pleased, and whilst
looking through it said repeatedly ' Good, very good !' Then
he gave me a theme of three bars, which I had to work out
in the same way, but this time to imitate at the fifth; out of
these I managed to fabricate three pages, working them in
every possible way. With this he was even more content,
saying he considered this exercise the most profitable of all;
I should, therefore, do altogether six two-part, which are the
most difficult, several three-part, and several four-part exercises of this kind, and then we should go on at once to the

fugue, which he said was not very different from these imitations. Five two-part exercises are at this moment finished; in the last one I showed him he found very little to change and nothing to blame. Besides all this he gave me the words for a Motet, which should contain first a chorus, then a quartet, and a final chorus with a *fugue*, for soprano, alto, tenor, and bass, without accompaniment. I have nearly finished it, and am wondering how it will please him; if you like, I will send you some of my work; consult Uncle Koch [1] as to how I shall manage about the postage. This is a true account of my studies up to the present. What pleases me best about Rinck is that he insists so much upon practical exercises, and thinks very little of mere theory; also, that he does not cling too much to the old rules: thus, he only forbids consecutive fifths when two greater fifths follow each other, one greater and one smaller fifth he willingly allows— that is to say, in several-part writing, for in two-parts it always sounds badly—his chief motto is: Lay no fetters upon Art. He is also very obliging: he is lending me the 'Cecilia,' the older volumes that I had not read, as well as the new ones, also the 'Iris' and 'Eutonia,' and of his music he lends me all I wish for. One thing more, during a walk Rinck asked me what my plans were after leaving here (N.B.— *he has now given me the fullest assurance that it will not be necessary for me to remain six months with him*). I told him our intention was that I should go to Paris from here; of this he highly approved, and promised to give me letters of introduction to *Cherubini* and *Meyerbeer*, whom he knows very well, the latter especially, and he will strongly recommend me to both; you will rejoice at this as much as I; a letter from Rinck to *these two* would be of the greatest use to me, for Cherubini is the Director of the Conservatoire, and you know how great the fame of Meyerbeer is just now in Paris. He will also give me letters to Ferdinand Hiller and other celebrated composers, whose names I cannot at present remember.

[1] The postmaster of Hagen.

. . . The first letter I delivered at Darmstadt was the one to Fräulein Mangold. The first reception was so dry and formal that I went home quite out of humour, but yesterday I was invited to a large party, where I enjoyed myself greatly. I made the acquaintance of Kapellmeister Mangold, of Concertmeister Mangold (an excellent violoncellist), and of two other Mangolds, one of them a very good violinist, and who, according to Rinck, must be quite a genius; there were several other gentlemen and many ladies. I had to play several times, and the two Mangolds and I have agreed often to play duets and trios together. The Kapellmeister, a very nice man, at once made the proposal, if I wished to attend the rehearsals of the orchestra, that I should go any morning at 10 o'clock to the Court Theatre. I went this morning, and my joy was quite indescribable. The orchestra consists of more than sixty members; they play like angels, I have never heard anything like it, and I must describe it more closely another time. To-day they played Beethoven's 'Eroica Symphony'— that is, indeed, a mighty composition—at times an icy cold shiver ran through me, but more of this later. Gottfried Weber received me *very kindly* (more of this later). Thank Mr. Thieme especially for both his letters, he has given me two very pleasant acquaintances by them, and please tell him I shall soon keep my promise and write to him about both persons. Now, my dear ones, farewell; you, dear father, do not work too hard, and take care of your health one and all, that we may all happily meet again. I promise faithfully that your loving admonitions shall not prove fruitless; never, I promise you, shall you grieve over my conduct. Greet Aunt Altgelt and all my relations, and kiss the little ones a thousand times. Your loving son

CARL HALLÉ.

N.B.—Write very soon and closer together, and more.

III

TO HIS PARENTS

(Translated from the German)

Darmstadt : July 23, 1836.

. . . I feel quite convinced that I can leave here at the end of three months, but Rinck has gone into the country for a week, so I could not give him your letter, nor can I tell you anything definite. During my last lesson, in the course of conversation, we spoke of Mangold, the violinist's, departure for Vienna *in the middle of September*, when Rinck said that I could go to Paris *at the same time*. Should he return tomorrow, which I do not expect, I shall be able to give you more positive news. I am very glad you asked him to give me a letter of introduction to Kalkbrenner ; he does not know him personally, but I think he will give me the letter. I have ordered a metronome at Schott's for Mr. Elbers, and received notice to-day that it had been sent off, but I did not ask them for an introduction to Kalkbrenner as you suggested, Rinck having promised to ask them for several letters for Paris for me, and, if he does so, it will have more weight ; I shall also ask him if he thinks Schott can help me to find a lodging in Paris. If Rinck comes back to-morrow I shall be able to tell you further of this also ; otherwise please write to me at once, so that I may answer you soon ; we must not delay, time passes so quickly that I can hardly believe I have been here six weeks. I shall certainly not go to Geisenheim, partly because I grudge the expense, but chiefly because it would interfere too much with my work. So, dear father, all your questions are answered. I am only surprised that you do not say a word as to how you liked Rinck's method of teaching, which I so fully explained ; please do not forget to give me your opinion of it in your next.

Now for your letter, dear mother : you begin by telling me that I must always be merry and cheerful—I do my utmost to obey the injunction, and I succeed pretty well. I have a good many diversions here, especially through my intercourse with

O

the Mangolds. Do not be afraid that I work too hard; no, what Rinck gives me to do I can easily get through without too much effort. I take a walk every day, generally towards evening. I have a better piano, and although I cannot call it good, it is a hundred per cent. better than the first old rattletrap, but I have to pay 15 kreutzers a month more for it. The great heat ceased so suddenly that it is almost cool now, and one has to be careful not to catch cold unawares, so I did catch a cold in my head, which only lasted a day. When I read Uncle Koch's letter I feared that Dr. Elbers was dead, and your confirmation of my fear has grieved me very much. For God's sake, beware of that dreadful smallpox, and let me know if there are more cases at Hagen. I cannot write to Mr. Elbers to-day, I really have no time, and should not like to send him a mere hasty scrawl, but in my next I shall certainly enclose a few lines to him. Your greetings to my *amiable* Hofräthin, to Rinck, and to Louis Flashoff I have already delivered, and am charged by all three heartily to return them.

Now, your letter also is answered, dear mother, and here comes my own mustard. But first I am going to take a little walk, in the Grand Ducal Park forsooth, and there, over a slice of cherry tart of a most delicate sort, shall meditate on what to say to you. So here you can make a pause, and wait until I have eaten my cake and have returned to my *wool-stuffed* sofa. . . . I will begin by telling you how I was received by Gottfried Weber. A few days after my arrival I went to his house at eleven o'clock in the morning, and was fortunate enough to find him; when I had given him Schott's letter, he kindly bade me sit down; whilst he was reading it I had a good look at him. Weber is a tall, strong-looking man, with a round, full face, very yellow and much scarred. He wore a large dressing-gown, a voluminous cravat tied loosely round his neck, and a white night-cap, which he never removed, as he has a perfectly bald head (so, at least, it seemed to me). When he had read the letter, he welcomed me once more, and asked if I

had begun my lessons with Rinck. I told him I had only
had one so far, and then I had to relate all that Rinck had
made me do, with which he was much satisfied, and praised
him for always proceeding to practise at once. He then
asked if I had already composed much. I said no; not
much as yet. He told me that was not right; that one
ought to compose a great deal from the first, and could study
the so-called thorough-bass style at any time. At the words,
' so-called thorough-bass style,' the fellow put on so sublime
a sneer, that his face must have looked just so whilst he was
writing his abuse of the thorough-bass style in his theory of
music. After a little further talk, he asked what I intended
to do after leaving Darmstadt, and when I told him of my
plan of going to Paris, he said he envied me. He invited
me to come and see him often, but so far I have not been
able to go again, and he also has been out of town. On
Monday or Tuesday I shall certainly go and try and sound
him whether he would give me a letter for Kalkbrenner,
should Rinck not do so. I go to the Mangolds nearly every
day. Carl Mangold, the violinist, and I have become intimate friends, and as often as we are together, we play duets;
sometimes, with the addition of an excellent violoncellist from
the Court apothecary, no! I mean from the Court orchestra,
we play trios. I have thus got acquainted with many works
hitherto unknown to me; for instance, I now know *all*
Beethoven's sonatas for piano and violin, nearly all his trios,
further, six trios by Reicha, and three trios by Prince
Ferdinand of Prussia, which are very fine, and many other
things besides. The 'cellist, Wilhelm Mangold, who has no
piano at his rooms, but lives just opposite to me, often comes
over with his bass tucked under his arm, and then we play
double sonatas by Beethoven, Onslow, &c., to our hearts'
content.

That under these conditions I feel quite in my element
you will easily believe. Next week we shall also play
quartets and quintets with pianoforte. On August 25 there
is to be a great concert in aid of the Beethoven monu-

ment, which will take place in the theatre, and probably last two days.

The Grand Ducal Kapelle is now in full rehearsal; none but Beethoven's compositions are to be performed. As often as I can find time, I go in the morning to the theatre to hear the rehearsal. I have now heard the 'Eroica' and the delicious Pastoral symphonies so often that I know them almost by heart; still, I go again and again, as I can never hear them enough. Now they are studying the great symphony with chorus, which I am most curious to hear. Such precision I had never heard in an orchestra, and had never thought it possible that such fine *nuances* could be obtained from such a numerous body; even the smallest indications were observed. They succeeded admirably in those crescendos which suddenly pass into *piano*, which are found almost exclusively in Beethoven's works. To be sure, Mangold, the conductor, takes enormous pains, one may say that he is indefatigable; for instance, at several rehearsals, before taking the whole orchestra together, he takes the first violins with only two of the other stringed instruments, and thoroughly drums their part into the first violinists, then he does the same with the second violins, with the violas, and with the 'cellos and five double-basses; thereby the quartet gets so perfect that you do not hear a single false note. The *pizzicato* is also something quite exquisite. In Beethoven's 'Eroica' symphony there is a great deal of *pizzicato*, even whole runs in unison, but I was never able to detect one instrument arriving a little late; each time it came like a spark, and the effect was most extraordinary.

I had almost forgotten one thing, about which Carl Mangold gives me no peace, and which I have promised to write to you about. He goes in the middle of September to Vienna, and absolutely insists upon my going with him there instead of to Paris. He says there are as many pianists in Vienna as at Paris, and that one has more opportunities of hearing great works, oratorios especially, than in Paris (this I doubt). Further, that it would be good for us both to

study composition again (he is going to take lessons from
Seyfried, especially in free style, although he has studied
harmony for years with his brother the Kapellmeister, who
had worked three years under Cherubini, and, either before
or after, with Spontini; he is exceedingly industrious, for a
whole year composed a fugue every day, and has acquired
such facility that he can produce a beautiful fugue in a
quarter of an hour).   However agreeable this would be, and
however much I should like to continue my intercourse with
one whose devotion, heart and soul, to music is greater than
I ever met with before, and, indeed, passes all belief, I still
prefer to go to Paris, and believe it would be more useful to
me.   Therefore, dear father, I beg you, in your next letter,
to put forward some good reasons why you prefer that I
should go to Paris, which I can read to him, as I have
always told him the decision rested entirely with you, and
have never shown myself averse from the project; for when
we are together I could wish to stay together always, and
still, I would sooner go to Paris.   Moreover, the cholera is
at Vienna, certainly a good reason for you, dear mother, to
insist upon my not going there.

I intended to tell you a delightful anecdote that I have
remembered since Mayence, but I have too little room, so
must keep it to myself for the present.   I notice that through
having to put off from one letter to another, things I wished
to tell you, I end by forgetting them, so if you remember
anything you wish to hear about, ask for it in your next
letter. . . .

IV

TO HIS PARENTS

(Translated from the German)

Darmstadt : August 15, 1836.

Beloved Parents,—If I were to delay any longer writing
to you, you might end by becoming anxious again ; I therefore sit down to write, if not a long letter, at least whatever
of importance I may have to tell you.

I cannot understand how it is I have so little spare time ; I get through the work Rinck gives me so quickly, that if I did nothing else, I believe I could be very idle; but I have borrowed from the Free Library (which contains many good works) Reicha's big book on Theory, also the 'French Musical Review,' by Professor Fétis, which is not only exceedingly instructive, but good exercise in French ; then the scores of several of Beethoven's symphonies, for which I have a ravenous appetite; then I am overwhelmed with music which people send me to look through, and expect me to play it to them afterwards; added to this comes the duet, trio, quartet, quintet, and septet playing, and the orchestra rehearsals which I hardly ever miss ; I could add several other items to the list, and it leaves me scarcely any time for letter-writing ; one has to take a walk occasionally to get a breath of fresh air, which is rather scarce here ; in short, if you consider all this, you will not take it ill if I do not write so often.

I have now copied for you, my dear father, my motet, and the first movement of a trio for violin, viola, and violoncello, which I have just finished, and that is why my letter is shorter than the previous ones, as I still have to work for Rinck.

I was exceedingly delighted, last Thursday week, at eight o'clock in the morning, to see old Günther suddenly enter my room. I had not expected him in the least ; he spent about an hour with me, gave me a great deal of news and your letter, dear father ; you might, however, with so excellent an opportunity, have sent me more than one letter. At nine o'clock we went off together to Rinck, who was hugely pleased to see his old friend and countryman. We spent a very pleasant morning with Rinck, breakfasted with him, and were invited by his wife to dinner next day. That dinner, and the afternoon that followed it, were the most enjoyable that I had had for a long time ; better-hearted people than the whole Rinck family would certainly be hard to find; and the whole conversation at table was as merry as it was interesting ; Rinck was in excellent vein, and told us a great deal about his musical opinions.

Your health was often toasted, and Rinck said at least twenty times: 'Now all I wish is that old Mr. Hallé were with us.' After dinner I had to play something; Rinck had not yet heard me. I first played the variations on 'Am Rhein! Am Rhein!' and I must say I had not played so well for a long time. That I had pleased Rinck, I guessed by the way he shook hands with me when I had finished; 'God preserve you,' was all he said. When I had rested a little, I had to play again, and this time I chose the first movement of Kalkbrenner's concerto, which pleased him very much.

At four o'clock, Günther, one of the Court orchestra named Soistmann, an old friend of Günther's who had come to see him there, and I, left Rinck's, took a walk, and then went to an inn and drank a couple of glasses of most excellent Bavarian beer in the garden (since then, I have often been to this inn, it is called the artists' tavern, as only musicians, painters, and such-like rogues frequent it, only artistic topics are handled there, and generally in a most interesting fashion); there we stayed until ten o'clock, when friend Günther started in the post-chaise for Heidelberg. I was very sorry I could not keep him here any longer, but he would not hear of it. I very much doubt if he will carry out the journey he had planned, as he already seemed in two minds about it.

Now for my Paris project. Rinck will write, as you will see by his enclosed letter, without fail to Kalkbrenner, as soon as he receives his address from Schott, to whom he wrote a fortnight ago, but as yet has had no answer, Schott being very dilatory in things outside his own business matters. We have both heard, and from different sources, that there may be difficulties in being taken as a pupil, as Kalkbrenner gives very few lessons, but we hardly believe that he will refuse the first request of Rinck, whom he knows well by reputation. Should he, however, refuse, I shall still go to Paris, as Rinck advises, on the chance of taking lessons with Hiller, Liszt, or Chopin; Hiller seems to be, according to what I have read in the 'Revue Musicale,' a tremendous performer, but simple and sincere. With him I could hardly

fail, as he is an intimate friend of Rinck, and would not refuse
him. On the whole I am not in the least afraid ; there are so
many first-rate pianists in Paris, that I shall certainly find
one amongst the number who will give me lessons. But I
do not doubt in the least that Kalkbrenner will accept me.
I have also spoken to Rinck about a lodging, and I shall now
tell you what I intend to do. I shall not write and ask
Schott to find one for me ; I have just told you that he has
kept Rinck waiting a fortnight for an answer, so you can
imagine how long he would be about this ; before he had
written to Paris and received an answer, and I had sent that
answer to you, the six weeks I still have to remain here
would have vanished. Rinck gives me letters to Schlesinger,
the music-seller, to the Abbé Mainzer (his pupil), and to
several other persons (besides the musical potentates), and is
procuring others from Schott. Louis Flashoff also gives me
two letters for friends of his from Essen who are in Paris ; one
of them I know personally since the time I was at Essen. . . .

By this post you will receive Rinck's latest work, which
he sends you as a little remembrance. He said it was only a
trifle, but he hoped you would accept it as a token of his
friendship. You will see that all the little preludes, especially
in the second volume, are charmingly worked out, and in the
whole collection there is a great deal of original and flowing
melody. In such work, and in such work only, is Rinck
really great, otherwise he is rather one-sided ; he has a few
phrases and figures which he introduces into all his works, so
if one knows a few of them and knows them well, one can
recognise a work of his at once. I still like his teaching, but
I see now that it could be a good deal better. If Rinck takes
a pupil from the very beginning, he must create a Babylonian
confusion in his head, so wanting in method is his teaching ;
he jumps quite without order from one subject to another ;
to-day he takes one thing, to-morrow another. I understand
him perfectly, because none of the subjects were quite unknown to me, and I rather like this habit of his, as it has
made me do a little of everything during these three months,

and will enable me to work by myself in Paris; but had I known nothing but what Rinck has taught me, I should have fared ill.

This may appear to you a contradiction of what I said in my second letter, but it really is not so, for, as far as I am concerned, I do like his method. The motet and trio I send you have Rinck's approval; in the trio he has not altered a single note, and I have written an Adagio to the same, as well as a motet for four male voices, but it will be impossible for me to copy either of them for you whilst I am at Darmstadt.

I beg you to show both things to our dear friend Atteau (to whom I send greetings, and a request that he will write to me), and then both of you criticise severely, and let me know what you disapprove of and what you like. You might have the trio written out so that you can try it over, but then I beg you to play it very softly and pay attention to every little sign, or else the effect is lost (the two half-notes in the seventh and eleventh bars must be played on one string and nicely drawn together). As you have now got a metronome, I shall just hunt about and see if I can find one here, to be able to indicate the time to you. In the middle movement in D of the trio you may relax the time a little, and this movement must be very well executed, and the crescendo on the first six notes well brought out. In the motet, the Adagio should be well sustained and sung with feeling. Rinck told me that the 'Holy, Holy,' in the third and fifth bars for tenor and bass might have been omitted; I have left them in to have your opinion. Now farewell, dear parents, I embrace you, and you will kiss the little ones for me. Greet all my relations and friends, and excuse me to those to whom I ought to have written. Write soon, but at greater length than the last time, to your loving son,

CARL HALLÉ.

N.B.—Between September 18 and 25 I shall start for Paris.

V

TO HIS PARENTS

(Translated from the German)

Darmstadt : September 8, 1836.

My dearest Parents,—In a few words I shall just tell you that I am still quite well, have safely received your letters, thank you heartily for the same, that I shall do all you recommend, that I am studying hard, practising harder (for very good reasons), moreover enjoying myself amazingly, have during the past two months made a number of pleasant and interesting acquaintances, am received in the best society, am much fêted, and lastly that I am sorry and glad to be going away from here again. 'These are the points I propose for your consideration during this sacred hour, but first let us, etc., etc.' I began by telling you that I was in good health, that is incontrovertible, so I need dwell no longer upon that point, but go on to the next. Your letters are all safely to hand. I found them at midnight on the 28th of last month, on my return home after a brilliant tea and supper party. I opened them at once, but delayed reading them until the next morning, my mind, head, and inside being still too replete with the varied pleasures of the evening. Bernard's letter pleased me best ; I was so glad to see the advance he had made in writing; his style is *very expressive*. That I thank Aunt Schulz most heartily for her humorous letter is self-understood ; that I do not answer it is not self-understood, but as soon as I get to Paris I shall try to make up for all deficiencies ; there I shall probably have much more time at my disposal than I have here, as I shall most likely only take one piano lesson a week ; first, because I do not think I shall need more than one ; and secondly, because they are sure to be barbarously dear. Rinck told me lately that a guitar-player from here, and only a middling one, gave lessons in Paris, and got six francs an hour, which makes 1 thaler 18 g. If that be true—if a middling lesson on a coffee-roaster cost so dear, what may not a pianoforte potentate charge ? I shall therefore—but halt, I see I have got off the road, and must make a big leap to get back to my forsaken Aunt Schulz. So, dear little aunt, or rather long aunt, should you perchance put your nose into this letter, do not be angry with me, do not be scandalised at my ill-breeding. Cornelius Flüss (ex-Doctor of Philosophy at Haspe [1]) I also sincerely thank for his second letter. This time I was satisfied with the length of it, but even at the risk of being called an ass, I cannot answer him now. I shall do so from Paris, and describe all its wonders, which I hope will satisfy him. . . . I am studying hard, and for the past few weeks have worked at nothing but fugues, at first three-part, and now four-part fugues, and shall do nothing else whilst I am here. Rinck's teaching pleases me less and less, but Rinck himself I like better and better. I practise harder and harder, and have bought some new music—for instance, Kalkbrenner's *Effusio Musica*, undisputably his best work, and Chopin's Variations on ' La ci darem' from ' Don Giovanni.' This is so dreadfully difficult, that I have to study it bar by bar, but I think that when I have overcome the difficulties (which will probably take a long time) I shall find it to be one of the most delightful works I know. These variations are far from being considered among his most difficult works, from which God preserve us !

My life here is exceedingly pleasant ; it is quite a new existence for me. The most delightful hours are those I spend in the house of Mr. von Plöennies (*medizinalrath*). One meets the whole artist-world of Darmstadt there : painters, musicians, poets—all artists are welcome. I have made many interesting acquaintances there, first among them Ed. Duller the writer, who lives here ; also a Doctor of Philosophy named Kringel, quite a young man, whom I shall meet again this winter in Paris. I was introduced by Kapellmeister Mangold, and since then have been invited several times a week to grand tea and other parties. A striking elegance reigns in the house, which is a little

----

[1] Small village near Hagen.

embarrassing at first, but one's shyness is soon dissipated by
the cheerful and easy tone which one hardly expects to find
allied with such magnificence. The central point towards
which all converges is certainly Mrs. von Plöennies. She is
a distinguished poetess, and moreover a very handsome and
most amiable lady, who enlivens the whole conversation. At
these parties the entertainment is most varied; either Duller
or Mrs. von Plöennies reads one of their latest compositions,
then there is music. I have had to play each time, on a very
fine grand piano, only a little hard to play on; duets and
quartets are sung, and so on; all this to a flowing accompaniment of wine and punch, whilst the palate is also most
delicately catered for. I always return home very well
pleased from one of these parties. You can therefore believe
that I am sorry to be going away so soon; but as regards
my studies I am glad, for I shall have time in Paris to chew
the cud of all I have devoured so quickly in these three
months with Rinck. Now my paper is coming to an end,
and, *par conséquence*, I must soon end also; it is time that I
returned to my fugue; but I must first, dear father, answer
your little observation on my trio. You say that in the first
movement one hears nothing of the key of D. That was a
gigantic oversight. If you will put on a pair of musical
spectacles, you will find that the whole second part of the
first movement is in D major. I am soon expecting your and
Atteau's criticism on both my compositions.

Now, dearest parents, *lebt recht wohl*. . . . Your ever
loving   CARL.

VI

TO HERR ELBERS

(Translated from the German)

Darmstadt: September 23, 1836.

Highly honoured Herr Elbers,—I was very delighted and
surprised, on opening the last letter from my parents, to
recognise, among the different letters they enclosed, one in
your honoured hand, though at the same time I felt abashed

that through my unpardonable neglect I had omitted to be
the first to write, in order to give you an account of all my
doings here ; so I read myself a severe lecture and made a
long face at myself for the rest of the day. Excuses I have
none. All the reasons I could give—such as too much work,
&c.—when seen in the right light, come to nothing. Therefore, I can only humbly ask your pardon, which, out of the
great and undeserved affection you have always shown and
proved to me, I confidently hope that you will grant.

At present, before leaving Darmstadt, I can only thank
you for your kind letter and the good advice and welcome
news that it contained, as well, most especially, for the letters
of introduction you were good enough to send. To write you
a long letter just now would be impossible, for I am surrounded by a most confused chaos (but not one out of Haydn's
' Creation ') as I am busy packing, and though, now and then,
I feel pretty comfortable in such moments of great disorder,
the comfort is not lasting. I have also some farewell visits
to make (a tiresome business !), and my passport to get. So
you see that I have not much time at command.

I can only, therefore, tell you briefly that the three
months I have spent here have passed very happily. I have
made many and very pleasant acquaintances, especially with
several members of the most excellent Court Orchestra. One
of them, a first-rate violoncellist called Mangold, I have often
played duets with, thus carrying on what I had begun with you
at Hagen. The Court Orchestra, which contains from sixty
to seventy musicians, is rather given to be idle during the
summer months, but, luckily for me, since my arrival there
have been rehearsals every morning from 10 to 1 o'clock
for two concerts in aid of the Beethoven monument, which
have just lately taken place. I have there heard Beethoven's
masterpieces, his symphonies, the second act of ' Fidelio,'
and his fantasia for pianoforte, orchestra, solos, and chorus,
given in the highest perfection. You will believe that
it was in the highest perfection when I tell you that the
Kapelle, certainly one of the best in Germany, has, for a

quarter of a year, studied these works regularly three hours a day.

I now clearly see that Beethoven's works are not, as it is usually considered, only capable of being appreciated by connoisseurs, but, when thus interpreted, even the musically uneducated who have minds in the least susceptible, must be impressed by them as by every work of the highest art.

I should be glad to speak with you more minutely about those performances, but I feel my incapacity to describe these sublime works of art with my pen, or to give the faintest idea of the impression that they made upon me. Therefore I shall remain silent, and reserve all I could possibly say for future verbal intercourse with you.

As to Rinck's method of teaching, I shall write to you fully when I am quietly settled in Paris. For himself personally, my worthy and never-to-be-forgotten master and friend, he is easily to be described. If you imagine the greatest goodness of heart shining through every feature and every act, combined with the greatest candour and simplicity of manner, and therewith, even in old age, an undimmed and glowing love of his art, you have his perfect picture. Certainly, seldom or never was a master more beloved by all his pupils. I have to thank him specially for introducing me to the artist world of Paris, through letters to Meyerbeer, Mainzer, Hiller, Schlesinger, and others. I now stand at the point for which I have been longing, when I shall come into contact with such celebrated members of the world of art. I am going to Paris with the highest expectations. What may happen to me there, how I shall be received, by whom I shall be taught, I shall in due course fully describe to you. Now my trunk calls me, and leaves me only time to beg you to recall me to the remembrance of your honoured wife, and to present my humble respects to her. Farewell, dear Mr. Elbers, and when next you have an hour of leisure, then pray give me the great pleasure of another letter from your hand. Sometimes remember in the far distance your devoted and obliged friend,   CARL HALLÉ.

VII

TO HIS PARENTS

(Translated from the German)

Darmstadt : September 23, 1836.

Beloved Parents,—To fulfil my promise of writing again before leaving Darmstadt, I sit down in the greatest haste to give you tidings of my perfect health and that I start to-morrow morning at 6 o'clock. I have barely five minutes to do it in, so do not take it amiss if these lines are very short. I am invited to dinner for the last time at the Mangolds (I dined with Rinck yesterday and enjoyed myself to my heart's content), and this afternoon I have several tiresome farewell calls to pay. With Louis' help I have luckily got my port-manteau packed. I have nothing contraband, my passport is in order, so I shall pass the frontier without difficulty. I have received the eighty R. thalers, which I shall change at Frankfort for *Napoléons d'or*. I return you my most hearty thanks for all the letters you have sent me. They will certainly be of great use to me. Everything that you have advised in your last letters I have either already accomplished or shall fulfil, therefore it is unnecessary to mention each separately. Now I can write no more; all further news from Paris. Only one thing: Do not be in the least anxious if my next letter is a little slow in arriving. I cannot write before I am settled in Paris, and the journey takes more than eight days, so my writing will be perforce delayed. But I stipulate that you answer my first Paris letter, at the latest, eight days after receiving it, else I shall think it lost and write to you again, and that would be a double postage. As to the address, I shall do as Uncle Koch advises. And now farewell, dear parents; wish me a happy journey, greet my uncle and aunts, kiss the little ones many thousand times, and continue to love your loving son,   CARL.

N.B.—Rinck intends to write to you again within the next eight days, but do not build upon it; he says himself that he would sooner compose a long fugue than a short letter. Adieu!

VIII

(Translated from the German)

Paris: October, 1836.

My dearest Parents,—At last I have arrived in good health and safety in this huge Paris! am already established in a lodging, have hired a piano, and in short am quite settled. All I shall tell you of my journey is, that I rested a day and a night at Metz, and just as long at Chalons, that I am none the worse, but rather fatigued and stiff, as one cannot help being after such a journey. This must be my whole description of it, as I have more important things to tell you, and especially to you, dear father—viz. about money matters. I shall explain everything fully, and then beg you to enter into it as fully in your answer.

The night before I left Darmstadt Rinck received an answer from Schlesinger, of Paris, which was very unsatisfactory on the whole; he said nothing at all about Kalkbrenner, and as to Chopin and Liszt, that they took pupils, but were both very much occupied. At the end of the letter he said: ' Living here is rather costly, but if a young man is economical he can live well for 200 frs. a month.' You can easily understand that this gave me a great shock, but as I heard at the same time that Schlesinger lived in great style in Paris (which is a fact), and perhaps judged of others by himself, I took comfort. Now that I am here, I see that it is not the living that is so dear, but, what with lessons, hire of piano, &c., that it will not be possible for me to manage on less than 200 frs. a month. This will give you as little pleasure as it gives me; but above all, do not think that I would treat it lightly—far from it. All my good-humour has gone to the deuce. I will explain more clearly how it is that I need so much. You know that, unfortunately, I am not very robust, and therefore require good and wholesome food. Now I hear from all sides that it would be very cheap to dine at restaurants, but that I must not be surprised if I am sometimes ill in consequence, as they do not cook fresh food every day, but often warm up what is left, even when it is half-spoilt. To get food and lodging in a private house is impossible here, as I am told, so I have taken a room in this hotel, the land-lady being a German, and dine at the table d'hôte, which is very good without being brilliant—rather like home cooking, my board and lodging coming to 100 frs. a month. This, according to Tilemann and Rumpe, is very cheap for Paris (in Prussian money it is 26 thalers 26 gr.). Now, I have no wood for the winter, which seems to be frightfully dear, and here neither coal nor turf is used. Then there is the washing. What these two last may cost I do not yet know. Piano hire is exceedingly expensive. As I am here for the purpose of studying the piano, I had to get, if not a good one, at least not a very bad one. I have found a tolerable instrument for 20 frs. a month; I could get none cheaper, even the worst were 15 frs. a month. Here we have come to 120 frs. Now for the lessons. How much they will cost I do not yet know. Kalkbrenner comes back at the end of this week, and I shall go to him at once. It is still doubtful, however, whether he will give me lessons. It seems he is enormously rich, and troubles himself very little with teaching; but I still have hope. Chopin and Liszt charge 20 frs. a lesson; Kalkbrenner, as I have heard, only 10 to 12 frs.; but I do not know if he makes an exception in favour of those who are studying professionally. Should he take 10 frs., if I go to him twice a week, as you desired, it will make 80 frs. a month, which, added to the 120, comes to a total of 200 frs. That leaves me not a penny of pocket money to go to the theatre and hear the great operas. This calculation certainly tends to destroy one's courage. There remains one hope for me—that of giving lessons. Here in Paris, the most second-rate lessons are paid 5 frs. an hour, and good teachers easily get from 8 to 12 frs. a lesson. Should I succeed in finding a few pupils, I could manage very well without greater sacrifices. Mainzer told me that four weeks ago he had been asked for a teacher for two pupils, who would

P

have paid 12 frs. Had I been here I could have got them.
At the same time he told me they were rare, as the competition was so very keen. As soon as he hears of any more he
will let me know. Perhaps I shall succeed when I am a little
better known here, for which I think I shall not have long
to wait, as an uncle of Tilemann's and a Dr. Düringe (a
German), to whom I had letters from Darmstadt, have
promised to introduce me to several families. Most of all
Kalkbrenner could help me to get known. Supposing I
should succeed, in a month or two, to give one lesson a day
even at 6 frs., it would make 150 frs. a month; that would
already be a great help. We may draw the following con-
clusions from these calculations: if, with the help of God and
Kalkbrenner's aid, I should succeed in becoming a good
pianist, I cannot fail, in this huge and wealthy Paris, to get
more pupils and at a higher price. If, later on, I should get
four pupils a day at 10 frs. each (which is very little in comparison with the first-rate pianists, and even with Mainzer,
who can be nothing very extraordinary, as he has no name
whatever in other countries, and who all charge 20 frs.), we
get a monthly income of 1,010 frs.; if I spend 250 frs. there
remains a clear balance of nearly 800 frs., or about 9,600 a
year. This result is grand, but not at all impossible. You can
calculate what a man like Chopin must earn who gives eight
or nine lessons a day at 20 frs. In three months' time I
shall surely find out if my calculations are correct or not.
Should they be so, then, dear father, I have the project, which
you will certainly approve, of making Paris my headquarters
for a length of time; for tell me any town in Germany, or
anywhere else, where it would be possible to earn so much,
and at the same time have such opportunities of perfecting
oneself in musical, and almost all other respects, as in Paris.
Of course, let us not forget that all this depends upon an *if*,
but an *if* that may very easily come true. Now I shall leave
this chapter, only begging you very earnestly to write to me
fully on the subject.

As I have still room, I will chat a little with you,

my unspeakably beloved ones, but of what? If I speak of myself, I can only tell you that I have the intensest longing for you and for my own country. Oh, how beautiful, how celestially beautiful, to be at home and in the midst of one's loved ones! What is Paris, with all its luxury and brilliancy, with its crowds of people in the dark and narrow streets where sun and fresh air hardly ever penetrate, with its slow-flowing, turbid Seine, compared with our lovely little valley with its pleasant little town, its clear and merrily-flowing river, its fresh air and brilliant sunshine, with its flowering meadows and green hedges and bushes, where nightingales and finches still sing their joyous song, long since driven away from here by the bustling multitudes whose only thought is gain! Each time I recall all this to mind I cannot keep back the tears. Could I but once walk hand-in-hand with you, the little ones and the dogs playing before us; through the garden, then by the fields to Alten Hagen; then back by the way of lovely Wiedey—only once!

I fear, I fear that I shall get home-sick; but I shall struggle against it with all my might, and should it overcome me, I shall turn my thoughts to the swift passing away of time; four months already have I spent away from you, and the rest will go by also.

I have worked myself into too soft a mood to go on writing. *Answer me within the next few days.* You cannot guess the longing with which I am expecting your next letter; and write much, describe all your doings, your daily life, how the uncle and aunts are getting on, and, mind, you must not forget what Bernard and Anna are doing, if he goes regularly to school, and how she passes her time; in short, everything; the merest trifles interest me now.

Farewell; write soon and at great length. Greet all relations and friends, embrace the two children, think very often of your loving CARL.

IX

TO HIS PARENTS

(*Translated from the German*)

Paris : October 18, 1836.

Dearest Parents, I did not expect a letter from you so soon, and my delight is therefore so much the greater; although Uncle Koch gave me a terrible fright by writing on the outside, 'This letter to be sent forward with the utmost despatch.' When I read this, I could not but think that it contained the news of some misfortune, but happily it was not so, and, on the contrary, I found that you were, God be thanked and praised, all in good health (only you told me nothing of *Mino's* doings; please do not forget in your next letter to speak of him).

First I must tell you of my own doings; that is easily done. I practise nearly the whole day long, and hardly anything but exercises, shakes, scales, and so on, and the rest of the time, for it is impossible to play without ceasing, I go over, and put into order, the work I did with Rinck, or, if ever *it stops raining for a moment*, I take a run through Paris and visit its sights. So far I have taken no lessons, but hope to do so in a few days, but not from Kalkbrenner. I shall tell you the whole story. The day after Kalkbrenner's return I went to see him at eleven o'clock ; he happened to be at home, and I was shown into an ante-room, where there were several people already assembled; when he had kept us waiting a considerable time, he appeared, wrapped in an ample dressing-gown. After he had spoken for a short time to the persons standing nearest to him, he came towards me; I stepped forward and was beginning to explain my business, but as soon as he heard I intended to become a musician, and had studied composition with Rinck, he asked me to wait until he had dismissed the rest of the company. I was pleased at this, as it would enable me to speak to him undisturbed. It lasted a good long time, but finally he had despatched them all, and I was able to make my request. When

I had done speaking, he said he regretted very much that it
was at present impossible for him to comply with my wish;
he had been seriously ill, had only just returned from the
Baths, and was still so weak that his doctor had strictly
forbidden him to talk much, a thing quite unavoidable in
giving lessons--in fact, he did look very ill. He had his
class at the Conservatoire, which he could not give up, and
that tired him so, that he had been obliged to give up all
other lessons. It was now my turn to express regret. Then
he said he would like to hear me play, to see how far I had
got on, and that he could perhaps recommend a teacher to
me. He took me into his sitting-room, where there was a
most beautiful grand piano, and I played him his own
Effusio Musica. He made several remarks about the *tempo*,
and said several times, ' very good,' ' first rate,' until I got
to a part where both hands had scales in octaves during
several pages; when I had finished them he stopped me,
and asked why I played the octaves with my arms and not
from my wrists? ' You are quite out of breath,' he said
(which was the case); *he* could play scales in octaves for an
hour without the least fatigue; and why had God given us
wrists? He was sure, if the Almighty had ever played the
piano, He would play from the wrist! He made several
other remarks; he said I held my fingers rather too high,
I must hold them closer to the keys, especially in *legato*
passages, to make them more finished, and obtain altogether
a rounder and more ringing tone; and as to the expression,
he gave me a good deal of advice, all very good, and worthy
to be followed. He then played part of the piece I had
played, to make it clear to me; after this, he began another,
and altogether *played for me more than half-an-hour.* You
can imagine my delight; it was the first time I had ever
heard a celebrated musician, and this half-hour has been of
the greatest use to me. In Kalkbrenner's playing there
reigns a clearness, a distinctness, and neatness that are
astonishing; in octave scales he has an immense facility and
precision, especially in the left hand; then he has a special

mode of handling the piano, particularly in melodious passages, which makes a great impression, but which I cannot describe to you ; the reason of it lies merely in that he keeps his fingers so closely over the keys. When he had finished, he told me to be very industrious, to avoid the mistakes he had pointed out, and that I would become a first-rate pianist; at present I should go to Osborne,[1] his best pupil, and who had quite his method of teaching (Mr. Elbers and I have played something of Osborne's, and, as far as I recollect, we liked it very much) ; I should tell him that Kalkbrenner had sent me to him and begged him to give me lessons ; when I had worked with him for some time then *he, Kalkbrenner, would give me some lessons with the greatest pleasure.* As often as I had studied a piece with Osborne I should come and play it to him, and if there was still anything wanting, he would point it out to me. I must also come and see him from time to time. That was kind, was it not ? and I shall certainly not fail to take him at his word.

Next day I went to Osborne (Tuesday, this day week) ; he also was out of town, and only returned on Saturday. On Sundays in Paris no one is ever to be found at home, so I went on Monday, yesterday, and luckily found him at home. He received me very amiably, and when I had told him my tale, he said I put him in a great perplexity ; that he gave lessons from early morning till night, and still he was most unwilling to refuse me. After a little more conversation he asked me to play something ; I did so, and he praised and blamed exactly in the same way as Kalkbrenner had done ; then he asked my address, and said he would write to me in a few days to say whether he had found it possible to arrange to give me lessons, and in this letter he would give me all particulars ; should there be any evening parties with music, he would introduce me with pleasure. I am therefore awaiting this letter ; should he delay too long, which I do not expect, I

---

[1] George Alexander Osborne (1806-1893), the well-known Irish pianist, teacher, and composer.

shall go to some one else. I have been here more than a fortnight, and have only been able to study by myself; but soon after my arrival, Mr. Probst of Leipzig, who lives here, and whose acquaintance I made through Mr. Tilemann's uncle, told me that if I had not learnt patience before, I should learn it here, and, in truth, it seems so. Neither Meyerbeer nor Hiller are in Paris, so I cannot deliver my letters to them. As to hearing many good works, it is not as we expected; at all the theatres there are only small operettas and ballets, even at the Grand Opera, where all the best and newest operas are generally given. A new ballet, *La Fille du Danube*, will probably have a hundred successive performances, so much does it please the Parisians; so there is but a poor prospect of hearing good music. All these things are not calculated to banish my bad humour; on the contrary, my longing for you and for my beautiful, peaceful birthplace grows ever stronger. *Christmas and New Year! O Gott!*

The only thing I am looking forward to is that Mainzer has promised to procure me the opportunity of often hearing Chopin and Liszt. I hope he will keep his word, for it would be of the greatest use to me.   CARL.

X

TO HIS PARENTS

(Translated from the German)

Paris: November, 1836.

Dearest Parents,—Your dear letters of October 23 only reached me, through Mr. Rumpe, on November 2. They have, therefore, been pretty long on the way, so I shall make no delay in answering them for fear you should get anxious again about me, your over-great love for your long-legged rascal making you so quick to take alarm. In this letter I have made up my mind not to write exclusively, as in the last two, about my studies, which would end by boring you, but of everything that comes across my mind, in a medley of wheat and tares, and you can disentangle it for yourselves

(N.B.—If you think it worth the trouble). I have just noticed that I have started with the master stroke of beginning to write on the wrong side of the page, but it does not matter. I shall hope to be able to close my letter all the same, and so go on in confidence. All the same, I must tell you that, God be praised and thanked, I have begun with Osborne, and have already had three lessons—one per week, which *is amply sufficient* (ten francs each). But I shall give you no further account of this, for where is the use of serving you with the sauce when you cannot judge of the meat? I know you trust me, and that I need not tell you continually that I am working hard. One thing, however, I must report. My manner of playing has to be entirely altered—not so much the expression, as my right reverend Aunt Christina, with an air of wisdom, opined; on the contrary, he paid me great compliments on this point. But it seems I had an abominable tone. You will, perhaps, not quite understand this, but as soon as I get back to Hagen I shall make it clear to you. I am making great progress already on this point, and during my last lesson he said several times: ' Je suis fort content de vous, vous êtes très-bon musicien.' (I have this moment received an invitation from Kalle to dinner at six this evening.)

I doubt whether, London excepted, there is another town in the world that can compare with Paris in any respect. Louis Flashoff would say it is a ' Gegenstand '—his favourite expression for anything grand. It gives me a curious sensation as often as I look from any height upon this immense agglomeration of stone. As far as the eye can reach, nothing but the sky and houses. One can never see the whole of Paris— some part is always lost in the distance. Everything in Paris is on a grand scale—manners and customs as well as the town itself; N.B., the prices too. Such a quantity of palaces, monuments, arches of triumph, one finds nowhere else. To describe it all is impossible; I should require much more time and much more paper. The finest building in Paris, and perhaps in all Europe, is the new church of the Madeleine. Only it hardly does for a church, nor was it originally meant for one. Napoleon, who began it, intended it for a Temple of Fame. It is built in the same Greek style (I believe after a temple of Minerva or Apollo at Athens), and so makes a curious impression in the midst of the modern houses and palaces that surround it. In Paris one has the best opportunities of studying the differences between the old Gothic and the Grecian styles, the first represented by the venerable cathedral of Nôtre Dame, and the second by this Temple of the Madeleine. Both are sublime masterworks, but, what an endless difference! The thrill one feels on entering a Gothic church like Cologne Cathedral is not experienced at the sight of this great temple, but a feeling of admiration for the grand old Greeks and for the days of antiquity passes through one. Under the high arches and vaulted roof of a Gothic cathedral one feels a certain sense (I at least do) of oppression, and breathes more freely when one returns to the open air. In this Greek temple everything is calculated to produce an agreeable and cheerful sensation ; the whole building seems so light, even smart, if that expression is not too trivial. In short, it represents the ideal of spirited beauty. So one could never picture a Gothic cathedral in a fine open landscape, but one can think of such a temple in the midst of the old Grecian land, with laurel groves and myrtle woods. Then it makes an unpleasant sensation to see the modish young bucks in their frock coats, white cuffs, kid gloves and walking sticks, wandering among the Corinthian columns and up the grand flight of steps. At every moment one expects to see a tall, stately Grecian figure step out and drive away these dandies, as Christ drove the money-lenders out of the temple.

I have already seen a most remarkable spectacle here, the like of which I shall never see again, viz. the erection of an Egyptian obelisk in the finest Place of all Paris and on the very spot—sufficiently remarkable on that account—where Louis XVI. and Marie Antoinette were executed. The obelisk was a present from the Pasha of Egypt to the present king, Louis Philippe, and was brought with immense trouble by ship to Paris. They had to raise the level of the Seine (how they did it I do not know, and cannot imagine) in order to bring it to the town. It is 72 feet high, consists of a single block of granite, and weighs over 500,000 pounds. Now, you can imagine the difficulty of placing such a mass on a pedestal twenty-four feet high. By means of a steam-engine it was brought from the quay as far as a wall, built on purpose close to the pedestal; then two hundred artillerymen, by means of ten windlasses and a great scaffolding which I cannot attempt to describe, raised it up. This raising lasted from ten o'clock in the morning to four in the afternoon, and all this time I stood, in company with three hundred thousand curious spectators, on the same spot, and certainly did not regret it. The obelisk is still veiled, so I do not know how it looks, but the top is somewhat damaged, as the old-curiosity mongers paid a ducat for each little particle they could get.

I could tell you a great deal more, but as the paper will soon come to an end, I shall say a little about myself; first I must tell you that I go to the theatre very often, as I have free entrance three times a week to the Grand Opera, by a curious combination of circumstances which I must recount. If an Austrian had not broken his leg at Châlons I should not have a free admission to the Grand Opera to-day; the poor devil lay at Châlons the day I stayed there, and as I knew of no hotel in Paris, I asked him if he could recommend one, and he told me of this one where I now am. At the table d'hôte here I made the acquaintance of a very nice man, called Ellisen, a painter, to whom I already owe much, and he introduced me to a family of the name of Kaselack, who are well acquainted with all the most famous artists, and have several tickets for every performance and always give one to me. Through these Kaselacks I have made the acquaintance of several other artists, for instance with the Opera composer Adam, and the first flutist in all Paris, Coninx; in short it was a lucky thing for me that that Austrian broke his leg at Châlons.

XI

TO HIS PARENTS

(*Translated from the German*)

Paris: November 28, 1836.

Dearest Parents,—You must be really angry with me,
now that I know I need pay no postage fee for my letters,
for not having answered your last letter sooner, and I acknowledge that you have certainly some cause for it; but on my
side I have some excuse for my delay; I would not write
before I could tell you how I had been received by Meyerbeer, a thing you were very eager to know; it is true I
cannot tell you yet (I will give you the reason directly), but
most probably before this letter is finished, which will be to-
morrow, I shall have seen him (with Parisians one can never
feel sure) and be able to tell positively if the famous composer of the 'Huguenots' has received me amiably or rudely.
Why I had not seen him sooner, as I think I have told you,
was because of his long absence from town; he has been
back about a fortnight; since then I have been three times
to his house, twice he was not at home, and the third time
there were so many people, to whom he was giving audience,
that I should have had to wait for more than half-an-hour,
and I had not the time to spare; now I have been informed
that he will receive me to-morrow at nine o'clock in the
morning, and I hope then to make the acquaintance of this
famous and remarkable man; I have seen him several times;
he is of middle height, rather lean, and stoops slightly, he
need not wear a label to proclaim that he is a Jew; that
any man can see, but also that behind his high and noble
brow many fine and glorious thoughts must dwell. Hiller,
for whom I also had a letter, is not in Paris; he has been at
Frankfort since the end of September, and, as I hear, will
hardly be back before the summer.

Now I shall tell you how it befel with the Leipzig letters,
and, thank God, have only good tidings to give. All those to
whom I was recommended, received me with so much hearti-

ness, not, as so often happens, with mere empty politeness. that I soon saw the great value of an introduction from Uncle Harkort. Especially Mr. Kalle and Mr. Thurneyssen were extraordinarily amiable; the first has invited me at least five or six times to dinner, and every Sunday evening to tea, and both he and his charming and beautiful young wife are always so kind and friendly, that I am in high spirits the whole day previous to going there. I always meet a large company there, consisting of French, Germans, English and Americans, and spend many a pleasant hour. Kalle has also told me, if ever I am in any difficulty, to apply to him at once and he would advise and help efficaciously. I have dined twice at the Thurneyssen's and am invited to a soirée for every Friday evening. I enjoy myself *very much* at their house also, and have made several pleasant acquaintances there, amongst them that of M. Scherbius, who is going to introduce me the day after to-morrow to Ferdinand Ries, who happens to be in Paris, at which I am immensely delighted; should he ask me to play I shall choose his own dear ' Am Rhein, Am Rhein.' The Thurneyssens must be very rich people; although the Kalles display great elegance, it is nothing to be compared to the luxury of the others; it is quite indescribable, but when I come home I shall have wonderful things to tell you of it, as well as of the tone and mode of Paris, that one has always read so much about.

Baron Eichthal also received me very well, and of him I have the greatest hopes from a musical point of view; he invited me a week ago, in a very amiable note, to dine with him on Wednesday (the day after to-morrow) and said he hoped to introduce me then to his friend *Chopin* ! So far I have neither seen nor heard Chopin, as all the soirées and concerts at which such artists play are only beginning now or a little later on. I have little fear but that once presented to Chopin by Eichthal he will invite me to his own house, and then I shall hear him not only once but several times. I also hope to be introduced to Liszt shortly, and Mr. Tilemann's uncle is going to make me known to Herz. So, by degrees, I shall get to know these people; things do not go quickly in Paris; one requires a boundless patience; so too with regard to the giving of lessons, which I thought would be so easy before I came. Up to the present there seems no prospect; principally as I do not know enough French to be able to teach. I hear from all sides that it is very easy to make a large fortune in Paris, when one has bitten one's way through, has made oneself known, and acquired a certain fame in the town; then every one rushes to you, and your hours are measured in gold; but it takes a pretty long time before one gets so far.

All the same, I still think it would be best, after I have quite completed my education, to return here for a considerable length of time; where so many others have been so fortunate, I, too, may perhaps succeed. I have now heard Kalkbrenner several times, and have paid him another visit, and shall go again one of these days, as I have studied twelve grand Etudes of his with Osborne, which I want to play to him. Last Sunday I heard him at a concert at the Hôtel de Ville; he played twice, first the Rondo, 'Gage d'Amitié' (which Mrs. Hennecke made me a present of), and then variations on a theme of Bellini's. I was very glad to hear him play a piece I knew, and to be able to discover in how much I am still wanting. He began the allegro of the Rondo at a speed that made my hair stand on end; he carried it on at the same pace, which he even increased towards the close, with such a bell-like clearness, and such great expression, that I cannot understand how any one could do it better; and still, Chopin and Liszt stand higher than Kalkbrenner. When next I see him I shall remind him of his promise to give me lessons, but should he not be willing to do so yet, I shall not insist, as Osborne's teaching pleases me very much, and Kalkbrenner's lessons will be more useful to me later on, when I have studied more; on no account shall I leave Paris without taking a few lessons from him, so as to be able to call myself his pupil.

You write to me, dear father, that by the end of January

I shall most likely, or certainly, have to return home; I know that my stay here costs a terrible amount of money, and that it cannot go on long, so I shall say no word against it, and shall rejoice to be with you again; but at the same time I am convinced that the object of my coming here will only have been half accomplished if I go away so soon; I should only have had altogether thirteen or fourteen lessons, and have arrived at the point where lessons from Kalkbrenner would be of the greatest use. I am making great progress, and Osborne praises me very much; he told me that during the winter I should study a concerto with him, and I believe that if I could thoroughly and perfectly study a concerto with such a master, so as to be able to play it anywhere, I should hardly need further lessons, but could perfect myself on the model of the great artists whom I have the opportunity of hearing; but, I believe, *only then.* However, if I must return home so soon I shall say no word against it, but shall even rejoice.

November 29.

I had got so far yesterday when the dinner-bell called me (at half past five). This morning at nine o'clock, dressed in my best, I went to Meyerbeer; at the door I met a Berliner, Rudolfi (whom I only know by name), who had also come to pay his respects. In the anteroom the servant received us with a shrug of his shoulders, and said he did not think we could be admitted, as Meyerbeer was composing, and had sent away a lot of people already; he went away and shortly came back with a very polite message that his master was so very busy that he could not possibly be disturbed, but begged us not to take it amiss, and to come without fail to-morrow morning at nine o'clock. This I shall certainly not fail to do, as I am convinced that I shall be well received, as was my friend Mangold who also brought him a letter from Rinck, and whose compositions he examined and corrected, and to whom he also often sends tickets for his operas. Most likely you do not know that Mangold is in Paris. I luckily persuaded him to come, but as he could not leave Darmstadt with me, he followed a fortnight later; we see each other very seldom, as he lives at half-an-hour's distance from me.   This is one of the disadvantages of Paris, the difficulty of seeing even one's best friends on account of the great distances; it would have been impossible for us to live together, the one playing the piano and the other the violin; we should have disturbed each other and made a veritable cat's concert of it.

You, dear mother, wish to be assured that I am not freezing here; I can do so.   Firstly, in my room I have no open fire, but a stove, a remarkable one made of *porcelaine*, but which warms the room very well; there is a fireplace, but as the landlord offered me a stove I accepted without hesitation; an open fire looks very nice and cosy, but one gets roasted on one side and frozen on the other.   Second, although the weather is very unpleasant, always raining and windy, it has been so warm that, although we are close upon December 1, I need no fire, but at the beginning of the month it was so cold that I could not do without one; I only wish it would remain warm, for wood costs a terrible deal of money here, and coal is unknown; two logs of wood cost almost a franc.

So you have had a concert at Hagen; as those concerts have given me so much pleasure from my earliest childhood, I take the greatest interest in them still, and you, dear mother, must positively give me all the details in your next letter; tell me what was given, and who played, and who sang; *please do not forget.*

Also the theatrical news, for I know your weakness, and that you will seldom have missed a performance.   Now, I shall look through your last letter to see if there is anything I have forgotten to answer, so just wait a little.   I have found nothing, and as you will be content with the length of this epistle, I shall promptly bring it to a close, first asking you to thank Mr. Elbers, with my best greetings, for his letter.   Mr. Selttinghaus of Altena is going back soon; if not too soon I shall charge him with several letters, not

only for Mr. Elbers, but for other persons to whom I owe
them. Now comes the accustomed usual ending. Dear
parents, farewell, write soon, greetings to all friends and
relations. I embrace you, the dear children, and the dogs a
thousand times; love me still, and think right often of your
loving   CARL.

XII

TO HIS PARENTS

(Translated from the German)

Paris: December 2, 1836.

Beloved Parents,—Selttinghaus's departure has taken me
so much by surprise that it is quite impossible for me to give
him several letters to take with him to Hagen. I went to
Rumpe's yesterday, the 1st of the month, to get some money,
and then learnt that Selttinghaus was leaving to-day at midday. As I have a lesson this afternoon and must practise for
it, I have barely time for a short supplement to my letter of
two days ago.

The morning after having written to you I went again
to Meyerbeer, and was at once admitted. As I expected,
Meyerbeer was extremely kind and amiable. He kept me
more than half an hour, inquired after Rinck and as to all my
studies, asked if I had yet composed anything, how I got on
in Paris, if I had heard the most eminent pianists, of whom
Liszt was the very first, and so on. When I told him that I
had neither seen nor heard Liszt, he said I must call again in
a few days, in the morning, and he would give me an introduction to him; Liszt was a very nice young man, who would
certainly receive me very kindly. How pleased I am that
Meyerbeer should give me an introduction to that original
fellow Liszt I cannot describe. This also is all very good
and satisfactory.

The same evening I went to dine with Baron Eichthal,
where I was very cordially treated, and where I heard—
Chopin. That was beyond all words. The few senses I had
have quite left me. I could have jumped into the Seine.

Everything I hear now seems so insignificant, that I would rather not hear it at all. Chopin! He is no man, he is an angel, a god (or what can I say more?). Chopin's compositions played by Chopin! That is a joy never to be surpassed. I shall describe his playing another time. Kalkbrenner compared to Chopin is a child. I say this with the completest conviction. During Chopin's playing I could think of nothing but elves and fairy dances, such a wonderful impression do his compositions make. There is nothing to remind one that it is a human being who produces this music. It seems to descend from heaven—so pure, and clear, and spiritual. I feel a thrill each time I think of it. If Liszt plays *still better*, then the devil take me if I don't shoot myself on the spot. Chopin is moreover a charming, delightful creature. He talked to me a long time, gave me his address and the permission to go and see him often, a permission he will not have given in vain.

But now, best of parents, I must stop, or Mr. Selttinghaus will be running away without my letter. Farewell. Mr. Selttinghaus will tell you how I am and how I live here. Greet all my friends and relations, and be assured of the lasting love of your son, CAROLUS.

XIII

TO HIS PARENTS

(*Translated from the German*)

Paris: December 19, 1836.

Dearest Parents,—For the last time this year I sit down to write to you, but this time you must be content with little; my letter to Uncle Harkort gives me some trouble, and I must also write to my old Rinck, to whom, of course, I wrote soon after my arrival here, but as yet have had no answer, so do not know if he is in good health, or dead, or if my letter never reached him, which I should greatly regret, for what would the good man have thought of me? With all this writing I must not neglect my studies, so you must

rest satisfied with a single sheet; there is, in fact, no need
for our writing much to each other, as I expect and hope to
be with you in nine or ten weeks, and how soon they will
pass! But first let me thank you, dear father, for having
granted me another month. I know that it will be difficult
for you, and therefore my gratitude is all the greater. I
shall do my utmost to make the month of great profit to me.
Of what shall I write? As I know that musical matters
interest you most, I shall begin with them, and tell you that
I have heard Liszt.

Meyerbeer gave me a kind, two-pages-long letter of
introduction to him, which did not fail in its effect.
When I went for the first time I did not find Liszt at
home, and was told he only received on Monday and Friday
afternoons from 2 to 5 o'clock. As I have a lesson on
Fridays, I had to wait till Monday—a week to-day—when
I went towards 3 o'clock. How curious I was to see this
man, who has so remarkable a fame, you can easily imagine,
especially as he has the reputation, even in his outward
appearance, of being a most original creature; and so I found
him. Liszt is the most original being in existence. When
I entered I found an assembly of thirty or forty persons,
among them many of the first artists of Paris, and even
several ladies, who had come to pay him homage (I had
noticed a great number of carriages at the door). He, the
fêted Liszt, came to me at once, and I gave him my letter.
When he opened it he glanced at once at the signature, and
seeing the name of Meyerbeer he shook me again by the
hand and kindly bade me sit down. I did not accept the
invitation, as there were forty persons in the room and only
ten chairs, all of which were occupied. He did not notice it,
spoke to me a little while, and then sprang off to some one
else. I then had time to look at him carefully, and saw that
I had not been told too much about the originality of his
outward appearance. His aspect is truly remarkable. He
is tall and very thin, his face very small and pale, his forehead remarkably high and beautiful; he wears his perfectly

lank hair so long that it spreads over his shoulders, which looks very odd, for when he gets a bit excited and gesticulates, it falls right over his face and one sees nothing but his nose. He is very negligent in his attire, his coat looks as if it had just been thrown on, he wears no cravat, only a narrow white collar. This curious figure is in perpetual motion: now he stamps with his feet, now waves his arms in the air, now he does this, now that. My hope of hearing him play in his own house was deceived. He has *no instrument!* I remained a few hours with him, until one after another the guests had left, then (*Donnerwetter!* here is a terrible blot! How it came I know not, but to copy the letter would be too tedious, so take blot and all!) I took my leave also. He accompanied me to the ante-room, and said that on Sunday (yesterday) he was giving a concert at the Conservatoire: that he would have given me a ticket with the greatest pleasure had he a single one left to dispose of, but he had given all his free tickets away, but if I cared to go to the rehearsal I must be there on Saturday morning at 9 o'clock, and that I must also come and see him very often.

I have now heard him twice: at the rehearsal, where he only played once, and at the concert three times, for I invested five francs in a ticket. When I heard him first I sat speechless for a quarter of an hour afterwards, in such a stupor of amazement had the man put me. Such execution, such limitless—truly limitless—execution no one else can possess. He plays sometimes so as to make your hair stand on end! He who has not heard Liszt can have no conception—literally no conception—of what his playing is. After having heard him my resolution was taken. 'Now you go straight home,' I said to myself, 'and grind frightfully for a couple of years, and if at the end of the time you have accomplished anything fit, you may come back here.' And so it shall be.

When I have worked very hard at home I shall certainly then return to Paris, I like it so well; so well, that already I

could wish to stay here for ever; and Paris is also the place
where one can earn money.

But now I must make a speedy end; time presses.
Lebt recht wohl! Keep well; I am so, and hope to remain
so. Spend a merry and happy Christmas, and think of me
(poor wretch!). Quickly and joyfully as those days flew
by formerly, so slowly and sadly will they crawl for me
now!

Adieu! *Lebt wohl!* Greet my relations and friends for
your true

CAROLUS.

Has Selttinghaus been to see you and delivered my
letters? I had forgotten to tell you that my lessons with
Osborne are going on satisfactorily. We are both well
pleased with each other. If possible, write to me again
before the end of the year. *Lebt wohl!* On New Year's
Eve drink a glass of punch for me! Here, dear mother, will
I answer your questions. 1. My clothes are still quite
good; I can appear before any man in them. 2. I have had
my hair cut twice. 3. Of course I always wear woollen
socks now; *à propos,* how cold is it now with you?
Write and tell me. 4. I have had to buy a tall hat; here it
is not proper to be without one; indeed matters are carried so
far that one is not allowed to enter the Tuileries Gardens
unless one wears a tall hat; the sentries send you back with
'On ne passe pas.' Now farewell, dear, good mother!

XIV

TO HIS PARENTS

(Translated from the German)

London: April 27, 1848.

My dear Parents.—Forgive me for not having written for
so long; courage failed me to do so; I could not make up my
mind to give only bad news, and of good news, alas! I had
none to give. The Revolution has dealt me an incalculable

blow, from the effects of which I shall have to suffer for a
long time. Paris is in a sad and pitiable state, and God
knows if it will ever recover itself; that my position there,
at least for the present, is quite lost, you will already have
guessed. All my colleagues are in the same case. I have
been here in London three weeks, striving hard to make a
new position, and I hope I shall succeed; pupils I already
have, although as yet they are not many. The competition
is very keen, for, besides the native musicians, there are
at present here—Thalberg, Chopin, Kalkbrenner, Pixis,
Osborne, Prudent, Pillet, and a lot of other pianists besides
myself who have all, through necessity, been driven to England, and we shall probably end by devouring one another.
During the last few days I have begun to hope, as I have
several times played in public with great success, and trust
soon to have got my footing. Until now, sadness has been
the order of the day, but, I assure you, my courage does not
fail me. My family has, of course, remained in Paris, and
you can easily fancy that, all alone, I do not feel very
happy.

O damnable Revolution!

Should things mend in Paris, I shall return there after
the London season; but should they remain in the same
condition I must of necessity establish myself here and bring
my family over, for in Paris one might starve—there will be
no thought of music there. In Germany, also, everything
seems in hateful disorder—madness is at home everywhere.
But do not grieve too much for me, my dear parents; sad as
things appear at the present moment, I am assuredly confident that I shall worry through, only it will cost some
trouble. Write to me soon, it will give me comfort. My
address is 28 Maddox Street, Regent Street, London.

What I wrote to you, dear mother, in my last letter, concerning the little drafts in case of need, remains unaltered,
only you must send them to my wife in Paris, as till now
I have but little money here, and left all I could in Paris.
I call courage and hope to your aid, as I do to my own.

Write to me, my dear, dear parents; as soon as things take a better turn I shall let you know; you may rely upon it.

Good-bye, father, mother, Anna; again good-bye, *lebt wohl*; keep in your loving thoughts your ever-loving and sad son and brother,

CARL HALLÉ.

XV

FROM MR. H. LEO

Manchester: August 4, 1848.

My dear Mr. Hallé,—According to your wish, I hasten to inform you of the state of things here, so that you may come to a decision on your return. . . . My opinion has not changed in the very least, and should you resolve upon coming to Manchester, it is my innermost conviction that your success will be complete. . . . . .

You will feel the delicacy of my position with respect to you. I should so heartily rejoice to have you here, and yet, believe me, I would not let myself be so swayed by selfishness as to give you advice against my own convictions. Were you my brother, I should say : Come to Manchester. All the same I cannot, and must not, accept the responsibility of the step. If you feel the courage and strength to trust Manchester with your fate, I believe you would do right, and would not regret it, but if you will not take the risk we must submit, and only beg you to give us credit for our good intentions. The post is closing; perhaps I shall write a few lines to-morrow if anything occurs to me.—Ever yours,

H. LEO.[1]

---

[1] My father had no access to the foregoing letters when writing his Memoirs, which he did entirely from memory.

XVI

[The following lines are taken from a letter from my mother to her sister at New Orleans.]

3 Addison Terrace, Victoria Park,
Manchester : 19 septembre 1848.

. . . . En attendant laisse-moi te dire que nous sommes à Manchester depuis le 6 de ce mois ; la dernière lettre de Mathilde t'a appris que Charles, ayant reçu de cette ville des propositions plus avantageuses encore que celle de Bath, s'était décidé à s'y fixer ; surtout en y trouvant des ressources musicales immenses il ne pouvait pas balancer entre ces deux villes. Voilà à peine un mois qu'il y est, et déjà nous pouvons espérer lui voir occuper bientôt une magnifique position (la moitié de son temps est pris par des leçons) ; on lui demande de toute part une série de Matinées Musicales dans le genre de celles qu'il donnait à Paris ; Mr. Leo, qui l'a décidé à se fixer ici, et qui est notre bon ange, me disait hier soir qu'elles lui rapporteraient au moins huit mille francs chaque année ; Mercredi dernier il a joué un concerto de Beethoven à la Société des Amateurs. Il a obtenu un magnifique succès ; jamais je n'ai vu un enthousiasme si grand et si général ; il a été engagé au concert même de jouer au prochain Festival de Liverpool ; son nom est tellement connu par toute l'Angleterre qu'un éditeur de Londres est venu hier à Manchester lui offrir de prendre toutes ses compositions à raison de 10 frs. la page gravée. . . . .

Si tu pouvais voir toutes les bontés de Charles pour nous ; son cœur lui inspire des supercheries charmantes, ainsi il m'avait écrit à Londres que Manchester n'étant pas une ville de plaisance, il ne pouvait trouver de maison meublée, et qu'il se voyait obligé de prendre la seule qui lui était offerte ; qu'elle était fort laide, ce qui le contrariait beaucoup. Notre vie devant être toute d'intérieur il aurait désiré nous donner au moins l'agrément d'être bien logé ; juge de notre joie, le soir de notre arrivée, de trouver une charmante petite maison, entourée de délicieux jardins, placée au milieu d'un parc, et ayant tout le confort des habitations anglaises, tapis partout, etc. etc. Ses élèves et cette bonne Mrs. Leo avaient, pour nous fêter, éclairé toutes les pièces, dans lesquelles se trouvaient de grandes corbeilles de fleurs naturelles; il fallait voir la joie de ce pauvre Carl, combien il jouissait en enfant de notre bonne surprise. . . . . Il m'est impossible, chère sœur, de te dire ce que j'ai éprouvé d'immense bonheur en ce moment, qui seul aurait suffi pour me faire oublier ces derniers six mois. . . . .

Les habitants de cette ville sont très bons; ils sont si fiers de posséder un artiste comme Charles qu'ils cherchent à deviner tout ce qui peut nous être agréable; toute la première société s'est empressée de venir nous voir, nous sommes accablés d'invitations et de visites. Nous avons trouvé en Mr. Leo un véritable père, il n'est pas possible d'être plus dévoués que lui et sa femme; ils ont su m'éviter tous les ennuis d'une installation en persuadant à un de leurs amis, qui partait pour l'Allemagne, de nous louer, pour 12*l.* par mois, la charmante petite maison que nous occupons. La vie est beaucoup moins chère qu'à Paris.[1]

---

[1] [*Translation*]

3 Addison Terrace, Victoria Park,
Manchester: September 19, 1848.

. . . . Meanwhile let me tell you that we have been at Manchester since the 6th of this month; Mathilde's last letter informed you that Charles, having received proposals from this town more advantageous than those from Bath, had decided to establish himself here, where, moreover, he finds such immense musical resources that he could not hesitate between the two towns. He has hardly been here a month, and we may already hope to see him occupy a magnificent position; half his time is taken up with lessons, and on all sides he is being asked to give a series of musical matinées like those he gave in Paris; Mr. Leo, who induced him to establish himself here, and who is our good angel, told me last night that they would bring him in at least eight thousand francs a year; last Wednesday he played a Concerto of Beethoven's for the Amateur Society; he obtained a magnificent success; I never saw such great and general enthusiasm; during the concert he was offered an engagement to play at

XVII

TO H. F. CHORLEY

Manchester : 23 août 1850,
Greenheys.

Mon cher Chorley,—Vous savez, j'espère, qu'avant mon
départ de Londres j'ai fait plusieurs tentatives pour vous
trouver chez vous, mais elles ont toutes échoué et à mon bien
grand regret ; car j'avais bien besoin de causer longuement
avec vous et de vous demander, une fois de plus, votre avis et
vos bons conseils sur le changement de résidence que je pro-
jette depuis si longtemps, sans avoir jusqu'ici pu parvenir à
l'exécuter.

Une bonne causerie vaut mieux qu'une longue correspon-
dance, mais malgré cela, si vous voulez bien me répondre

the forthcoming Liverpool Festival ; his name is so well known throughout
England that a London publisher came to Manchester yesterday to offer
to take all his compositions, at the rate of ten francs the printed
page. . . . .

If you could only see all Charles's goodness to us ; his heart inspires
him with charming deceits ; thus he had written to me to London that
Manchester, not being a city of pleasure, he had not been able to find a
furnished house, and had been obliged to take the only house that had
been offered to him, and that it was a very ugly one, which annoyed him
greatly, for our life here having to be entirely a home-life, he would have
wished at least to give us the pleasure of being well-lodged. Judge of our
delight, the evening of our arrival, to find a charming little house surrounded by delicious gardens, situated in the middle of a park, and with
all the comforts of an English habitation, carpets everywhere, &c., &c.
His pupils and good Mrs. Leo, in order to welcome us, had lighted up
all the rooms, in which were placed large baskets of flowers ; you should
have seen poor Charles's joy, how he rejoiced like a child at our glad surprise. . . . . It would be impossible, dear sister, to tell you the immense
happiness that filled me at that moment, which would alone have sufficed
to make me forget the past six months. . . . .

The inhabitants of this town are very kind ; they seem so proud of
possessing an artist like Charles, that they try to guess what would give
us pleasure ; all the best society hastened to call upon us ; we are overwhelmed with invitations and visits. We have found a real father in Mr.
Leo, it would be impossible to be more devoted than he and his wife are to us ;
they managed to spare me all the annoyance of furnishing by persuading
one of their friends, who was going to Germany, to let us, for 12l. a
month, the delightful little house we occupy. Life is much cheaper than
in Paris.

quelques mots aux questions que je compte vous adresser, j'en tirerai toujours grand profit, et vous en serai bien reconnaissant, croyez-le-moi.

L'idée de me fixer à Londres a tellement mûri dans ma tête, que je commence enfin à croire que je le mettrai en exécution cet hiver; il me semble du moins que je ne pourrai jamais trouver un moment plus favorable; la mort de madame Dulcken et le départ de Bénédict doivent laisser, momentanément, un vide qui rendra peut-être une prompte réussite plus facile.

Si j'hésite encore un peu, c'est uniquement parce que ma position ici est réellement très belle, et l'idée de la perdre, sans retrouver bientôt une au moins équivalente, me tourmente à cause de ma famille qui est nombreuse, comme vous savez. Vous comprendrez donc, mon cher Chorley, pourquoi je demande à mes vrais amis, et je vous compte parmi eux, de m'aider de leurs conseils et de m'indiquer, autant que cela se peut, les moyens qui pourraient rendre ma réussite plus prompte et plus facile. Je connais trop peu le terrain de Londres pour pouvoir vous faire des questions précises, excepté pourtant celle-ci : à quelle époque me conseillez-vous de venir ? Serait-il nécessaire pour moi d'arriver avant le mois de janvier ou février ? Pour tout le reste je m'en remets à votre obligeance ; je suis persuadé que tous les conseils que vous pourrez me donner, vous me les donnerez, et je vous promets de les suivre avec reconnaissance. Si vous pouvez entrer dans des détails, même sur le quartier que vous me conseilleriez d'habiter, faites-le, je vous prie ; vous me pardonnerez mon indiscrétion, j'espère, en faveur de l'importance de la question.

Ce que je vous demanderai encore, mon cher Chorley, c'est que si vous doutiez de ma réussite à Londres, de me le dire en ami et sans détour, et pour vous mettre plus à même de pouvoir le faire, je vous dirai franchement, entre nous, que je gagne ici de 1200l. à 1300l. par an, ce qui vous expliquera aussi mon embarras.

Je vous répète, mon cher Chorley, que tous vos conseils

seront reçus avec reconnaissance, et laissez-moi espérer que vous ne m'en voudrez pas de vous causer tant d'ennui.

Mille compliments affectueux de ma femme et de

Votre sincèrement dévoué ami,

CHARLES HALLÉ.

H. F. Chorley, Esq.[1]

[1]

[Translation]

Manchester: August 23, 1850, Greenheys.

My dear Chorley,—I hope you are aware that, before leaving London, I made several attempts to find you at home, but they were all in vain, to my very great regret; for I wanted greatly to have a long talk with you; and to ask your advice once more as to the change of residence that I have so long projected, without having yet been able to put it into execution.

One good conversation is worth more than a lengthy correspondence, but nevertheless, if you will have the goodness to answer a few words to the questions I shall put to you, I shall always greatly profit by them, and shall be very grateful, believe me.

The idea of establishing myself in London has so ripened in my mind that I begin to think that I shall carry it out this winter; it seems to me, at least, that I could never find a more favourable moment; the death of Madame Dulcken, and Benedict's departure, must leave a momentary void which may, perhaps, make a prompt success more easy. If I still hesitate a little, it is solely because my position here is really a very good one, and the thought of losing it, without soon finding at least an equivalent one, torments me on account of my family, which is a large one, as you know. You will understand therefore, my dear Chorley, why I ask my true friends, and I count you among them, to aid me by their counsels and to indicate, as far as may be, the means that might serve to render success more prompt and more easy. I know too little of the *terrain* of London to be able to ask you precise questions, excepting this one however: At what time of the year should you advise me to arrive? would it be necessary for me to come before the month of January or February? As to all the rest, I trust in your good nature; I know that you will give me all the advice you can, and I promise to follow it with gratitude.

If you can enter into details, even as to the part of the town that you would recommend me to reside in, do so, I beg of you; you will forgive my indiscretion, I hope, in virtue of the importance of the question.

Another thing I would ask you, my dear Chorley, is that if you have any doubts as to my success in London, you will tell me so as a friend, and without circumlocution, and to place you more in a position to do so, I will tell you frankly, between ourselves, that I earn between 1,200*l*. and 1,300*l*. a year here; this will explain my hesitation.

I repeat, my dear Chorley, that all your advice will be received with gratitude, and let me hope that you will bear me no ill-will for giving you so much trouble.

A thousand affectionate compliments from my wife and from your sincerely devoted friend,   CHARLES HALLÉ.

XVIII

TO — GLOVER, ESQ.

[The following is one of the first letters my father ever wrote in English. Up to this time his correspondence, even with the managing director of the Concert Hall, had always been carried on in French or German ; but from the date of his arrival in Manchester he had perseveringly taught himself English, carrying on the study principally in the omnibuses, on the way to and from his pupils' houses. Every morning he left home with a dictionary or grammar in his pocket, and by the autumn of 1850 he could write as follows :]

Manchester : September 13, 1850.
Greenheys.

Dear Sir,—Allow me to present you my best thanks for the copy of your ' Jerusalem,' which you have had the kindness to send me, and the perusal of which will certainly give me a very great pleasure.

As to the execution of your work at the next Xmas concert, I think you should apply to the directors of the Concert Hall, as I have only to conduct, but not to make the choice of the performance, and if they accept your proposition, I for myself, will very readily join them.

Excuse my bad English, and, believe me, dear Sir,

Yours very truly,

CHARLES HALLÉ.

— Glover, Esq.

XIX

TO HIS MOTHER

(*Translated from the German*)

Greenheys, Manchester :
April 10, 1851.

My dear Mother,—I have let many fête-days pass without sending you my good wishes, but I have perfect confidence that you have not been angry with me, as you know my busy

life too well.   But your birthday I will *not* pass over, but
wish you such a joyful day, and in this wish all my family
unite, that you may desire to have very many more to come.
I also shall be a year older to-morrow, and expect a very
pleasant day, for, as my birthday present, we shall have
the christening of our fat Fred, who seems almost able to
run to church by himself, and is sure to make faces at
the priest during the ceremony.   Ernst is coming purposely from London to make music for me in the evening; we are all well and hearty; we shall see many good
friends, so I have every right to expect a very pleasant day
of rest.

Your dear letters, which always give me the greatest
pleasure, are looked forward to with eagerness, and they are
always too short for me, and give me too few details of your
life, which I should be so glad to follow step by step; once
for all, believe me that the minutest details are interesting to
me.   It is a blessing for you that Bernard [1] is here, who, I
hope, sends you the amplest news of everything that happens;
where should I find the time for it?   In spite, however, of
my being so busy, the new arrangement works so well that I
am never over-tired, but always get to work with eagerness
and pleasure, which formerly I could not have said.   Bernard will also have informed you of the changes that will
take place next month with regard to Mathilde; the thing
may be considered fortunate, but for my poor mother-in-law
the separation from her daughter will be very painful, and I
doubt if she will get over it.

Next week I go for a little while to London, but shall
return here in the beginning of May for the wedding.   The
day before yesterday I played there, and, thank God! with
the usual success.   The news of your musical doings amused
me very much—by all means go on with them.   Now, dear
mother and dear Anna, *lebt recht wohl*. Desirée, Mathilde, the
four children send you their best love, and I beg you to give

---

[1] His younger brother.

mine to all my dear friends and relations. Write very soon
to your loving son and brother,

CARL.

P.S.—In your next letter, my dear mother, I beg you to
give me an idea of the state of your finances, that my mind
may be easy,

XX

TO FERD. HILLER

(*Translated from the German*)

Manchester: July 31, 1851.

My dear Hiller,—Through Ernst. I heard a few days ago,
with joyful surprise, of your arrival in London, and to-day I
received the card you sent me by young Mr. Cleather, which
I took as a proof that you still remember me. Therefore, I
ask you at once, how long are you staying in London? It is
my intention to take my wife for a few days to London that
she may see the Exhibition, and if I only knew how long you
meant to stay I should arrange this excursion so as to meet
you there.

It would give me so much pleasure to spend a few hours
with you, and to hear full details of your new and beautiful
position; we have much to relate on both sides; nine years
have passed since I saw you last, and they have brought much
and taken much away; the few days I spent at that time
with you, and the hearty kindness of your hospitality, belong
to the dearest and pleasantest of my recollections. Write to
me soon, dear Hiller, and let me know when I must start
in order to be able to tell you by word of mouth how much I
care for, and esteem you.

To our speedy meeting, therefore. My wife adds her
kindest remembrances to my own.

Your faithful friend,

C. HALLÉ.

XXI

TO ERNST

(Translated from the German)

Manchester: August 10, 1851.

My dear Ernst,—Mr. Kaufmann is at last on the wing and starts to-morrow, and with him the long-desired shirts, to which I wish all possible success. Before we speak of anything else I must, by my wife's orders, give you a few explanations, as follows : the number of them is eight, and the cost 5*l*. 9*s*., which makes for each specimen 13*s*. and a fraction, as it was estimated. Mr. Kaufmann is therefore commissioned to return you 11*s*. The shirts are all well cut, and, it is to be hoped, will fit well, only the front buttons are not *all* put on aright, and do not quite exactly face the buttonholes ; that you will have to get remedied ; we only discovered the blunder to-day, or it would have been set right here. As a final clause let me add, that should the quality of the linen, or anything else, not please you, I am ready to keep them myself. Your own pattern is returned with them.

Now let us have done with the shirts !—First let me beg you to interest yourself in our good friend Kaufmann ; it is, I believe, his first visit to Paris, and you can give him many useful hints. I am also giving him a few lines for Heller, perhaps for Lehmann as well, and if you can make him acquainted with a few others capable of furthering the object of his visit to Paris—to amuse himself—I shall be much beholden to you. As a capital viola-player he deserves all one's sympathies, and certainly he is a very good fellow.

I see in to-day's 'Musical Work' that you are going to travel and give concerts in Switzerland, and that Stockhausen goes with you. I envy you both, and should like to be of the party. One of these days we must really treat ourselves to such a little freak, and do a little artistic travel together ; if it does not amuse the public, it certainly will amuse us so well, that we may forget the noble public altogether. I imagine we should have great fun.

Before you undertake the Swiss journey I hope to hear from you; write at length, how you are, what your further projects are after Switzerland, and above all, when we may hope to see you in England again; if you intend to return with the fogs, or think of other winter quarters. Write about it all fully for once in a way, just for the sake of novelty, and you shall be praised. Joking apart, you know how much it is our wish to be able to follow you, at least in thought, and a long letter would be taken as a real proof of friendship.

In anticipation of your questions, I inform you at once that all my family are well, the children have got rid of the whooping-cough, and my wife is well and hearty. The only one who gives me great anxiety is my brother; since his return the cough and hemorrhage have recommenced, and I think he will have to leave England.

I am making the most of the comparatively quiet time, and work very hard, so as, if possible, to produce something; for when, next month, the treadmill of lessons begins anew, everything else comes to a stop.

What are *you* doing? Did I dream of a quartet that you began long ago, or did you speak of it? Anyhow, I ask how far you have got with it. I should also be glad to hear of Heller's work; induce him to write to me again.

Now, farewell, dear friend, and receive, with our heartiest greetings, our best wishes for your happiness and contentment. A thousand kind messages to Eckert, Frank, &c., &c., and write soon to your true friend,   HALLÉ.

Mathilde has safely reached New Orleans.

XXII

TO STEPHEN HELLER

(Translated from the German)

Manchester: August 10, 1851.

My dear Heller,—These lines will be delivered to you by one of my best friends here, Mr. Kaufmann, and you would oblige me greatly, by doing your utmost to further his intention of amusing himself during the eight days of his first visit to Paris. He is a nice, clever, and musical young man. Treat him therefore as you would wish me to treat one of your friends.

And now let me ask how things have gone with you during the long time that we have not seen, and still less written to each other. From time to time I have heard through Ernst that you were well, but that was all, so you see that there is many a hiatus to fill up; let me hope you will repair them here and there, and I shall be grateful.

How often I curse my own laziness in letter-writing I cannot tell you, for otherwise I hope I should not be so entirely cut off from my old friends as is now the case; to say nothing of the fact that it gives them the full right to lose confidence in me; but should this ever happen to you, then think of the old days, and believe that I am always unchanged and the same, that is to say that I have never felt so closely drawn, nor attached in such true friendship, to any man as to you. You will perhaps say : 'il n'y parait pas,' but all the same it is so.

Above all give me news of your work, dear Heller. Of course I know what has been published in England since last year, but I suppose that is not all; what has become of the Sonata (in B if I am not mistaken) of which you played the beginning to me in London ? You were yourself, and with full cause, so very satisfied with this opening that I hoped you would not rest until it was completed; if it is actually so, do come out with it, nor let us, who are so well-disposed, pine any longer for it in vain.

Of the published works I like best the charming 'Berceuse,' the exhilarating 'Chasse,' and the delicious little piece on Mendelssohn's 'Minnelied.' I play them often ; I like the others also, and produce them often, but the first are my special favourites. But give us something greater, dear Heller, something to work at, otherwise we shall get lazy. Things are going sadly in the musical world, a penury reigns which you know better than I ; to whom shall we turn for comfort ? Therefore, out of compassion, you should come to the rescue ; it is your bounden duty, for you are the only one to whom the faithful can look for help.

Next winter, most probably in January, I shall certainly see you in Paris, if only for a short time ; let us hope we may live through some of the old days again : I am still ready to come to you at night, with a bottle of champagne under my cloak, and under such circumstances to play through the 9th Symphony again. But I will not speak of next January as if until then we were to be dead to each other ; on the contrary, write to me, and you shall see that I also will mend my ways.

Ernst will have imparted to you news of all that has occurred here of interest, also that M. has married our brother-in-law M., and that they have arrived safely at New Orleans. Of musical events there have been few, but I am anxious to know the effect of Gounod's opera ; the most certain part of it will be a duet between Davison and Chorley. As I hear, Berlioz has greatly praised Thalberg's opera—oh, weakness ! *La plume est donnée à l'homme pour déguiser sa pensée.*

Adieu, dear Heller, and *lebe wohl !* My wife sends you her kindest greetings, and still hopes to see you some day at Greenheys. Write soon, *bleibe gut.*

Your faithful and true friend,
HALLÉ.

XXIII

TO MR. RENSHAW

Manchester : 14 août 1851,
Greenheys.

Mon cher Renshaw,[1]—Je pense, comme vous, que les morceaux que Beale nous nomme sont vieux comme le monde, mais que faire ? Il y a un trio dans ' Il Flauto Magico ' (' Dunque il mio ben non vedrò più ? '), que vous pourrez proposer, mais je ne crois pas qu'il y en ait dans ' Le Prophète,' plutôt dans ' Les Huguenots ; ' mais c'est surtout contre les Duos

---

[1] Director of the Manchester Concert Hall.

qu'il faut se révolter : nous les avons eus quatre cents fois au moins, et il doit y en avoir d'autres dans le monde, peut-être y en a-t-il dans 'Le Prophète,' et certainement dans 'Robert' ou 'Les Huguenots.' Je ne connais pas plus Mlle Fischer que vous ; pourtant, je pense que pour le concert où Mme Sontag chantera nous aurons plutôt besoin d'un chanteur que d'une chanteuse, et pour cette raison je préférerais Stigelli ; qui aurons-nous encore ?

L'air de Stradella, celui de 'Saffo' et les Spanish Songs seront intéressants ; Tamberlick devrait chanter autre chose que l'éternel 'Tesoro ;' 'Le Piff, paff' n'ira qu'avec accompagnement d'orchestre, que nous n'avons pas pu obtenir la dernière fois lorsque Formès voulait le chanter. Tamberlick chante l'air de 'Fidelio' très bien, pourvu que cela fasse de l'effet dans un concert ; proposez-le-lui toujours.

Quant aux ouvertures, je pense que pour le premier concert celles de 'Preciosa,' 'Fra Diavolo' et 'Nozze di Figaro' suffiront ; mercredi prochain nous en essayerons quelques nouvelles pour le second. Du reste j'approuve parfaitement votre programme, et si vous venez mercredi à la répétition nous pourrons en causer encore.

Mille amitiés de

Votre bien dévoué

CHARLES HALLÉ.[1]

---

[1]

[Translation]

Manchester : August 14, 1851, Greenheys.

My dear Renshaw,—I think, with you, that the pieces Beale proposes are as old as the hills, but what can we do ? There is a trio in 'The Magic Flute '('Dunque il mio ben non vedrò più ?') which you might suggest, but I do not think there is one in 'Le Prophète,' rather in 'Les Huguenots ;' but it is especially against the duets that we must rebel, we have had them four hundred times, at least, and there must be others in existence, perhaps there are some in the 'Prophète ' and certainly in 'Robert 'or 'Les Huguenots.' I know no more of Mlle. Fischer than you do, but I think that for a concert at which Madame Sontag is to sing we rather need a male singer than another lady, and for this reason I should prefer Stigelli ; whom have we besides ?

The air of Stradella, the one from 'Saffo,' and the Spanish songs will be interesting ; Tamberlick ought to sing something else besides the eternal

XXIV

TO ERNST

(Translated from the German)

Manchester: September 19, 1851.

My dear Ernst,—I must hasten, if I am to send you a line from Greenheys before you have taken flight, I hope with renewed strength and vigour, from your quiet Bougival to heaven knows what corner of the world. The story of your sufferings, old friend, touched me more than I can say. I felt for all your annoyances, but I have the firm conviction, that just this idyllic *Hühnerleben*[1] and the complete rest have been your best cure, and that our friend Roth has had an easy task. But try to let this cure suffice, a repetition of it might be terribly tedious; everything in moderation, even an idyll in Bougival.

Your life lately could, it seems, be described in a few words, and so indeed could ours, as far as outside events are concerned; always the same eating and drinking parties, the same chess and whist parties, only in the latter there has been a slight interruption, friend Stern having gone for three weeks to Frankfort, to recover from the delights of too much lobster, but he is expected home to-morrow, and all will be the same again.

My brother still causes me great anxiety, and I am now convinced that the English climate would destroy him entirely if he remained here much longer; therefore he starts for Italy

'Tesoro;' 'Piff, paff,' would only do with orchestral accompaniment, which we were unable to procure last time, when Formes wanted to sing it. Tamberlick sings the air from 'Fidelio' very well, provided that it prove effective in a concert room; propose it to him, anyhow.

As to the overtures, I think that for the first concert those of 'Preciosa,' 'Fra Diavolo' and 'Nozze di Figaro' will suffice; next Wednesday we shall try some new ones for the second. For the rest I perfectly approve of your programme, and if you will come to the rehearsal on Wednesday we can talk of it further.

A thousand kind regards from your very devoted

CHARLES HALLÉ.

[1] Leading a life like the fowls.

in October. most probably to some town in Sicily, and I hope
he may return in a few years quite recovered and strong
again ; all the doctors promise it ; may they be right ! This
is for the present the only cloud on our horizon, but you will
believe that it is a very dark one. We have good news of
M., she seems to be pleased with her new life, and to have
made many friends ; greetings to you I must not forget.

Our friend the viola-player and shirt-carrier seems to
have enjoyed himself right well in Paris, but much regrets
not to have seen you at all, and Heller only once ; please tell
the latter that I was astonished to hear from the aforesaid
friend viola-player that he had reproached Heller for not
having kept his promise to send me news of Gounod's opera ;
a promise which Heller denied, and with good reason. I
knew quite well he made no such promise, and cannot understand through what confusion of ideas Kaufmann had come to
such a conclusion. I laughed heartily at the mistake. After
this explanation I hope Heller will bear me no further grudge
but will write to me soon ; urge him to do so, the man has no
idea what pleasure he would give me. Of late I have busied
myself more than usual with his works, for instance his great
(B minor) sonata suddenly became quite clear to me, and
delighted and touched me much. I had not previously gone
into it so deeply. I had found many beauties but had not
entirely lifted the veil from them all. It now appears to me
as his greatest and most complete work, and one which, without exaggeration, has in my opinion few rivals of its kind ; it
makes me eager to talk to Heller about it, and almost to ask
his pardon for having been so slow in arriving at this conviction, but how can one make it clear in words that one understands a piece of music ? one can only give the assurance without being able to offer proof ; therefore I hope during this
winter, by playing it to him, to give him such a proof. I
have made up my mind in short to go to Paris in February,
at last, even if only for a few weeks, and I promise myself
many pleasant hours with Heller during the time.

Now to come back to yourself. I was much pleased to

hear that you had the good intention to employ your quiet
time in Bongival in composition, and hope you will com-
municate the result at our next meeting. How is the quartet
getting on? I shall perhaps have one also to pester you
with, at least I am working at one, and, naturally, your playing sounds continually in my ear, and helps me greatly.

Sivori was here lately, at the Free Trade Hall, but caused
little *furore*; such rubbish as the man plays now I had never
heard, and really, as an artist, felt ashamed of him. Sainton
played a fortnight ago at the Concert Hall, where, at last,
we also had Madame Sontag. Spohr's ninth concerto, first-rate,
only the double-stopping in the *finale* did not quite succeed;
moreover I find this *finale* very empty and tiresome.

The news that Hiller has accepted the Paris post and, I
believe, the London one as well, I had already been told, as a
secret, by Stern, only I do not clearly understand the matter;
in the German papers it is said that he is *chef d'orchestre*; you
call him general music director, and Stern tells me he will replace Lumley, who, for the future, will merely look on, and does
not intend to conduct again; if this be true, I do not think
the situation will be a very pleasant one. If you see him in
Paris please recall me to his memory.

Now, enough gossip for to-day; exert yourself on your side,
old friend; write, above all, that you have quite recovered, and
do not forget to make me acquainted with your plans, so
that I may be able to write to you from time to time. Greet
all friends and acquaintances for me, and it is self-understood
that all from here most heartily do the same by you. *Leben.
sie wohl und glücklich!* Your faithful   C. HALLÉ.

XXV

FROM HENRY F. CHORLEY

13 Eaton Place, W.
October 20, 1851.

My dear Hallé,—My holiday is now over. Is yours
coming to come? or have the young Manchester ladies caught
hold of you, and won't let you go? I wish we could have met

somewhere in Italy, because there is something in
the air of that country which makes me more agreeable
than I am anywhere else; however, so completely this
year have I proved the value of it as a prescription,
that I think I shall try it again next year, in spite of the
dirt, and in spite of the dust, and in spite of the heat,
and in spite of the fleas. Perhaps this next time I may be
more lucky in finding company. I came home by Genoa,
Turin, over the Mont Cenis, to Lyons, Paris, where I stayed
about nine days, and arrived at home on Saturday night with
literally not enough money to pay my cab! Paris seemed
very full. I saw Mme. Viardot twice, who had come from
the country to nurse M. Scheffer, who is very ill. She
seemed well and in cheerful spirits, and she spoke of Berlin
in January, and then of coming to England immediately,
with some view, I fancy, of passing a large part of her time
here. It really seems to me that, if this be the case, considering the lost prestige of the Philharmonic Concerts and the
offence which Mr. Ella has contrived to give, that something,
with the means in our reach, betwixt a grand orchestral and
a chamber concert, might be given in the way of entertainment—say a subscription of six—to which the public would
respond, and which might be made choicer than anything of
the kind in being. *Pensez-y.* I saw M. Meyerbeer in Paris,
who seemed to me more cowardly and cautious than ever,
and saw, I think, at a distance, M. Heller, looking very old
and white-haired and savage. What else I have seen and
heard is all written, and most of it printed, in the *Athenæum.*

Since I came back I have seen no one, save Benedict,
who looks very wretched, and says he has lost half his fortune
in these American failures, and Miss Gabriel.—I fancy Mrs.
Sartoris is in London for the winter, but I have hardly washed
myself clean or unpacked myself, or read my letters, and so I
have not yet asked at her door where she is. In fact, I merely
send this as a card to announce my return, and so with best
love to Mme. Hallé (no offence to Mme. E.) and to the children,
believe me to be ever yours,   HENRY F. CHORLEY.

XXVI

FROM STEPHEN HELLER

Paris : 2 janvier 1854,
12 Rue Saint-Georges.

Mon cher Hallé,— . . . D'Ernst, je n'en sais rien sinon que j'ai appris son projet de visiter l'Angleterre. Il a donné des concerts en Allemagne avec beaucoup de succès. Eckert est nommé Maître de Chapelle à l'opéra de Vienne et il commencera ses fonctions le 1er avril. Il est à Paris, où il donne quelques leçons de chant, entre autres à Mlle Cruvelli. F. devient toujours davantage ce qu'il a promis depuis longtemps ; voilà au moins un homme qui ne trompe pas les espérances qu'il a fait concevoir à ses amis. Il est morose, ennuyé, maladif et mécontent de tout le monde. Cet ensemble réjouissant est racheté par les résultats extraordinaires qu'il a obtenu, et obtient encore, de son commerce intime avec les somnambules d'une lucidité garantie, et avec des tables et des guéridons prophétiques et révélateurs. Gouvy est en Allemagne, où ses symphonies, me dit-on, obtiennent beaucoup de succès. Bohn est un peu souffrant toujours ; il travaille, mais en secret, et on ne sait pas ce qu'il fait. C'est toujours un excellent garçon. . . .

Berlioz est revenu d'Allemagne, enchanté des orchestres et des publics allemands. Il va y retourner au mois d'avril. Il n'a rien fait de nouveau. Voilà mon sac à nouvelles vidé. J'ai eu l'honneur de voir ce matin M. X., qui restera un mois à Paris ; il a même laissé espérer un plus long séjour parmi nous. Grâce à son extérieur faible et délicat il sait se donner un faux air de Chopin. La santé peut lui manquer ; le talent manque certainement. D'ailleurs un pareil artiste se porte toujours trop bien. Ceci n'est pas très chrétien, mais les vrais artistes sont un peu païens ; il ne serait pas malheureux s'ils étaient tout à fait ' Haydnisch,'[1] sans porter préjudice à tous les Beethoven modernes qui pullulent au dire de certains gens.

---

[1] A play on the German word ' haidenisch,' heathen.

Je termine, et je te prie de dire mes amitiés cordiales à Mme Hallé et de croire à l'amitié sincère de ton dévoué

STEPHEN HELLER.[1]

XXVII

FROM MR. J. ELLA

London : November 3, 1854.

Dear Hallé,—I am just home from a three months' ramble in Switzerland and France. All the musical news *there* has long ago reached you through the various channels—*M. World, Athenæum,* &c.—I saw both Chorley and Davison at Paris, and had a long discussion with them *separately.* I was one of the four *témoins* at the wedding of Berlioz, and I am

---

[1]   [*Translation*]

Paris : January 2, 1854.

My dear Hallé,— . . . I know nothing about Ernst, except that I heard of his project of visiting England. He gave concerts in Germany with great success. Eckert is appointed conductor at the Opera at Vienna and enters upon his functions on April 1. He is in Paris, where he gives singing lessons, to Mlle. Cruvelli among others. F. is daily becoming more like what he always promised to be ; here, at least, is a man who does not betray the hopes he has led his friends to conceive. He is morose, disappointed, sickly, and ill-pleased with all the world. This agreeable *ensemble* is redeemed by the extraordinary results he has obtained, and still obtains from his intimate commerce with somnambulists of guaranteed lucidity, and with tables and standishes of the prophetic and revelatory order. Gouvy is in Germany, where his symphonies, they tell me, meet with great success. Bohn is still rather ailing ; he works, but in secret, and no one knows what he is doing. He is always an excellent fellow.

Berlioz has come back from Germany, enchanted with German orchestras and audiences. He is going to return thither in April. He has done nothing new. Now I have emptied my newsbag. This morning I had the honour of seeing M. X—— who will remain in Paris a month ; he even held out hopes of a longer stay among us. Thanks to his feeble and delicate appearance he manages to give himself a false air of Chopin. He may be wanting in health—he is certainly wanting in talent. For that matter, such an artist as he always enjoys too much health. This may be somewhat un-Christian ; but all true artists are a trifle heathenish ; it would be no misfortune if they were altogether ' Haydnisch,' without prejudice to all the modern Beethovens that swarm around us, according to some people.

Now I must make an end, and beg you to present my cordial regards to Madame Hallé and to believe in the sincere friendship of your devoted

STEPHEN HELLER.

happy to say that he is in better spirits, with only one wife to provide for. Ernst is enjoying a passive matrimonial existence with a florid amount of maternal eloquence *ad lib.* I am scarcely sufficiently settled to make any visits, and have not yet been to the Prince of Waterloo's soirées—Jullien; you know that he has purchased a *château* near Waterloo? I meant to call on Molique to inquire after your pupil, my next *débutante*. *Arabella*[1] is doing wonders on the Continent, *selon ses amis.* I dined last week with Massart, and was charmed with his wife and her talent.

Remember me to your good lady and tell her I hope she *may* live long enough to see me go to the quartet-conspiration with her, as predicted. Alas! the war will make us feel, next year, its direful consequences. Send me the dates of your concerts, and tell me if you seriously contemplate engaging Vieuxtemps at one of them. I saw the L.'s in Paris, *en route* from Switzerland. Odd enough, they and my party were in Martigny—they going to and we coming from Chamounix—on the same evening, and both parties heard a Prussian officer (engineer) play Beethoven's 'Son. Pathétique,' Mendelssohn's March, and the Sonata in A flat, *con Marcia funebre!* very well indeed! I can never forget the impression! Lovely, mild night, full, bright moon, sitting outside the auberge after dinner, in a valley surrounded with peaks of St. Bernard, &c., &c.

Heller was looking a *little* grey; I saw La Clausen, she is working, but not yet married. Her *fiancé* I frequently met, at Galignani's. The Guides band has created quite a *furore.* Men ply them with beer and champagne; the life they lead, if recorded, would be a curiosity in ventures—*chez les Anglais et les Anglaises.* If all fail, I will try a moustache and uniform, and enter the bonds of matrimony. Again, best regards to Madame Hallé and the children and believe me yours faithfully,   J. ELLA.

So Anderson invited you to Osborne! Better late than never.

---

[1] Miss Arabella Goddard.

XXVIII

FROM RICHARD DOYLE

Stafford Club, Albemarle Street :
November 5, 1857.

My dear Hallé,—Your not having turned up in this part
of the world makes me fear that the influenza may resemble
me in one respect, that of paying very long visits. I hope it
is not the case, and that Mrs. Hallé and yourself have both
long since forgotten that there are colds in this life. Also I
should like very much to hear that your little Charley is
quite well.

Since I came to town I have been leading a very quiet
life, scarcely seeing any body or thing. London looks very
dark and 'muggy,' the weather being seasonable and November fogs the fashion. The public seems getting tired of
talking about India, and gladly clings hold of the 'big ship'
for a change. When the news of the failure in the attempt
to launch her became known, it gave as painful a shock to
every one as did the first intelligence, two months ago, of
General Havelock's being obliged to retire on Cawnpore.

'Tom Brown' tells me, in a letter, that his sister, Mrs.
Senior, was to arrive last Monday in town. I have not yet
been to see if it is an 'accomplished fact.' I have seen
Watts, and after all he has not been, and does not go, to
Lord Lansdowne's. It appears that the scaffolding required
for his fresco would so interfere with the comfort of visitors,
who are now at Bowood, that the Marquis has written to
propose that he should put off going to work till spring.
And this after Watts, with much pain to himself, had given
up the Art Treasures, and your kind invitation, solely on the
ground that the preparations for the fresco in London would
require all his time. Such is, &c.

I hope Mr. Fairbairn is very well, and that the executive
committee are as well as can be expected under the circumstances. Have many of the pictures gone home? Is the
exhibition building so changed that its best friend would not

know it again? Does the pike man cry 'two pence' with the same cheerful tone as before, or is his voice dashed with melancholy at the thought of the 'days that are no more'? Is my favourite lamp-post as firm and steady in the legs, and as light-headed as of yore?

The Duke of Devonshire, by the way, was rather annoyed at not getting his pictures sent back at once, as he wanted them hung in their places while the party was at Clumber, and I see a letter in the *Daily News* to-day complaining of the writer's pictures not being returned to him.

Please tell Mrs. Hallé that the reading of her letter was the pleasantest French lesson I have had for a very long time. Ever sincerely yours,   R. DOYLE.

P.S.—This being Guy Faux Day the streets are full of guys, but instead of Cardinal Wiseman being, as usual, the popular representative of the character a sepoy seems 'the thing.' Here is one I have just seen in Bond Street.

Nov. 7 (another P.S.).—I forgot to post this on Thursday, and have had it in my pocket for two days. For the next few days my address will be Strawberry Hill, Twickenham, Surrey.

XXIX

TO HIS MOTHER

(*Translated from the German*)

Greenheys, Manchester:
October 22, 1858.

My dear Mother,—It seems incredible, but it is none the less true, that only the desire of writing fully and at great length, to tell you how happy I was during my stay with you, and with what pleasure I think of the too short time spent with you, has been the very cause of my not writing at all. It seemed to me quite impossible only to send you a few lines, and so I fell into the old habit of procrastination, and days, weeks, even a month, have flown by so quickly that I can only think of them with amazement. Regret in such cases always comes too late, but be assured, and you will readily believe me, that only stress of work in making up for lost time and preparing for the coming season has kept me silent so long, and certainly no lack of good-will, nor of love and gratitude for the happy hours you made me enjoy.

No, never did a visit to you do me more good than this last one; from the first to the last hour it was beautiful: I really revelled in the remembrances of my happy childhood, and I am now almost glad that a month has passed since my visit, and brings us so much the nearer to the next one, which I can only wish may resemble it in *gemüthlichen*, homely, and peaceful joy.

I found all my family in the best condition on my return, strengthened and invigorated by sea-bathing; the little ones had much to tell of donkey rides and other pleasures, and they amuse us often with their very comical recollections. They have now got used to their Manchester life again, and are all working hard at their lessons. In what concerns my own business, I found the time I had allowed myself for preparation for my first concert, which took place on September 15, all too short; my whole orchestra had to be re-organised, and I have really had not a minute's rest. Besides this, the new choral society, of which I had laid the foundations before my departure, had to be brought to completion, and in this I have got so far that its first concert, Haydn's 'Creation,' takes place this very day, with the unheard of number of 1,600 subscribers, and an orchestra and chorus of 300. I have just come home from the very satisfactory final rehearsal, and am full of expectation for this evening. My chamber music concerts will recommence on November 25, the St. Cecilia in a fortnight, *und so geht der alte Trödel wieder los.*

But now as to the surprising and saddening news of Cornelius'[1] illness, how truly it went to my heart you, and he especially, will easily understand; I cling unspeakably to the good old honest friend; his strong constitution makes me hope that he has already overcome the disease, whatever it may be,

---

[1] Cornelius Flüss, the greatest friend of his childhood.

and I hope to God that I do not deceive myself. Give me further news of him soon, as I cannot overcome a certain feeling of uneasiness; greet him most heartily from me, and exhort him, in my name, in future not to trust too much to the strength of his constitution, but, like weaker mortals, to take a little care of himself.

Another thing I am anxiously awaiting tidings of is your threatened removal; I hope such an annoyance is not really before you—for the dear home has become so cosy—but should it come to that we shall have to take counsel together, and after all, one's well-being does not depend upon one's walls.

The hour of the concert will soon strike, and I have still much to do, so I finish for to-day, with my love to you and Anna, and greetings to Uncle Koch and his wife and children, to dear Aunt Altgelt, to Cornelius and his wife, to Baldewein, to Gustav Butz, Friedrich Wolff—in short, to all who remember me with affection, and of whom I think so often. Write to me soon and much.

Your loving
CARL.

Of course, best love from all here. The enclosed 10*l.* note will soon be followed by another.

[The Aunt Altgelt mentioned in the foregoing letter was my grandmother's eldest sister. Married at the age of sixteen, after two short years of happiness she was left a widow at eighteen, and from that date, refusing all offers of marriage, she devoted herself to her young husband's memory and to the care of her child. This little girl, Minna Altgelt, after some childish illness at four years of age, which was mismanaged by the local doctor, fell into confirmed ill-health, and became almost totally paralysed, and her life, until the age of thirty-six, when death mercifully put a term to her sufferings, was a continued martyrdom to herself and to the poor mother, whose own life was absorbed in daily, anxious care and solicitude for her stricken child.

Minna Altgelt was, perhaps, the most gifted member of a gifted family, and the more crippled and helpless her mortal

frame became, so much the brighter did the flame of her intellect
appear to shine.   Unable to raise her hands more than a few
inches from her lap, she yet taught herself to use them in a
remarkable manner, and her delicate embroideries were the
admiration of all who saw them, although she could only slowly
draw the silken thread through the fabric in lengths of two or
three inches at a time.

Passionately fond of music, she often had herself carried to
the homely 'Concordia' concerts, the chief musical society of
the little town.   These concerts were frequently followed by an
assembly ball, and when Minna Altgelt felt well enough she
would sometimes remain after the concert to watch the dancing
for an hour ; on these occasions the young men would crowd
around her couch, so brilliant, so full of wit and charm was
her conversation.

Not the least interesting feature of her individuality was her
reputed and firmly-credited gift of second sight, several curious
instances of which have survived at Hagen up to the present day.
So firmly did her family and friends believe in this attribute of
hers that during my father's first long absence from home, whenever my grandmother had been left an unduly long time without
news of him, she would refrain from going to see Minna, fearing
she might have, through her mysterious gift, some ill-tidings to
impart.   Minna would then send her a message, 'Tell Aunt
Caroline she need not be afraid to come and see me—I have *seen*
nothing, all is well at Paris.'

As will readily be believed, the poor invalid's room, filled
with plants and flowers, and made gay with the song of birds and
by every contrivance the ingenuity of love could invent, was the
centre round which the whole family life revolved.   She was the
confidante, the receptacle for the troubles, the joys, the love-
affairs, and the secrets of half the parish.

On my father's second return to Hagen from Paris it was to
her he confided the secret of his engagement to my mother, some
time before he divulged it to his parents, and entrusted to her
safe-keeping a beautiful miniature, by David, of his betrothed.
This portrait Minna hid in the recesses of her work-table, a perfect labyrinth of drawers and shelves, specially constructed for
her crippled state, which always stood beside her sofa.   It was
a subject of perplexity to all the other young members of the family
why my father, during the whole period of his stay at Hagen,
never left Minna's presence on his daily visits to her, without

making a profound bow to her work-table ; and no one, they say, who had once seen it, could ever forget the exquisite smile with which Minna Altgelt watched her young kinsman's chivalrous act of homage to the concealed image of his future wife. In 1844 Minna Altgelt died, and her mother survived her for more than thirty years.]

XXX

TO HIS WIFE

Londres : 3 mai 1859.

Hier j'ai d'abord répété avec Wieniawsky, ensuite j'ai assisté chez Joachim à la répétition des quatuors de Beethoven qu'il jouera mercredi ; c'était magnifique, j'ai rarement eu un plus grand plaisir. Cela m'avait donné une rage de travailler telle que j'ai joué depuis mon dîner jusqu'à une heure du matin, et voudrais pouvoir recommencer aujourd'hui.[1]

XXXI

TO THE SAME

Glasgow : 1er février 1860.

Il y avait beaucoup de monde hier, dans une salle charmante que je ne connaissais pas encore. . . . tout a bien marché. Le concert a fini avec la sonate dédiée à Kreutzer, après laquelle on nous a jeté—un bouquet, que tous deux nous avons regardé avec pas mal d'étonnement. Vieuxtemps ne bougeant pas, je l'ai ramassé pour le lui offrir devant le public, mais il ne voulait pas l'accepter ; alors je suis allé bravement dans la chambre des artistes et je l'ai donné à— Madame Vieuxtemps.[2]

---

[1] [*Translation*]

London : May 3, 1859.

Yesterday I first rehearsed with Wieniawsky ; then, at Joachim's, I assisted at the rehearsal of the Beethoven quartets that he is to play on Wednesday ; it was magnificent, I have rarely had a greater treat. It gave me such a rage for work that I practised from dinner-time until one o'clock in the morning, and wish I could begin again to-day.

[2] [*Translation*]

Glasgow : February 1, 1860.

There were a great many people yesterday, in a charming room that I had not seen before . . . everything went well. The concert ended with

XXXII

TO THE SAME

Lundi.

Que deux mots aujourd'hui : j'ai trois leçons à donner, une
autre répétition pour ce soir, et il faut que je travaille encore
cette fichue musique anglaise qui ne vaut pas le diable et
cependant est d'un difficile incroyable.   C'est vraiment une
pitié de se donner tant de mal pour des choses qui n'en valent
certes pas la peine ; mais comment refuser de jouer à un
concert *anglais* à Londres ? J'aurais été écartelé au moins dans
le 'Times' . . . J'arriverai mercredi dans l'après-midi et j'ai
demandé à D. de changer la répétition du vendredi au jeudi,
car j'aurai probablement à repartir jeudi soir.[1]

XXXIII

TO THE SAME

Baden-Baden, 17 août 1860,
Hôtel de Hollande.

Je suis depuis hier à Baden ; le temps était magnifique hier
quand je suis parti de Heidelberg, ce qui m'a décidé, et j'ai
rencontré ici Berlioz, Richard Wagner, Danton, Sivori, Wolff,
Cossmann, Piatti, et plusieurs autres vieilles connaissances.
Avec Berlioz j'ai passé presque toute la journée d'hier : nous
avons parcouru toute la partition d' 'Armide,' et, de souvenir,

the Kreutzer sonata, after which we were thrown a bouquet, which we
both looked at with no little astonishment. As Vieuxtemps did not budge.
I picked it up and offered it to him before the public, but he would not
accept it ; then I went bravely into the artists' room, and I gave it to
—Madame Vieuxtemps.

[1]   *[Translation]*

Monday.

Only two words to-day ; I have three lessons to give, another rehearsal
this evening, and I must work again at that wretched English music that
is not worth a rap, and yet is incredibly difficult.   It is really a pity to
give oneself so much trouble about things that certainly are not worth it—
but how can one refuse to play at an *English* concert in London ? I should
have been drawn and quartered, at the least, by the *Times* . . . I shall
arrive on Wednesday afternoon, and I have asked D. to change the
rehearsal from Friday to Thursday, as I shall probably have to leave again
on Thursday evening.

toute celle d' 'Iphigénie,' et j'ai appris bien des choses que je
ne connaissais pas et qu'il sait de tradition ; il m'a montré
des effets que je n'aurais pas pu trouver seul, je suis donc
bien content de l'avoir vu. Je t'écris dans ce moment chez
P., que j'ai rencontré ce matin. . . . Nous venons d'avoir une
longue conversation au sujet du théâtre à Manchester ; il est
plus que jamais persuadé de la possibilité de la chose, et
croit que ce serait une bonne chose pour Manchester et pour
moi.[1]

XXXIV

TO THE SAME

Paris : 19 août '60,
Hôtel du Louvre.

. . . A Baden j'ai encore rencontré Mme Miolan et son
mari, et Wieniawski avec sa femme ; j'ai de plus assisté à
une répétition d'un grand concert, que Berlioz a dirigé et
où il a répété une grande partie de 'l'Orphée,' ce qui m'a
bien vivement intéressé ; j'y ai encore appris bien des effets
que je ne connaissais pas : ce pauvre Berlioz du reste m'a
fait une peine énorme ; jamais je n'ai vu un homme changé
comme lui, et à moins d'un miracle il sera certainement dans
la tombe avant un an d'ici. Il le sait lui-même, et il en
parle avec une tristesse qui navre le cœur. Il était si content de me voir et de pouvoir parler musique à cœur ouvert ;

[1]
[*Translation*]

Baden-Baden, August 17, 1860,
Hôtel de Hollande.

I have been at Baden since yesterday ; the weather was magnificent
when I left Heidelberg, which helped me to decide, and I have met here
Berlioz, Richard Wagner, Danton, Sivori, Wolff, Cossmann, Piatti, and
several other old acquaintances. I spent nearly the whole day yesterday
with Berlioz ; we went through the score of 'Armida,' and, from memory,
the whole of 'Iphigenia,' and I learned many things that I was ignorant
of and which he knows by tradition. He showed me effects that I should
never have discovered by myself. I am therefore very pleased to have
seen him. I am writing in P.'s room, whom I met this morning . . . We
have just had a long talk about the Manchester Theatre ; he is more than
ever convinced of the possibility of the scheme, and thinks it would be a
good thing for Manchester and for me.

il m'a dit que de longtemps il ne s'était senti aussi bien que pendant ces deux jours. . . .

Je vais aller à la découverte de Heller maintenant, j'espère qu'il est à Paris; ce soir je compte aller entendre 'Fra Diavolo' à l'Opéra Comique, à moins que Heller propose autre chose.[1]

XXXV

TO THE SAME

Royal Hotel, Princes Street, Edimbourg:
dimanche ('61 ?)

Le concert d'hier a été un grand succès et j'aurai 60*l.* pour ma part, ce qui vaut la peine; il y avait un public vraiment admirable et toute l'aristocratie de 40 milles dans la ronde y était. La duchesse était bien fâchée de ce que je ne puis aller à Dalkeith, mais elle espère qu'une autre fois je pourrai m'arranger de manière à y passer une semaine.

Les X. avaient invité une vingtaine de personnes pour la soirée, de sorte que j'ai dû jouer un peu malgré ma fatigue et avaler une douzaine de ballades écossaises. Il y avait une Mrs. —— qui m'a fait passer le plus terrible quart d'heure dont je me souvienne de longtemps; figures-toi une assez vieille femme, fort extraordinaire dans sa mise, avec une voix de basse comme celle de Formès, qui se tient

---

[1]

[Translation]

Paris: August 19, 1860.
Hotel du Louvre.

. . . I also met at Baden Mme. Miolan and her husband, and Wieniawski with his wife; moreover, I assisted at the rehearsal of a grand concert, which Berlioz conducted, where he rehearsed a great part of 'Orpheus,' which interested me keenly; I again learned many effects that I did not know before. Poor Berlioz, however, gave me the greatest pain; I never saw a man so changed, and, but for a miracle, he will surely be in his grave before this time next year. He knows it himself, and speaks of it with a sadness that pierces one's heart. He was so pleased to see me and to be able to open his heart in talking of music; he told me he had not felt so well for a long time as during those two days. . . .

I am now going to hunt for Heller, I hope he is in Paris; this evening I intend to go and hear 'Fra Diavolo' at the Opéra Comique, unless Heller has something else to propose.

debout, seule, au milieu du salon et, sans aucun accompagnement, chante, sur des mélodies improvisées avec toute espèce
de vieux trilles et hoquets, quelques-uns des poëmes de son
frère, et pas des plus courts. Il m'a pris une telle peur
d'éclater de rire que vraiment j'en étais presque malade.[1]

XXXVI

FROM STEPHEN HELLER

Paris : 5 déc. 1861.

Mon cher Hallé,—Ta lettre m'a fait un très grand plaisir :
je devrais dire, une joie. D'abord j'obtiendrai ce que j'ai
désiré, et puis c'est à ton amitié et à tes démarches que je
dois cette réalisation. Merci, cher ami, bien sincèrement
d'avoir usé de ta position et de ton influence en faveur de ton
vieux camarade. Ce que tu me dis de la solidarité de la
maison Chappell me tranquillise. . . . Tu me connais assez
pour savoir que je ne suis pas homme à regarder au gain.
Néanmoins je dois te dire, que ce n'est pas pour moi que je
désire gagner un peu de ce vil métal si nécessaire. Depuis
plusieurs années je suis aussi obligé de soutenir plusieurs
membres de ma famille, qui ont tout perdu. Mais, avec mes
compositions, surtout si je parviens à être un peu mieux rétri-
bué (comme c'est déjà le cas en Angleterre, grâce à toi) à

[1]

[*Translation*]

Royal Hotel, Princes Street, Edinburgh:

Sunday ('61 ?).

Yesterday's concert was a great success, and I shall have 60*l.* for my
share, which makes it worth while; the public was truly admirable, and
all the aristocracy for forty miles around was there. The duchess was
very sorry that I could not go to Dalkeith, but she hopes that another
time I can arrange to spend a week there.

The X.'s had invited about a score of people for the evening, so that I
had to play a little, in spite of my fatigue, and to swallow a dozen Scotch
ballads. There was a Mrs. ——, who made me spend one of the most
terrible quarters of an hour that I can remember for a long time; imagine
an oldish woman, very extraordinary in attire, with a bass voice like that
of Formes, who stands up, alone, in the middle of the room and, without
any accompaniment, sings to improvised melodies with all sorts of old-
fashioned shakes and hiccoughs, several of her brother's poems, and by no
means the shortest of them. I was seized with such a fear of bursting
into laughter that it nearly made me ill.

Paris, et à avoir quelques élèves bien payans, je pourrais m'en tirer. Je ne suis arrivé à un bon résultat qu'en Allemagne, où les éditeurs de tous les pays désirent avoir de mes ouvrages. Si j'avais ici un artiste de ta force, j'y serais arrivé également. Mais c'est toujours l'ancienne histoire. Je compte 3 catégories de musiciens et amateurs, sous ce rapport : la 1re me joue bien ; c'est une catégorie peu nombreuse ; la 2de me joue mal ; elle est bien plus nombreuse ; la 3me ne me joue pas du tout ; celle-ci est de bien loin la plus nombreuse. Oui, il y en a qui jouent bien quelques-uns de mes morceaux ; quelques professeurs, quelques petites filles, qui jouent surtout très vite ; quelques amateurs, qui aiment Chopin, Schumann, Mendelssohn, qui me font l'honneur de me laisser suivre ces maîtres. Mais tout cela n'est pas animé, ni assez simple, ni assez riche, ou simple où il faudrait être riche et riche où il faudrait être simple ; sentimental où il faut être chaud et affectueux ; puissant au lieu d'être aimable ; pesant aux endroits legers, et *vice versâ*. Tu es resté mon idéal de pianiste, parce que tu n'exagères rien. C'est là qu'on reconnaît les maîtres dans tous les arts. Tu ne seras jamais emphatique (chose horrible dans toutes les manifestations de l'art), boursoulé, larmoyant, affecté ; car tu ne veux ni faire pleurer les roches, ni dompter les animaux féroces, ni soulever les montagnes ; tu as le sentiment *vrai*, voilà tout dire. Moi, je réunis tout en ceci. Les grands écrivains, les grands peintres ont eu le sentiment vrai, ni plus ni moins. L'artiste qui va au-delà, comme celui qui reste en deça manque également son but. J'ai eu horreur les pianistes modernes tout en reconnaissant leurs grandes qualités. Mais ces qualités, à quoi reviennent-elles ? En vérité je ne les ai pas entendu jouer la plus facile des sonates de Beethoven de manière à me contenter, de manière à me donner l'idée de l'auteur. Le *grand* Rubinstein a joué chez moi plusieurs ' Waldstücke ' (en mi entre autres). Quel style ! quelles exagérations des endroits moins saillants, et quelle négligence dans les passages plus importants ! On sentait l'ennui de ses doigts agiles et puissants qui n'avaient rien à mettre sous les dents, à peu près comme

lorsqu'on donne à l'éléphant du cirque une simple saladière à
engloutir. Il a joué à Saint-Pétersbourg ma Tarantelle en la
bémol, enjolivée de traits d'octaves, de trilles, etc. etc. Si
ces gens l'osaient, ils en feraient de même avec Beethoven.

S. HELLER.[1]

1   *[Translation]*

Paris : December 5, 1861.

My dear Hallé.—Your letter gave me very great pleasure—I might say,
joy. First of all I shall obtain what I desired, and then it is to your
friendship and to your exertions that I shall owe this realisation of my
wishes. I thank you, dear friend, very sincerely for having made use of
your position and of your influence in favour of your old comrade. What
you tell me of the solidity of the house of Chappell tranquillises me. . . . You
know me well enough to be assured that I am not a man who looks for gain.
Nevertheless, I ought to tell you that it is not for myself that I desire to
earn a little of that vile metal that is so necessary. For several years I
have had to support several members of my family who had lost their all.
But, with my compositions, especially if I succeed in getting better remuneration in Paris (as, thanks to you, is already the case in England), and
with some pupils who would pay me well, I cou'd manage. I have obtained
a good result only in Germany, where the publishers of all parts wish to
have my works. If I had an artist of your quality here I should have done
equally well. But it is always the same old story. I divide artists and
amateurs into three categories on this head. The first play my things
well—this is but a small category; the second play them badly and are
far more numerous; the third do not play them at all, and are the most
numerous of all. Yes, there are a few who play some of my pieces well.
A few professors, a few little girls, who play very fast above all things, and
a few amateurs, who like Chopin, Schumann, Mendelssohn, and who do
me the honour to let me follow these masters. But all these are not very
animated, nor simple enough, nor ornate enough, or they are simple where
they ought to be ornate, and ornate where they ought to be simple; sentimental where they should be warm and tender; powerful instead of amiable,
heavy in light passages, and *vice versâ*. You have remained my ideal of
a pianist, for you never exaggerate. That is where one recognises the
master in every art. You are never emphatic (a horrid thing in any
manifestation of art), bombastic, whimpering, affected; for you neither
wish to make rocks weep, nor to tame wild beasts, nor to move mountains;
you have *true* sentiment, and that is everything. I sum up everything in
that. The great writers, the great painters had *true* sentiment, nothing
more and nothing less. The artist who goes beyond, and he who stops short
of it have equally missed their aim. I hold modern pianists in horror
while recognising their great qualities. But these qualities, what do they
amount to? Of a truth, I have not heard them play the easiest of Beethoven's sonatas in a manner to content me, to give me the composer's
meaning. The *great* Rubinstein played several 'Waldstücke' at my
house (the one in E among others). What a style! What exaggeration of

XXXVII

[Letter to a Manchester Paper]

February 13, 1862.

The remarks of your musical critic on yesterday's concert must lead your readers to believe that the introduction of 'Cadenzas' into Mozart's concertos is optional with the performer. I feel sure you will allow me to remove such an impression, and to inform the writer of the paragraph as well as your readers that in all concertos by Mozart, in five out of the six written by Beethoven, and in almost every other instance (Mendelssohn excepted), 'Cadenzas,' the place for which is distinctly marked and prepared for in a peculiar manner known to all musicians, cannot be dispensed with without destroying the symmetry of the work, or involving its mutilation. It is hardly necessary to explain that the object of these 'Cadenzas' is to recapitulate the principal ideas contained in the movement, at the conclusion of which they are introduced; to condense them, present them in a new form, and, in short, to give a *résumé* of the whole work. That this has perhaps in no instance on record been done in a more masterly manner than by Mr. Stephen Heller yesterday, all musicians at the concert will readily acknowledge.

Far from being an 'intrusion,' or a violation of 'the principle which demands respect for the creations of genius,' the composition of 'Cadenzas' is therefore in strict accordance with the intentions of our greatest composers, and has always been regarded as one of the severest tests of the musician's faculties.

Thanking you for the space you have kindly allowed me, I remain, yours very obediently,   CHARLES HALLÉ.

the less salient parts, and what negligence in the more important passages! One felt the boredom of those agile and powerful fingers that had nothing put into them, as when they give the circus elephant an empty salad-bowl to swallow. He played my Tarantelle in A flat at St. Petersburg, ornamented with octave passages, shakes, &c., &c. If such people only dared they would do the same to Beethoven.

STEPHEN HELLER.

XXXVIII

TO HIS WIFE

6 Arlington Street, London :
dimanche, 13 avril '62.

Jamais le voyage de Manchester à Londres ne m'a semblé plus court qu'hier ; Heller et Joachim étaient gais comme des pinsons et nous nous sommes bien amusés. En arrivant j'ai installé Heller dans ses appartements, qui lui plaisent ; ensuite j'ai donné deux leçons, j'ai retrouvé Heller et Joachim à dîner au Wellington, et le soir j'ai eu ma soirée payante chez Mr. Cook, où j'ai joué quatre sonates de Beethoven pour dix personnes, de sorte que je suis rentré assez fatigué. . . .

Heller vient d'arriver et désire écrire quelques mots sur la 4ᵐᵉ page ; je finis donc. . . .   Ton   CHARLES.

Chère Madame,—Carl me laisse cette page, pour vous écrire un mot. Je voudrais vous remercier encore de toutes les amitiés dont vous m'avez entouré pendant mon séjour à Manchester. Des mots, je n'en veux pas dire, mais vous savez que je sens vivement, et que je n'ai jamais connu de plus vive joie que de pouvoir être reconnaissant et affectueux. Je vous ai voué ces sentiments-là, et je les garderai toujours. Vous savez déjà que nous sommes arrivés sains et saufs. Maintenant j'attendrai mon sort dans cette belle et affreuse ville.

Je voudrais déjà vous y voir, pour la trouver plus habitable. Je vous prie de dire mes amitiés à Mlle M., L., à C. et à toute cette charmante marmaille dont vous êtes l'excellente et digne gardienne. Que Dieu vous garde, c'est mon vœu le plus sincère. Votre dévoué

STEPHEN HELLER.[1]

[Translation]

6 Arlington Street, London :
Sunday, April 13, 1862.

. . . The journey from Manchester to London never seemed shorter to me than it did yesterday. Heller and Joachim were as merry as larks, and we amused ourselves greatly. On arriving, I established Heller in his

XXXIX

TO THE SAME

6 Arlington Street :
21 avril '62.

Je comprends tes inquiétudes sur la Nouvelle-Orléans, mais il ne faut pas les exagérer ; le Nord n'y est pas encore ; et comme la ville même ne saurait guère se défendre, n'étant pas fortifiée, il n'y aura certes pas d'excès, ce sera une simple occupation ; de plus il n'est pas probable que ceux qui peuvent s'en aller resteront à attendre les événements. Broadwood est en Ecosse jusqu'à samedi, de sorte qu'il ne peut pas me donner des nouvelles. . . .

Nous avons passé une charmante soirée chez les Sartoris avec Millais et Browning ; Heller a beaucoup joué et très bien. . . .[1]

rooms, which please him ; then I gave two lessons, and rejoined Heller and Joachim at the Wellington for dinner. In the evening I had a paid private concert at Mr. Cook's, where I played four of Beethoven's sonatas to ten people, so that I came home rather tired. . . .

Heller has just come in and desires to write a few words on the fourth page ; so I must end. . . .

Your CHARLES.

Dear Madame,—Carl leaves me this page to write you a word. I should like to thank you again for all the marks of friendship you bestowed on me during my stay in Manchester. I am not a man of many words, but you know that I feel keenly, and that I have never known a greater joy than that of being grateful and affectionate. Those feelings I have consecrated to you, and they shall be yours always. You already know that we arrived safe and sound. Now I shall await my fate in this beautiful and frightful town.

I wish you were already here, to make it a little more habitable. I beg you to give my compliments to Miss M., to L., C., and to all that charming brood of which you are the excellent and worthy guardian. That God may have you in His keeping is my sincerest wish.

Your devoted STEPHEN HELLER.

[Translation]

6 Arlington Street :
April 21, '62.

I understand your anxiety with respect to New Orleans, but you must not exaggerate it ; the North has not arrived there yet, and as the town could hardly defend itself, not being fortified, there would certainly be no excesses, it would be a simple occupation ; moreover, it is not probable

XL

TO THE SAME

6 Arlington Street :
27 avril 1862.

Ne manques pas de me dire par quel train vous allez arriver, et si c'est décidément jeudi ou vendredi, car pour venir te chercher il faudra peut-être que je change quelques leçons, ce dont il me faut naturellement prévenir mes élèves la veille. Cependant je n'en ai presque pas jeudi, à cause de l'exposition ; je suis un peu tenté moi-même d'acheter un billet de trois guinées pour pouvoir y aller ; je pourrais tout de même être au chemin de fer à temps ; je voudrais voir aussi ce qu'on fera pour Costa ; il a tenu bon et ne conduit pas la musique de Bennett qui est dévolue à Sainton, qui a consenti de la diriger ; cela commence à faire un brouhaha épouvantable, le 'Daily Telegraph' a eu un 'leading article' contre Costa d'une violence extrême, disant qu'il est temps de lui prouver que l'Angleterre peut se passer de lui ; le 'Daily News' en a fait de même, mais moins rudement, et il n'y a pas de doute que les autres journaux ne l'épargneront guère ; reste à savoir comment le public se comportera. Meyerbeer est arrivé, mais je ne l'ai pas vu encore.

Heller et moi nous jouerons le concerto de Mozart au Crystal Palace samedi prochain, on nous offre les mêmes 'terms' que la Société de Londres ; Heller est enchanté, d'autant plus qu'il a vendu hier une nouvelle édition de ses études pour 20 livres, sur lesquelles il ne pouvait guère compter ; il se sent donc en fonds, et regarde Londres d'un tout autre œil. Pour moi, cela me fera quatre concerts dans la semaine. . . .

Chorley veut réellement donner un 'fancy ball' le mardi de la semaine du Handel Festival, et j'ai dû lui promettre de vous en prévenir dès le lendemain, ce que j'ai fait. Je crois qu'il

that those who can get away will stay there to await events. Broadwood is in Scotland until Saturday, so he can give me no news.

We spent a charming evening at the Sartoris's with Millais and Browning ; Heller played a great deal and very well. . . . .

est fou, car figures-toi un bal *dans ses appartements*,[1] et si on
ne danse pas, figures-toi nous tous assis tranquillement à côté
les uns des autres dans toutes sortes de costumes ; je lui ai
dit que j'irais en ' Christy minstrel '—Chorley lui-même sera
en Apollon, naturellement.

J'ai reçu hier au soir une invitation des Prinsep à dîner
aujourd'hui ; je crois que cette fois je dois y aller, à cause de
Charlie et de Watts ; le temps est superbe, et le jardin sera
agréable sans doute. Je dois d'abord faire toute espèce de
répétitions surtout avec Heller chez Broadwood ; il a fait un
nouveau point d'orgue pour le concerto de Mozart, que nous
n'avons pas encore essayé, et nous avons demain la répétition
avec l'orchestre.[2]

[1] Chorley's house, 13 Eaton Place, West, was exceedingly small.

[2] *[Translation]*

April 27, 1862.

Do not forget to tell me by what train you will arrive, and if you have
decided upon Thursday or Friday, as in order to meet you at the station I
may perhaps have to change some lessons, of which I must warn my pupils
the day before. I have hardly any, however, for Thursday, on account of
the Exhibition ; I am rather tempted to buy a 3-guinea ticket myself
to be able to go there ; I could anyhow be at the station in time. I should
also like to see what will happen to Costa ; he has held his ground, and
will not conduct Bennett's music, which has devolved upon Sainton, who
has consented to conduct it. This is beginning to cause a tremendous
uproar ; the *Daily Telegraph* had a leading article of extreme violence
against Costa, saying that it was time to show him that England could do
without him ; the *Daily News* took the same line, though less roughly,
and there is no doubt that the other papers will not spare him ; it remains
to be seen what attitude the public will take up. Meyerbeer has arrived,
but I have not yet seen him.

Heller and I are to play the concerto by Mozart at the Crystal Palace
next Saturday ; they offer us the same terms as the London Society.
Heller is enchanted, all the more so that he sold a new edition of his
' Studies ' yesterday for 20*l.*, which he had hardly expected ; he feels himself in funds, and looks upon London with quite another eye. As to me,
that will make four concerts in the week. . . . .

Chorley really means to give a fancy ball on the Tuesday of the
Handel Festival week, and I had to promise to let you know at once,
which I have done. I think he is mad, for just imagine a ball *in his
rooms*, and if there is no dancing, imagine us all quietly seated side by
side in all sorts of different costumes ; I told him I should go as a ' Christy
Minstrel '—Chorley himself will appear as Apollo, naturally. I received an
invitation last evening from the Prinseps to dine with them to-day ; I

XLI

TO THE SAME

6 Arlington Street : 29 avril '62.

J'ai emmené Heller chez les Prinsep hier ; il n'y avait personne que Doyle, et aucune dame que Mrs. Prinsep ; la maison même n'est pas encore arrangée. Le temps était superbe, et jamais je n'ai vu un homme plus charmé que Heller ne l'était de Watts, de Doyle, des Prinsep, du jardin, et de tout enfin.

Watts veut voir tout ce que Charlie a jamais fait, aussitôt qu'il sera ici, et m'a promis de me donner alors ses meilleurs conseils sur les maîtres qu'il faut lui donner. Apporte donc tous ses dessins, même si cela donne beaucoup d'embarras ; c'est trop important. Watts approuve beaucoup qu'il s'est tant occupé d'anatomie cet hiver ; c'est vraiment l'homme dans lequel, comme artiste, j'ai le plus de confiance, et je suis bien heureux qu'il montre tant d'intérêt pour Charlie.[1]

---

think I ought to go this time on account of Charlie and Watts ; the weather is splendid, and the garden will doubtless be very agreeable. I have first every kind of rehearsal, especially one with Heller at Broadwood's ; he has composed a new cadenza for the Mozart concerto, which we have not yet tried, and we have the orchestral rehearsal to-morrow.

[1]

[*Translation*]

6 Arlington Street,
April 29, 1862.

I took Heller to the Prinseps yesterday ; there was no other guest but Doyle, and Mrs. Prinsep was the only lady. The house itself is not yet in order. The weather was splendid, and I never saw a man more charmed than was Heller with Watts, with Doyle, with the Prinseps, with the garden and with everything.

Watts wishes to see everything that Charlie has ever done, as soon as he comes to town, and he promised that he would then give me the best advice he could as to the masters we must give the boy. Therefore, bring all his drawings, even if it gives a great deal of trouble ; it is very important. Watts highly approves of his having studied anatomy so much this winter. Watts is certainly the man in whom, as an artist, I feel the greatest confidence, and I am very happy that he takes so much interest in Charlie.

XLII

FROM ERNST

(Translated from the German)

Nice: May 21, 1862.

Dear Friend.—I have just finished a letter to Chorley in which I begged him to tell you that I would write to you in a few days. But 'je prends mon courage à deux mains,' in spite of fatigue and excitement, and do so at once, for I will no longer delay to tell you how glad I am that you have joined the friends who are venturing upon my enterprise. You must feel a certain satisfaction in contributing to the success of a project in which, a few years ago, you took the initiative. Let me thank you to-day (which I hope Roth has already done for me), and at the same time assure you that my joy at your participation would have been complete had your kind offer been sent to me by yourself; although on the former occasion I thought it right for different reasons not to accept it. It is now five years since misfortune overtook me, and much has changed since then. In compliance with our friend Chorley's wish, I have already sent you my quartet by post; I hope it is now in your hands, if not, kindly claim it at Chappell's in New Bond Street. Notwithstanding the other hopes attached to it, I can assure you that the appreciation, if only in part, of my work by the public would fulfil the innermost wish of my *artist's heart*, and be the greatest satisfaction the efforts of my career could obtain.

Under your direction, and with artists so great as those London can offer, I am certain of the most perfect interpretation, and, in the event of ill-success, my disillusion would be all the bitterer.

I have no special remarks to make. I hope you will be able to read the score; it is very unequally written out, according to the greater or lesser degree of my suffering. To your judgment and insight I leave it, whether the scherzo is to follow the first movement or the *andante* (as it is written); since I sent it off the thought has occurred to me to let it follow the first movement, as it would serve to make the contrast greater between the *allegro moderato* and the *andante*.

But one thing more—pay special attention to the part in the last movement commencing with *poco a poco più lento*, and continuing to the *poco a poco accell. e crescendo*. I should like it to be played almost *rubato* and with great *abandon*. The whole of the last movement with the greatest possible swing.

I cannot tell you, my dear Hallé, with what impatience I am expecting a letter from you. In our youth art brought us together. After five years' separation and almost entire cessation of our former so intimate intercourse, she again stretches out her hand to unite us once more. May you seize it as eagerly as I! Write to me soon. With real joy I shall hear of all that concerns you and your family. Do not be chary of news, tell me of all our mutual friends, and of the present state of art in London.

Your old and true friend,

ERNST.

A thousand greetings to all yours, and the same from my wife.

XLIII

FROM THE SAME

(Translated from the German)

Nice: June 13, 1862.

Dear Friend,—The good news contained in your kind letter gave me all the more pleasure that it arrived at a moment when the ill-luck, that has followed me so long, had just dealt me another blow. Can you believe it, that yesterday morning, between four and five o'clock (almost the only hour during which I slept, and indeed I had had a light burning until then) we were robbed, in the very room in which we slept. The value of the articles stolen is at least 1,000 frs., and besides their material worth they were precious as remembrances. Among them a large watch, which, together with its wooden stand, was taken from under my very nose, from the table beside my bed. The whole day we had commis-

*saires de police, juge d'instruction, procureur impérial, com-
mandant des gens d'armes,* and *gens d'armes* in the house, to
search the premises and take our depositions. Up to the
present, the wooden watchstand has been found on the ground
floor, but has led to nothing further. It has been such a
curious robbery that it gives rise to all sorts of conjectures
and solves none of them. All this has excited and distressed
me so much that I have spent a terrible night, and this
morning early I received your letter; you can imagine how
welcome it was. A thousand thanks for it, and a thousand
thanks to you all for your sympathy.

I accept with great gratitude the offer for my quartet, so
delicately put. . . . With regard to the time of publication,
it would be advantageous to me if it could be deferred until
late autumn, as some musical friends in Vienna propose to
organise a performance of it, for which the summer season is
not suitable, and it would lessen the interest of the public if
the work was already printed and at every one's disposal.

The kind offer of a concert at which my quartet shall be
played, and the form it is to take pleases me greatly, and it
is a matter of course that Chappell's shall have the right to
perform it afterwards as often as they like. The good God
grant that its reception may be such as to make them wish
to exercise the right frequently . . . And now let me tell
you that what you say of the impression my composition
made upon you on reading it through, greatly pleased me,
and I shall be enchanted if you think as well of it after
having heard it. Write to me, I earnestly beg of you, as
soon as ever you are able to tell me your opinion.

Need I assure you that the two names Joachim and
Piatti delighted my artist's heart, and that the thought of the
first public performance of my work being in such hands
filled me with the liveliest hopes?

Thank them for the care they are going to bestow upon
me, which you have already promised in their name. In
your next letter I should like to hear what artists you have
chosen for the second violin and viola.

My health, I am sorry to say, is no better, and only the importance and interest of the circumstance enabled me to overcome the agitation of spirit, and the pain in my fingers and arms which long writing produces. The day before yesterday I took my first sea-bath, but could not continue them.

I close my letter with repeated thanks to my friends, particularly Chorley and Chappell; the latter's letter I have received and shall write to him soon. Hearty greetings to your dear wife and children, from myself and my wife.

Your old friend,   ERNST.

XLIV

FROM THE SAME

(Translated from the German)

Nice : June 29, 1862.

Dear Friend,—I am just at present in a series of very painful days, else I should have acknowledged sooner the receipt of the 100*l.*, and not have let two days intervene before expressing my great joy at the success of the concert, and the gratitude and emotion that filled me at hearing of such a widespread expression of good-will and sympathy.

Even to-day it is impossible for me to write at any length; therefore I beg you, dear Hallé, to be the interpreter of my most heartfelt thanks to all those (*à commencer par vous*) who, in one way or another, have proved their sympathy for me. As soon as I feel better, I hope to be able to write to each separately. The unprecedented composition of the quartet enchanted me. I beg you at the first opportunity to embrace them all four, and their instruments as well. That which my dear old friend, the great master Molique,[1] did for me, pleased me above all.

I received letters from Lehmann, Chappell, and Joachim senior; greet them all for me; letters will follow, as soon as I am a bit better, to each in turn. The weather is so un-

---

[1] Molique played the second violin in the quartet.

usually bad here that since my first sea-bath, I have not been able to take another. No trace of the thieves; appearances seemed to point to a maid-servant, but nothing could be proved. Lehmann sent me the *Times*; many thanks.

I can write no more. I greet you and yours a thousand times. Your old, faithful   ERNST.

P.S.—I am very, very ill, my dear friend. Forgive my brevity. You would oblige me much by sending me some of the papers that have notices of the concert.

XLV

FROM H. F. CHORLEY

13, Eaton Place, W.
Tuesday, August 19, 1862.

My dear Hallé,—Thank you very much for all the trouble you have taken. Thank you *more* for your *wilfulness* (I had meant *willingness*) in offering me a great help. The specimens are very queer, but are full of humour, nothing in them that *you* could not play at first sight.[1]

I shall be back (D.V.) on the 11th of October, and before my return I shall have the illustrations copied so that any one can read them. They are just now rather chaotic, as Sullivan played from a figured bass sometimes. I have a syllabub (*hus*) ready to send to Mr. Worthington, in case it is the habit of the institution to announce matters beforehand. This I hope to hear from him ere I go, which will not be till the 26th.

I am glad you liked the Prologue. It was murderously ill-spoken. I should have sent it at once to the Manchester papers, only, as I planned going thither, I did not choose to put myself forward *for to go philanthropically*, after the fashion of the holy * * * ! Perhaps, however, they might like to have it, and, if you think so, I send you a copy.

I am dead *beat*, having used up my last scraps of energy

---

[1] Mr. Chorley was about to give a lecture on music in Manchester in aid of the Cotton Famine Fund.

in making this opera-book for Sullivan. It is worth while, for what he has written is delicious, with a sort of 'perfume' about it (I can get at no better word), which I have found in the fancies of no other English composer. So, good-bye till October 11, and thank you. Best regards all round, from ever yours truly,

HENRY F. CHORLEY.

XLVI

TO HIS SON CHARLES

Greenheys: September 28, 1862.

My dear Charlie,—Your first letter from 'foreign parts' has duly arrived this morning, and gives us great pleasure, as it contains nothing but satisfactory news. I had only one fault to find with it, namely, that it was not *dated*, which, as your mamma is sure to keep all your letters most preciously (and if she did not I might, perhaps, have that weakness myself), would render the chronological order most difficult to preserve if persevered in; therefore you are herewith requested to put the proper day of the month in all future letters, and --the next time you *leave off* writing, you might, perhaps, spell 'off' with a double f, if Mrs. Appell supplies you with sufficient ink. There! We arrived here all safe and sound at about a quarter to eleven on Friday evening, and found the house in excellent order; my room looks exceedingly well, and more comfortable than ever. We have all got over the fatigue now, but to-day there are great lamentations in the house, as none of the boxes sent off from Cowes on Thursday have arrived yet, thanks to M., who had the bright idea of omitting the direction, so that the supply of clean linen, &c., has run awfully short, and the two boys are sporting the maids' collars, without which they could not have gone to church.

The fowls, chickens, and the dog are all quite well, and send compliments; the dog is really very nice and no 'beast,' but had very nearly come to a premature end yesterday. He is

so very lively that the boys thought they had better chain him
up, so they got a cord, made a running noose at one end and
put the poor dog's neck in it; of course, being so very lively,
he soon strangled himself most effectually, got into 'agonies,'
and began to foam at the mouth, upon which he was declared
mad. and I was just considering if I might not shoot him
with your peashooter, when Mrs. C.'s servant fortunately
found out the cause of the poor animal's behaviour, and at
once released him and us all from our anxiety. This is the
only event I have to relate from here to-day. . . .

Mamma is writing to you also, so that you will have enough
to read to-day; do not think that I am going to spoil you
often as I do now, but be sure that I expect to be spoiled,
and hope that you will write often and much.

God bless you, my dear boy. With love from us all,

Your loving father,

CHARLES HALLÉ.

XLVII

TO THE SAME

Greenheys: October 2, 1862.

My dear boy,—Your mamma tells me this minute (a quarter of an hour before post time) that nobody has written to you
to-day; I hasten, therefore, to send you a few lines, as otherwise you would be without news until Monday, to say that
we are all well. . . .

You have got fairly into harness now; try only to have
your lessons not too far off from your house; long distances
won't be pleasant at all during the winter.

What are you drawing now at the Museum? please let
me know, so that I may, in mind, see you at work. It appears
that Chappell will want me at the end of this month already,
so that I shall soon have a look at you and at your work, for
you must take me to the Museum whenever I come.

Your long letters make us all very happy; continue to
write as much as you can, you will prevent many 'agonies.'

Yesterday evening the children gave me a party in the schoolroom, which I like so much. . . .

Your affectionate father,

CH. HALLÉ.

XLVIII

TO HIS WIFE

Londres: 26 mars 1863.

J'arrive à l'instant (dix heures du soir) de Windsor et je vais te raconter ma journée avant de me coucher. J'y suis arrivé à deux heures ; Ruland avait fait préparer un excellent luncheon dans sa chambre, pendant lequel il me disait que nous irions ensuite faire un peu de musique en haut dans la salle de Rubens (où il y avait deux pianos) et que peut-être nous aurions la visite de la Princesse de Wales, qui savait depuis deux jours par Lady Augusta Bruce que je devais venir aujourd'hui. Un peu après trois heures nous sommes montés et avons commencé à jouer à quatre mains ; au bout d'une demi-heure un domestique est venu porter une petite lettre de Lady A. Bruce à Ruland, dans laquelle elle lui disait que les députations du Lord Mayor, etc., etc. étaient arrivées si tard que cela mettait fin au projet de la Princesse de venir nous entendre. J'étais naturellement contrarié, mais cependant content de ce que la Princesse s'était occupée de moi. Après un autre quart d'heure Lady Augusta Bruce est venue elle-même, et s'est montrée la gracieuseté même ; c'est une bien aimable dame, aimant la musique passionnément ; j'ai dû lui jouer une sonate de Schubert, une de Beethoven, et Dieu sait combien de petits morceaux de Bach, Mendelssohn, Heller, etc. Elle ne nous a quittés qu'à six heures passées, et alors nous sommes redescendus chez Ruland. A peine installés dans sa chambre, un domestique est venu avec l'agréable annonce : 'The Prince and Princess of Wales wish to see Mr. Hallé.' Nous sommes montés alors en toute hâte dans les appartements privés (Ruland pour me présenter), et pendant que nous attendions devant la porte que le domestique nous annonce, la Princesse Alice, avec le Prince Louis, qu'on avait évidemment fait chercher aussi, nous ont passé pour entrer chez le Prince. La Princesse Alice s'est arrêtée et m'a serré les mains d'une manière bien affectueuse, en me disant qu'il y avait si longtemps qu'elle ne m'avait vu.   Un moment après nous les avons suivi, et le Prince de Wales, après m'avoir donné un *shake-hand* cordial, m'a présenté à sa femme, de la beauté et de la grâce de laquelle on ne peut se faire aucune idée par les photographies. Il n'y avait là que le Prince et la Princesse de Wales, la Princesse Alice et le Prince Louis, Ruland et moi, et j'y suis resté jusqu'à sept heures et demie, tantôt faisant de la musique, tantôt causant de la manière la plus familière et la plus agréable de toute espèce de sujets. Pendant la conversation le Prince de Wales m'a prié de lui acheter trois pianos, deux grands, les meilleurs que je puisse trouver, pour sa maison, 'un pour en bas, et l'autre pour en haut,' comme il me disait, et le troisième un petit en 'maple wood and green silk,' dont il veut faire cadeau à la Princesse Alice. Quand enfin on nous a congédiés, il a rappelé Ruland au moment où je sortais de la porte, pour lui demander si je viendrais à Londres pendant quelque temps cette saison, et quand Ruland lui a dit que j'y étais déjà et que j'y resterais il a répondu : ' Ah, j'en suis bien content.' Il me semble donc évident que la Princesse me demandera de lui donner des leçons ou que le Prince a quelques intentions sur moi, car jamais il ne m'aurait demandé de lui acheter trois pianos si cela devait en rester là, et la remarque à Ruland disait clairement qu'il aura besoin de moi. Ruland et Becker sont tous deux de la même opinion et bien contents, je t'assure. Je suis plus avancé que Becker maintenant, car il n'a pas encore parlé à la Princesse de Wales, tandis que j'ai été assis à côté d'elle pendant une heure. La journée n'a donc pas été perdue ; puisse le récit te faire quelque plaisir.'

[Translation]

London : March 26, 1863.

I have at this moment (10 p.m.) arrived from Windsor, and I will relate my adventures before going to bed. I arrived there at two o'clock ; Ruland had an excellent luncheon ready in his room, during which he told me that

XLIX

TO THE SAME

Darmstadt : mercredi matin,
8 sept. 1863.

Nous sommes toujours avec ce bon Becker ; il avait tellement compté sur une longue visite qu'il a été vraiment im-

we should go up to the Rubens room afterwards (where there are two pianos) to make a little music, and that we should perhaps receive a visit from the Princess of Wales, who had known for the last two days, through Lady Augusta Bruce, that I was expected to-day. A little after three o'clock we went upstairs and began to play duets. Presently a servant came in with a little note from Lady A. Bruce to Ruland, to tell him that the Lord Mayor's deputation, &c., &c., had arrived so late that they had put an end to the Princess's intention of coming to hear us. I was naturally a little disappointed, and yet pleased that the Princess had thought of me. After another quarter of an hour Lady Augusta Bruce came in and was graciousness itself; she is a very amiable lady, passionately fond of music. I had to play a sonata of Schubert's, one of Beethoven's, and heaven knows how many little pieces by Bach, Mendelssohn, Heller, &c. She only left us at past six o'clock, and then we went back to Ruland's room. We were hardly there when a servant came in with the agreeable message ; 'The Prince and Princess of Wales wish to see Mr. Hallé.' We went in all haste to the private apartments (Ruland to present me), and as we were waiting at the door to be announced, Princess Alice and Prince Louis, who had evidently also been sent for, passed us to go into the Prince's room. Princess Alice stopped and shook hands with me very affectionately, saying it was a very long time since she had last seen me. A moment later, we followed her in, and the Prince of Wales, after shaking hands cordially, presented me to his wife, of whose beauty and grace the photographs give no idea. There was no one present but the Prince and Princess of Wales, Princess Alice and Prince Louis, Ruland and I, and I stayed until half-past seven o'clock, either making music, or joining in familiar and most agreeable conversation upon all manner of subjects. The Prince of Wales asked me to buy him three pianos, two grands, the best that I could find, for his house, ' one for downstairs, and the other for upstairs,' as he said, and the third, a cottage piano in ' maple wood and green silk,' which he means to give to Princess Alice. When at last we were dismissed he called Ruland back, just as I was going out, to ask him if was going to London this season for any length of time, and when Ruland told him I was there already and meant to stay, he said : ' Ah, I am very glad.' It seems evident, therefore, that the Princess means to ask me to give her lessons, or that the Prince has some intentions concerning me, or he would never have asked me to buy him three pianos. Ruland and Becker are of the same opinion, and greatly pleased, I assure you. I am further advanced than Becker, for he has not yet spoken to the Princess of

possible de le laisser déjà, et la Princesse a, de son côté, rendu notre départ impossible jusqu'ici. Lundi matin, après avoir expédié ma lettre, elle m'a fait dire qu'elle reviendrait de Francfort à quatre heures et espérait me voir de suite à Kranich-stein, le château qu'elle habite pendant l'été, à une distance de deux milles à peu près de Darmstadt. Nous y sommes allés, Becker, C., et moi, mais Becker devait retourner en ville et C. s'est fait promener dans le magnifique parc par notre fiacre pendant le temps de ma visite. La Princesse a été on ne peut plus aimable et m'a gardé jusqu'à près de sept heures, elle a fait chercher son *Baby* pour me le montrer, nous avons fait beaucoup de musique ensemble ; le Prince Louis est venu nous écouter en fumant son cigare *dans le salon*, et avant de la quitter elle m'a dit que comme le lendemain elle avait la visite de la Reine, elle comptait me voir mercredi (aujourd'hui) pendant d'autant plus de temps, et hier elle m'a fait dire d'être chez elle à deux heures aujourd'hui. La Reine et la Princesse Hélène sont venues hier avec elle en ville, pour voir son petit palais et celui qu'elle fait bâtir ; pour aller au premier elles passaient la maison de Becker, en voitures découvertes ; C. et moi nous étions à une fenêtre du rez-de-chaussée et toutes les trois nous ont envoyé les saluts les plus aimables, la Reine se retournant plusieurs fois quand elles avaient passé déjà. Elle a de suite dit à Becker, qui les attendait au palais, qu'elle m'avait vu ainsi que sa mère.[1] . . .

Wales, whereas I have sat beside her for an hour. So my day was not wasted ; may this account of it give you pleasure.

[1]

[*Translation*]

Darmstadt : Wednesday morning,

September 8, 1863.

We are still with our good Becker ; he had so counted on a long visit that it was impossible to leave him sooner, and the Princess has also made our departure impossible until now. On Monday morning, after I had despatched my letter, she sent me word that she would come back from Frankfort at four o'clock, and hoped to see me afterwards at Kranich-stein, the castle she inhabits during the summer, about two miles from Darmstadt. Becker, C. and I went there together, but Becker had to go back to the town, and C. drove about the magnificent park during my visit. The Princess was most amiable and kept me till near seven o'clock. She sent for her baby, to show him to me. We made much music together ;

L

TO THE SAME

Hagen : 13 septembre 1863.

Hier matin, à dix heures, nous sommes arrivés en bonne santé chez ma mère et nous l'avons trouvée, Dieu merci, bien portante. . . . Tante Altgelt avec tante Koch n'ont pas tardé à venir nous voir. Tu peux te figurer leur joie en voyant C. Tante Altgelt est toujours la même, elle n'a changé en rien et est aussi active et forte qu'elle était il y a vingt ans, et bonne, comme tu le sais; c'est vraiment une femme merveilleuse.

Après dîner j'ai fait avec C. une promenade, accompagné du fidèle Cornélius, qui a engraissé d'une manière prodigieuse ; nous sommes montés d'abord sur le Goldberg et C. a été émerveillé de la beauté de la vue, et du charme de ce cher et paisible Hagen ; puis nous sommes descendus, et je lui ai montré la maison et la chambre dans laquelle je suis né, l'école dans laquelle j'ai été élevé, l'église dans laquelle j'ai fait ma première communion, la maison de notre bon pasteur Zimmermann, les différentes maisons que nous avons successivement habitées, la maison de Cornélius et la chambre dans laquelle nos pauvres pères, Cornélius et moi, nous attendions tous les dimanches l'heure de l'église, la salle où j'ai joué pour la première fois en public, et ensuite tous ces chers endroits où nos jeux d'enfance se passaient, et que je porte tous dans mon cœur ; où nous faisions, Cornélius et moi, nos Robinsonades, où nous cherchions des papillons, où nous herborisions lorsque la passion de la botanique nous avait

Prince Louis came to listen, smoking his cigar *in the drawing-room*, and before I left she told me that as she expected a visit from the Queen next day, she would hope to see me again on Wednesday (to-day) for a longer time, and she sent me word yesterday to go to her at two o'clock to-day. The Queen and Princess Helena came with her to town yesterday, to see her little palace and the new one she is building. On their way to the former they passed before Becker's house, in an open carriage. C. and I were at a window on the ground floor, and they all three bowed to us most amiably, the Queen turning round several times after they had gone by. She immediately told Becker, who was awaiting them at the palace, that she had seen me, and his mother as well. . . .

pris, où nous apprenions à connaître les étoiles, où nous
rêvions ensemble tant de choses, dont si peu se sont réalisées,
et où cette amitié d'enfance s'est formée qui ne pourra jamais
finir.   Ah, que ces souvenirs sont bons, et comme ils atten-
drissent le cœur—je sentirai longtemps l'effet de cette visite—
nous le sentirons tous—je n'ai eu qu'une pensée hier pendant
tout ce pèlerinage, pensée qui comprend tout, c'est que Dieu
veuille que mes enfants puissent un jour, en pensant à leur
père, sentir ce que j'ai senti hier, et ce que j'éprouve toujours
ici.   Je ne puis rien ajouter à cela.[1]

LI

FROM SIR WILLIAM FAIRBAIRN

[A great friend of both my parents was the venerable Sir
William Fairbairn, the eminent engineer.   He was a regular

[1]
[Translation]

Hagen, September 13, 1863.

We arrived here, in good health, at ten o'clock yesterday morning at
my mother's, and found her well, thank God . . . Aunt Altgelt, with Aunt
Koch, did not delay to come and see us. You can picture their delight at
seeing C. Aunt Altgelt is just the same, she has not changed in the least
and is as strong and active as she was twenty years ago, and good as you
know her to be; she is really a marvellous woman. After dinner I went
for a walk with C., accompanied by the faithful Cornelius, who has grown
prodigiously stout; we first went up the Goldberg, and C. was delighted
with the beauty of the view and with the charm of this dear, peaceful,
Hagen; then we came down, and I showed him the house and the room in
which I was born, the school where I was educated, the church in which I
made my first communion, the house of our good pastor, Zimmermann, the
different houses in which we had successively lived, the house of Cornelius
and the room in which our poor fathers, Cornelius and I, used on Sundays
to await the hour of service, the room in which I first played in public,
and then all the dear spots where we played our childish games, every one
of which I carry in my heart; where Cornelius and I played at Robinson
Crusoe, where we caught butterflies, where we collected plants when the
passion for botany had seized us, where we learnt to know the stars, where
we dreamt of so many things, so few of which have come to pass, and
where that friendship was formed which can never have an end. Ah, how
good are these memories, and how they stir one's heart! I shall long feel
the effects of this visit—we shall all feel them—I had but one thought
during all this pilgrimage, a thought that contains all things; it was that
God might grant that one day my children, in thinking of their father, may
feel as I felt yesterday, and as I always feel when I am here. I can add
nothing to that.

attendant at my father's concerts, and it was always a pleasure
to my mother when, from her box, she could see his beautiful
snow-white head towering above his fellows, as he entered the
Free Trade Hall accompanied by his gentle wife; greatly
pleased was she, therefore, to receive the following characteristic letter from her old friend the morning after one of
the great Thursday concerts.]

Manchester: December 2, 1863.

My dear Mme. Hallé,—There is an old saying that—

> Music hath charms to soothe the savage breast,
> To soften rocks.

In that I agree so far as regards the former, but I never knew
it make any impression upon the latter. One thing I however know, and that is that Mr. Hallé, in his intensity of
thought and his love of the sublime in sound, is the very
essence of harmony. In fact, he

> Floats upon sound, and rides upon its echo!

Such were my feelings the other evening as I watched his
motions. I perceived that every movement was in unison
with a volume of sound, that appeared to descend from the
heroic to die in strains of melody upon the ear.

Music is certainly an exquisite art, and the liquid tones
of the human voice, when in harmony with tuned instruments,
become the more sensitive as they recede from the sonorous
to the more subdued tones that affect the passions and touch
the heart. Even old as I am, I felt all these sensations, as I
allowed the music full and unrestricted scope during the
time I watched the movements of our able and exquisite
leader. On that occasion I gave full rein to my imagination,
at least so far as to fancy that I perceived the very notes
issue from his fingers, as he spread them abroad to the right
and left of the performers. There is magic in that wand
that he wields so tunefully, but there is more in the liquid
tones, as he so cleverly diffuses them over the heads of his

audience with the art and power of a magician!   Like an
old Scotch song :

> His very step has music in it,
> As he comes up the stairs!

So I think of the leader of Hallé's Concerts!
  Believe me, my dear Madam,

Yours faithfully,
W. FAIRBAIRN.

[The life of Sir William Fairbairn has been written, and
his achievements in his craft recorded, but the number of
those who have a personal recollection of the simplicity and
charm of this noble specimen of one of nature's truest gentlemen is getting smaller year by year.   Nothing was more
delightful than to hear him talk of his early days in Scotland,
and of his first arrival in Manchester as a young mechanic.
He told me once that his golden rule, and his advice to all
young men, had always been to ' work hard and spend little ';
that when he first got work in England his wages were
eighteen shillings a week, and he managed to live on sixteen
shillings; and so he had gone on through all the struggles of
his early life, always ' working hard and spending little.'

His memory carried him back to the very first years of
the century, and he remembered old customs of Scotland that
lingered in the country-places, and had a strange flavour of
antiquity and lawlessness about them.   Once, when a little
lad, he was driving cattle with his father, and stopped at a
remote wayside inn for refreshment.   The landlord poured
out the drink, and ere he set the glass before each guest
raised it to his own lips—a relic of the courtesy that required
the act as a proof that there was nothing harmful—neither
drug nor poison—in the cup!]

LII

FROM JOSEPH JOACHIM

(*Translated from the German*)

October 12, 1864 !

Dear Hallé,—Only a hasty greeting before I leave Dublin.
. . . Belfast, Hotel Royal. Since writing this, my dearest
friend, I have been through the whole South of Ireland, and
am to-day, October 12, at Belfast, where we remain till Saturday to give three concerts. Belletti has given me your
scolding! Had I been able to write as you wished, you would
have had news of me long since, but to say 'No' to your
renewed amiable offer was more difficult. When one is bound
by an engagement efforts are unavailing, and in spite of the
call of friendship, one must stay under the yoke. I console
myself with the belief that the time will come when I shall
be freer.

On my homeward journey I shall trust to see you, and to
spend a day with you and yours, if it can possibly be
managed, but I shall write of this from Dublin, where we
return on the 22nd (after Ballymena and Londonderry). As
to your proposal for March, I can say nothing so long beforehand. I must, before all, see how the winter at Hanover
suits me, but I shall certainly let you hear from me from
time to time during the winter, as I do not wish distance to
make us strangers, or that our *shake* in the Kreutzer Sonata
should chime together less precisely than before!

The wonderful scenery of Ireland and the delicious air
have refreshed and strengthened me. I have seldom seen
such rich beauties of nature; it would have delighted you also.

Jenny Lind's singing is unique. She is one 'by the
grace of God,' and a charming travelling companion into the
bargain. Pardon my hieroglyphics—thanks to a bad steel
pen. Certainly most difficult to decipher.

Your faithful and obliged   JOSEPH JOACHIM.

LIII

TO HIS WIFE

Mansfield Street : dimanche, avril 1866.

Tu as su par la lettre de Charlie hier, que mon portrait et celui de B. sont positivement reçus à l'Académie, ce qui me fait espérer que les autres le seront aussi, car la ' Beatrice' est certainement encore mieux peinte ; voilà donc notre bon garçon devant le public et lancé, et je ne doute pas de son succès ; que le bon Dieu le protège dans sa carrière—je sens comme si la mienne était finie maintenant, car je ne prends plus d'intérêt, et je ne pense plus, qu'à son succès.[1]

LIV

TO ONE OF HIS DAUGHTERS

Hagen : September 7, 1866.

My dear Slave,—And I am sadly afraid the appellation is but too true, and that my poor young thing has to work with brain and body like the blackest nigger that ever was, and I can only say in return that her old Pa is more grateful to her, especially for the ever cheerful way in which she does her work, than he can express.

You will all be glad to hear that I found grandmamma, on the whole, better than I ventured to hope. She certainly is somewhat changed, looks a little thinner and older, but nobody would take her to be seventy. It seems that from the moment she knew I was coming she brightened up wonderfully. I am therefore glad that I did come. They all say

---

[1]

[Translation]

Mansfield Street : Sunday, April, 1866.

You know by Charlie's letter of yesterday that my portrait and B.'s are positively accepted at the Academy, which makes me hope that the others will also be taken, as the ' Beatrice' is certainly even better painted ; so now our dear boy is before the public and fairly launched, and I have no doubt of his success. May the good God protect him in his career. I feel as if mine had come to an end now, for I take interest solely in, and think only of his success. . . .

here that this short visit will help her safely through the winter.

But now I had better relate all that has befallen me since I last wrote from London, for the little note from Calais contained very few words, and I do not even feel quite sure if you ever received it. On Tuesday evening the weather got so very bad in London, the rain falling in torrents and the wind blowing very hard, that I made up my mind not to cross that night, and preferred remaining in Mansfield Street and save the expense of the hotel at Dover, not, however, without having asked cook if she could undertake to call me at six o'clock, and have my breakfast ready at half-past six, as the train started at 7.25, both which she promised faithfully. In the morning when I awoke I thought there was rather too much daylight for six o'clock. I looked at my watch, and, to my horror, found that it wanted only eight minutes to seven. I jumped out of bed, I rang frantically and shouted ' Cook ! cook !' all over the house, and, after a while, heard a voice from the top of the house answering, ' Coming.' What could I do but dress in the most fearful hurry, without shaving, send her for a cab the moment she appeared, jump into it in a towering rage, jump into the train, which was just starting, reach Dover two hours later (the train stops at no stations), and find myself on board of the steamer, which even in port jumped up and down like mad, *without having had a morsel to eat or even a drop of water to drink?* What do you say to that ? And what I most regret is that I had not time even to scold cook and Anne as they deserved, neither of whom spoke a syllable.

The crossing was very rough, but as before getting under steam I had just time to eat a sandwich and drink a glass of brandy and water (the only drink they seemed to have), I felt more comfortable and kept well all the time, although we were more than two hours before reaching Calais. Louis Gassner[1] was on board, acting as courier to a newly-married young couple, who went to Switzerland on their wedding

---

[1] An old servant.

tour. The young husband suffered fearfully and was a sight
to behold, and as his young wife was quite well and could
nurse him, he must have felt rather ashamed, I dare say.
There was a whole school of young ladies on deck, about
eighteen in number, under the guidance of a stout, merry-
looking (at starting), old French schoolmistress. They were
all laughing and joking before the vessel moved, but, poor
things, how they dropped off one after the other, the mistress
setting the example, before we were ten minutes on our way;
not one of them escaped, and they were lying about in all
possible and impossible positions, and were rolled about by
the sailors like so many sacks. I borrowed a waterproof coat
from a sailor, in spite of which I got wet through, for as it
did not cover my head, and the waves came constantly down
upon that unlucky member, they gradually soaked my collar,
cravat, waistcoat, and, by degrees, I felt the wet creeping
down lower and lower, whilst at the other extremity we stood
always about ankle-deep in water. Fortunately, salt water
does not hurt; otherwise, my luggage being registered to
Cologne, and I therefore having to travel a whole day and
night in this wet state, it might have been the worse for me ;
as it is, I feel quite well and all right, but it was certainly
not *comfortable*.

It was about half-past five a.m. when I arrived at Cologne.
I went to the Hôtel du Nord, which is nearest to the station,
and was not sorry to get my wet clothes off and to go to bed
for a few hours. I left again at 11.20 for Hagen, after having
sent a telegram to my good mother to announce my arrival,
which telegram we are still anxiously awaiting. I hope it
will come before I leave again. At the station I got into the
midst of a regiment of 'Landwehr' (militia), returning to
their homes from the late war, and such a row I never heard
before ; such singing, such shouting—I believe I am half
deaf still. They seemed to have been at the station, which
was cram full, for a long time already, as they were in full
song, and there, and afterwards in their carriages till Düsseldorf, where I left them, they repeated incessantly the follow-

ing spirited and patriotic lines, singing them well, too, and
with proper emphasis :

> Die Landwehr hat Ruh,
> Die Landwehr hat Ruh ;
> Und wenn die Landwehr Ruhe hat,
> So hat die Landwehr Ruh !

(I append a literal translation for those that might miss
the point otherwise):

> The Landwehr has rest,
> The Landwehr has rest ;
> And when the Landwehr *has* rest,
> Then *has* the Landwehr rest !

Undeniable, and logic and patriotic sentiments equally
sound. Who can wonder now that the Austrians have been
beaten by a people capable of such efforts in poetry? It
took a long time to get those noisy warriors into their
carriages, but then, when the platform was comparatively
empty, there was one little incident which I shall not easily
forget. Three poor peasant women, dressed in decent black,
went slowly along the train, arm in arm, the middle one
crying and seemingly supported by the two others, but all
three with such sad faces, and looked once more into every
carriage, as if they still hoped it might not be true, and they
might discover their lost one, for whom they were already in
mourning, in some corner.

At Düsseldorf the regular troops were also expected to
make their entry that day on their return, and the whole
town seemed to be one huge flag and wreath ; every house
was covered with all sorts of garlands, flowers, and flags, the
Prussian one always at the top; all the people were in the
street, and altogether it was a most exciting scene. Between
Düsseldorf and Hagen I passed a train which contained a
regiment of cavalry with some guns, the engine and every
waggon being also decorated with flags and wreaths, and
such shouting from our train to theirs, and such answering !

This was the last incident worth relating ; at the station

I found Clara, who had been since the day before at every train to look for me; she brought me to my mother, and what our meeting was you can imagine without my telling you anything about it.[1]

The soldier Koch has not returned yet, but he has been made lieutenant on the battlefield, and as for harrowing details, I have got so many already that they will take me a good long time to tell you *viva voce*. For to-day I think I have written enough, and will therefore end by telling you how happy I was to have such good accounts of you all. . . . Give my best love to all round, Canon Toole included, and kiss all the little ones for me. I continually pray, as dear mamma used to do, that God may keep you from all dangers, illness, and accidents! Your loving father,

CHARLES HALLÉ.

LV

TO ONE OF HIS DAUGHTERS

Hagen: Sunday morning,
September 9, 1866.

My dear L.— . . . There is nothing talked of here but the war; and it certainly is very interesting to see real accounts from the battlefield in the letters from the soldiers themselves; harrowing details I have got in plenty; enough to satisfy M., and I shall relate them faithfully on my return. I shall also bring a lot of local newspapers, in which many of the soldiers' letters I spoke of are printed. It is now proposed that to celebrate the peace, on a given night, a huge bonfire shall be lighted on the top of every mountain in all Prussia; which would certainly be a fine sight if one were in a balloon; they will soon set the whole world in a blaze.

Soldiers pass through here every day, and people come miles and miles to see them for a second and shout themselves hoarse. At Düsseldorf the other day an immense hotel near the station was really very fine to behold; you know what a lot of windows these hotels muster; in this

---

[1] This was my father's first visit to Hagen after the death of my mother.

case every window had a small balcony entirely covered with
flowers and leaves, and in every corner of which there was
a tiny Prussian flag, something like this:

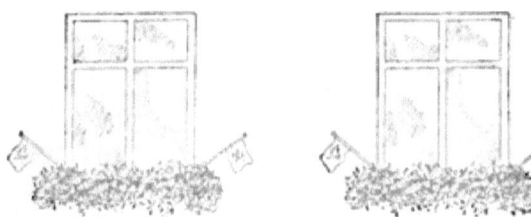

imagine more than a hundred windows like this, but you can
have no idea how pretty it looked.

I must tell you that from Düsseldorf to Elberfeld I helped
an old, kind-looking lady into the same carriage with me;
soon after starting I saw her busy at work trying to open
the window, which proved a very stiff one; so I got up,
crossed over to her side, and opened it for her, upon which
she said: 'danke, danke, schönstens, es ist sehr warm,' and
then struck by a sudden idea, and smiling most benignly,
she repeated several times with great emphasis: 'mooch,
mooch, mooch,' so, to please her, I answered 'very mooch,'
and then our conversation dropped, the old lady being evidently much pleased with the display of her English.

Hagen has wonderfully changed since we were here, new
streets and new houses have sprung up on all sides; there
are many changes in the people too, and the number of my
old friends keeps diminishing steadily; soon there will be
none left, and very sad it is. . . .

With best love to you all in general, and to your own
little self in particular, I remain your affectionate father,

CH. HALLÉ.

LVI

TO ONE OF HIS DAUGHTERS

Hagen: Monday, September 10, 1866.

To-morrow I am going to take grandmamma and Aunt
Anna, Aunt Altgelt, Aunt Koch, and Clara on an excursion

to Altena, the birthplace of my mamma, and which none of them have seen for twenty-nine years : therefore as we start at half-past seven in the morning, and shall probably not be back before seven in the evening, I write a few lines to-day, which, if I leave on Wednesday, will be the last you will receive—from here at least.

We go by train to-morrow, the distance being about twenty miles, and I cannot tell you how happy they all seem at the idea of seeing once more the place where they were so happy in their childhood. I hope the weather will be fine. To-day it is so-so ; not raining, but threatening.

We spent the afternoon and evening yesterday at the Kochs, and very pleasant it was. I shall bring you some very fine old Dutch china, which has been in our family at least a hundred years, and is, I think, very valuable : a big milkpot, a coffeepot, a sugar-basin, tea-canister, three cups, but only one saucer. The packing will be the awkward thing, but I hope I shall bring it all safe.

The soldier Koch is at Hanover now with his regiment, and is likely to be kept there for some months more. He wrote yesterday, and gives very bad accounts of the reception they have met with in Hanover ; the ladies turning their backs upon them when they meet them in the streets, and altogether they seem to be treated as enemies, and feel very uncomfortable, so it is not all quite serene. . . .

Good-bye, my dear M. Sunday I shall be with you in any case. Is it not very strange that, although I am very happy to be with grandmamma, I should be so impatient to find myself again in the midst of my dear— rascals ? A thousand greetings from all here, as usual.

LVII

TO ONE OF HIS SONS

Springkell : September 20, 1866.

My dear G.—Cheer up, old boy ! The time will soon pass away, and Christmas will be there before you think of it.

And now let me tell you that I am very glad indeed that

you write so frankly all you feel about the school. By all
means continue to do so; it makes me very comfortable;
although, of course, I am very sorry that you should both feel
so unhappy, you are quite right to tell us all your likes and
dislikes. . . . You are equally right in wishing to give it a
fair trial, for sometimes first impressions are wrong and do
not last, and suddenly to be thrown amongst entire strangers
is never pleasant. I remember the doleful letters I wrote
when I first was sent to Paris, and how some years later I
thought I could live nowhere else.

Ask B. to keep his temper for his dear mamma's and my
own sake, and to be cheerful when the boys tease him. A
good laugh will disarm them, and then they will soon leave
him alone or be friends with him ; and among so many boys
there must be a few nice ones, which undoubtedly you will
soon find out. For the present devote all your energies
to learning ; try to do that well, so that if you go back to
the other school you may have gained upon the other boys.

Now do as I have often done in similar cases, and think
of stages by which you can see how quickly the time flies.
The first stage may be our return to Manchester—that will
bring you nearer Christmas ; then comes my first concert,
and so on. Never look to the most distant time, but always
to one of these intermediate stages, and the time will seem
much less long. . . .

And now, my dear boy, or rather my dear boys, I end as
I began with—Cheer up ! There are many hard things in this
world which we must bear like men, but in your case it will
only be for a very short time if it does not mend, and that
ought to be a comfort.

LVIII

FROM STEPHEN HELLER

Paris: 18 oct. 1866,
54 Rue N.-D. de Lorette.

Mon cher Hallé,— . . . Je suis resté à Paris, Berlioz
aussi ; le reste s'est envolé à tire d'aile, qui en Suisse, qui

aux bords de la mer. Berlioz est aussi bien souffrant, bien plus que moi. Il est tout cassé, usé, et ne fait que geindre, le pauvre homme. A peine qu'on reconnait l'ancien Hector, si fringant, si batailleur, pourfendant ses adversaires, et quelquefois les ailes de moulin.

Je termine, et t'envoie mes plus sincères amitiés, qui ne se sont jamais affaiblies. Tel que j'ai été, je suis et je serai toujours. Ton   STEPHEN HELLER.

Mes amitiés à tes enfans et à Henry Broadwood.[1]

LIX

TO ONE OF HIS DAUGHTERS

Osborne : December 28, 1866.

I will only report shortly the events of the day, as Sahl promises that you will receive this letter on Sunday morning; there is no chance of your getting one to-morrow. I got to London at six in the morning, having slept a few hours in the railway carriage between Crewe and Rugby, and reached Cowes about a quarter past three, where I found the excellent Sahl at the landing place (East Cowes) waiting for me. He took me at once to Osborne, where I am still; on the way we met the Queen driving with Princess Helena, who both bowed and smiled most graciously. At Osborne I found an excellent luncheon prepared for me in Sahl's room, saw Sir John Cowell who manages the household, and was informed by him that I was to have General Grey's apartments (not in the Palace, thank Heaven, but in the first

[1]
[*Translation*]

Paris : October 18, 1866,
54 Rue N.-D. de Lorette.

My dear Hallé,— . . . I have stayed behind in Paris, Berlioz also; the rest have taken wing, some for Switzerland, some for the seaside. Berlioz is very ill, far worse than I am. He is broken, used up, and does nothing but lament, poor man. One can hardly recognise the old Hector, so fiery, so warlike, cleaving his enemies, and sometimes charging at windmills.

Thus I end, and send you the expression of a sincere friendship that has never faltered. What I have been, that I am, and shall ever be, your
STEPHEN HELLER.

My remembrances to your children and to Henry Broadwood.

house near the big gate); everybody was very polite, and at
five o'clock I received the message that the Queen wished to
see me at half-past five. I had, therefore, to go to her
just as I was, there being no time to go back to General
Grey's house; fortunately Sahl lent me a clean collar, mine
being rather dirty from travelling. At half-past five I was
ushered into a small boudoir, and after a minute the Queen,
Princesses Helena, Louise, and Beatrice, and Prince Leopold
came in, were also awfully kind and polite, made me play
lots of things, and kept me till seven o'clock. The thing
was extremely interesting and agreeable, but I shall tell you
all about it on my return. Sahl had ordered dinner for us
two in his room, in order to avoid dressing, but to-morrow I
shall have to breakfast, &c., with the household. Between
luncheon and the visit to the Queen Prince Leopold came to
fetch me to his room, where we were as jolly as two larks.
I must add that there was not a single attendant with the
Royalties all the time I was with them, which made it all
the more pleasant. What is going to happen to-morrow I
do not know, except that breakfast is at half-past nine.

LX

TO ONE OF HIS DAUGHTERS

Osborne : December 29, 1866.

My dear L.—You have written me such a nice letter,
which I received by the second post this evening, that I
think it is only proper I should answer it as soon as possible,
especially as you want so much news. I have given M. an
account of yesterday, so I may go on with to-day's events.
Between breakfast and luncheon, after I had written a few
letters in order to substitute the ' Elijah' for 'Iphigenia' on the
10th, Sahl and I went out for a walk as far as West Cowes,
stepped on board the Queen's yacht for a few minutes, and
had a look at the American yachts, which are rather ugly.

We returned to Osborne just in time for luncheon ; the
party at meals consists of the Duchess of Athole, Lady

Caroline Barrington, Lady Susan Melville, Miss Cavendish,
Sir Thomas Biddulph, Sir John Cowell, General Seymour,
Baron v. Schroeter, Mr. Lake, Dr. Sahl, and myself; the
eating is good, and the company very cheerful and not at all
stiff, and, like well-bred people, they all make a point of
being very polite to me.

After luncheon, Sahl being busy, I went with Baron
v. Schroeter (who has the little Prussian [1] prince in charge)
down to the shore in the grounds to have another look at
the American yachts, which came there that the Queen
might have a look at them, and to salute her. The Queen,
with a large party, was also at the water's edge, but we, of
course, kept aloof. At half-past four o'clock we turned in
again, at five your letter came, and I had just opened the
envelope when I was called to the Queen; I saw her, with
all her children, in the same room as yesterday, and remained
till about half-past six o'clock; nothing could be pleasanter,
except that I had rather too much to play. Once more in
Sahl's room I took your letter out of my pocket to read it,
when a message came from Princess Helena, or rather
Princess Christian, as she is now called, if I would be kind
enough to come and see her in her room. So off I trotted
again, and after a little chat she asked if I would play a few
duets with her, or if I was too tired? Of course we set to
work again, and it was five minutes to eight when she gave
me leave to go; there was just time to dress, and your letter
had actually to wait till after dinner before I could at last
read it. The Queen takes most kindly to music; she has
suggested many of the pieces I played, and now I am no
longer anxious about the choice, but may play just what
suits me.

Altogether this is an extraordinary visit, but when shall
I get away from here? there is the rub; the Queen speaks,
and Princess Helena speaks as if I were going to stop here
for ever, and as for little Prince Leopold, he has got such an
affection for me, that he follows me about the house from

[1] The present German Emperor.

Sahl's room to Lake's room, and takes me off to his own whenever he has a chance. The little Prussian is a lovely boy and very droll; we had a grand scene with him in the Queen's room this evening; he came in just when I was about going away, and the Queen wanted him to make me a bow ; he was too shy and resisted, so she asked him what his mamma would say if she heard he was so impolite, but this had no effect; she, however, insisted upon it, so at last he looked at her and said: 'No, I won't.' And then it became a hard struggle between them until he gave in, drew himself up, and made me a deep bow. It was a charming scene, the Princesses and Prince Leopold laughing most heartily. But I really must go to bed. I hope to-morrow to be able to say when I shall be back ; in the meantime a thousand kisses to all of you from your loving father,

CH. HALLÉ.

LXI

TO HIS ELDEST DAUGHTER

December 30, 1866.

I have no idea if this will reach you to-morrow, but I hope so, that I may at least tell you before the end of the old year, that I shall begin the new one in spirit with you all, although for the first time I shall be away from you all, and not hear your dear voices wish me happiness. Arrangements have already been made for me to play again to the Queen in the afternoon and in the evening in the drawing-room, and I cannot upset them. On Tuesday, however, I shall be off and reach you most probably by the night mail, as I shall have something to do in London on account of all these concert changes.

This day has of course been a quiet one ; there is no music going on here on Sundays, and I have only seen Prince Leopold of the Royal Family ; I do not know yet, however, what may happen in the evening.

At three o'clock this afternoon the owners of the American yachts came up to Osborne to be shown over the place.

One of them, Bennett, is a fine young man, a real giant; the others are precious ugly. I do not think that they were received by the Queen, but I went out for a walk with Baron von Schroeter and Sahl, so do not know. I have not a bit of news to give you, but enclose the monogram of Princess Helena for the boys, the other side being at the same time an autograph.

I hope you will make some punch, and good punch too, for all of you to-morrow evening, and kiss all the children, big and little, for me, and also that you will drink my health as I shall drink yours if I get a chance.

LXII

TO THE SAME

December 31, 1866.

I am not to leave Osborne before Wednesday morning, the Queen wishing to see me again this afternoon at half-past five o'clock, to spend the evening with the Duchess of Athole and the other ladies (perhaps the Princesses), and to play to her, for the last time, to-morrow evening after dinner instead of this evening.

So I cannot be at the rehearsal on Wednesday evening, and this makes me as busy as a bee, writing to D. and arranging matters. . . . I shall now arrive on Wednesday night between two and three o'clock, and reserve all further news till then; this is a visit which the Queen is sure not to forget, and it will keep me in her good graces for ever.

LXIII

FROM STEPHEN HELLER

Paris: 17 avril 1867,
54 Rue N.-D. de Lorette.

Mon cher Hallé.—Tu es dans une déplorable erreur si tu crois que je te dois une lettre. Non pas que cette dette, si elle existait, me coûterait d'acquitter; au contraire; mais c'est qu'il y a différence du tout au tout: c'est toi qui depuis plusieurs mois me dois une lettre, que je t'ai écrite vers la fin de l'an passé. J'y ai parlé de mes dernières publications, et j'ai exprimé le désir d'en avoir ton opinion.

J'ai reçu la visite de l'étonnant animal que tu m'as recommandé.[1] Il a gambadé sur un seul pied, il a baragouiné avec lui seul dans une langue, qui m'a donné la certitude que les différents sons et cris des animaux représentent des mots, qu'ils comprennent entre eux. Lorsque cette incompréhensible créature se mettait tout à coup à jouer la sonate en ut dièse mineur, j'avais l'impression comme si je me trouvais devant le Palais des singes du Jardin des Plantes, et que je voyais tout à coup un de ces horribles habitants descendre d'un barreau, auquel il était suspendu par la queue, et se mettre à un piano pour y jouer du Beethoven.

J'ai aussi éprouvé sa mémoire. Il a pataugé, et même il a mis du sien, de façon à me faire croire qu'il sait plus qu'il n'en a l'air, mais il avait en effet assez retenu pour me surprendre. Il est évident qu'il y a là une aptitude extraordinaire. Mais, après tout, je ne puis, avec la meilleure volonté, m'y intéresser beaucoup. Je ne sais si je me trompe, mais je crains que son *cornac* le maltraite et joue le tuteur tendre devant le monde. C'est un chef de saltimbanques, beaucoup moins gai que Bilboquet, qui me donne sur les nerfs. Trouves-tu ces gambades, et tout ce manège d'idiot, de possédé, naturel? Depuis Barnum j'ai une extrême défiance contre les merveilles américaines. Ce qui est sûr c'est la faculté musicale de ce malheureux. Avec toute ta lettre je ne sais rien de particulier sur toi. Tu es devenu tellement occupé et affairé qu'on ne parvient plus jusqu'à toi. Cependant ce n'est pas mon intérêt qui t'a jamais manqué. Il est vif et sincère.

Quant à moi, je ne me ferais pas prier pour écrire souvent et longuement, mais les encouragements m'ont manqué. Il est vrai que je n'ai rien que du temps ('er hat nichts als Zeit'), comme dit Jean Paul dans les 'Flügeljahre,' et que toi, tu as toutes sortes de choses, excepté du temps.

---

[1] A half-witted negro youth, known as 'Blind Tom,' possessed of remarkable musical gifts.

Je t'excuse et—j'en gémis.

Adieu ; portes-toi bien, dis mes amitiés à ta famille et crois à l'inaltérable amitié de ton vieux

STEPHEN HELLER.[1]

[1]

[*Translation*]

Paris : April 17, 1867,
54 Rue N.-D. de Lorette.

My dear Hallé,—You are making a deplorable error if you think that I owe you a letter. Not that the debt, if it existed, would cost me anything to pay ; on the contrary ; but the truth of the matter is that you owe me the answer to a letter I wrote you towards the end of last year. I spoke in it of my last publications and expressed the wish to have your opinion of them.

I have had a visit from the extraordinary animal you sent me. He gambolled on one leg, he talked to himself in a jargon, that made me feel certain that the various sounds and cries of the lower animals represent words, which they understand among themselves. When this incomprehensible creature suddenly began to play the sonata in C sharp minor, I had an impression as if, when in front of the monkey-house at the Jardin des Plantes, I had seen one of its horrid inhabitants suddenly descend from the bar where he had been swinging by his tail, and sit down to a piano to play Beethoven.

I also tried his memory. He floundered, and even put in something of his own, in such a way as to lead me to think that he knows more than he seems to do, but still he had remembered enough to surprise me. It is evident that his aptitude is extraordinary. But, after all, with the best good-will, I cannot interest myself much in him. I do not know if I am mistaken, but I am afraid that his keeper ill-treats him and plays the tender guardian before company. He seems a master-acrobat, far less cheerful than Bilboquet, and acts upon my nerves. Do you believe those gambols, all that idiot and demoniac business to be natural? Ever since Barnum I have had an extreme distrust of these American marvels. One thing is certain, the poor wretch's musical faculty. After reading all your letter I know very little about yourself. You have become so busy and so much occupied that one can no longer get at you. It is not my interest in you that has ever failed. It is lively and sincere.

As for me, I should have needed no entreaties to write often and at length, but I met with no encouragement. It is true that I have nothing but time (er hat nichts als Zeit), as Jean Paul says in his 'Flügeljahre,' and you, you have all sorts of things, except time.

I excuse you—and I suffer from it.

Adieu, keep well, remember me to your family and believe in the unalterable friendship of your old   STEPHEN HELLER.

LXIV

FROM ROBERT BROWNING

19 Warwick Crescent,
Upper Westbourne Terrace, W.: May 14, 1867.

My dear Hallé,—All thanks for your invitation, which I shall profit by if I possibly can.

I want to explain to you why in all probability I shall be away from your music [1] for once; it is foolish, I know. My son goes to college at Michaelmas and has to work so hard in order to matriculate at Balliol, where he wants to go, that he *cannot* spare even one morning a week, and I have got so used to have him with me that I can't bear sitting alone. Next year, if all goes well with us both, I shall assuredly do the nearly one thing I thoroughly enjoy now. Ever yours truly,
ROBERT BROWNING.

LXV

FROM STEPHEN HELLER

Paris: 3 décembre 1871.

Mon cher Hallé,—Ta lettre m'a fait bien plaisir, et tu m'as rendu un signalé service en me mettant en relations avec un éditeur honnête homme, *rara avis.* . . .

La Sonate de Wagner est idiote. On est d'autant plus étonné de la transformation immense de cet homme. Quand peut-il avoir écrit cette épicerie? On dirait qu'il n'avait alors connu, je ne dirais pas Beethoven, mais pas même une sonate de Hummel, Dussek, voire même Kalkbrenner, qui a donné de jolis spécimens dans ce genre. Ce dernier au moins connaissait son piano.

Quand on sort d'une belle représentation d'un opéra, ou d'une exécution parfaite d'une symphonie, on aime à s'en remémorer le plaisir, en parcourant la partition au piano. C'est ainsi que j'ai fait après t'avoir entendu jouer la Nocturne et la Barcarolle de Chopin. Je n'avais pas jugé ces deux ouvrages à leur valeur. Je les avais entendu rarement, et

[1] My father's Pianoforte Recitals at St. James's Hall.

incomplètement, et je n'ai pas été tenté de les lire moi-même, étant effrayé des difficultés qu'elles présentent.

Ton exécution véritablement incomparable a complètement modifié mon opinion. Interprétés de cette façon on reconnaît leur grand mérite, leur grande valeur ; ils sont dignes de Chopin. C'est pour la centième fois que je me suis désolé sur les conditions désastreuses des œuvres de musique.

Elles restent à l'état de lettre morte, si elles ne trouvent un grand artiste de bonne volonté qui se charge de les faire comprendre et aimer.

Le peintre n'a pas besoin d'interprète. Un cadre et de la lumière lui suffisent.

D'après ta lettre tu es en ce moment par monts et par vaux. Ne travaille pas trop, ne deviens pas trop riche et tâche de donner de temps à temps à ton meilleur ami un dimanche comme le dernier à Paris. Ton vieux

STEPHEN HELLER.[1]

[1]

[*Translation*]

Paris : December 3, 1874.

My dear Hallé,—Your letter gave me great pleasure, and you have rendered me a signal service by introducing me to an honest publisher—*rara aris*. . . .

Wagner's sonata is idiotic. One is all the more astonished at the immense transformation of the man. When can he have written this sample of grocery ? One would say that when he wrote it he did not know, I will not say Beethoven, but even one sonata of Hummel's, Dussek's, or even Kalkbrenner's, who has given us some pretty specimens in this style. The latter, at any rate, knew the piano.

When one comes away from a fine performance of an opera, or the perfect execution of a symphony, one likes to recall the pleasure by going through the score on the piano. This I did after hearing you play Chopin's ' Nocturne ' and ' Barcarolle.' I had never judged these two works according to their value. I had rarely heard them, and incompletely, and I had never been tempted to read them myself, being frightened by the difficulties they present. Your truly incomparable execution entirely modified my opinion. So interpreted, one recognises their great merit, their great value ; they are worthy of Chopin. For the hundredth time I lamented over the disastrous position of works of music. They remain a dead-letter unless they can find a great artist of good-will, who takes upon himself the task of making them understood and liked.

The painter has no need of an interpreter. A frame and daylight are sufficient for him.

According to your letter you must be at this moment among valleys and

LXVI

Hagen: September 3, 1879.

. . . Charlie is indeed very lucky and I quite envy him, but the time to the beginning of October seems very short, and probably he will not be able to spare a day for Munich, but it might be useful to him, as I don't think he knows anything about the present German painters. If he goes I recommend him to look at one, 'Christ in the Temple' (the smaller one of two pictures of the same subject in the German part of the exhibition). He will thank me for having drawn his attention to it, for he will seldom in his life have enjoyed such a good laugh.

We had the Sedan anniversary yesterday, and I had to go to a supper at the 'Concordia' and to sit upon the same chair from half-past eight until half-past one o'clock—a somewhat dreary performance.

What has been the result of the Grosvenor exhibition this season? Has it been satisfactory?

LXVII

Copenhagen, Hotel d'Angleterre: April 8, 1880.

Dearest M.—Here I am; the day before yesterday I read, to my surprise, that the Princess of Wales was also on her way to Copenhagen, and I am very glad to be here just at the same time. To-day is the King's birthday, and the whole town in a state of uproar; I am to go to the palace to-morrow morning, and to play there at a matinée either on Sunday or Monday.

The town seems very fine, but the country from Korsör here is very ugly. I shall see Gade this afternoon, which will be a great pleasure.

mountains. Do not work too hard, do not become too rich, and try, from time to time, to give your best friend another Sunday like the last in Paris. Your old   STEPHEN HELLER.

At Hanover, I spent a most agreeable day with Hans von Bülow, who was charming, and I had a great success into the bargain. In the evening he, Bülow, gave a supper which must have cost him a year's salary (he is now in the service of the Duke of Meiningen).

LXVIII

TO THE SAME

Copenhagen : April 12.

I have been twice with the Queen and Princess, and yesterday afternoon played for two hours for them and the King; they are the most simple and pleasant people I have met with for a long time; the Princess, of course, being delighted with the joke of seeing me hand her letter to the Queen in her presence.

Gade also is most amiable; I see him daily, he trots me about, and to-day I am dining with him. On Thursday I shall be in Hagen, and I think I shall go from there to Louviers, unless I get letters which show me that I must get back to London at once. My love to everybody.

LXIX

TO THE SAME

Vienna : October 9, 1880.

Dearest M.—I cannot remember having ever spent more interesting days than these last few ones. Brahms is the most delightful and good-natured creature imaginable, and what a musician ! He knows everything, has everything in his library, and seems quite happy when he can talk about musical curiosities, or about works and certain points in works, which must interest every musician. We have dined together every day at the coffee house ('Der Igel') where Beethoven used to dine, spent a few hours afterwards in talk, met again in the evening and remained together till midnight.

Then I have made the acquaintance of Pohl, the author

of a most remarkable biography of Haydn, and keeper of
the musical archives here; he is a charming, warm-hearted
man, and has shown me all his treasures, autographs without
number, and such interesting ones! MS. scores of Beethoven's,
Mozart's, Haydn's, Bach's Symphonies, Concertos, unpublished works even; it would have been worth my while
to remain months in those rooms.

Nottebohm is another remarkable man and writer on
musical matters, who is in possession of the most curious
MS. sketches of Beethoven's sonatas, which have helped me
to decide several doubtful passages in some of them, about
which I have often quarrelled with Bülow and others.
Richter, Hellmesberger, Brüll, Hanslick, and many others,
are all delightful people, and I feel very sorry that go I must
on Monday. The weather is delightful into the bargain.

LXX

TO HIS DAUGHTERS

Leipzig, Hotel Hauffe: October 14, 1880.

Dearest M. and N.—You have both been very good and
written to me, very amusing letters too, although the sky-
light adventure must have been far from amusing to you. I
hope all is right again by this time, and that umbrellas are
no longer necessary indoors.

My stay in Vienna has been wonderfully interesting;
Brahms has taken to me like a duck to the water (of which
I feel not a little proud); he hardly ever left me, and on
Monday afternoon even went to the station—a very long way
indeed—to see me off. I shall have a deal to tell when I am
once back in London.

I left Vienna on Monday at 2.10 P.M., and arrived here
on Tuesday morning shortly after seven. Yesterday morning
at nine o'clock I had the rehearsal, which went off very well,
and to-night at half-past six is the concert, which I wish
was over already. I play a Beethoven Concerto and several
small pieces by Chopin; at the rehearsal the audience (there
is rather a large one at the rehearsals here) was very *polite*

to me; nevertheless, I am a little nervous just now. The band, I am happy to say, is not quite equal to our Manchester band; that is a fact.

Yesterday evening I saw the celebrated 'Meiningen' actors in Shakespeare's 'Winter's Tale'; they certainly play wonderfully well without having any really great actors; it is the perfection of 'ensemble,' and very striking.

To-morrow, early, I am off for Dresden, where I play on Saturday evening, quite alone, with only a few songs. On Sunday evening I shall be at Hagen, where I must remain a few days, and I shall reach London on Thursday evening next, or perhaps on Friday, to go off to Manchester on Saturday, the first concert taking place on Monday, the 25th.

Good-bye, dear girls, and give my love to the boys.

LXXI

TO ONE OF HIS DAUGHTERS

66 Elbenfelden Street, Hagen :
March 19, 1881.

Dearest M.—If by chance any one of you said yesterday, between one and two o'clock, 'Now the Dad is in Mopsa's [1] arms,' that one was much mistaken, for at that time—don't be alarmed, for there was nobody hurt—I was contemplating the wreck of our train between Verviers and Bleyberg, and a more perfect smash I never saw: the engine lying on its back, all the carriages off the line, some of them shattered, the rails being driven through the luggage vans and looking out at the top, and the line itself, from straight as it had been, twisted, with all the sleepers, into a curve for more than a hundred yards. Well, there is much to be grateful for, for not a soul had even a scratch, and I cannot say that I was alarmed for a moment; all the bumping over the sleepers—and it was severe—left me perfectly cool. I cannot say as much of some of the other passengers nor of the guards. A few looked like ghosts. We had then to be sent

---

[1] A favourite little dog of my grandmother's.

X

back to Verviers by a train coming from the opposite side, and later on we were despatched over the wrong line, and altogether I reached Hagen at half-past six o'clock instead of one. I was thankful for having been alone, without one of you, or else I might not have remained so cool.

Here I have not even mentioned the matter, as Granny might feel upset. I am happy to say that I found her as well as I could possibly wish. Anna, Bertha, and Mopsa are equally flourishing, the latter young lady rather inclined to get somewhat stout.

LXXII

TO ONE OF HIS DAUGHTERS

Vienna : Hotel Imperial,
April 2, 1881.

Dearest M.—So I have at last played in Vienna, and may say that I have every reason to be pleased. I played Beethoven's Concerto in E flat and three pieces by Chopin, and after each performance I was recalled five times to the platform. People are very complimentary, and if we were not so near Easter I might certainly play again ; as it is, I may be sure to be welcomed another time. At Prague, three days ago, I was even recalled seven times as a rule, and had a great mind to take a chair and sit down on the platform for greater convenience. Here the calls do not mean an 'encore,' they are merely complimentary.

What has Gladstone been doing to Dizzy ? I have not seen much of the papers.

LXXIII

TO THE SAME

Greenheys : October 23, 1881.

My dear M.—The Huddersfield Festival was really a great success, and the people most enthusiastic. 'Faust' never went so well yet. Lloyd certainly sang better than ever, and so did Miss Davies ; Santley was splendid too, although a little fatigued at first. . . .

I send you two Huddersfield and one Bradford papers, which will tell you the whole story. How things grow! I cannot help thinking now often of the evening when I asked you if you could not help me by translating 'Faust,' and now people have actually come from Ireland to Huddersfield merely to hear it. I have seen them with my own eyes. They had been ruefully sea-sick, and said they would not mind being so again the next day if they could hear 'Faust' once more.

LXXIV

TO THE SAME

Hagen: April 10, 1882.

Dearest M.—I also have nothing to report, except that the weather is splendid, although the nights are very cold, that we are all well, and that the 'Easter Fires' yesterday evening were extremely fine.

To-morrow being my birthday, I am sure you will all think of me. It is getting rather serious, but, thank God! I feel as capable and as fresh for hard work now as in my youngest days.

May it last so a little longer!

LXXV

TO THE SAME

April 11, 1882.

Dearest Mats,—You have been the spokeswoman for the others, so I must thank you for all the good wishes you have sent me. This is the first birthday I have spent in Hagen since the year eighteen hundred and *thirty-six !* and indeed I feel ' I know not how,' as Margaret sings in 'Faust.' I have received all manner of small presents and lots of flowers, but the first thing I saw when coming out of my bedroom this morning was Mopsa, standing on her hind legs, with a big sugar heart dangling from her neck on a beautiful pink ribbon. It is a grand day for her. . . .

I was sorry to hear of Henri Lehmann's death. One more old friend gone!

April 12, 1882.

My birthday has passed without any serious effects upon my health, and I hope now to stand the next few days manfully also. The weather is finer than ever—almost too good to last until Sunday.

LXXVI

TO ONE OF HIS DAUGHTERS

11 Mansfield Street: August 29, 1882.

. . . Yesterday I went to Birmingham to hear a rehearsal of Gounod's ' Redemption '—not a very beautiful work—and came back in the evening to have an interview to-day with Grove. I had found a letter here from him informing me that the Prince of Wales offered me the professorship of the first pianoforte class in the Royal College, and I had to show him by my engagement-books how impossible it was for me to accept. He understood at once, and was sorry. They mean to open next year.

I return to Birmingham this evening, in time for the concert, at which a new work by Benedict—' Graziella '—is to be given. It seems that he fainted the other day at a rehearsal, in spite of which he insists upon conducting it himself.

Gounod was very nice and kissed me, *à la française*, which I thought unnecessary. Gade is there also, and it is altogether an interesting meeting. Poor Costa looks awful, but gets through his work in spite of his illness; there is indomitable pluck in the old fellow.

LXXVII

TO THE SAME

August 31, 1882.

Since I wrote last I have been to Birmingham and heard the first performance of Gounod's ' Redemption.' My first impression was more than confirmed; it is a dull work and monotonous in the extreme. . . .

Yesterday evening I came on to Preston, where everything is in confusion, the Duke of Albany being too ill to make his promised visit.

LXXVIII

TO THE SAME

Bull and Royal Hotel, Preston : [1]
September 7, 1882.

Dearest M.,—Two of your letters—the last from Cortina and the first from Pieve—have reached me here together. I was most happy to read your description of your excursions to Caprile and Agordo, and could not help reading the whole letter to Straus. It must have been delightful.

I cannot say as much for Preston, although the weather has become fine since yesterday. First of all, I have caught a horrid cold, and, secondly, I have to deal with a committee that makes many mistakes in the management, and none of us derive any pleasure from the concerts. Just imagine that the performance of ' Elijah ' was announced to commence at half-past eight o'clock—certainly an unreasonably late hour —but the doors could not be *opened* to the public before *a quarter past nine*, because the hall was not ready! You can fancy the row that was going on. We began the performance at 9.30, whilst the people were streaming in, and, of course, for a long time not a note could be heard, much to our disgust. We had not finished until past midnight, in spite of having made no interval.

Yesterday's concert began at the equally stupid hour of 4.30 o'clock, and we ended in perfect darkness, no arrangements having been made for lighting the gas. The crowds of roughs, through which we have to fight our way to and from the concerts, always on foot, are most unsavoury. The processions seem remarkably stupid. So, altogether, I am not in the best of tempers. However, it comes to an end to-morrow afternoon, and perhaps Straus and I may often have a good laugh together over the whole affair.

Another thing : rehearsals are quite out of the question,

---

[1] On the occasion of the Preston Guild Festival.

as there is no room and no time for them, so that nothing goes as it ought to do.

I suppose by now you are in Venice, and I need hardly say that I should be only too happy to come to you, but up to the present I hardly know what to say about it. I shall certainly not be able to leave London before the 12th or 13th, so much I see, and I have an absolute craving for some good music. I may say that it is a necessity for me to hear some good performances before beginning my work again, otherwise I might become a 'ganache,' like so many others. So I meant to give myself a week or ten days of running in search of what may be interesting at Munich or Vienna, according to the répertoire; then, before coming back to England, I must spend a little more time at Hagen. Still, I hope that between the two I may find a week to spend with you, about which I shall write later.

LXXIX

TO ONE OF HIS DAUGHTERS

Hagen : July 22, 1884.

I am still here. Yesterday evening, when my luggage had already been taken to the station, I felt that I could not tear myself away, and sent B. to fetch my bag back.

I shall never be able to give anybody an idea of what I feel here, of the immense longing for the past and for so many dear faces, all at rest. Not to speak of poor dear granny, I can stand before the house of Cornelius, vainly trying to persuade myself that I shall never see him again. I really think sometimes that I should feel happy if I could live here altogether, so you may imagine if I find it hard to go away.

LXXX

TO THE SAME

Bayreuth : July 26, 1884.

'Parsifal,' yesterday, made a very deep impression upon me, much more so than before, and I shall see it again to-morrow with very great interest. After all, one has no idea in England of such a performance, and one ought to come here every year to learn what can be done—every detail is so perfect. The musical pleasure is not paramount, but there are very fine and powerful effects in it, and it is interesting throughout, and much less crude than ' Siegfried ' and 'Tristan und Isolde.'

I have not seen Liszt yet and begin to doubt if I shall see him ; the fact is, I don't like his *entourage*.

LXXXI

FROM STEPHEN HELLER

Paris: 4 mars 1885.

Mon cher Hallé,—Depuis trois mois et demi j'attends la ' longue causerie ' dont tu m'as parlé dans ta dernière lettre. Dis-moi de tes nouvelles. Si les espérances dont tu me parlais ne peuvent se réaliser, dis-le avec courage. J'ai toujours l'espoir que je pourrais un peu travailler. J'ai passé deux mois à faire une petite mazurka, et encore avec l'aide d'un musicien qui rectifiait mes notes. Le Docteur Wecker parle encore de ' quelque temps.' Oh Dieu ! je n'y crois guère. Voilà dix-huit mois que je suis soumis à un traitement incessant. Je m'y rends *tous les jours*. Je me dis si dans six mois il n'y a pas un mieux sensible, il faut abandonner tout espoir. . . . Je m'ennuie, cela c'est certain. Je ne puis lire mes chers livres, qui m'ont consolé de tant de peines. Je ne puis parcourir mes chères partitions de Symphonies et de Quatuors qui m'ont fait passer des heures ravissantes. Je ne puis lire les journaux, ni les lettres d'une écriture fine. Cela fait que l'ennui me fait dormir quelques heures durant le jour. Cependant il y a pour certaines choses un peu d'amélioration. Je distingue mieux les traits d'une physionomie inconnue ; les aiguilles d'une pendule, si elle n'est pas loin de mes yeux—toutes choses que je n'ai pu faire il y a six mois.

Si tu fais un voyage pendant les vacances, tâche donc de

passer quelques jours à Paris avec moi. Je voudrais savoir quelque chose de ta vie, de tes concerts, voyages, etc.

Adieu, mon ami. Ecris-moi.

St. Heller.[1]

LXXXII

FROM STEPHEN HELLER

Paris: 13 mars 1885.

Cher Hallé,— . . . Mes yeux vont un peu mieux—hélas! bien peu. Ce que j'écris est devant moi, pâle, effacé, voilé. Mais je ne suis point *arengle*, et Dieu veuille au moins me laisser ce que j'ai. Quand je pense aux malheureux que je vois chez le Docteur, je dois rendre grâce à Dieu. Oh! mon ami, si peu fortuné qu'on soit, il y a toujours une plus grande infortune, qui vous est épargnée. Tout est relatif. Fontenelle, âgé de quatre-vingt-dix-huit ans, ne pouvant ramasser

---

[1]

[Translation]

Paris: March 4, 1885.

My dear Hallé,—For three months and a half I have been waiting for the 'long talk' of which you spoke in your last letter. Give me news of yourself. If the hopes of which you spoke cannot be realised, say so with courage. I still have the hope of being able to work a little.[2] I spent two months over a short mazurka, even with the help of a musician to rectify my notes. Doctor Wecker still speaks of 'some time.' Oh, God! I hardly believe in it. For eighteen months I have undergone an incessant treatment. I go to him *every day*. I tell myself that if in six months there is not a material improvement, I must give up all hope. . . . I feel dull—so much is certain. I cannot read my beloved books, which have consoled me in so many troubles. I cannot go through my beloved scores of the symphonies and quartets, that have made me spend many a charming hour. I cannot read the papers, nor my letters if the writing is small. So weariness makes me sleep several hours during the day. Nevertheless there is a slight amelioration on one or two points. I can distinguish the features of an unknown face better; I can see the hands of a clock if it is not too far from my eyes—things that I could not do six months ago.

If you come abroad during the holidays, do try to spend a few days in Paris with me. I should like to know something of your life, of your concerts, travels, &c.

Adieu, my friend. Write to me.

Stephen Heller.

[2] Heller was losing his sight.

un éventail qu'une belle interlocutrice avait laissé tomber, s'écria : ' Oh ! que je regrette mes quatre-vingts ans ! ' Si je devenais aveugle, que je regretterais mes yeux d'aujourd'hui ! Adieu, ami ; au revoir.

St. Heller.[1]

LXXXIII

TO ONE OF HIS DAUGHTERS

Grand Hotel, Paris :
April 17, 1885.

It does not do to see old friends again, and my visit to X. has made me sad. If I am as much changed in mind and body as he, I ought to be locked up.

Heller looks very old too, but is fresh in mind, and as pleased as a child to have me here. He consents to the Testimonial, after a hard struggle, so my object is gained, and when I come back we shall set to work at once.

LXXXIV

TO GEORG LICHTENSTEIN

(Translated from the German)

June 8, 1885.

My dear Lichtenstein,—Best thanks for your kind letter. And now, in haste, a few lines about our old friend, Heller. For the past two years he has been almost totally blind. He

---

[Translation]

Paris : March 13, 1885.

Dear Hallé,— . . . My eyes are a little better—alas ! very little. What I have just written is before me—pale, effaced, veiled. But I am not quite blind, and may God leave me what I have. When I think of the poor wretches I see at the doctor's, I may well render thanks to God. Ah, my friend, however little fortunate one may be, there is always some greater misfortune which one has been spared. Everything is relative. Fontenelle, at ninety-eight years of age, being unable to pick up a fan which a fair lady he was talking to had dropped, cried : ' Oh, how I regret my eighty years ! ' If I were to become *blind*, how I should regret my eyes of to-day !

Farewell, friend. *Au revoir !*

St. Heller.

sees but a glimmer of light, can find his way in the street, but can no longer work, cannot set down a note on paper, has not a single pupil, and is so near want that for the past nine months (with the help of a few friends) I have had to support him.

He has now consented to accept a public testimonial, and you will probably in the course of a few days see an appeal from me in the *Times*, which I shall also send to the Edinburgh papers. Sir Frederick Leighton, Robert Browning, and I form the committee, but I should like to form a sub-committee in all the principal towns, and with regard to Edinburgh I hope you will give me your aid.

He has given pleasure to so many that I may hope to collect in all England a sum of 2,000*l.*, which would purchase an annuity of 300*l.* Always yours,

CHARLES HALLÉ.

LXXXV

TO THE EDITOR OF THE 'TIMES'

The Composer Stephen Heller

11 Mansfield Street,
Cavendish Square: June 1885.

Sir,—A distinguished artist, the eminent composer, Stephen Heller, whose name is a household word to all lovers of music, has been overtaken by a terrible affliction—almost total blindness. His solitary life is darkened, and the pursuit of his art, his only happiness, is henceforth closed to him.

The sorrow of Mr. Heller's personal friends for the calamity that has befallen him will, I feel sure, be shared by the general public, and I have no hesitation in asking you, sir, to allow me to make it known that it is intended to offer him some more substantial mark of our sympathy, and of the high estimation in which he has always been held among us, than a mere expression of condolence in words.

A small committee, composed of Sir Frederick Leighton,

P.R.A.. Mr. Robert Browning, and myself, has met to consider what form our testimonial shall take, and it has been decided that, if the necessary funds can be raised, a small annuity shall be purchased for M. Heller, that his declining years may, at all events, be spared the cruelty of any possible pecuniary embarrassments arising from his misfortune.

So many will doubtless be glad of the opportunity thus afforded to repay, in some measure, their debt of gratitude to Stephen Heller for the pleasure his exquisite music has given them, that we feel confident our appeal will be responded to without further words on my part, and I have only to add that subscriptions to the 'Heller Testimonial Fund' will be received by Messrs. Coutts, 59 Strand ; by Messrs. Forsyth Brothers, Deansgate, Manchester, and by me.   I am, &c.,

CHARLES HALLÉ.

LXXXVI

FROM STEPHEN HELLER

Paris : 1 juillet 1885.

Cher Hallé,— . . . Voilà ce que je puis te dire au sujet de l'acte de naissance.   Je suis né de parens israélites, qui se sont convertis à la religion catholique lorsque j'avais 12-13 ans, je crois.   Je crois être certain d'être né le 15 mai 1813-1814.   Mon nom était *Jacob* Heller jusqu'au jour où je devins chrétien catholique, et mon nom devenait Stéphan (Istvan en hongrois) d'après le nom de mon parrain qui était, je crois, le Bürgermeister de Pesth.

Le baptême eut lieu dans le Leopoldstadt (faubourg), à l'église de ce quartier.

J'ignore les prénoms de mon père avant le baptême.   Il s'appelait après Franz Bénédict, et il était, je crois, dès ma naissance teneur de livres, ou caissier, dans une fabrique de draps d'un riche israélite, nommé Kanitz.   C'est donc probablement dans les registres de la commune ou synagogue israélite qu'il faudrait rechercher mon acte de naissance. J'ajoute que j'ignore le nom de famille de ma mère.

Dr Jacob Heller était le fils d'un autre frère de mon père,

plus âgé que lui. Il s'appelait Bernard H. et il était professeur de l'école israélite. Il était resté juif, et ne frayait pas avec mon père, ni avec l'eter, à cause de la conversion. Ladite veuve J. Heller (Anna) n'est pas d'origine juive. Ce doit être une excellente personne qui a été très bien avec ma sœur Marie, morte (célibataire) il y a cinq ou six ans. Cette dame a un frère, qui m'a paru dans une certaine circonstance (a la mort de ma sœur) un brave homme et un homme d'ordre. Mme veuve Heller pourra s'adresser à ce frère pour l'affaire. . . .

Voilà tout ce que je puis te dire, cher Hallé. Quant au reste, ce que tu me dis est vraiment fort beau. Déjà aujourd'hui avec un peu de travail je pourrais vivre sans soucis et tracas. Je voudrais te voir délivré de cette pierre d'échoppement qui obstrue la route.

Ton ami des anciens jours comme des derniers.

ST. HELLER.

J'ajoute un mot. Dans cette confusion je commence à douter si nous avons été baptisés dans l'église de Leopoldstadt ou une autre. Il me semble que cette église était située *Gottengasse*. Je n'étais pas si jeune alors, et j'avais au moins douze ans. Je me rappelle que peu de temps avant cet acte j'ai eu une singulière conversation avec mon père. Il me raconta les persécutions et la haine des chrétiens envers les juifs. Et comme j'exprimais ma compassion il me dit que j'étais juif moi-même. Grande fut ma stupéfaction. Je n'en savais rien, car rien dans la maison ne le fit soupçonner ; du moins je ne le remarquai pas. Je me mis à pleurer. Mon père me prit dans ses bras, et me dit, 'Mon *Cobi* (Jacob), ces malheurs seront détournés de toi. Tu deviendras chrétien, et nous tous également.' Lorsque je fus préparé au baptême par le curé, il dit à mon père, 'Votre enfant est né chrétien : il n'est imbu d'aucune pensée juive.' C'est mon père qui m'a raconté cela. Depuis il n'a plus jamais parlé de cette épisode de ma vie.

Mon unique espoir est maintenant dans les souvenirs de

ma cousine. Mais ma sœur était aussi d'une nature absorbée, distraite, et n'ayant pas l'idée de la vie pratique.[1]

[1]   *[Translation]*

Paris : July 1, 1885.

Dear Hallé,— . . . Here is all I can tell you about the certificate of my birth : I was born of Jewish parents, who were converted to the Catholic religion when I believe I was twelve to thirteen years of age. I believe I can certainly say that I was born on May 15, 1813-1814. My name was *Jacob* Heller until the day that I became a Catholic, and my name was changed to Stephen (Istvan in Hungarian), after my god-father, who was I believe the Burgomaster of Pesth.

The baptism took place in the parish church of the Leopoldstadt quarter.

I do not know what were my father's fore-names before his baptism. Afterwards he was called Francis Benedict, and he was from the time of my birth, I believe, book-keeper or cashier in the cloth-factory of a wealthy Israelite of the name of Kanitz. It will therefore probably be in the parish register or in the Jewish Synagogue that the certificate of my birth must be looked for. I may add that I do not know my mother's family name.

Dr. Jacob Heller was the son of an elder brother of my father. His name was Bernard Heller, and he was a professor in the Jewish College. He remained a Jew, and held no intercourse with my father, nor with Peter, on account of their conversion. The widow, J. Heller (Anna), you refer to is not of Jewish origin. She must be an excellent person, and was on good terms with my sister Marie, who died (unmarried) five or six years ago. This lady has a brother, who seemed to me on a certain occasion (at my sister's death) to be a good, steady-going man. Madame J. Heller might obtain her brother's help in the matter. . . .

That is all I can tell you, dear Hallé. As to the rest, what you tell me is very satisfactory. Already, with the addition of a little work, it would enable me to live without care or anxiety. I should like to see you free of the stumbling-block that obstructs the way. Your friend now as in times past,

STEPHEN HELLER.

I add another word. In this confusion I begin to doubt whether we were christened in the Leopoldstadt church or in another. I fancy that the church was in the *Gottengasse*. I was not so young at the time—I was at least twelve years of age. I remember that a short while before the ceremony I had a remarkable conversation with my father. He told me of all the persecutions of the Jews by the Christians, and of all their hatred. And when I expressed my compassion, he told me that I was myself a Jew. Great was my stupefaction. I knew nothing of it, and nothing in our home would have made one suspect it—at least, nothing that I had ever remarked. I began to cry. My father took me in his arms and said : ' My *Cobi* (Jacob), these misfortunes will be averted from you. You will become a Christian, and all of us as well.' When I was being prepared for

LXXXVII

TO GEORG LICHTENSTEIN

(Translated from the German)

11 Mansfield Street, London:
July 7, 1885.

My dear Lichtenstein,—Pray let me know if you have sent the statement respecting Heller's birth to Pesth, and if your brother, or some one else, will take the matter up in earnest, and if you hope to be able to obtain the certificate. The Testimonial Fund is getting on not at all badly. You wrote that you had received nearly 15*l.* I have therefore credited you with 14*l.*, which brings my total to 1,392*l.* 11*s.*, which is sure to reach 1,400*l.* to-day, so that only some 600*l.* are still wanting.

I intend to publish the first list of subscribers in the *Times* at the end of this week, so kindly send me word by then the exact amount you have received, so that we may make a good show!

Next Sunday I go to Hagen for a week to see my sister, and must then come back here in the hope of soon getting the whole thing finished.

Do your best therefore to get that certificate, or I shall be in a pickle!

Ever yours,

C. HALLÉ.

LXXXVIII

FROM STEPHEN HELLER

Paris: 20 juillet '85.

Cher Hallé,—Je suis bien aise d'apprendre que tu n'as pas songé à t'adresser au public allemand. Je ne puis t'apprendre rien de nouveau. Je ne puis me souvenir de

---

baptism by the rector, he said to my father, 'Your child is a born Christian; He is imbued with no Jewish sentiment whatever.' My father repeated his words to me. He never again spoke of that episode in my life.

My only hope now lies in the memory of my cousin. But my sister was also of a vague and dreamy nature, and with no idea of the workaday side of life.

choses que je n'ai jamais su.   Mon père ne parlait jamais de
ses affaires, et même je le voyais peu, de sorte que les choses
qui sont connues dans des familles bien ordonnées et bien
constituées me sont restées à jamais inconnues.—Je crois
être sûr que mon père s'appelait Ignace, encore plus que
ma mère s'appelait Aloysia et qu'elle abhorrait son nouveau
nom de Scholastique, et nous défendit de la nommer ainsi.
Je n'ai aucune souvenance d'une adoption d'une de mes
sœurs par l'oncle Peter.   Ni mon père ni ma mère n'était
Hongrois.   Ils sont venus de la Bohême, et ils étaient ce
qu'on appelait chez nous *Deutsch-Böhmen*.   Leur langue
était l'allemand.   Puisqu'on a trouvé Ign. et Aloysia, on
doit me trouver aussi.

   Pour aujourd'hui je termine.   Bientôt je t'écrirai de
nouveau, car je ne dois pas craindre de te fatiguer.

                    Ton   St. Heller.

   Peut-être ne m'a-t-on pas dit la vérité sur toutes choses.
L'éducation et la manière de traiter les enfants chez les juifs
de l'ancien temps, et notamment dans un pays comme la
Hongrie, alors si peu avancé, a été quelque chose d'inconce-
vable de nos jours.   Pas d'entretien intime, familial, expansif.
Les pères jouaient une manière de Jéhovah ; insondables,
mystérieux, taciturnes et toujours prêts à punir.   Les mères
seules étaient douces et tendres envers les enfants.   Ainsi
était ma mère.   Mais lorsque je jouissais de cet ineffable
bonheur d'être entouré des soins d'un amour maternel,
j'étais trop jeune pour les comprendre.   L'enfance n'a pas
d'entrailles, et elle récompense les bontés sublimes de la mère
par une sorte d'ingratitude inconsciente et cruelle dans son
enfantillage irresponsable.   Lorsque j'arrivai à l'âge où je
pouvais rendre amour pour amour, je fus arraché des bras de
ma mère.[1]

                              Paris : July 20, '83.
   Dear Hallé,—I am very glad you did not think of addressing yourself to
the German public . . . I can tell you nothing fresh.   I cannot remember
things that I never knew.   My father never spoke of his affairs, in fact I

LXXXIX

FROM STEPHEN HELLER

Paris: 28 juillet 1885.

Mon cher Hallé,—Ma plus grande joie était d'abord de te
savoir délivré de ce cauchemar d'acte de naissance.[1] Puis,
en continuant de lire, j'apprends la belle réussite de ton
œuvre, œuvre d'amitié, s'il en fût jamais. Comme cela prouve
ton influence, ton pouvoir dans ce grand pays, ton activité,
mais par-dessus tout ton affection pour ton vieux frère d'armes !
Nous avons toujours servi sous le même drapeau, dans ce
qu'on appelle les armes savantes, dans le corps du génie. Je
t'en prie, ami, va clore cette œuvre. . . . Les raisons pour
te demander de l'arrêter sont : 1° Il ne faut en rien forcer
la note. Le résultat obtenu est très beau ; pourquoi en
vouloir un résultat encore plus beau ? Le mieux est l'ennemi

saw him but little. So that matters which are known in well-regulated
and well-ordered families, remained for ever unknown to me. I am almost
sure that my father's old name was Ignatius, and still more so that my
mother's was Aloysia, and that she abhorred her new name—Scholastica—
and forbade us ever to use it. I have no recollection of the adoption of
one of my sisters by my Uncle Peter. Neither my father nor my mother
were Hungarians. They came from Bohemia, and were what is called
Deutsch-Böhmen. They spoke German. If they have found Ignatius and
Aloysia they ought to find me also.

That is all for to-day. I shall soon write again as I need have no fear
of wearying you. Yours,

ST. HELLER.

Perhaps I was not told the truth about all things. The education
and the treatment of children among the Jews in those days, and notably
in a country like Hungary, then so little advanced in civilisation, was
something quite inconceivable nowadays. No sort of intimate, familiar
family intercourse. The fathers were a kind of Jehovah, inscrutable,
mysterious, taciturn, and ever ready to punish. The mothers alone were
sweet and tender to their children. So was my mother. But when I
enjoyed the ineffable happiness of being the object of maternal care and
love, I was too young to appreciate it. Childhood is heartless, and it pays
back the mother's sublime goodness with a sort of ingratitude that is unconscious and cruel in its irresponsible childishness. When I came to the age
when I could return love for love, I was torn from my mother's arms.

[1] My father had had infinite trouble to get the necessary certificate of
Heller's birth, for the purchase of his annuity.

du bien, dit un proverbe. 2° Plus la chose va, plus les chances augmentent de voir les journaux français et allemands en parler, et en faire des gloses. Cela peut devenir pour quelques *reporters* d'art un article amusant, cancanier ; les uns seront pleins d'une pitié humiliante, les autres seront malicieux ; ceux-là approuveront, ceux-ci critiqueront, et ils défendront leur opinion. Si chétif que soit mon personnage, un chroniqueur à bout de ressources, un rédacteur ou *reporter* sans thème, ou sans ouvrage, s'empare de tout ce qui peut lui donner matière à un article ou à un entrefilet. En France on ne comprend guère ce qu'on appelle là-bas un Testimonial, etc. Ici on regardera cela comme une de ces souscriptions que le ' Figaro ' ouvre de temps en temps au profit d'un maçon tombé d'un échafaudage. En Allemagne c'est encore pis.

Je pense que si tu abrèges, ou plutôt si tu fermes la souscription, que les journaux ne publiant plus rien, on oubliera plus vite. Je tremble à l'idée de ce qu'un journaliste français pourra faire de tout cela. Je t'assure que je serais, avec le produit annoncé et les quelques appoints cités, parfaitement à l'abri de tout besoin.

Ton but est donc, et déjà, atteint. Assez là-dessus.

La nouvelle de la mort de Henry Forsyth m'a profondément affligé. C'était la perle des éditeurs. Jamais je n'ai eu affaire à un pareil, et je n'en aurai jamais à un homme semblable. Il a eu toutes les qualités désirables, et je ne l'oublierai jamais.

Je ne vois plus et je termine, mais j'écrirai bientôt, sans attendre une lettre de toi. J'ai vu ce matin pendant 3 minutes seulement, Mme D. Je lui ai communiqué le contenu de ta lettre. Elle en a été profondément touchée, surtout de tes paroles : que de nous deux le plus heureux, c'est toi.

C'est une noble parole qui doit t'être comptée ici-bas et là-haut.

Ton ami,
ST. HELLER.[1]

[1] *[Translation]*

Paris : July 28, 1885.

My dear Hallé,—My greatest joy was to learn that you were delivered

XC

FROM STEPHEN HELLER

Paris: 7 août 1885.

Cher Hallé,—Tu as le don de me rassurer, tâche difficile, j'en conviens, où tu réussis admirablement. Ainsi dormirais-

from that nightmare of a certificate.[1] Then, on reading further, I saw the great result of your labour, a labour of friendship, if ever there was one. How it proves your influence, your power in that great country, your activity, but above all your affection for your old brother-in-arms! We have always served under the same flag, in what may be called the scientific branch of the service—the engineers. Now I pray you, friend, bring your good work to a close . . . The reasons why I beg you to stop are : 1st, a thing must never be overdone. The result obtained is very good ; why endeavour to improve upon it ? The proverb says : *Le mieux est l'ennemi du bien.* 2nd, the longer the thing lasts, the greater the chance that the French and German papers will get hold of it and make their comments. It might become for some art-reporters the subject of an amusing, gossipy article ; some would be full of humiliating compassion ; others would be malicious, some would approve, others would criticize, and all would defend their opinions. However insignificant a personage I may be, a chronicler at the end of his resources, an editor or a reporter in want of a subject or in want of work, lays hold of whatever may furnish him with an article or a paragraph. In France, what you call a testimonial, &c., is hardly understood. Here it would be looked upon like one of those subscriptions opened from time to time in the *Figaro*, in aid of a stonemason who has fallen from a scaffolding. In Germany it is far worse.

I think that if you curtail, or rather if you close the subscription list at once, if the papers publish nothing more, it will be the sooner forgotten. I tremble at the thought of what a French journalist might make of it all. I assure you that with the sum announced, and the small additions quoted, I should be perfectly sheltered from want.

Your object is therefore attained. Enough thereon.

The news of Henry Forsyth's death afflicted me profoundly. He was the pearl of publishers. I never had to do with his equal, and I shall never meet with such another man. He had every desirable quality, and I shall never forget him.

I can no longer see and must stop, but I shall soon write again, without waiting for a letter from you. I saw Madame D. for three minutes this morning, and I gave her the contents of your letter. She was profoundly touched, especially by your words : that of us two, the happier is yourself.

It was a noble saying, which will be repaid you here and hereafter.

Your friend,

STEPHEN HELLER.

[1] Of Heller's birth, for the purchase of his annuity.

je sur les deux oreilles, comme tu le dis, si je n'étais autrement empêché par des raisons de santé. Mais rien n'est plus
ennuyeux pour soi et pour les autres que de parler de ses
maux, dont, du reste, personne n'est entièrement exempt.

Tu m'as fait bien rire en me demandant si je suis sûr
d'être né. Par le ciel, c'est à en douter. Je pense avec
commisération aux recherches laborieuses du biographe futur
pour fixer définitivement la date de ma naissance, comme cela
s'est vu pour d'autres *grands hommes!* Tu es très occupé
en ce moment, donc je ne t'écris que ces quelques lignes. Je
me réserve le droit de t'écrire quand j'aurai besoin de
m'épancher dans un cœur fraternel. Mais je ne te tracasserai
pas. Je causerai avec toi, car je n'ai personne qui me comprend. Hiller me disait un jour : 'Personne ne comprend
personne.' C'est un peu pessimiste.

A bientôt. Ton

ST. HELLER.[1]

XCI

FROM THE SAME

Paris : 30 septembre 1885.

Mon cher Hallé,—Je ne m'attendais pas de si tôt à une
lettre de toi, pensant bien qu'après une longue absence et à

---

[1] *[Translation]*

Paris : August 7, 1885.

Dear Hallé,—You have the gift of reassuring me, a difficult task, I
allow, but one in which you succeed admirably. Therefore I should sleep
on both ears, as you say, were I not prevented from doing so by reasons of
health. But nothing is more tedious to oneself and to others than to talk
of one's ailments, from which, indeed, no one is wholly exempt.

You made me laugh by asking me if I am sure that I was ever born?
By Heaven, one might doubt it. I think with commiseration of the
laborious researches of my future biographer to establish the date of my
birth, as has happened before in the case of other *great men!* You are
very busy at present, so I shall only write a few lines. I reserve the right
to write to you whenever I feel the need of unbosoming myself to a fraternal soul. But I shall not tease you. I shall chat with you, for I have no
one here who understands me. Hiller once said to me: 'No one understands any one.' That is somewhat pessimistic.

Farewell for the present,

Yours,

ST. HELLER.

la veille de grands concerts tu serais bien absorbé par mille soins nécessaires. Le plaisir de recevoir de tes nouvelles a donc été d'autant plus grand. Tes occupations ne t'ont pas empêché de penser à ton ami.

Ton séjour a été une vraie joie pour moi ; l'amitié, l'affection et la satisfaction de l'artiste ont également trouvé leur compte. Tout ce que tu nous a fait entendre, à moi et à madame D., reste dans nos souvenirs comme une des plus parfaites manifestations d'un art accompli. Madame D. en parle à tout le monde. Moi, j'écoute, et je me dis : je sais tout cela depuis bien longtemps ! Conserve encore bien des années cette force et ce pouvoir, c'est mon vœu, et cela sera, car tu aimes l'art, et rien n'a pu entamer ou amoindrir en toi cette noble passion. Ainsi tu joueras prochainement mon petit opuscule. Ce n'est pas pour toi, c'est pour moi que je prierai. Quant à ' l'affaire,' tout est bien, ce que tu as fait, ce que tu fais et ce que tu feras. Je serai désormais à l'abri de tout souci. Je me donnerai, avec l'aide de Dieu, le petit supplément qu'il me faut, et qui achèvera ce que Horace appelle si judicieusement la *médiocrité dorée*. C'est tout ce que désirait ce sage immortel, et ce que je me permets de désirer à mon tour. Tu me promets une visite pour le mois de mars. C'est une longue échéance. C'est le cas de dire : qui vivra, verra.

J'espère vivre et te revoir. Je te serre la main et je suis ton ami,   St. Heller.[1]

Paris : Sept. 30, 1883.

My dear Hallé,—I did not expect a letter from you so soon, knowing that after a long absence and on the eve of great concerts you would be absorbed by a thousand necessary cares. The pleasure of receiving news of you was therefore all the greater. Your occupations did not hinder you from thinking of your friend. Your visit was a real joy to me ; friendship, affection, and the satisfaction of the artist, were all equally contented. Everything that you made Madame D. and me hear remains in our memory as one of the most perfect manifestations of accomplished art. Madame D. talks of it to everybody. I listen, and I say to myself : I knew all that long ago ! May you long preserve that power and that ability, that is my prayer, and you will do so, because you love your art, and nothing has ever been able to weaken or diminish that noble passion. So you are soon going to play my little work. It is not for you, but for myself, that I

XCII

FROM STEPHEN HELLER

Paris : 8 octobre 1885.

Mon cher Hallé,—Merci de ta bonne lettre ; je m'empresse de t'annoncer que le tout est arrivé à bon port. L'appoint que tu m'envoies sera bien venu pour boucher les petites brèches ouvertes par certaines dépenses d'hiver, telle que le vulgaire bois de chauffage, objets de literie, vêtements chauds et autres articles qui nous rappellent les conditions de l'existence matérielle et triviale.

Trivial tant qu'on voudra, il est bon de ne pas grelotter et de faire réparer des cheminées qui fument et que le propriétaire, animal cruel et avare par état, refuse de prendre à son compte. Je ne sais pourquoi je me souviens en ce moment d'une quittance drolatique que le directeur d'une Maison des Pauvres avait adressée à un donateur de cette maison. La voici : ' Mit dankbaren Herzen bescheinige ich hiermit, dass ich von Ihnen erhalten habe 8 Bettdecken, 12 Paar wollene Strümpfe, und 9 Paar Stiefeln, mit welchen wieder viele Thränen getrocknet worden sind.'

Je suis bien content que l'impromptu a plu ; *es hat ausgesprochen*, comme disait Rob. Volkmann quand il parlait d'une exécution d'un de ces morceaux.

Oui, c'étaient là de bonnes heures que nous avons passé le mois dernier. Je me sens depuis porté pour le travail. Une grande jouissance musicale produit toujours cet effet sur moi. Les grandes exhibitions de célèbres gymnastiques du piano

shall pray. As to the 'affair,' everything is right, what you have done, what you are doing, and what you will do. I shall henceforth be sheltered from all anxiety. With the help of God, I can give myself the trifling supplement to complete what Horace so judiciously calls a *golden mediocrity*. That was all that wise immortal sighed for, and in my turn, it is all that I desire.

You promise me a visit in the month of March. The date is a late one It is really a case of saying : he who lives will see.

I hope to live and to see you again. I press your hand and I am your friend,

ST. HELLER.

me laissent froid comme les mélodrames des théâtres du Boulevard, qui font verser à un public inculte des torrents de larmes.

Moi, je suis ému et ravi d'une belle scène, simple, naturelle, qui est puisée dans le cœur, et rendue avec art. Cet art est celui qui me touche, qui m'émeut. C'est ce que j'ai senti quand tu as joué Beethoven, Chopin, Brahms et Schubert.

Je te serre la main et t'envoie mille amitiés.

St. Heller.[1]

XCIII

FROM THE SAME

Paris: 8 novembre 1885.

Mon cher Hallé,—Je m'empresse de t'annoncer que j'ai reçu une lettre d'une maison de banque, qui a évidemment

---

[1]

[*Translation*]

Paris: October 8, 1885.

My dear Hallé,—Thanks for your good letter. I hasten to announce that everything came safely to hand. The remittance you sent will serve to stop many little gaps made by certain winter expenses, such as the vulgar firewood, bedding, warm clothing, and other articles that remind us of the conditions of material and trivial existence.

Trivial it may be, but it is good not to shiver and to be able to cure a smoky chimney, which the landlord, a cruel and rapacious animal by nature, refuses to repair. I do not know why I am reminded at this moment of a comical receipt addressed by the master of a poorhouse to a benefactor. Here it is: ' With a grateful heart I beg to acknowledge your gift of eight blankets, twelve pairs of worsted stockings, and nine pairs of boots, with which many tears will once again be wiped away.'

I am very glad the impromptu pleased; it *spoke out*, as Rob. Volkmann used to say in speaking of the execution of his works.

Yes, those were famous hours we spent together last month. Since then, I have felt impelled to work. A vivid musical pleasure always produces that effect upon me. The great exhibitions of certain celebrated gymnasts of the piano leave me as unmoved as do the melodramas at the theatres of the Boulevards, which cause an uncultivated public to shed torrents of tears.

As for me, I am moved and ravished by a fine scene, simple, natural, sprung from the heart, and rendered with art. That is what I felt when you played Beethoven, Chopin, Brahms, and Schubert.

I press your hand and I send you a thousand greetings.

St. Heller.

trait à la rente attendue. Je copie la lettre pour toi, afin de te faire connaitre le style financier en usage. 'MM. Seillière, Banquiers, 58 Rue de Provence, avisent M. S. Heller qu'ils ont reçu de MM. Coutts de Londres un crédit en sa faveur.' Cette littérature n'est peut-être pas exquise, mais elle ne manque pas de charme. Je suis trop indisposé aujourd'hui et je me rendrai demain, lundi, chez ces messieurs. Je crois me rappeler que tu devais monter le 'Mors et Vita' de Gounod. Dis-moi à l'occasion si ton impression première ne s'est point modifiée depuis. Je te dis adieu pour aujourd'hui. Porte-toi bien et penses quelquefois à ton ami et frère.

ST. HELLER.[1]

XCIV

FROM THE SAME

Paris : 21 décembre 1885.

Mon cher, bien cher ami,—Non pas à cause du Jour du Nouvel An que je t'envoie ces lignes. Il n'y a pas de jour où je n'aie une bonne pensée pour toi. Je désire pour toi toutes les prospérités, toutes les satisfactions du corps et de l'âme. Réussis en tout ce que tu fais, et sois toujours entouré d'amis affectueux, sincères, intelligents et aimables. Je sais que c'est beaucoup demander à la vie. Mais, que je voudrais, que je voudrais que ce lot te soit échu !

[1]

[Translation]

Paris: November 8, 1885.

My dear Hallé,—I hasten to announce that I have received a letter from a bank, that evidently refers to the expected annuity. I copy the letter so as to make you acquainted with the financial style in vogue. 'Messrs. Seillière, Bankers, 58 Rue de Provence, advise M. S. Heller that they have received from Messrs. Coutts, of London, a credit in his favour.' This literature may not be exquisite, but it is not wanting in charm. I am too ill to go to-day, but I hope to visit these gentlemen to-morrow, Monday. I think I remember that you were to give Gounod's 'Mors et Vita.' When you have an opportunity, tell me if your first impression has not been modified. Farewell for to-day. Keep well, and sometimes think of your friend and brother,   ST. HELLER.

Je te serre la main et je reste jusqu'à mon dernier souffle ton ami, dans toute l'étendue de ce grand mot : un ami.

ST. HELLER.[1]

XCV

FROM THE SAME

Paris: 3 janvier 1886.

Cher Hallé,—Tu n'as besoin de nulle excuse de ne pas m'écrire plus souvent. Je sais que tu es au feu, devant l'ennemi : je veux dire, devant le public, monstre insatiable et impitoyable, qui veut satisfaire ses appétits et ses gloutonneries pour l'argent qu'il donne. Cela demande un grand soin, et beaucoup de temps. J'ai eu un véritable plaisir d'apprendre que tu as joué la canzonette en mi bémol. Il y a de bonnes choses, il y en a que j'aurais mieux faites plus tard. Je crois qu'il y a beaucoup d'auteurs dans le même cas. L'imagination est peut-être plus fraîche et plus hardie lorsqu'on est jeune. Le goût, le discernement, l'expérience s'acquièrent avec les années. Les deux choses réunies produisent les œuvres parfaites.

Puisse ton projet de venir à Paris au printemps se réaliser.

Ton meilleur ami,

ST. HELLER.[2]

---

[1] [*Translation*]

Paris: December 24, 1885.

My dear, very dear Friend,—It is not because of New Year's Day that I am sending you these few lines. Never a day goes by but that I have a kindly thought of you. I wish you every prosperity, every satisfaction of soul and body. May you succeed in all you undertake, and be ever surrounded by affectionate, sincere, intelligent, and amiable friends. I know this is asking a good deal from life; but I wish—how I wish !—that this may be the fate allotted you !

I press your hand, and I remain, until my latest breath, your friend, in all the compass of that great word—a friend.

ST. HELLER.

[2] [*Translation*]

Paris: January 3, 1886.

Dear Hallé,—You need no excuse for not writing oftener. I know that you are under fire, before the enemy—I mean before the public; an in-

XCVI

FROM THE SAME

Paris: 3 avril 1886.

Mon cher Hallé.—Je te remercie bien de m'avoir si tôt donné de tes nouvelles. Je me disais bien que tu aurais une mauvaise traversée, le jour était affreux. Il faut que tu sois vraiment né marin, pour ne pas avoir été malade.

Oui, c'étaient quelques jours charmants, qui me laisseront encore pendant longtemps des souvenirs pleins de sérénité et de bien-être. Tu étais, ou tu paraissais, cette fois un vrai flâneur, sans affaires, sans souci, sans préoccupation. Tes flâneries étaient non aux Boulevards mais Rue des Martyrs, chez ton vieil ami, et tu y apportais la plus affectueuse et la plus aimable humeur qu'un ami et un malade peuvent désirer. Je n'oublierai pas non plus les deux Sonates que tu as dit avec une admirable perfection, reconnue même par une adepte aussi enthousiaste que partiale de Rubinstein. Tout le monde ne voit pas ce qu'il peut y avoir de faux rubis et de fausses perles dans une parure habilement et ingénieusement montée.

Moi, je demande la simplicité, la sincérité et la vérité dans une œuvre d'art, et dans l'interprétation artistique de quel genre qu'elle soit. Cette vérité et cette sérénité je les trouve dans ta manière de jouer Beethoven.

Tu es plus libre en disant les maîtres modernes, et en cela encore je te donne raison. Ils ne sont pas aussi sûrs de ce qu'ils ont fait que les anciens. On peut—avec tact et

satiable and merciless monster that insists upon satisfying its appetite and its gluttony for the money it pays. This gives much trouble, and takes time. I learnt with real pleasure that you had played the canzonet in E flat. There are some good things in it; there are some that I should have done better later. I think many authors are in the same case. Imagination is perhaps fresher and bolder in youth. Taste, discernment, and experience come with years. The two united achieve perfection.

May your project of coming to Paris in the spring be realised.

Your best friend,

ST. HELLER.

mesure—un peu les accommoder à sa propre individualité. C'est ce que tu fais, et je t'approuve.

On commence un peu à gouailler tout le bruit ridicule qu'on a fait du grand Ex-virtuose.[1] Il paraît qu'il a joué chez Erard comme un enfant, mais qu'on y a tout de même répandu des larmes d'attendrissement. Le public parisien commence à rire de lui-même, car le vrai caractère du Parisien est frondeur. Il aime d'abord le fracas, les arcs de triomphe, les transparents et puis il éteint tout, en soufflant les mots les plus mordants et souvent très justes dans leur cruauté. Le dieu d'hier n'est bientôt qu'un pantin dont il s'amuse à cœur joie. Adieu pour aujourd'hui.

Je suis toujours ton

ST. HELLER.[2]

[1] Liszt.

[2]

[*Translation*]

Paris: April 3, 1836.

My dear Hallé,—I thank you for so speedily sending me news of yourself. I expected you to have a bad crossing, the weather was frightful. You must be a born sailor not to have been ill.

Yes, those were charming days, and have left a serene and lasting memory behind them. You were, or you seemed to be this time, a true holiday-maker, without business, care, or preoccupation. But you did not seek your pleasure on the Boulevards, but in the Street of Martyrs, with your old friend; and you brought him the most affectionate and the most amiable humour that a friend and a sick man could desire. Nor shall I forget the two sonatas which you rendered with admirable perfection, acknowledged even by a disciple of Rubinstein, as enthusiastic as she is partial. It is not every one who can see how many false rubies and sham pearls there may be in a set of jewels cleverly and ingeniously mounted.

I ask for simplicity, sincerity, and truth in a work of art, and in its artistic interpretation, in whatever style it may be. This truth and this serenity I find in your playing of Beethoven.

You are freer in your rendering of the modern masters, and there again I agree with you. They are not so sure of what they have done as the ancients. One may—with tact and within due limits—bend them a little to one's own individuality. This you do, and here again I am with you.

People begin to mock at all the ridiculous fuss that has been made over the grand *ex-virtuoso*. It seems he played like a child at Erard's, and yet people wept with emotion. The Parisian public is beginning to laugh at itself, for the true character of your Parisian is to jeer. He begins by enjoying a tumult, triumphal arches and illuminations, and then he extinguishes it all by giving vent to the most biting words, often very accurate

XCVII

FROM THE SAME

Paris : jeudi, 15 avril 1886.

Mon cher Hallé,—Rien qu'un petit bonjour que j'ai envie de t'envoyer. J'espère que tu es bien portant et de bonne et belle humeur, comme tu l'as été à Paris.

De ma santé—rien de nouveau à dire.

D'après quelques réclames dans les journaux français notre grand Roy François Liszt jouit là-bas des mêmes triomphes et ovations qu'à Paris. Il a eu cependant à essuyer quelques observations dans certains journaux parisiens qui manquaient complètement de respect, et qu'on pourrait qualifier comme offuscantes. Francisque Sarcey notamment l'a rudement malmené et l'appelle un banquiste ! C'est dur de passer ainsi de l'apothéose à la Roche Tarpéienne !

Mais notre vieux fou tombe de cette roche sur ses pieds comme les chats ; il en peut être un peu étourdi, et brille peu après de tout l'éclat de son génie tapageur et extravagant.

Je voudrais que tu me dises quelque chose sur tout cela.

Adieu, cher ami ; je te serre les mains.

Ton vieux
STEPHEN HELLER.[1]

in their cruelty. The god of yesterday speedily becomes nothing more than a puppet with which he amuses himself to his heart's content.

Adieu for to-day.

Ever your
ST. HELLER.

[1] *[Translation]*

Paris : Thursday, April 15, 1886.

My dear Hallé,—I only want to wish you good-day. I hope you are well, and in the same good and happy mood as when you were in Paris.

As to my health—nothing new to say.

According to some of the accounts in the French papers, our great monarch, François Liszt, is enjoying the same triumphs and ovations with you that he did in Paris. Nevertheless, he had to endure certain observations in some of the Paris papers that were altogether wanting in respect, and might even be qualified as stinging. Francisque Sarcey, for one, mauled him rudely, and called him a charlatan. It is hard to pass thus from apotheosis to the Tarpeian Rock !

XCVIII

FROM STEPHEN HELLER

Paris : 3 août 1886.

Cher Hallé,—Je suis bien content d'avoir de tes nouvelles. Je vis maintenant du souvenir de ces jours que j'ai passés avec toi. Ils ont été bien charmants! Nous avons bien causé, et tu paraissais d'une humeur très heureuse. Je ne sais si j'en avais l'apparence; mais, crois le bien, j'ai été bien content, bien satisfait et bien heureux.

Tu as soif après le piano, dis-tu. Eh bien, c'est une sensation délicieuse, si on peut l'étancher, bien entendu. Tu le peux, et tu sais préparer ce breuvage divin qui te rafraîchit, te réconforte, et que tu serviras à ceux qui éprouvent aussi cette noble soif. Soûle-toi donc de bonne et belle musique, et verse-en de copieuses rasades à tes amis.

Voilà donc ce pauvre Liszt disparu à son tour de ce monde, qui lui a offert des jouissances, faites pour satisfaire les ambitions et les appétits les plus robustes. Que la paix soit avec lui, qui n'a rien tant aimé que le bruit !

Notre petit cénacle du petit Véfour regrette ton absence. . . .

Mille choses affectueuses,

St. HELLER.

Je t'envoie deux volumes de Guy de Maupassant, où tu trouveras plusieurs contes remarquables. On peut beaucoup avoir à redire de son choix de sujets, et de son trop grand penchant pour les choses scabreuses. Mais c'est une riche organisation; un talent puissant et original, un conteur de premier ordre.[1]

But our old madman falls from the rock on his feet, like a cat—he may be stunned for a moment, but shines again directly in all the effulgence of his noisy and extravagant genius.

I wish you would tell me a little about it all.

Adieu, dear friend, I press your hands.

Your old

St. HELLER.

[1] [*Translation*]

Paris: August 3, 1886.

Dear Hallé,—I am very glad to have news of you. I live upon the re-

XCIX

FROM THE SAME

Paris : 15 mars 1887.

Cher Hallé,—Je suis bien content de recevoir de tes nouvelles, mais, comme tu le penses, bien affligé, bien peiné de la nouvelle de la mort de ce bon et excellent Hecht.[1] Oh, oui ! tu as raison ; qu'est-ce la vie de cette terre !

Je comprends ton embarras de chef d'orchestre, étant privé de la collaboration d'un second aussi intelligent et dévoué que l'était le regrettable Hecht. Je lui aurais prédit une longue vie, une verte vieillesse. Il était fort, il était gai, actif, aimant la vie, le travail, et dans une position aisée, à ce qu'on m'a dit. Pauvre femme ! pauvres enfants ! Ah ! je suis bien affligé de cette mort, comme de celle de Forsyth, que j'estimais de tout mon cœur. J'ai connu deux éditeurs (race que j'abhorre, car j'en ai connu un grand nombre de véritables malfaiteurs) que je porte au cœur. C'était Forsyth, et c'est

membrance of the days that I spent with you. They were very charming. We had some good talk, and you seemed in a very happy humour. I do not know if I appeared so, but, believe me, I was very content, very well satisfied, and very happy.

You say you have a thirst for the piano. Well, it is a delightful sensation, if one can quench it, that is to say. You can do so, and you know how to prepare this divine beverage which refreshes and revives you, and which you can pour out for those who feel the same noble thirst. Inebriate yourself well, therefore, with good and beautiful music, and serve copious bumpers of it to your friends.

So poor Liszt, in his turn, has disappeared from this world, which had offered him joys enough to satisfy the most robust ambitions and desires. May he rest in peace, who loved nothing so well as noise and tumult.

Our little circle at the ' Petit Véfour' regrets your absence.

A thousand affectionate greetings,

ST. HELLER.

I send you two volumes of Guy de Maupassant, wherein you will find several remarkable stories. One may find much to object to in his choice of subjects, and in his predilection for doubtful topics, but his is a rich organisation, a powerful and original talent ; he is a story-teller of the first rank.

[1] Mr. Edward Hecht, for many years my father's chorus-master and intimate friend.

Edwin Ashdown, un brave et généreux homme, un homme
d'esprit et de cœur, sans aucune affectation de bienfaiteur et
de bénisseur, mais qui agit bien et grandement, sans phrases.

Je ne suis pas sorti de ma chambre depuis les premiers
jours de janvier. Tu jugeras, d'après cela, combien je suis
souffrant pour rompre ainsi toutes mes habitudes. Que je
serai heureux de te revoir, et de ré-entendre cette voix si
amicale, si connue, si liée à toute ma vie passée et présente !
Je n'ai pas bien saisi le passage de ta lettre où il est question
de l'Exposition Anglaise. Est-ce que cela augmentera ou
diminuera ton activité ? Prends-tu part à la musique officielle
des fêtes, ou jouiras-tu des loisirs d'une interruption de tes
travaux habituels, en te tenant éloigné des productions
gouvernementales avec grosses caisses, tambours et panaches
militaires et civils ?

On dit ici des merveilles de la Symphonie en sol mineur
de Saint-Saëns. Elle a été jouée à Londres, je crois. Qu'en
sais-tu ? On l'a exécutée trois fois au Conservatoire avec un
succès d'enthousiasme, et déclarée son chef-d'œuvre.

Assez bavardé. Porte-toi bien ; conserve ta bonne humeur
—cela vaut mieux que les visites et les remèdes des plus
grands médecins.

Ton invariable ami pour toujours,   St. Heller.[1]

---

[1]   *[Translation]*

Paris: March 15, 1887.

Dear Hallé,—I am very glad to have news of you, but, as you can
imagine, very much grieved, deeply pained to hear of the death of that
good and excellent Hecht. Ah, yes! you are right: what is this earthly
life ?

I can understand your embarrassment as a conductor at being deprived
of so intelligent and devoted a collaborator as was the regretted Hecht.
I should have predicted for him a long life, a green old age. He was
strong, cheerful, active, fond of his life, of his work, and in fair circumstances, as I have heard. Poor wife! poor children! Ah! I am much
afflicted by this death, as I was by that of Forsyth, whom I esteemed with
all my heart. I have known two publishers (a race which I abhor, for I
have known many who were real malefactors) for whom I have a warm
feeling. One was Forsyth, the other is Edwin Ashdown, a good and
generous man, a man of heart and intellect, with no affectation of being a

C

FROM THE SAME

Paris : 30 mai 1887.

Mon cher Hallé,—Rien qu'un petit bonjour, parce que je me sens un peu mieux ce matin, ayant été si souffrant la nuit passée. Alors, se retrouvant encore debout, respirant, mangeant un peu, buvant, lisant le journal, on a ressaisi le sentiment de la vie ; la petite flamme, tout à l'heure si faible, s'est ranimée—on est heureux . . . tant l'homme tient à la vie et à ses sensations. Ton aimable fils m'a envoyé une photographie de mon portrait. Madame D. en est enchantée. Elle trouve bien du talent à ton fils, et moi aussi. . . .

Il aurait fallu mettre en bas : ' Photographie d'après un portrait de Ch. Hallé fils,' et mon nom. Je l'aurais donné à Brandus et à Hamelle pour l'exposer à leur vitrine. Tu es maintenant dans le coup de feu. J'aurais voulu être à tes cotés. Amitiés.   Sr. HELLER.[1]

benefactor or a patron, but dealing fairly and liberally, without unnecessary talk.

I have not been out of my room since the early days of January. You can judge how ill I must be thus to break off all my habits. How happy I should be to see you and to hear your friendly voice again, so well known, so bound up with my past and present life ! I did not quite understand the passage in your letter referring to the English Exhibition. Will it increase or diminish your activity ? Are you going to take part in the official music of the *fêtes*, or will you enjoy the leisure of an interruption of your habitual labours, by holding aloof from official functions, with their big drums, kettle drums, and civil and military pageants ?

Great things are said here of Saint-Saëns' Symphony in G minor. It has been given in London, I believe. What do you know about it ? It was played three times at the Conservatoire with enthusiastic success, and declared to be his masterpiece.

Enough chatter. Keep well; preserve your cheerful humour. It is worth more than the visits and prescriptions of the greatest doctors.

Your ever faithful friend,   ST. HELLER.

[1]   [*Translation*]

Paris: May 30, 1887.

My dear Hallé,—I wish you good morning, feeling a little better after a very bad night. So, finding oneself still erect, still alive, eating a little, drinking a little, able to read the paper, one takes hold of life again ; the little flame, so feeble just now, revives again. One feels happy . . . so

CI

FROM STEPHEN HELLER

Paris : 8 juillet 1887.

Cher Hallé,—Que fais-tu ? Que deviens-tu ? Toujours dans la musique jusqu'au cou ? Que Dieu te conserve telle puissance de travail, car c'est un grand bonheur si ce n'est en même temps une nécessité. La chaleur ici est intense ; j'en souffre moins, car je ne sors pas, étant toujours confiné chez moi, et forcé à l'immobilité.

Quand tu auras le temps, le loisir, la disposition, tu m'écriras quelques notes sur ta vie, sur tes affaires, sur tes projets. Peut-être même viendras-tu passer un jour ou deux à Paris ; alors j'apprendrai de vive voix ce qui m'intéresse tant de savoir.

Le pauvre L. Comppey est parti de ce monde. Il a été un très grand ami et propagateur de ma musique. Il n'avait pas d'élève, ni de petit élève, ni d'arrière-petit élève (il comptait des générations d'élèves) qui ne connût une grande partie de mes ouvrages. Mais nous ne nous voyions que deux ou trois fois par année, et nous n'avions aucune relation qu'on peut qualifier d'intime ou d'amicale.

C'est l'inverse d'autres qui sont des vrais amis, intimes, serviables, affectueux et sympathiquement dévoués à ma personne, et qui sont indifférents, froids et muets pour l'artiste, c'est-à-dire pour ses œuvres.

Ainsi va le monde. Il y a des choses excellentes, mais rien n'est complet ni parfait. J'attends l'autre monde. Je

closely does man cling to life and to its sensations Your amiable son has sent me a photograph of my portrait. Madame D. was delighted with it. She sees great talent in your son, and so do I. . . .

It should have been inscribed : 'Photograph of a portrait by Charles Hallé, the younger,' and my name. I should have given it to Brandus and to Hamelle to show in their shop-windows. You are now in the heat of battle. Would I were by your side. Yours,

STEPHEN HELLER.

m'y achemine en tapinois, et avec une curiosité un peu
craintive. . . .

Ton fidèle

St. Heller.[1]

CII

FROM THE SAME

Paris : août 188

Cher ami,—Que je suis heureux de te savoir si bien
installé, si content du pays[2] que tu habites en ce moment,
et que tout cela semble te donner une sérénité d'esprit, et un
bien-être physique qui se trahit clairement dans ta lettre.
Quant à moi, je ne puis pas te parler des frais ombrages et
des brises fortifiantes de la mer ; elles font défaut à la rue de
Laval, et il y en a encore moins rue Victor Massé.[3] Il y a

---

[1]

[*Translation*]

Paris : July 8, 1887.

Dear Hallé,—What are you doing ? What has become of you ? Still
up to the neck in music ? May God long preserve this power of work in
you, for it is a great happiness, if it is not at the same time a necessity.
The heat here is intense. I suffer less from it as I do not go out, being
entirely confined to my room in a state of immobility.

When you have time, opportunity, and inclination, you will write me a
few words about yourself, your affairs, your projects. Perhaps you will
even come for a day or two to Paris ; then I shall hear from your own lips
all that it so much interests me to know.

Poor L. Couppey has departed this life. He was a great friend and a
great populariser of my music. There was not one of his pupils, or grand-
pupils, or great-grand-pupils (he counted his pupils by generations) who
did not know my works. But we only saw each other two or three
times a year, and held no intercourse that could be termed intimate or
friendly.

It is just the reverse with others who are true friends, intimate,
serviceable, affectionate, and sympathetically devoted to my person, but
who are indifferent, cold, and mute to the artist—that is to say, to his
works.

So goes the world. There are excellent things in it, but nothing complete nor perfect. I am waiting for the other world. I am advancing
towards it shyly, and with a somewhat timid curiosity. . . .

Your faithful

St. Heller.[1]

[2] Warsash, on Southampton Water.
[3] The name of the street was changed from Laval to Victor Massé.

Z

toujours une vive opposition contre l'auteur des 'Noces de
Jeannette,' et le principal opposant est un riche loueur de
voitures de la rue, qui organise la révolte, et dépense beaucoup
d'argent pour des banderoles en percale, avec l'inscription :
'Cette rue s'appelle Rue de Laval.' Mais je crois que force
restera au Conseil Municipale, cette collection d'enfants
terribles, qui nous imposeront bientôt des changements bien
autrement graves, si les bonnets-de-coton conservateurs et
bien-pensants les laissent faire avec une colère timide et une
indignation inactive.

On ne peut pas dire de ma santé la phrase habituelle des
bulletins de santé : *Le mieux* (ne pas lire le vieux) *persiste*.
C'est absolument le contraire. J'aurais désiré t'envoyer de
ces beaux *Dandies* de cigares, chamarrés d'argent et de galons.
Je te garde les trois uniques que j'ai ; Dieu pourvoira à
l'avenir !

J'ai eu un véritable plaisir en apprenant que ton brave
fils a vendu tous les tableaux qu'il avait exposés. C'est
charmant, un artiste qui renait de deux côtés. Il recueille
les honneurs du bon travail, il amasse des couronnes de
laurier, et du vil métal qui donne de si bonnes choses.

Certes, tu ne peux compter pour une victime de la
Révolution de juillet ! Et Dieu en soit loué. Tu as accompli
une vie de travail, d'honneur, de succès, et ayant donné du
savoir, de l'instruction, du talent à une nombreuse famille, tu
as encore pu ériger un monument à l'amitié ! A une
prochaine fois ; mille poignées de main.

St. Heller.[1]

[1] [Translation]
Dear Friend,—How glad I am to know you so comfortably installed,
so content in your present quarters ; you seem to have gained an increase
of serenity of spirit and a physical well-being which clearly betray themselves in your letter. As for me, I cannot speak to you of cool shades or
of the invigorating breezes of the sea ; they are wanting in the Rue de
Laval, and still more so in the Rue Victor Massé. There is still a violent
opposition against the composer of the 'Noces de Jeannette,' and the
principal antagonist is a rich job-master in the street, who organises the
rebellion, and spends a great deal of money in calico streamers, with the
inscription, 'This street is called Rue de Laval.' But I think the Municipal

CIII

FROM THE SAME

5 septembre 1887.

Cher ami.—J'ai reçu le volume, il y a quatre ou cinq jours, et je t'ai écrit aussitôt pour t'en remercier. Mais, croyant que tu aurais quitté la campagne pour quelque voyage que tu fais d'ordinaire, j'ai envoyé ma lettre à Manchester, où tu la trouveras sans doute. Je suis très content d'avoir une nouvelle lettre et de voir que tu vas bien, et que tu te reposes encore ; si cela me va de te voir encore une fois cette année —je le crois bien. Et ne serait-ce qu'un jour d'arrêt à Paris, tu aurais toujours une ou deux heures pour moi ?

Mon état est déplorable. J'ai des jours et des nuits où la vie m'est indifférente. D'autres où je végète—mais je ne suis jamais bien.

Ce livre de Nottebohm m'intéresse énormément. Seulement je dois le lire à petites doses et à grands intervalles ; je travaille dans ma mémoire (tant qu'elle m'obéit) les ouvrages dont il parle, et cela me fatigue beaucoup. Comme il se répète infiniment, et qu'il veut être très clair, il devient

Council will have the last word. That collection of *enfants terribles* will soon impose far more serious changes upon us, if our well-intentioned conservative 'night-caps,' with their timid rage and inactive indignation, allow them to have their way.

As to my health, I cannot quote the habitual phrase of bulletins of health : 'The improvement continues.' The exact contrary is the case.

I should have liked to send you a few of those fine *dandy* cigars, all rigged out with silver and stripes. I am keeping you the last three ; Heaven will provide for the future ! It gave me real pleasure to hear that your good son had sold all the pictures he had exhibited. It is charming to see the artist born again in another mould. He is reaping the honours of good work, he will amass crowns of laurel, and of that vile metal that purchases so many good things.

Certainly, you cannot be counted among the victims of the Revolution of July ! And God be praised for it. You have accomplished a life of labour, of honour, of success, and having given knowledge, instruction, and talent, to a numerous family, you have yet found means to erect a monument to friendship ! Till we meet again a thousand shakes of your hand !   ST. HELLER.

un peu fatigant. Mais c'est d'un poignant intérêt, et je te remercie bien de me l'avoir envoyé.

C'est dur de se séparer d'un enfant, et pour une contrée si lointaine! Comme on s'applique d'être malheureux pour être heureux! Il y a quelque chose de mystérieux et d'insondable dans le cœur, et dans l'esprit de l'homme.

Ton adresse actuelle m'est très difficile à écrire (encore plus à retenir) et résonne à mes oreilles d'une façon disharmonieuse. Je n'aime pas *Warsash*; j'aime encore moins *Titchfield*, mais je trouve horrible *Hants*, qui veut dire Hampshire, je le sais; cette façon anglaise d'abréger me déplaît énormément. Idiosyncrasie. Mille amitiés tendres et fraternelles.

St. Heller.[1]

---

[1]

[*Translation*]

September 5, 1887.

Dear Friend,—I received the volume four or five days ago, and I wrote at once to thank you. But, thinking you had probably left the country for one of your usual journeys, I sent the letter to Manchester, where you will probably find it. I was very glad to receive another letter, and to learn that you are well, and still resting yourself. If it will suit me to see you again this year? I should rather think so. And if you only pause for a day in Paris, you would still have an hour or two for me.

My state is deplorable. There are days and nights when life becomes indifferent to me. There are others when I vegetate, there are none when I feel well.

Nottebohm's book interests me enormously. Only I can only take it in very small doses and at long intervals; I go over in my memory (so far as it obeys me) the works of which he speaks, and it tires me greatly. As he repeats himself continually, and as he wants to be very clear, he becomes rather fatiguing. But it is keenly interesting, and I thank you heartily for having sent it to me.

It is hard to part with a child, and for so distant a country![2] How miserable one makes oneself in order to be happy! There is something mysterious and unfathomable in the heart and mind of man.

Your present address is very difficult to write (and still harder to remember), and sounds most inharmoniously to my ear. I do not like *Warsash*, I like *Titchfield* still less, but I find *Hants* horrible; it means Hampshire I know, and that English fashion of abbreviation displeases me enormously. Idiosyncrasy.

A thousand tender and fraternal greetings. St. Heller.

[2] Referring to the departure of one of Sir Charles Hallé's eldest sons for South Africa.

CIV

FROM MR. LUDWIG STRAUS

(Translated from the German)

Manchester: January 1, 1888.

Dear Mr. Hallé,—You asked me if I could not tell you verbally what I wished to write to you.

I strove hard to do so when I drove home with you from the Concert Hall rehearsal, but it would not pass my lips. But it is my duty not to leave you in ignorance, and to make the matter known to you in time, so as to enable you to make the necessary arrangements.

It is a greater pain to me than I can express, to sever a connection[1] that has been so full of artistic and personal satisfaction. During the sixteen years that I have had the honour of working under your bâton, I found in you not only a master, to whom I looked up with pride, and whose guidance it was ever a pleasure to follow, but also the kindest and most considerate of friends. With gratitude and satisfaction I look back upon the past—much as we played Wagner and Berlioz, no discord ever disturbed our intercourse—full of thankfulness and affection shall I remain so long as I have life. Never would it have occurred to me to leave an association that contented me so fully, had not my health, during the past three years, been so uncertain, and my joints so unmannerly as to protest energetically against the continuance of my former activity.

The doctor says, and I have long felt, that the sudden changes from a hot concert-room to a chase after a cold railway compartment, and the fatigue consequent upon the combination of a Manchester and London life are no longer practicable for me. I must therefore restrict myself to London, where I shall hope still to have much musical and friendly intercourse with you, and that the sacrifice I make

---

[1] Mr. Ludwig Straus was leader of my father's orchestra during sixteen years.

and the avoidance of exposure and exertion may keep within bounds the threatened recurrence of acute rheumatism.

I shall earnestly and faithfully fulfil the obligations of this season—alas, my last one with you—and remain always, with all my heart, your grateful and true

LUDWIG STRAUS.

CV

TO MR. LUDWIG STRAUS

(Translated from the German)

January 2, 1888.

Dear Mr. Straus.—What can I answer you? Although you had occasionally given me hints which caused me sad forebodings, I feel to-day as if a totally unexpected blow had fallen upon me, and I feel it deeply!

Your state of suffering touched me too nearly, and has moved me too deeply, to allow me to make any attempt to induce you to reconsider your decision; but its consequence will be to rob me of a great part of the pleasure I took in my concerts. You must know this yourself, for you know how closely you have been identified with my musical life. That I shall not lose your faithful friendship I know right well, but the cessation of our constant collaboration will create a sense of loneliness in me that I can never hope to lose. Your kindly expressions of friendship—I may say of attachment—have moved me deeply, and I shall keep your letter as a precious memento. To me also it is more than satisfactory to be able to say that never during the long course of years has the slightest shade of discord arisen between us.

I really feel this too keenly to be able to write at length, and must wait until we meet to say more. If you know me well—and I dare hope you do—you will understand how it is with me.

In true friendship I remain,

Ever yours,

C. HALLÉ.

CVI

TO MR. LICHTENSTEIN

January 30, 1888.

My dear Lichtenstein,—The article about Heller[1] is very good. The annuity gave him close on 300*l.* a year; his latter days were therefore free from financial care. No time for more.

Ever yours,

C. HALLÉ.

CVII

TO ONE OF HIS DAUGHTERS

Hotel d'Angleterre, Rome :
April 8, 1889.

. . . To speak of what we see here is impossible ; there is too much, and the impressions are too strong. What strikes me is the amazing number of things that have been discovered since 1870, and the changes in the Forum, Coliseum, &c., &c., through the recent excavations. It is wonderful to think that when we were last here some of the most beautiful statues in the Vatican were still buried underground. What may not be hidden still !

The weather, I am sorry to say, is atrocious ; rain, rain and cold, is the order of the day.

The principal things we have seen already are : St. Peter's, half of the Vatican, the Coliseum, Pantheon, the Capitol with its two museums, the Forum Romanum, Forum Trajanum, Temple of Vesta, San Paolo fuori le mure, a lot of triumphal arches, the Trevi and other fountains, and so on and on. The hotel is very comfortable and the service excellent. We have a remarkable guide—quite a character —who boasts of intimate acquaintance with Cardinal Manning, Prince Jerome, the King, and a few other small people. Thanks to him we saw the King, the Queen, and the Crown

---

[1] Heller died on January 14, 1888.

Prince drive in three different carriages yesterday, as he knows their habits. We also visited the Quirinale yesterday, with its gorgeous but very stiff and cold rooms. Altogether we are not idle, and we shall have more to tell when we come home than to write now, for which there is hardly time.

Let me know when you return to London; and when you are there please get a good piano at once, for I shall have to practise like a slave from the first day of my arrival.

Best love from both of us to all of you, great and small!

CVIII

TO ONE OF HIS DAUGHTERS

Rome: April 10, 1889.

Yesterday has been the worst day, rain from morning till night, but, nevertheless, we have seen many beautiful things and enjoyed ourselves. Mr. Bliss, for whom we had a letter from Lady Herbert (through Mrs. Grimshawe), took us through a part of the Vatican which is not generally shown, the Archives, Library, and Christian Museum, in which are splendid paintings by Pinturicchio, especially in what are called the Borgia rooms, and he showed us also an old, precious MS. life of St. George, with wonderful illustrations by Giotto. We were there hours, and took Miss Goodwin with us, who was most grateful. After luncheon I went to see Lord Dufferin. I saw the Bishop of Trebizond also, who had been away, and he will try to help us to an audience with the Pope, but there will be no chance until after Easter.

We meant to go to Naples to-day and had secured rooms in the Grand Hotel, when yesterday evening some people from Dublin, who knew both of us and who had returned from Naples the same day, told us there had been four cases of typhoid fever in the hotel, one of which had ended fatally on Monday. You can imagine that I countermanded the rooms at once. I have now telegraphed to the Bristol Hotel, the one high up in the healthiest situation, and if I get a

favourable answer we shall go to-morrow. Naples seems to
be crammed.

Newton is here also; I had a chat with him yesterday.

And now we shall set to work again, so I send you our
united love.

CIX

TO THE SAME

Hôtel Bristol, Naples: April 14, 1889.

Your, Louisa's and Anna's dear letters reached me yesterday evening and were none the less welcome for being late.
All your good wishes do me good and I thank you heartily
for them. May it do you good also to know that I am
supremely happy, and feel as if I had nothing more to desire
in this world.

We left Rome on Thursday afternoon, arrived here at
about seven o'clock (Italian railways are punctual now), found
good rooms, with a view upon Vesuvius and Capri and all the
rest of it, and had the pleasure of a good reception from the
smoking mountain, which showed a great deal of deep red at
regular intervals, so regular that milady for a long time would
maintain we saw a huge revolving light. On Friday we
spent the greater part of the day at the Museum, which seems
to me more interesting than ever, and afterwards took a drive
over the Pausilippo and back by Virgil's Tomb and the
Chiaja, which was full of carriages of every description; it
was most delightful. Yesterday we spent the day at Pompeii.
The weather was beautiful, and we were both in raptures. It
is and remains the most wonderful place in the world, and
you have no idea how much has been brought to light since
we were here last. One house, which has been unearthed for
the German Emperor, contains most remarkable pictures,
fresh as if painted yesterday. Another, laid bare only a fortnight ago, has garlands of flowers, fruits, with lizards and
birds, painted upon a black ground, too delicious for words!
There is one little bird, pecking at a grape, before which we

stood and could not tear ourselves away. In the evening we
had a thunderstorm, which we did not mind, as we go to
roost before ten o'clock to recover from the fatigues of the
day; but this morning there is another with rain and hail,
and that is much more serious, for probably we shall be unable
to do anything but go to the Museum again, which, however,
we could only half finish on Friday, so there would be no
harm in that, provided it cleared up afterwards, which, unfortunately, seems doubtful.

I have not told you that on Wednesday afternoon in Rome
we took a drive into the Campagna to see two extraordinary
tombs, which I do not think you saw. They are wonderfully
preserved, with remarkable pictures and decorations. On
returning, we crossed another carriage, heard shouts, and
who should jump out but Hamilton Aïdé, Schuster, and
Crawshay! You can imagine that we had a long chat.
They came from Naples, and Aïdé and Schuster were to leave
the next day for Florence. Crawshay has a house in Rome.

The next morning old Newton came with a message from
Mrs. Story, asking us to an afternoon tea with Mrs. Cyril
Flower and Mrs. Eliot Yorke, but, of course, we could not
accept, as we were leaving at one o'clock. We shall undoubtedly see the Storys when we return.

That is as much as I have to tell up to the present.
When I return I shall be more eager for work again than
ever, and shall enjoy the music amazingly.

CX

TO ONE OF HIS DAUGHTERS

Hotel d'Angleterre, Rome:
April 22, 1889.

I will try to relate our *faits et gestes* since my last letter
in the fewest words possible, for the weather is so splendid
that one grudges the minutes spent indoors.

On Friday afternoon we got to the station at Naples
half an hour too soon, but found every carriage full of

Italians, who had crammed in all their luggage with them. We were quite in despair, when a kind porter asked if we would like to travel in the Pullman Car, and then for a few francs we had a beautiful compartment to ourselves, and got comfortably to Rome without loss of luggage.

Shortly after nine we were at the hotel, and found cards from Lord Wilton, who had called twice during the day, and came again half an hour after our arrival to invite us to dinner next day with Boehm and Lord Dufferin. (At Naples I received an invitation from the Lord Mayor of London to meet Lord Dufferin at dinner at the Guildhall. The world is really very small !)

Boehm is staying at this hotel, and Lord Wilton at the ' Europe,' close by. The dinner was very pleasant.

Saturday we walked about and drove on Mount Pincio in the afternoon. Yesterday at 10 o'clock we went to High Mass at St. Peter's, which was sung by a Cardinal under the dome, not before the real high altar, but before one on the side of the crypt towards the entrance. The Papal Choir sang, and most beautifully, although the music was the reverse of sacred. After Mass the relics were shown from one of the balconies high up, all the people kneeling, and in fact the whole ceremony was most impressive. In the afternoon we saw a good many things, and at a quarter to five we heard Vespers at St. John Lateran's splendidly sung, the Bishop of Trebizond officiating.

But this morning at 7.30 we were present—think of that —at the Pope's own Mass in the Vatican ! And we shall never forget it ! It was celebrated in the ' Salle du Consistoire,' a beautiful room, by the Pope in person, without music, of course, and lasted from 7.30 to 9 o'clock. He is very old and shaky, poor dear, and his voice is tremulous, but I never heard Mass said with such reverence and deep expression. It sounded as if he read it for the first time and was overwhelmed by its sublimity. The effect was indescribable. At the same time there was much simplicity about the whole act; no show of cardinals, &c., &c.; there

were only a few priests with him, and of course some Swiss
Guards, whose costume is much spoilt by their having
adopted the German 'Pickelhaube.'

When we came back to the hotel we were very glad to
have breakfast, for we had got up between five and six o'clock,
and were at the Vatican punctually at seven, having had
nothing to eat.

Since then we have seen that wonderful villa 'Farnesina,'
with Raphael's Galatea, and other marvels, the Palazzo
Corsini, the Church of St. Cecilia in Trastevere, and this
evening we shall see the Coliseum lighted up with Bengal
fires. In fact, we live in Fairyland!

CXI

TO A FRIEND

Manchester: February 26, 1890.

My dear ——.—I have been so terribly busy the last few
days that I could not find a moment to write to you. Your
last letter naturally interested me very much, and the
Edinburgh outcry against me highly amused me. In the end
people will see that I could not give up the Reid Festival without telling them the reason. Had I not done so, they would
have imagined all sorts of reasons except the right one—viz.,
the bad attendance at the concerts. You know how often
during the past three years I have spoken to you about the
empty benches, and I should not have gone to Edinburgh
this year had it not been the double jubilee. Now the public
know the reason—the only reason—of my staying away, and
with that I am content. For the rest, I said no word about
'want of appreciation,' or of want of love for music, as you
yourself can testify. That has been gratuitously attributed
to me. I contented myself with the simple facts, and could
not possibly add 'thanks for the bad attendance!' I now
know that during the last few years the Professor contributed
towards the expenses. When I wrote I felt sure of it, but

had no positive proof. Can any one under such circumstances expect me to come again?

Also I cannot regret that I pounced upon the critics. They deserved it too richly, and one cannot *always* let them have the last word. That I had to attack your friend I am sorry for; but why did your friend never think into what a false position he put you through his ignorance and impudence? For *your* sake I am glad to have said what I did say, and on this point to have separated you from his stupidity. The frame of mind of such a man, who out of pure ignorance would, as it were, spit upon a work of art as divine as the Apollo Belvidere or the Venus of Milo, will ever remain incomprehensible to me. Respect for art, and the greatest masterpieces, I expect from every man, and from a so-called critic especially, and above all that the critic should have some knowledge of what to all men of the craft is irrefutable. Most likely the man in question never heard that both concertos, the E flat and the violin concerto,[1] stand at an unattainable height. Oh, thou rhinoceros!

Why did you not educate him better? Warn him for his own sake.

But let us leave the Edinburghers alone, and let me rather ask you once again if you cannot come to one of my Manchester concerts? On March 6 we give 'Faust.' Make an escapade for once and come. It will give us great pleasure, and the performance will interest you very much. Write soon, and with kind regards to your ladies, believe me, ever

Your old friend,

CHARLES HALLÉ.

CXII

FROM MR. LUDWIG STRAUS

(Translated from the German)

Cambridge: March 29, 1894.

Dear Sir Charles,—Among the noble-hearted friends and artists who have united to honour and distinguish me, I read,

_____
[1] By Beethoven.

though not in black on white, your *caro nome*. I am compelled, in the fulness of my heart, to thank you for your friendly sentiments, and for lending the power of your name to the twice 'seven before Thebes,' or rather, before Cambridge. Your noble wife brought the united beautiful gift, imbedded in a wealth of lovely red and yellow roses and wonderful lilies of the valley.

Our common labours, stretching over so many years, in the realms of symphony and chamber music came vividly to my mind, as well as the many pleasant hours we had spent together.

If only you had not been the terrible Pontifex Maximus of 'sixty-six,' who, during so many railway journeys, had so unmercifully treated me, poor neophyte !

Keep me ever in your good and friendly thoughts, and let me thank you again for your participation in this beautiful artists' demonstration.[1] With all my heart, ever yours,

LUDWIG STRAUS.

CXIII

TO MR. LUDWIG STRAUS

(Translated from the German)

Greenheys, Manchester: April 1, 1894.

My dear Mr. Straus,—Your very kind letter stirred me deeply and awoke many delightful recollections. Those were happy times we spent together, adorned with how much artistic pleasure, and never shadowed by the slightest cloud !

Our modest gift has the only merit of proving that your comrades think of you, and in what high esteem they hold you. As such a proof you will value it.

My wife, who happens to be here, has told me many

---

[1] Fourteen artist-friends and colleagues of Mr. Straus had given him on the occasion of his retirement a silver tea service and tray; on the tray the fourteen signatures of the donors, Lady Hallé, Joachim, Paderewski, Piatti, my father, &c., were engraved in *fac-simile*.

pleasant things of you, and the pleasantest of all was that she found you so much better. Your kind letter awakened a longing for a good long game of 'sixty-six,' with a cigar-accompaniment—not taking into consideration that I have to revenge myself for many defeats—and I hope you will soon allow me to seek you out in your home. I shall have a fortnight's holiday on the 14th of April, which I shall spend in London, and I shall take the liberty of proposing a day to you. It will certainly do us both good to have a real long chat together.

Greet Fräulein Ida for me, and believe me with the old, tried friendship, yours,   CHARLES HALLÉ.

CXIV

FROM MR. LUDWIG STRAUS

Cambridge: April 4, 1894.

Dear Sir Charles,—I was heartily pleased to see your handwriting again and to learn how kindly you are mindful of me.

I am leading a life of idleness, and have not made sufficient progress in the eating of macaroni to thoroughly master, or enjoy, the *dolce far niente*. I can still blow the cigar-smoke into the air, and still remember the difficulties of 'sixty-six': to secure the safety of the ten.

'Batti, Batti,' but come, and thus give great pleasure to your old, true friend,   LUDWIG STRAUS.

I am longing for a line to say what day you can propose.

CXV

TO MR. LUDWIG STRAUS

(*Translated from the German*)

London: April 18, 1894.

My dear Straus-gral,[1]—Who could resist? I shall arrive at 12.30 on the 23rd and ready for anything!

[1] This mode of address is evidently an allusion to their studies of *Parsifal*.

Your promises of 40 [1] and so on remind me of Molière and his doctor, who promised him thirty years of life if he would obtain for him a certain favour from the king. Molière answered: 'Mon bon docteur, je serai amplement récompensé si vous ne me tuez pas.' Just so; I may say to you that I shall be pleased if I come out of the fray with a whole skin, but I am ready for the fray.

So farewell till Monday. Your old and faithful friend,

CHARLES HALLÉ.

---

[1] A term in the game of sixty-six.

DIARIES AND NOTES OF TRAVEL

I

EXTRACTS FROM DIARY KEPT BY SIR CHARLES HALLÉ
IN THE YEARS 1855–6

[*Translated from the German.*]

December 12, 1855.

Rehearsal at the Concert Hall in the evening. Haydn's B Major Symphony, Overture, *Ossian*, Gade, the second movement of Berlioz's Symphony, 'Harold in Italy' ('Marche des Pélerins'), and a triumphal march by Best, for next week's concert. Tolerably satisfied with the orchestra, but still further convinced of the necessity of the intended reforms. Gade's overture is pretty and shows good intentions, but is wanting in strength and in breadth of idea. In the present dearth, however, its appearance must be accepted with thankfulness. Berlioz's movement carried me back to the dear old days, and therefore, perhaps, gave me exceptional pleasure. But how fresh, even at the present day, is the old master's, Haydn's, Symphony!

December 18, 1855.

The necessity of engaging a trumpet-player for to-morrow evening's concert took me to the theatre, where a pantomime rehearsal was going on. Knowles, in his usual abrupt manner, spoke to me of a plan which certainly deserves consideration. He proposed that I should ask the committee of the New Free Trade Hall if, and on what terms, they would let it to me for a year, or for a shorter or longer period, and that he and I should make use of it together.

A A

December 19, 1855.

Molique arrived towards four o'clock and accompanied me in the evening to the Concert Hall. His presence fired the violinists, and altogether the performance was not unsatisfactory. The effect of the whole was marred by the laughable figure and manners of the singer, which were not redeemed by any artistic qualities. A clarinet concerto in A by Mozart was capitally played by our excellent clarinettist, Grosse. The composition, although by Mozart, is such a grandfatherly production and so lengthy that the finale had to be left out, not to try the patience of the public beyond endurance. Mr. Best had come from Liverpool to hear his march, and introduced himself to me after the concert, but it was impossible to find anything agreeable to say about his composition.

December 20, 1855.

To-day's concert, the third, was not quite so well attended. The approach of Christmas, the cold weather, and Jullien, who is performing his hocus-pocus for the first time at the theatre, were perhaps the reasons that militated against it. The programme was as follows: Quartet, C major, Mozart; sonata with violin, C minor, Beethoven; pianoforte quartet, F minor, Mendelssohn; violin duet, G minor, Spohr; Barcarolle, Frühlingsglaube and Erlking, Schubert and Liszt. Molique was very well disposed and played splendidly. The duet was played by him and his pupil Carrodus in a masterly fashion. The concert was quite satisfactory, with the exception of the viola player, who caused us great anxiety. I was tolerably content with myself, but have often played better.

December 21, 1855.

Molique and Tolbecque left for London this morning at 9 o'clock; Lucas remained till 5. During the day I busied myself with the buying of Christmas presents, and in the evening the Christmas-tree arrived; it is a stately one.

December 22, 1855.

The preparations for Christmas continue. The children are very busy on their side, and the whole house is full of secrets. M. is not quite well, but I hope she will be all right

by Monday evening, so that we may be able to enjoy the
feast in the old accustomed manner.

December 23, 1855.

Dined with Mr. Henry Higgins. After dinner, with
him and Mr. Renshaw, we held an improvised meeting,
under Higgins's presidency, upon the affairs of the Concert
Hall, and brought them into order. My proposal and stipu-
lation was that, instead of the irregular and approximate
fortnightly rehearsals of two hours' duration, there should in
future be one rehearsal the day before the concert, and of
longer duration. The concerts must therefore be changed
to Thursday, and dates fixed longer beforehand. Everything
was willingly granted, whereupon I withdrew my resignation.

Very busy in the evening decorating the Christmas-tree.

December 24, 1855.

The dear, familiar Christmas Eve made us all, great and
small, very happy. The gifts to the children were rich, and
their delight filled our hearts with joy. The children had
again prepared a small tree for us in their school-room,
and pleased us, moreover, with little gifts of needlework,
drawings, and dear letters. Until 10 o'clock they revelled
in their happiness, which was to begin anew the next
morning. I received a nice present from Mr. Stern,
the 'Conversation's Lexicon,' in twenty-three volumes, and
Mendelssohn's 'Lieder ohne Worte,' beautifully bound, from
an anonymous but well-known hand. I gave my wife a neat
gold bracelet and necklace, which greatly pleased her.

December 25, 1855.

On this Christmas Day the children made closer
acquaintance with their new treasures, and I, during the
time, went over some new music. Gade's 'Spring Fantasia,'
a very thoughtful and pleasing work. Schumann's 'Paradise
and the Peri' truly surprised and entranced me; of all his
works not one has so deeply interested me; it has great
poetic charm; melody and harmony are new and very fine.
It is a pity that the poem is somewhat monotonous, and

must probably diminish the effect of the music, because it requires too many slow *tempi*. Began Marschner's ' Vampire.'

December 26, 1855.

Practised Molique's trio diligently, and continued Marschner's ' Vampire.' At the Concert Hall rehearsal in the evening I announced the renewal of my engagement to the members of the band, which was received with jubilation ; further, the changes in the regulations concerning the performances and rehearsals, which also met with approval. Afterwards, with the quartet alone, went through Berlioz's symphony, ' Harold in Italy,' and brought the three first movements to a satisfactory point. After the rehearsal I went to the first performance of the pantomime, ' St. George and the Dragon,' the unbounded stupidity of which annoyed me ; public taste in England is still rather backward. The performance of ' Elijah ' at the Concert Hall is fixed for January 22, and Banks's concert at Ashton-under-Lyne postponed to the 23rd.

December 27, 1855.

Spent a few hours of the day very pleasantly ; Canon Toole (a Catholic priest), a very nice, enlightened, poetry and art-loving man, brought the children a big magic-lantern, and many interesting pictures were thrown upon a white sheet fastened to the wall. Before Canon Toole left us, a remark about Shelley led to a theological discussion between him and Miss C. What a sharp contrast—an unbeliever and a Catholic priest !

December 28, 1855.

Finished reading Marschner's ' Vampire.' The work contains many beauties, and exceeds in true worth many of Meyerbeer's operas which enjoy such a far greater celebrity. It is to be regretted that so many of the incidents seem copied from the ' Freischütz.'

Piatti writes that his wife is better, and he hopes to be able to come on Wednesday. Received a letter from Chester ; they do not want a Beethoven Sonata for their concert on January 2, but something lighter.

December 29, 1855.

An article in the *Manchester Guardian*, under the title, ' Mr. Hallé and the Concert Hall,' speaks of the new regulations which I made known to the orchestra. The directors most likely will not approve of this publicity, but it is necessary and useful for the whole institution. The *Guardian* also draws attention to Molique's trio.

Began to write the score of Méhul's G minor Symphony. The work seems fresh and interesting.

For some time past I have read a great part of Schlosser's ' Welt-Geschichte,' and have much enjoyed the solid worth of the work; the craving after knowledge and learning has strongly revived in me; I thirst for a quiet time when I can better satisfy my longing for reading.

December 31, 1855.

The last day of the year; a day on which there was little work to do, I spent it quietly and co-ily in the midst of my family. Made music, and read a good deal. In the evening delighted the children very much by making them some weak punch before they went to bed, and making them drink the health of their grandmamma, their parents, and their aunts. The few hours before midnight I spent in alternately reading Schlosser and conversing with my wife, and so peacefully and quietly ended the year.

January 1, 1856.

At midnight peacefully and contentedly greeted the New Year with a glass of punch. The children were all quietly wrapped in slumbers free from care; we parents went the rounds to give them each a first loving New Year's kiss. The past year has brought us many joys and much good, and has had few shadows: may the coming one be as favourable. Seldom has the looking back been so pleasant, and though there have been many cares, they are none of them discouraging.

January 2, 1856.

Started for Chester at 8.45, and went to the Royal Hotel. At 11 looked up Mr. Gunton to talk over the performance of the ' Messiah,' which must take place without a rehearsal.

Mr. Gunton is organist at Chester, and in the absence of an
orchestra had undertaken to accompany the 'Messiah' on the
organ. Upon my natural inquiry as to whether the chorus
was safe, I received the surprising answer that he had never
heard them; so that conductor, chorus, solo-singers and
organist for a great performance met for the first time in
the hall, and at the moment of commencing the concert!
Nevertheless everything went well; the chorus was excellent
(from Liverpool), the organist also, the solo-singers, Madame
Rudersdorff, Miss Messent, Miss Dolby, Mr. Lockey, and
Mr. Thomas altogether left very little to be desired, and so
the conducting was not unpleasant. A young bass-singer,
Cuzner, made his *début* in the air 'Why do the Nations,'
and gave proof of a good voice. After the morning concert
wandered through the quaint old town, and visited the famous
cathedral, where the carved wood-work of the choir is specially
remarkable. In the streets the arcades over the foot-ways
struck me most. At the evening concert I played Liszt's
'Lucia,' Caprice in E by Mendelssohn, 'La Truite' by
Heller (as an encore, impromptu by Chopin); two 'Lieder
ohne Worte' by Mendelssohn, and a waltz by Chopin.

January 3, 1856.

Left Chester at 9.10 and reached home at half-past 11,
where I found Molique and Piatti waiting for me; both
had arrived the previous evening. The concert was very
gratifying, and gave me personally great enjoyment. Programme.—Trio, Beethoven, Op. 70, No. 2; sonata with
violoncello in A, Op. 69, Beethoven; trio in F, Op. 52.
Molique; Souvenir d'Ems. Romanza, and 'Les Fiancés,'
petit caprice for 'cello, Piatti; Serenade, Op. 56. Heller, and
Mazurkas in B, F minor, and C, Chopin. Beethoven's two
magnificent works were played as perhaps we had never
played them before; Molique's new trio is highly interesting,
and made a deep impression. Molique was recalled, and
the dear good man was as much moved by the affection with
which we had played his work as by its reception by the
public. For me it will always remain a pleasant recollection

that I have, so to speak, brought this trio to light. Piatti's little solos were, as usual, played in masterly style. I, too, was satisfied with my playing, in spite of a little slip of memory in Heller's Serenade. Both friends left for London at 4 A.M. Piatti was anxious about his wife, and Molique went to bear him company. I sought my bed at 1 o'clock, very tired.

January 4, 1856.

The *Guardian* and the *Examiner* have very laudatory articles on the concert, especially on Molique's trio, so that the apprehended danger that unfamiliarity with the work might cause dissatisfaction with it, and thus affect its reception in London, is happily averted. Set my library in order, and sent a quantity of books and music to Anderson, the bookbinder. In the evening continued to write the score of Méhul's symphony, and busied myself choosing the works for the next concert.

Put the last touch to the corrections of the first twelve sonatas by Beethoven for the new edition.

January 5, 1856.

To-day's *Athenæum* attacks Jenny Lind pretty severely for her rendering of the solos in the 'Messiah;' Chorley's personal likes and dislikes seem to have an influence upon his pen, without his will or knowledge. Wrote some more of Méhul's symphony; the first movement is half finished; the ideas are fresh and noble; but the workmanship and power are not very interesting, but somewhat trivial.

January 6, 1856.

Ella writes that he wishes to give some lectures on music in Manchester; he seems to have already entered into the matter with Mr. Andrews, who referred him to me. I have promised to use my influence, and have asked for more particulars. Busy with a mass of correspondence that had got into arrears. Mr. Banks, who came to inquire about the programme for his coming concert, told me he had heard Jenny Lind in the 'Messiah' at Liverpool; according to him she has fallen off, and the applause, though still great, was not to be compared with the enthusiasm of former days.

January 7, 1856.

For the next concert I have chosen the sonata by Beethoven, Op. 27, No. 2, never yet played by me in public, and am working hard at it. Spohr's trio in F will also be given, and require some preparation.

Have finished the fourth volume of Schlosser's 'Welt-Geschichte,' thus terminating the history of the old world, which was rich in enjoyment.

January 8, 1856.

Have finished the sketch of the programme for four private concerts to be given during the winter months, and have sent it to Mr. Higgins for perusal; it contains much that is new and interesting, and I shall be pleased if it is accepted, although I have prepared much hard work for myself by it. Ella writes that he has already given up the intention of giving musical lectures in Manchester. He has not yet decided to give concerts before Easter, and maintains that everything in London is at a standstill, except Jenny Lind, who seems to monopolise the public.

Have written to Molique to consult him as to the best construction for the new platform that is to be erected in the Free Trade Hall.

January 9, 1856.

Began the Andante of Méhul's symphony, which seems to be very simple.

Busied myself with the analysis of Spohr's trio in F, and the Beethoven sonata.

Began to read about the Arabs in Schlosser.

January 10, 1856.

Chappell, the publisher, has at last consented to allow my new edition of Beethoven's sonatas to proceed in chronological order, instead of in the arbitrary order, or rather disorder, of Moscheles' edition. I have commended him much for it. The analysis of Spohr's trio for the next programme is finished and sent to the printer.

January 11, 1856.

Have half finished a long letter to my mother, which will give her great pleasure, as it contains a full description of our Christmas doings. The children had an invitation to Professor Scott's,[1] but were kept at home by the cold weather, so after dinner I consoled them by playing with them for a whole hour—building palaces, lighthouses, and such like with their little wooden bricks. In the evening I worked at the symphony, and practised. A duet for piano and violin upon 'William Tell,' by Osborne and de Beriot, which I shall have to play next week with Mr. Cooper, vividly reminded me of a *soirée* at Madame Huët's fifteen years ago, when I played it with Alard.

The thought of going once again to Paris and playing at the Conservatoire has greatly occupied my mind to-night.

January 12, 1856.

Auguste Gathy writes from Paris asking for biographical notes for an article on me in his 'Musical Lexicon.' He congratulates me upon the situation I have won in England.

In the evening worked hard at Méhul's Andante, so as to be rid of it, as my interest in the work begins to diminish.

January 15, 1856.

Left for Wakefield at 12.10. Before starting I bought a good edition of the 'Vicar of Wakefield,' and by its perusal changed an otherwise tedious day into a very pleasant one. The place itself is most prosaic, dark, and smoky, as are all English manufacturing towns, and in no way answers nowadays to Goldsmith's description. I arrived at 4 o'clock and went to the Strafford Arms—a very old-fashioned building, with old-fashioned management and service. I met there Mr. Perring and Mr. Wynn, who take part, like me, in to-night's concert. They are both indifferent singers, but possessed of a certain amount of instruction, and very much in earnest. The givers of the concert—Mr. Cooper and Miss Milner—only want talent to make them very good artists. The concert took place at 8 o'clock at the Exchange Rooms—

[1] Principal of Owens College.

a large hall with good acoustic, and before a large audience.
My share of the programme consisted of Osborne and de
Beriot's duet, the Finale of Lucia, by Liszt, Caprice in
E Major, by Mendelssohn, and Heller's Truite (as an encore,
Lied ohne Worte in A, by Mendelssohn), variations from
Beethoven's Kreutzer Sonata, and an impromptu and two
waltzes by Chopin. The appreciation of the public, among
whom was the former celebrated singer, Miss Wood, was flat-
tering. The first duet, however, did not go well at all. After
the concert I took a stroll through the principal streets of
Wakefield, and returned to the hotel, where I had a tolerably
long conversation with Mr. Perring.

January 16, 1856.

Finished the ' Vicar of Wakefield ' in bed this morning,
and therefore rose late. At 12.30 started for Leeds in company with Mr. Perring and Mr. Wynn. The programme
was identical with that of last evening. I had even greater
success than the day before, and after Chopin's Waltz had to
play two Mazurkas (in B and C Major). An Erard piano
was sent to both places for me. During the day I went to
an exhibition of French paintings, and was specially struck
by the powerful conception and vigorous execution of Rosa
Bonheur's picture of the Horse Fair. The grouping of the
spirited, snorting horses is wonderful, and there reigns a
mighty lifelikeness in the whole work. Very remarkable is the
new, nearly completed, town hall—a building that does honour
to the town of Leeds, and that will have few rivals in England.

Bought a fine-bound Virgil (in Latin) with the date of
1548, also an English translation of Juvenal and Persius.

January 17, 1856.

Left Leeds at 7.20 and arrived at Greenheys towards
10 o'clock. Piatti and Sainton arrived at 3 o'clock, and we
began the rehearsal for to-night's concert at once. Programme:
Trio in F, Op. 123, Spohr; Sonata quasi Fantasia, Op. 27, No. 2,
Beethoven; trio in B, Op. 97, Beethoven; Variations *à la
Monferine*, piano and violoncello, Hummel; *Morceau de Salon*,
violin in D, Sainton. The trio in B gave us special pleasure,

and made a great impression on the public, as also did the
Sonata, which I played with a little hesitation. During the
concert we were pleasantly surprised by a little supper of
oysters and champagne, arranged by some friends. Heron,
the Town Clerk, presided at it. Piatti and Sainton left again
at 4 A.M. After the concert we entertained ourselves for a
time with the game of cannonade.

January 18, 1856.

Very busy the whole day, so that I felt the fatigue of the
previous day's exertions doubly. Dinner at Mrs. Grundy's,
where I met Professor Scott and his wife, with the poet C.
Swain, and spent a very interesting evening. Some little
pieces I played to them were gratefully welcomed.

January 19, 1856.

In the few free moments my pupils left me I practised
hard the duet for piano and viola on themes from 'The
Huguenots,' by Thalberg and de Bériot, as I have to play it
next week at the concert with Mr. Blagrove. Very unpleas-
ing and uncongenial work, which I have to force myself to.
In the evening choral rehearsal at the Concert Hall for
the 'Elijah' which takes place next Tuesday. In precision
of intonation the chorus leaves much to be desired, but I
have tried to give them an idea of the importance of *nuances*,
and in this I have partly succeeded. At any rate, they have
become more attentive. But, so long as the chorus does not
have regular practice, good results cannot be expected. To
this end, let us hope, the new Free Trade Hall will soon
contribute.

January 20, 1856.

A letter from Molique, with a very good plan for the
building of the orchestra in the Free Trade Hall. I am
entirely satisfied with it, and hope to get it adopted. Sainton
writes he can accept an engagement at the Concert Hall for
February 21. I offered an engagement, through Molique,
for the same date, to Miss Leusden, recommended to me by
Hiller. She seems to be a very good contralto. Mr. and
Mrs. Troost and Mr. Kyllmann visited us in the morning.

The latter criticised the too rapid speed of the *tempo* of the Finale of the Beethoven Sonata at the last concert, and he may have been right.

At 3 o'clock I dined with the Charles Souchays, and spent a most agreeable afternoon. A noble and intellectual family, such as one rarely finds. During dinner, among other things, much talk of the pleasantness of the life in many parts of Germany, and the beauties of my birthplace, which they knew by report, were sung by me. Later, I played some short, delicious pieces of Heller's, which led to some very interesting conversation. A letter from Mendelssohn was read, in which he expresses the opinion that words are vague, and capable of many interpretations, whilst music renders feelings with precision. Against this there is very much to say. Altogether, the letter seems to me more ingenious than true. Then Heine was much talked of, and I had many anecdotes to tell of our former close acquaintanceship in Paris. When the conversation turned upon painting, Mrs. Souchay asserted an opinion, against which I protested, that a painter can only reproduce the impression of what he has actually observed in nature. For instance, he could only paint the sorrow on a human countenance that he had really seen there.

January 21, 1856.

Worked again at that fatal Thalberg duet, and looked more closely through the three Schumann trios, in order to choose one for the next concert. The third seems to be the best.

In the evening choral and orchestral rehearsal of 'Elijah.' Of the solo singers only Miss Birch put in an appearance. The chorus did better, and the orchestra was really good, and so the performance promises to be satisfactory.

January 22, 1856.

Went to Mr. Blagrove in the morning to arrange for a rehearsal for this afternoon, and then to Mr. Peacock to lay the plan for the orchestra before him, which met with his entire approval. We went together to the new building, which is pretty well advanced, and I was much surprised by the size and beauty of the different rooms. But it seems to me that in the great hall the space allowed for the orchestra is too small, and especially is it to be feared that the desire of gain, or, at any rate, of material profit, will not be brought into accord with the necessary arrangements for real artistic purposes.

The performance of the 'Elijah' this evening was in many respects satisfactory, though the soloists left something to be desired. According to old-established custom, the public gave no sign of approval throughout, which naturally was not encouraging to the performers.

January 23, 1856.

The concerts that have lately taken place in the surrounding towns have given me the notion of attempting a so-called *tournée* myself, and I have already written to Sainton and Piatti about terms.

At 6 in the evening started with Miss Poole, Miss Manning, Miss Wilkinson (a young pupil of Garcia's), Mr. Blagrove, Mr. Frank Bodda, and Banks in an omnibus from the Mosley Arms Hotel for Ashton-under-Lyne for a concert. This was largely attended by a somewhat raw and unintelligent public; the reaction upon me was such as to make me very dissatisfied with my playing, and altogether I could not work myself up to concert pitch. We returned in the same omnibus, and I reached home very tired at midnight, and with the fear that the Broadwood piano I had sent there might be injured by the dampness of the hall.

January 24, 1856.

The programme of to-day's concert in Bury was the exact counterpart of last night's. The public quite as numerous, but very intelligent and appreciative. I have seldom played better; my pieces the same as last evening: Beethoven's Sonata in C. Op. 53, Thalberg and de Beriot, Heller's Truite, and the Finale of Lucia by Liszt. The duet pleased so well that part of it had to be repeated, and after Liszt's Fantasia

I had to play Mendelssohn's 'Volks' and 'Frühling's Lied' as an encore. The whole evening, as well as the drive there and back, was very pleasant, and reconciled me to the whole undertaking.

January 25, 1856.

Sainton writes that he usually gets 30 guineas a week during a *tournée*, and leaves it to me to decide what I shall give him; this would be very acceptable, but the project cannot be realised before the coming season as it requires too much preparation, for which I cannot spare the time. We shall see later on. Piatti sent an undecided answer.

Third concert to-night : at Cheetham, in the new Town Hall. Very empty room. The programme the same as last night and the night before.

January 26, 1856.

Studied the second Schumann trio (F major) and Heller's 'Wanderstunden' and 'Nuits Blanches' for the next concert, and the last-named filled me with the intensest pleasure. Later went through some of Bach's Motets, which are to be tried next Monday at the St. Cecilia.

January 27, 1856

Worked at the analysis of Schumann's trio for the next concert, in which I proffered the opinion that the German element contained in Schumann's works, and which has some affinity with the spirit of Jean Paul, militates somewhat against a right understanding of them in other countries. Worked at the trio itself, as also on the little Heller things. Some of Schumann's 'Noveletten' I played through with delight.

January 28, 1856.

Finished the analyses of the trio, and also of Beethoven's A minor Sonata. Op. 23, and took them both myself to Sever, who was greatly pleased with the first. Ordered at Mr. Hulme's a large mirror for our drawing-room as a surprise for my wife.

The St. Cecilia was not well attended, most likely on account of the cold and bad weather; the Bach Motets caused great interest, and promised us many pleasant hours.

They will be studied with affectionate industry. After the
meeting went with Mr. Hecht, Dr. Finckler, and Mr. Wydler
to the Clarence, where we chatted agreeably for an hour or
two. On the way back I asked Dr. Finckler to give me
some lessons in Latin, and so fulfil a long-cherished wish,
and we fixed next Friday evening for the first lesson.

January 29, 1856.

Worked diligently for the next concert. The trio by
Schumann pleases me more and more. Also the Noveletten
become clearer and dearer to me; the ear becomes accustomed
to some rather considerable harshness. An Étude by Kullak,
'Les Arpèges,' I played through, which promises to be a
brilliant and pleasing drawing-room piece. Went through
some parts of Bach's Mass with astonishment and admiration.
In the evening wrote a few pages of the score of Mozart's
9th Concerto in G major.

II

EXTRACTS FROM DIARY KEPT DURING SIR CHARLES AND LADY HALLÉ'S FIRST TOUR IN AUSTRALIA IN 1890

Wednesday, May 28, 1890.

On Friday morning, the 16th, at about 9 o'clock, we
arrived safe and sound at Williamstown, the port for Melbourne, and were met on board by Mr. and Mrs. Poole, Mr.
Otter (in whom I recognised a former assistant at Chappell's,
and also at Schott's), a representative of the *Argus*, and
several other people. I received also a few letters of welcome,
amongst which was one from Mr. Gurnett, my former pupil,
and now musical critic of the *Argus*. The Captain went with
us on shore, and we travelled together to Melbourne by rail,
which took us about three-quarters of an hour. Here the
Captain put us into a queer-looking cab, into which we got
from behind, and on the way to the hotel we drove first to the
Custom-house, where the polite secretary, to whom I had a
letter from Mr. Cashel Hoey, told me that he had given orders
already on the previous day to pass all our luggage unex-

amined. At the hotel we found our rooms ready for us. Wilma told me that whilst I was at the Custom-house our cabby had held a conversation with her through the open window, addressing her at once as ' Milady,' and telling her he felt sure we should have a great success ; he would be proud to drive us to the concerts, and hoped that on our return to England ' You will speak well of us,' meaning the public of Melbourne, himself included. At 1 o'clock the Captain called and took me to the head office of the P. and O. Company, where the manager in the most obliging manner secured for our return journey the very best cabin on the *Arcadia* ; he also gave me a few good Manilla cigars, and offered me his further services in the most amiable way. Our luggage arrived shortly after, minus a large box, which, however, turned up next day, having caused us much anxiety in the meanwhile. At 3 o'clock a deputation from the resident professional musicians presented us with an illuminated address ; other people called to welcome us ; a very good semi-grand Bechstein was brought in from Allan's, the largest musical firm here, and at 7 o'clock the Captain came to dinner, and we spent a most enjoyable evening together. The next morning I was interviewed by Mr. Hart, one of the staff of the *Argus* paper. Toole, who is staying at this hotel, paid us a visit, and offered us boxes for his theatre. Santley also came and told us of his disagreeable adventures. On Monday, the 19th, at 4 o'clock, we were received officially by the Mayor and welcomed to Melbourne in the Town Hall.

On Tuesday I left cards and letters at the Governor's, the Prime Minister's, and the Chancellor's of the University, and saw the two latter gentlemen. Thursday, the 22nd, the day of our first concert, we did not go out, and denied ourselves to all visitors. We dined at 3 o'clock, and drove to the Town Hall at a quarter to 8. We were rather curious to learn how the public would like us, and were glad to find a very full room, representing 243*l.* 18*s.* Lord and Lady Hopetoun arrived punctually to the minute, the accompanist playing ' God Save the Queen ' vigorously on

the piano as they entered. When they were seated I mounted
the platform to play the Waldstein sonata, and was received
with much and prolonged applause, which was renewed
vehemently after each movement, and at the end I was recalled
twice. Wilma's first piece, the 'Fantaisie Caprice,' created a
perfect *furore*, and she was recalled four times. She was in
excellent form, and I really believe that I never had heard her
play so well, with such grace, such passion, such marvellous
perfection, and such mastery. It was a thing to be remembered, and no wonder that the public was amazed. The whole
concert was a grand triumph, and made us think that we are
quite safe here. During the interval Lord Hopetoun came to
speak to us, and was very amiable. He is almost a boy still,
hardly twenty-eight, and seems lively. We had to promise
him that we would dine at Government House on the following Sunday. The papers next morning sang our praises to
the echo, and we collected them to send home. Saturday,
the 24th, the Queen's Birthday, was very rainy and disagreeable. We received an invitation to Government House for
9.30, and previous to that I dined with the Gurnetts to meet
some of the principal musical men here. Mr. Otto Linden, a
pianist, Herr Scherch, both with their wives, and several
others, dined, and many more came immediately the dinner
was over. Mr. Linden said a great deal about the advantages
the whole profession had derived from my 'Practical Pianoforte School,' which it seems has been adopted throughout
Australia.

At 9 o'clock I fetched Wilma and drove with her to
Government House. The throne-room is really splendid, and
the party was a brilliant one. Lady Hopetoun talked a long
time with Wilma, and proved very charming, simple, and shy.
We made many acquaintances, amongst others that of the
Austrian Consul, Herr Carl Pinschoff, a most charming man
and a true Viennese, a great friend of Brahms, and formerly
of Wagner, having always lived in musical circles and married
a singer, Mlle. Widemann.

Sunday, the 25th, we lunched with Sir William Clarke.

There were a few more guests: Colonel Waddington, Aide-de-camp to the Governor, some others, and the captain of a sailing vessel, who proved to be from Manchester and a nephew of Sir James Watts; I have forgotten his name. He told us that one of his passengers, a few days after leaving England, had gone raving mad, so that he had to fasten him up. The laws of this country do not allow a madman to be landed, and so the captain does not know what to do with him, and fears he will be saddled with him for a long time. This house is a perfect marvel for the size and number of the entertaining rooms, and also for the number of admirable bed-rooms, which Lady Clarke showed us. But this is not to be wondered at, as they are amongst the very richest people in Australia. We dined with the Hopetouns, who were most amiable. We had great fun in the evening with a tame opossum, a very nice beast, and a curious parrot. Lady Hope-toun made us promise to lunch with her on Wednesday, when she would show us her horses, her kangaroos, and her emus.

The concert on Monday was very full, and our success greater than ever. On Tuesday evening the same crowd and the same most flattering success. Wilma gets heaps of the most beautiful baskets and bouquets of flowers, much to her delight, and when we drive home the whole carriage is full of flowers.

Friday, May 30, 1890.

On Wednesday afternoon, after our luncheon with Lord and Lady Hopetoun, which was very agreeable, Wilma had a reception, and many people called—so many, that at 6 o'clock she was quite exhausted. At Government House we had been much amused by the kangaroos and the three emus, the funniest beasts we ever saw. A lady has sent Wilma two emu eggs, very big and curious, as a souvenir from Melbourne. The concert yesterday, our fifth, was fuller than any of the others, the receipts exceeding 400*l.* There was not a place empty in the whole hall, even the platform being crowded, and much money was refused at the doors. It appears that the next one, to-morrow, will be equally crowded. All the

papers are most sweet; we shall keep and take them home.
This morning we were photographed. At 2 we received
letters from England, as we had done on Friday, and were
very happy.

Saturday, May 31, 1890.

To-day Mr. Poole brought me the instructions for the
next fortnight. They are: June 4. Geelong; 5th, Melbourne;
6th, Ballarat; 7th, Melbourne; 10th. 12th, and 11th. Melbourne; in the same week as the last three dates there will
be a concert at Sandhurst, the date of which is not fixed yet.
On the 19th we commence at Sydney, arriving there on the
16th, so as to get two days' rest before beginning. The
weather to-day is fine and warm.

Tuesday, June 3, 1890.

The concert on Saturday was again crowded; the platform had been made narrower, and thus about three rows of
reserved seats gained, the first row being, nearly in its entirety,
occupied by twenty blind people who were treated to the
concert by Lady Clarke. After Wilma's first solo there came
an extraordinary shower of bouquets down upon her; half the
platform was full of them, and it took several people to pick
them up. After my last solo three very handsome bouquets
were thrown at me also, with which I walked off proudly.
On Sunday we took luncheon with the Austrian Consul. The
day was fine, and we walked to the railway station and took
return tickets to Windsor, where he lives. We passed Richmond and other stations with well-known English names, and
on arrival drove in a hansom to his house. His wife is on
a visit to her mother in Vienna. He has two nice little
daughters, of whom his sister-in-law takes care. The captain
of the *Sperber*, a German man-of-war, Herr von Foss, took
luncheon with us, and was very entertaining. He had
taken Stanley and Emin Pasha to Zanzibar, and was at the
banquet after which Emin walked out of the window instead
of the door, and had his celebrated fall. The captain is a
charming man of most polished manners. Two other gentlemen were there, nice people also.

B B 2

Thursday, June 5, 1890.

Yesterday morning Captain Briscoe paid us a visit, to our great surprise; he had only just arrived. He is to go to the concert with us this evening, and afterwards stay for supper. At 1.25 P.M. we left for Geelong, where we arrived at 3; were received by Mr. and Mrs. Poole, Otter and Rose, and drove to the 'Grand Coffee Palace.' Shortly after we had settled in our sitting-room a mouse descended by the window curtain and took up her quarters in a cottage piano, where later on we heard her rummaging amongst the wires. The view upon the harbour and the sea was rather fine. The concert at the Exhibition Theatre, a very draughty place, was crammed full, not a seat being vacant, and the applause was tumultuous. Geelong seems a very primitive place, and we had to walk through a long garden, into which carriages cannot enter, to get to the theatre. Fortunately, the weather was fine; if it had been raining we could hardly have got there at all. We left again at 10.15 this morning and arrived at Melbourne at 12. To-morrow we have a concert at Ballarat, and on Saturday here again; the one in Sandhurst is given up, or at all events postponed for the present.

Tuesday, June 10, 1890.

The concert on Thursday last was again satisfactory in every respect. Friday morning we left for Ballarat, the celebrated gold-mining place. We arrived at 3 after a somewhat tedious journey through an uninteresting country, very thinly inhabited. Strange and weird-looking were a multitude of trees, bereft of all foliage and of all bark; they are killed by an incision made near the ground, called bark-ringing, after which they die, and in a year's time fall to the ground, thus saving the trouble of felling them. We found Craig's Royal Hotel a very small place, but the eating was much better than we expected. Ballarat lies 1,500 feet higher than Melbourne, and is therefore somewhat colder. It is a beautiful town, with broad streets and fine clean houses, most of them surrounded by splendid gardens. The concert was a curious affair, the

house crammed to suffocation, in the cheaper places by crowds
of miners who actually roared their applause. Unfortunately
we had again much to suffer from draughts, the place being
a theatre, and a rather dilapidated one; I was most anxious
on account of Wilma, but fortunately she has not suffered
much from it. On Saturday morning we left again at
11 o'clock, but before then the President of the Associated
Miners (himself one of them) and the Inspector of Mines
called to present Wilma with a little piece of gold, as a
memorial of Ballarat, and they offered, if we paid another
visit to the place, to take us to the mines and show us everything worth seeing. We returned to Melbourne at 2.15, and
had our eighth concert in the evening. A very full house
again, and the usual success. The programmes had gone
astray, and every piece had to be announced by Herr Scherek,
the accompanist.

Sunday we spent at home, reading and writing letters to
England, declining to see any visitors. Yesterday, Monday,
Mr. Poole came to give me the dates of the first six concerts
at Sydney, where he was going in the afternoon. The
Chancellor of the University had invited me to meet him
and the council at half-past 1 o'clock, which I did, and then
aired my views about the Chair of Music. They seemed
much impressed with what I said, and asked me to revise the
paper which they had sent out to candidates, and strike out
those of the conditions I could not approve of, which I have
promised to do. In the evening the Liedertafel gave me a
reception, or a ' Social ' as they call it, and presented me with
a beautifully got-up address (to Sir Charles and Lady Hallé).
The President, Judge Casey, is a very nice man, and the
conductor, Mr. Hertz, extremely clever, to judge from the
excellent way in which the Liedertafel, about 120 strong,
sang. The quality of the voices, the ensemble and nuances,
all were as good as could be wished for. All the evening I
sat on a raised platform between the President and Baron von
Müller, a celebrated botanist, who has been in Australia
upwards of fifty years, and has explored it from east to west.

It is curious that he and another gentleman, who was present last night, should have lived, fifty years ago, under a tent, in the midst of a bush and surrounded by kangaroos, on the very spot on which Melbourne stands now; so rapid has been the growth of the town. I made the acquaintance of Mr. Hayter, a Government Statist, who has sent me a most interesting book on the population of Victoria. It shows that before 1835 there was not one white man in the whole province, but about 5,000 aborigines; by May 25, 1836, there were 177 whites, by November 8 of the same year 224, two years later there were 3,511, and by April 3, 1881, 849,438. This shows what a new country it is; in 1841 there were in the whole province only 1,190 dwellings, and in 1881 their number was 179,816. The population of Melbourne falls short of that of Manchester, without Salford, and the wonder is that so many concerts can be given in so short a time; but then, there are no poor people here at all, and a beggar is not known.

To-day is a good day for practice, and I must say that the contact with a new public has done us much good, and has put fresh musical life into us. Playing so constantly in England as we do, it becomes a matter of routine, and loses its interest; here we are quite astonished to find that we take a real interest in every concert, in every article in the papers, and we certainly do our very best. It is a great satisfaction to witness the breathless attention with which these large crowds listen to us; there is not the least exaggeration in saying that you might hear a pin drop; and never a soul stirs before the last note is played.

June 11, 1890.

The concert last night was full, without being crowded. The wretched weather must have detained many. Mr. Wilson, from Ballarat, a son of the late Canon Wilson, of Manchester, this morning sent Wilma a box full of specimens from the different gold mines; they are extremely interesting and gave her much pleasure. Two gentlemen travelled 500 miles yesterday to hear us and are returning to-day, but wish to shake hands before they leave. A letter from Sandhurst

speaks of the impatience with which we are expected there,
but it is doubtful if we can go. Mr. Wilson called at twelve
o'clock with a little daughter, aged fourteen, who played for
me, and very well too. She is to be sent to England, and I
could honestly encourage him to do so. The two gentlemen
from Hamilton came also. One of them proved to be the
nephew of the celebrated chess-player, Horrwitz, whom I
knew long years ago, and the other, a Mr. Palmer, a nephew
of Heller, the well-known 'prestidigitateur.' They were in
raptures over the concert and are remaining for to-morrow's.
As it was Wilma's reception-day, we had crowds of people in
the afternoon—amongst them several of our fellow-passengers
from the *Valetta*. A quiet dinner and an hour's 'sixty-six'
concluded the day. Of course, we both practised to-day as
on every other day.

June 14, 1890.

We remained at home on Thursday, and had a most
brilliant concert in the evening, with a crowded audience.
A little girl presented Wilma with a violin, full-size, made of
violets. We heard from Mr. Rose that at his hotel a party
of twenty-five are staying, who have come hundreds of miles
from the bush for our last three concerts here.

Yesterday, Friday, was a wet day, but we had to go to the
University at 2.30, which the Chancellor wished to show us.
It was very interesting, but a great fatigue, so many different
buildings had to be visited. In the museum we saw a curious
freak of nature, the skeleton of a young man, who, from the
knee downwards had only one leg and one foot, although
from the knee upwards he was formed like other people.
Curiously enough the skeleton had been prepared by the
father of Eugène Sue, the novelist, who was a distinguished
doctor. One of the professors came from Manchester and
knew me, of course. The great hall of the University is a
beautiful place—not quite finished yet—with fine oak carv-
ings and bronze chandeliers. We had to take wine with the
Chancellor, who had escorted us everywhere in full academical
costume, in his private room, and very good Australian wine

it proved to be. On our return to the hotel, we found the long-desired letters from home, and were very happy, all the more so that they brought only good news. In the evening I went for the first time to the Yorick Club, of which I had been made an honorary member, and met there the Town Clerk, Mr. Nisbett, Mr. Hart, and several other gentlemen, with whom I spent two hours very pleasantly.

To-day Wilma is not so well, probably in consequence of our trudging about in the wet University grounds yesterday, and I wish this evening's concert were over. Altogether the salutary effect of the long sea-voyage seems on the wane and I long to be afloat again. Yesterday a long telegram from Lord Carrington informed me that he and Lady Carrington will, after all, be at our first concert in Sydney, his intended inland journey having been put off on account of some floods. At the same time he asked us to dinner on Thursday next, which invitation we accepted by telegraph. At three o'clock this afternoon we went to the orchestral concert in the Town Hall to hear Haydn's 'Clock' Symphony and Beethoven's 'Leonora' Overture. We would gladly have stopped at home if all the newspapers had not announced our visit. We were conducted in state to two enormous armchairs in front, one on each side of a passage, so that we could not even talk together.

June 16, 1890.

The concert on Saturday was perhaps the most successful of all; the hall was crammed and the demonstrations of the public as enthusiastic as possible. A floral tribute was offered to Wilma on the part of her compatriots, which was extremely handsome and costly; a thousand pities that it must fade away. Altogether, we were extremely gratified, and the people cheered us in the street when we left the hall. We can be sure of a hearty welcome on our return.

To-day we leave at 4.55 P.M. The weather is fine, but people tell us that the night will be very cold and uncomfortable. We have to change at 11.20.

June 21, 1890.

The journey from Melbourne to Sydney was very tedious, the carriages very uncomfortable, and we had to change at eleven o'clock at Albany, where the N.S. Wales line begins. We got up pretty early, and had a very bad breakfast at Mittagong. On Wednesday, the 18th, our first concert was given, after we had been debating the whole day if it ought not to be postponed, for since the previous day or two Wilma had been suffering from rheumatism in the middle finger of her left hand, which made playing very painful and almost impossible. Poole was in a great state of excitement and anxiety, and finally we arranged that I should let him know at six in the evening if the concert was to take place. At the last moment and with her usual pluck Wilma decided that she would play, and never did she play more divinely. Our success was enormous, but how glad we were when it was over!

On Thursday afternoon the Mayor received us in the Town Hall at 3 P.M. He sent his carriage for us, and, with Mrs. Burdekin, met us at the top of the outside stairs—she, a very handsome and ladylike woman, presenting Wilma with a splendid bouquet. The Mayor himself, a man of enormous wealth, is charming, and has most friendly, winning manners. We were conducted upstairs to the first of a long suite of reception rooms, where we took our stand, and immediately after the presentations began. We had to shake hands with about 800 people, the *crème* of the society here, including the Speakers of both Houses, Ministers of State, Consuls, &c., &c. They all passed us, went through the suite of rooms, and found their way to the other side of the building, where, in another suite of rooms, refreshments were served, and to which we also were conducted when we had done with the shaking of hands. The whole thing was admirably managed, much better than at Melbourne, and no speeches were delivered. The two suites of rooms are on both sides of the large hall, in which the huge organ is being erected, for the completion of which Mr. Best is waiting here. The hall is really a grand and splendid one, all white, and of noble proportions; I cannot recollect one in Europe to match it. People hope we shall be able to give a few concerts in it when we return from Brisbane, but that seems doubtful.

We left at 5 o'clock, the Mayor conducting us to the carriage. Shortly after we had to dress to drive to Government House, where dinner was at 7 o'clock, to enable us to attend the second part of the Liedertafel's Jubilee Concert. Lord and Lady Carrington had been at our concert the previous evening, but could not speak with us, as they were perched high up in the gallery over the clock. It is impossible to be more nice, hearty, and amiable than they were. After dinner we drove to the Exhibition Building, waited a few minutes in the carriages for the end of the first part, and then made our entrance, Lord Carrington giving his arm to Wilma, and I to Lady Carrington, the people standing up, and 'God Save the Queen' being played. The Liedertafel, about 120 strong, sang uncommonly well, but the solos were not to our taste. The Exhibition Building has a railway on one side, and a tramway, worked by steam-engines, on the other, both whistling almost every minute, which spoils the effect of music considerably.

After Wednesday's concert Wilma's finger got worse, and medical aid became indispensable. Dr. Scott Skirving, recommended by Lady Carrington, a Scotsman, who knew us well from the Reid Concerts, was very nice; he said that if she were an ordinary woman he should prescribe complete rest, but as this in her case was out of the question he would try a compromise. We stopped at home all day, receiving plenty of visitors, and a deputation from the German Club, to offer me the honorary membership and to invite us both to a 'Maskenball' next Friday.

Sunday, June 22, 1890.

Yesterday morning, on trying her finger, Wilma found to her sorrow that it would be impossible for her to play in the evening. Placards had therefore to be put up in the town,

and the announcements made in the evening papers to the
effect that the concert was postponed, in spite of which large
crowds collected in the evening to find the doors of the hall
closed.

Monday, June 23, 1890.

When the doctor came yesterday he found Wilma's finger
much improved, but insisted upon her giving it entire rest
until Thursday, for fear of a relapse. The concerts have to
be postponed therefore, and the announcement to that effect
appears in this morning's papers. It is a great annoyance,
but it cannot be helped. Sydney strikes us as much more of
a town than Melbourne; there are finer streets, beautiful
buildings, splendid shops, and altogether it looks more
civilised and home-like.

Wednesday, June 25, 1890.

On Monday afternoon Mrs. Burdekin sent us her carriage
at half-past 2 o'clock for a drive. The weather was fine, but
a little too windy, and there was a deal of dust. We drove
to South Head, one of the two heads through which the
harbour is entered and upon which the lighthouse stands.
The view is beautiful in the extreme; the harbour winding
through the green hills, and, being dotted here and there
with little islets, is unlike anything we have seen before; it
is like an immense river, expanding at intervals into lakes,
and being surrounded by upwards of a hundred bays. From
the South Head it forms an enchanting panorama, extending
for many miles up to Sydney. Close to the spot where we
were Captain Cook landed, and for the first time hoisted the
English flag; Botany Bay is also very near; altogether, it
was a most interesting drive. Before we left the hotel we
had letters from home, to our great joy, as we only expected
them the following day. All the news was good, thank
God!

June 26, 1890.

Wilma's finger is getting better and better; nevertheless,
the doctor does not seem quite sure that the exertion of
playing this evening, and afterwards at so many concerts,

will not do it harm. She thinks it will not: we must hope
for the best, but I feel anxious. The weather has been very
bad to-day; rain from morning to evening. Yesterday afternoon there came more letters from home, much sooner than
we could expect them; one to Wilma from Mrs. Ewart with
good news of Winzi.[1] She strongly urges that we should
give a concert at Colombo on our return journey, and offers
to arrange everything. On inquiry at the P. and O.'s office,
I find that the *Arcadia* will stop there from twenty-four to
thirty-six hours; so we can do it, and I will telegraph to
that effect. In less than eight weeks we shall be on our way
home, and very glad of it.

June 27, 1890.

In spite of the pouring rain, the concert last night was
crammed, and our success very great. Wilma played beautifully, and, thank God, the exertion has had no ill effect. So
we hope we may now go on without further interruption.
The two sonatas of Beethoven's seemed to please most last
night; they were certainly listened to with breathless attention and vehemently applauded.

July 1, 1890.

Last Saturday has been the rainiest day we have had yet;
it poured from early morning till 7 in the evening without a
single moment's interruption. Then it cleared, which was a
good thing for the concert. Both on Friday and Saturday
the hall was crammed, and the applause as warm as we could
possibly wish for. Wilma received a most beautiful flower-
basket, and an enormous laurel wreath, big as a cart-wheel,
with the letters H and N in white and red camellias, which
are still fresh to-day.

Sunday we dined with Sir Alfred Stephen and his two
amiable daughters. He is a remarkable and very gentle-
manly old man of nearly eighty-eight, with a very fresh
mind. In the absence of Lord Carrington he acts as Governor,
and seemingly does not find that it overtaxes him. He was
full of anecdotes, and very sprightly. As a compliment to
Wilma he had read up the history of violin-making, and

<hr>

[1] Lady Hallé's dog.

knew more about it than either she or I; he confessed, however, that his learning was not a day old, but protested that
he would not forget it again.

On Monday, yesterday, the weather was fine, and we took
a walk through the Domain and the Botanical Gardens to
Farm Cove Harbour, a most enjoyable promenade. The
Gardens are wonderfully interesting; we saw there an incredible variety of palm and other exotic trees, some looking
most fantastical and forming beautiful groups. The view
upon the harbour is very fine, the gardens are beautifully
kept, and as they are quite near to our hotel we shall go there
often, weather permitting. The concert was crowded; long
before the commencement the notice was put up at the box
office : ' Standing room only.' After the concert we went for
an hour to a ball which was given by the Mayoress, not in
her own house but at some very spacious Assembly Rooms.
It was a brilliant scene, well lighted, and there was a substantial supper. Gentlemen and ladies danced with infinitely
more animation and energy than is ever seen in England, and
we watched them with much amusement. Some of the young
ladies were extremely handsome, and most of them well
dressed. We left at half-past 11.

July 1, 1890.

Concerts on Tuesday and Wednesday full, and animated
as usual; there is nothing new to be said about them.
Wilma's finger fortunately keeps well enough not to hinder
her playing, although it is not yet quite in its usual state.

Yesterday afternoon we walked to the 'man-of-war steps,'
where Captain Foss was already waiting for us with his boat
to take us to the *Sperber* for tea. It is a small warship, but
very interesting. The captain's cabin is small but rich in
curiosities picked up in many countries, especially in Africa.
There were spears and arrows, many of them poisoned, and
some from the newly-discovered Pigmy race, curious shields,
damascened swords, and so on. We had bad tea, excellent bread
and butter, and very good champagne at this very odd hour.
He then took us over the whole ship, explained all her fight-

ing power, and especially the torpedoes, the most wonderfully
clever things, which, as he said, can do everything but speak.
At 5 o'clock we were on the bridge when the flag was lowered
and saluted militarily by the captains, officers, and the men
who had been called out for ' flag parade.' It was nice to see.
The boatswain who called the men out had the most unearthly
voice ever heard, something between the trumpeting of an
elephant and the grunting of an ox. The captain told us
laughingly that the boatswains seek in honour to outdo each
other by the terrific voices they can produce from their throats.
Before we left we signed our names in the captain's autograph
book, on the same page, at his request, where Stanley and
Emin Pasha had written their names. Singularly enough he
showed us the photographs of the wife and two daughters of
our former friend, Prince Frederick of Schleswig-Holstein,
afterwards Prince de Noer, who died some years ago. Shortly
after five the captain took us back to the steps in his boat in
two minutes, and five minutes later we were at the hotel.

July 10, 1890.

Both the last concerts in Sydney, on Friday and Saturday,
were crowded, the one on Saturday particularly so, and will
long be remembered by us. Lord and Lady Carrington, who
had only returned the same afternoon, were there, and sat on
the platform close to the piano. Wilma got bouquets after
every one of her pieces ; but after the last, when we thought
the flowery tribute exhausted, there came such a shower of
them from all sides that the whole air seemed filled with roses
and other splendid flowers that were thrown from the galleries,
right and left, as well as from the reserved seats, many of
which struck Lord Carrington as well as me. The whole platform was in a short time covered with them, Lord Carrington
and I being very busy in picking them up ; but to gather
them all was impossible, and Wilma on leaving the platform
had literally to walk over roses.

Next day we started for Brisbane. At the Sydney station
we had a disappointment, for a special carriage which had been

promised to us by the Chief Commissioner of Railways, Mr.
Eddy was not forthcoming, and the ordinary one, reserved for us,
was the reverse of comfortable. The journey, one of thirty-six
hours, was therefore very fatiguing, and a long telegram from
Mr. Eddy, which we received on the road, and in which he
expressed all his regret at the misunderstanding, brought us
little comfort. We arrived at Brisbane at 6.20 on Tuesday
morning, the 8th, very tired, and went to bed soon after having had some tea at the Bellevue Hotel, where we are staying.
What we had seen of the country between Sydney and here
had been extremely uninteresting and very monotonous.
Brisbane looks cheerful, and of course brand new, for thirty
years ago there was not a house there. Now we have fine
Houses of Parliament just opposite our windows, we look down
upon splendid Botanical Gardens, and going out we walk
through broad and regular streets with very grand buildings
here and there, all very fine, but not interesting. Yesterday,
at half-past 2, we were received by the Mayor at the Town
Hall, the funniest ceremony we ever were at. The concert in
the evening was very full, and the Centennial Hall, in which
it took place, is very good and free from draughts. The
Governor, Sir Henry Norman, was there with his suite. The
audience applauded us a good deal, but I am afraid that the
music we play is a little beyond them, although the papers
this morning are in raptures. We have concerts this evening,
to-morrow, Saturday, Monday, and Tuesday, and return to
Sydney on Wednesday next, arriving on Friday morning.
Since our arrival at Brisbane the weather has been very fine,
only with a little too much wind and, consequently, dust. We
have now reached the furthest point from England; when
we leave here we shall have the feeling of getting nearer and
nearer home.

July 12, 1890.

The weather yesterday was lovely; Wilma and I took a
long walk, first to the town to post our letters, and then
through the Botanical Gardens, which are fine, although they
cannot be compared to those of Sydney. One part, a pool of

water surrounded with bamboos more than 50 feet high, is eminently characteristic of the tropics: it is a perfect picture.

The two concerts have gone off well, but without interesting us in the least; we don't feel in our element, and shall be glad to turn our backs upon Brisbane.

July 14, 1890.

Saturday afternoon we took another walk through the Botanical Gardens, and found them more interesting than before. The variety of trees is quite astounding; some, like the bottle-tree, look perfectly ridiculous. We returned again yesterday, and discovered the aviary with a collection of fascinating birds; also a fine fernery. Being Sunday, the gardens were crowded, and we were much stared at, too much for our comfort. The public on Saturday evening was warmer, but not so numerous as before. I am afraid Brisbane has been a mistake of our managers. To-day the weather is splendid, bright sunshine and warm. So at 1 o'clock we took a carriage and drove to 'One Tree Hill,' from which we had a really beautiful view. The drive there was very fine; first along the Brisbane water and then through woods with innumerable birds. The houses we passed were all of them built upon poles (like the *Pfahlbauten* of old) as a protection against gigantic ants, which visit this country frequently. The extent of country we saw from the top of the hill was enormous; a little before us, on our left, we had the whole of Brisbane, the houses of which looked like so many big square stones; through the whole plain, densely wooded everywhere, the river was gliding in ever so many zigzags; in the distance, twenty-five miles away, we saw the town of Ipswich, very white, and nearly everywhere the horizon was bounded by a range of picturesque mountains of a beautiful dark-blue colour, leaving, in a few places, a glimpse of the ocean open. The air was wonderfully clear, and we enjoyed the drive immensely.

July 15, 1890.

The concert was crowded last night, and the enthusiasm greater than previously.

July 16, 1890.

Luncheon with the Governor, Sir Henry Norman, yesterday was very pleasant. Nobody was present except Captain Baden-Powell and Mr. Wilson, formerly Postmaster-General, but now in opposition—a great music-lover, a violinist himself, who writes on music for the papers. Government House is small, but neat and well-situated, the gardens in front of the house descending to the river. We were glad to eat well-cooked viands after a whole week's fare at this hotel. The concert in the evening was again very full. It has much interested us to watch the growing interest of the public. The applause during the last two concerts has been very different: much more genuine and spontaneous than at the first. It would not take long to educate them, and to make them appreciate the best music. Before us, nobody had ever played them a sonata by Beethoven, or any other really good music. In the afternoon I had a visit from old Toole—a dear and pleasant man.

July 18, 1890.

The journey back to Sydney has been as pleasant as the one to Brisbane had been disagreeable. We had special carriages, good beds, and a special gentleman to attend upon us and all our wants. We played many games of 66, and were altogether jolly. We arrived at 5.10 this morning, and experienced a feeling of intense relief in getting into our snug, clean rooms again. While at breakfast I heard that poor Mr. Best has had a bad fall down a high staircase (after a dinner given to Mr. Toole): has hurt his side very badly, and has already been a fortnight in hospital. The opening of the organ and the Centennial Hall is therefore postponed, and not likely to take place before the second week of August. Lady Carrington had sent us most pressing invitations by letter and telegram to Brisbane to stay with them at Government House during our present visit, but we had to decline them, as we could never have been masters of our time, which, with so many concerts on our hands, is a matter of absolute necessity.

July 21, 1890.

To-day we drove to Coogee's Bay. It is a charming place. and the colour of the sea most beautiful. To-morrow I am to be entertained at dinner by the Athenæum Club, whilst Wilma will dine at Government House. The restored cable brought the news of H. M. Stanley's marriage and Lydia Becker's death.

July 22, 1890.

The concert was crowded yesterday, and very successful. We hear that for the next, which takes place at 3 P.M. to-morrow, the plan is already closed, as all the tickets are sold. Wilma went this morning to a Chinaman's shop and bought a few small things. The Chinaman, Geeong Tarr, a mandarin, has asked us to supper after one of the concerts, and we shall go on Friday evening. It will be a new experience. I went out in the afternoon, and, passing a music shop, I saw in the window the old lithograph of the ' Musical Union,' with myself at the piano. Whilst I was looking at it the owner of the shop came out and addressed me very politely, telling me that this very morning he had sold another copy of the same.

July 23 1890.

The dinner at the Athenæum Club yesterday evening was well attended, and President Dr. Tarrant a pleasant man. The Mayor sat on his left, and I, as the guest of the evening, to his right. The eating and drinking were good : one soup, *bêche de mer*, a novelty to me. It was very much like turtle. After dinner the president made a speech, to which I had to reply, and then a little concert was performed, of which I have kept a programme. It was rather curious, on account of the exuberance of feeling displayed. Just as I was going Mr. Hünerbein, a member of the club, begged me, together with about twenty other gentlemen (amongst whom was the Mayor) to go with him into another room, where we found more champagne, tea and coffee, and where lots more speeches were delivered. The Mayor and he then escorted me to the hotel, the night being very fine.

July 25, 1890.

The concert on Wednesday afternoon was the most crowded of those we have had here. The Carringtons were present again. In the evening we went to see 'A Doll's House,' by Ibsen: a very strange and not altogether satisfactory play. It was well acted, Miss Janet Achurch being especially good.

July 28, 1890.

After the concert on Friday evening we took supper with Mr. Geeong Tarr, the Chinese mandarin—a very pleasant little man, who had prepared a grand spread for us. Mrs. Tarr, an Englishwoman, was in the country. Geeong Tarr is a very wealthy man and a great benefactor to the poor—not merely the Chinese poor, but of all nations. Some years ago the Emperor of China sent for him and made him a mandarin (although he was a Christian), together with three of his ancestors.

August 3, 1890.

On Monday last we gave our last concert at Sydney, a matinée, which was crowded. During the interval Wilma was presented with a lyre-bird in silver as a souvenir of some of her Sydney admirers. It is a beautiful thing, and she is greatly pleased with it. We left Sydney at 5 o'clock on Tuesday, and arrived at Melbourne at midday on Wednesday. On Thursday we heard from Mr. Poole that the four concerts next week are to be with orchestra. Yesterday morning I rehearsed Weber's 'Concertstück' with the Victorian orchestra, and they did very well. The Chancellor of the University came to see me on Friday morning, to thank me for the advice I had given them with regard to the Professorship, which the Council seemed inclined to follow. Mr. Marshall Hall, from Oxford, has the best chance of being appointed.

August 7, 1890.

The 'Emperor' Concerto made a great impression last evening, and altogether the concert was very pleasant. It was full, but not crowded, and the little orchestra does its best.

August 10, 1890.

The Beethoven Concerto on Thursday evening had an immense success. Wilma played it splendidly. It was very well accompanied, and the enthusiasm of the band was touching to behold.

Yesterday I had a rehearsal of Beethoven's C Minor Concerto. I went also with the band through the Adagio from Spohr's 9th Concerto (without Wilma), because the clarinet parts were missing, and I had written them out from memory, so it was necessary to see if they were what was wanted. At half-past one I went to the Mayor's luncheon at the Town Hall. The Premier and several other Ministers, the Speakers, and many members of both Houses were there—altogether about fifty people. I sat between the Premier and the Chairman of the 'Harbour Trust,' who hails from Radcliffe, near Manchester, and was therefore a sort of acquaintance. The luncheon proved to be a sumptuous dinner, and lasted till half-past four. Many speeches were delivered, some quite political and very amusing, and my health was proposed (at the Mayor's request) by Mr. Carter, a prominent member of the House of Commons here, and a very good speaker, who did it very well, and whom it was a pleasure to answer. Some of the speeches by members of the Opposition having been rather violent, falling foul of the Premier and Government, I began my answer by saying how interested I had felt in listening to them, and how it had seemed to me that music was the basis of all of them, for we musicians knew well that discords were the great charm of harmony. This was much applauded, and altogether I got pretty well out of my troubles. When I left Mr. Rose was waiting to conduct me to the branch establishment of Broadwood's here, which was to be inaugurated yesterday. There I found thirty to forty musicians, writers, and friends assembled, and a large array of bottles of champagne. Speeches were made, healths drunk, and prosperity wished to the new establishment, which indeed promises well. I returned to the hotel at about 6 o'clock, rather exhausted and not too well

prepared for our farewell concert in the evening. This, however, went off splendidly, and was a glorious finish to our
season here. There was not an available standing-place in
the whole of that big Town Hall (larger than the Manchester
Free Trade Hall), and many hundreds had to be turned away.
It was an exciting evening, and no one can wish for greater
ovations than those that were accorded us. We sent to the
hotel a whole cab-full of beautiful flowers, amongst them a
large lyre in violets and white flowers from the Victorian
orchestra, which we esteem highly. It was an evening to be
remembered, and we may be sure of a good reception if ever
we come back to Australia. The feeling of satisfaction when
we sat down to our supper, surrounded by our flowers, was
very pleasant, and sent us to bed tired, but happy. We were
to have had luncheon with the Austrian Consul to-day, but
we sent an excuse yesterday, and were very glad we did so,
this day of absolute rest having been very enjoyable.

August 11, 1890.

We had a very pleasant dinner at Government House,
returning at 10 o'clock. To-day we are in all the bustle of
packing up, and at 4.40 P.M. we leave for Adelaide.

August 13, 1890.

On Monday morning our beautiful goldfinch died in
Wilma's hand, to our great grief. The last two days it had
been ailing, but we hoped it would get better again; we
were very sorry indeed. If, according to Hector Malot, great
affection for animals is a sign of insanity, then Wilma and I
are a very insane couple.

I fetched our tickets for the *Arcadia* at the P. and O.
office, received a few visitors, and at 4 o'clock we left the
hotel, taking leave of Mrs. Menzies and her daughter, who
had been very kind to us. At the station we found many
friends, and Mr. Pinschoff travelled with us to Adelaide.
The journey was most comfortable; at 7 in the morning we
had a first-rate breakfast, with very fine fish, at Murray
Bridge, and at 10.20 we arrived in Adelaide. The country

became very beautiful on nearing Adelaide; we saw a great extent, with the sea in the distance. Chief Justice Way, who had ordered our rooms at the Botanic Hotel, received us at the station (with several other people), and sent us off in his carriage. Half-an-hour after our arrival I was interviewed by the reporters of the two papers, and then we had an exciting scene. We had put our two white sparrows upon a balcony and in the sun, when suddenly a beautiful canary bird came and settled near their cage, most eager to talk to them; it clung to the outside, hopped away, came back, stuck its head through the wires, and evidently tried to get to them. It was not at all afraid of us—even hopped into our sitting-room and out again; so at last we put a small cage in its way, with the door open and seed in it, and after a while it went in and Wilma caught it very cleverly. Now we have six birds again, and this one is a beauty—it has probably escaped from somewhere, for canaries are not found in Australia.

Yesterday evening we dined with Lord and Lady Kintore and a small party. After dinner there was a grand reception and a concert of Australian music, arranged in our honour, followed by a little operetta, very well acted and sung by four amateurs, and composed by Mr. Sharp, another amateur.

To-day at 11 o'clock the Mayor received us in the Town Hall, and we had to go through the ceremony of handshaking, as in the other towns. The town organist played us a piece on the organ—a fine instrument, but the piece was not interesting. Now we are going to dress for the first concert here, and after it we shall be serenaded by the Liedertafel.

August 14, 1890.

The first concert here was a great surprise to us. Adelaide boasts of being a very musical town, and the Town Hall, not a very large one, was half empty. True, the weather was bad, but so it has been in the other towns often enough without a similar result. Those that were there made noise enough, and we are curious to see what to-night may bring.

Lord and Lady Kintore were there, and were announced to be there; so they do not draw here either. At 10.30 the Liedertafel—a very small body of fifteen or sixteen members—serenaded us, and I had to stand on the balcony, where it was bitterly cold, to listen to their not remarkable singing.

August 15, 1890.

Last night's concert was little better attended than the first, and our managers cannot have derived much profit from it. It seems that Adelaide is the least musical town in Australia; the next concerts will show. The last one, on Tuesday next, is announced to be a *matinée*; so in all probability we shall be able to go on board the same evening, which will be delightful.

August 17, 1890.

Last evening the house was crowded, and the demonstrations as lively as possible. Strange that we should have had to conquer the public of Adelaide by degrees, after all our triumphs in the other towns. Lord Kintore and his daughters were there again.

August 18, 1890.

The luncheon with Chief Justice Way yesterday was extremely pleasant. He has a charming house and a delightful garden with a fernery; besides this a splendid collection of birds, which we admired a long time. A beautiful squirrel and a parrot, spinning round and round for the amusement of the visitors, were very comical. Before luncheon we took a drive of more than an hour, which was very enjoyable; the situation of Adelaide is fine, the range of hills forming a beautiful background. The most interesting thing we saw were aloes in flower; it is said that they flower only once in a hundred years, so we were particularly lucky. The flower grows on a tree, from thirty to forty feet high, with many little side branches, and shoots up in a single day or night. It lasts a very short time and then the aloe dies, exhausted with the effort of producing it. It is very extraordinary, but not beautiful. We also saw an enormous haystack on fire, causing a loss of 2,000*l*.

In the evening we went to hear the Cathedral choir; they sing really well and have beautiful voices. Afterwards we had supper with Mr. Arthur Boult, who has taught the choir; he hails from Manchester; his father was one of the directors of the Concert Hall in 1849, and I believe one of the members of the first committee of the Classical Chamber Music Society. There were a few more people, amongst whom Mrs. Kennion, the wife of the Bishop of Adelaide, who knew me from Edinburgh.

August 19, 1890.

The house was pretty full last night, but there were empty places here and there. This morning Poole settled everything, and we are now prepared to start, this afternoon's concert being the last.

We are invited to a ball at Government House, but shall wisely abstain.

August 21, 1890.

The last concert has been given, the whole Australian tour is ended, and we are in the good ship *Arcadia*, homeward bound. The concert was crowded, and the ovations like those in Melbourne and Sydney. In the morning I had tried in vain to buy a diamond-sparrow for Wilma, to replace one that had flown away; on our return from the concert we found six of them, sent by the Chief Justice, who had heard from Mr. Pinschoff of our loss. As I had bought a zebra-finch and two mannikins, and Mr. Rose had brought two more zebra-finches, we travel now with no less than sixteen birds, all beautiful and most amusing. We spent the last evening at the hotel, Pinschoff dining with us, and were very merry. Fourteen boxes had been sent off to the *Arcadia* in the morning, and only three remained to follow the next morning. At half-past 9 we were at the station, the Consul, Mr. and Mrs. Poole, and the advance-agent Henry accompanying us on board, as well as two gentlemen from the P. and O. office; one a Swede, Mr. Kilman. The weather was beautiful, and we reached the *Arcadia* before 11 o'clock, and then had about two hours

of great anxiety, as none of our luggage had arrived.
Steam-launch after steam-launch came, brought passengers,
all the mail-bags, but not a scrap of our luggage. The
bell had rung for strangers to leave, and, as we could not
possibly start on a month's journey without even a shirt to
change, we were on the point of returning to Adelaide,
although it meant the loss of a fortnight, the giving up of
the pleasure of spending a little time in Italy, and many
other disagreeable consequences, when a steamer, despatched
to the shore on purpose by our excellent Swede, at last
brought our treasures and changed our despair into contentment. We then took leave of all our friends, who cheered
us from their boat, and bade adieu to Australia. In all
probability we shall return next year.

The *Arcadia* is a splendid ship, of immense size, beautifully fitted up, and going so easily that we do not feel even
the slightest trembling from the motion of the screw. We
have indeed been liberally treated by the P. and O. Company, for we have three cabins to ourselves. The deck is
of immense size and makes a splendid promenade. There
are two music-saloons, a grand smoking-room, and altogether
the accommodation is vastly superior to that on the *Valetta*.
One great advantage is that the first-class is in the fore-part
and not behind the funnels, so that we never get the smoke
and shall feel the breeze much better. The Captain, Andrews,
is much more bluff, and perhaps less kind and obliging, than
our dear Briscoe was, but a very nice man all the same. The
number of passengers is small, perhaps only from forty to fifty.

September 1, 1890.

At 8 o'clock this morning we crossed the line, just four
months after our first crossing it. The weather is perfection,
cool and pleasant; we enjoy the deck more than ever.
Either to-morrow evening or on Wednesday morning very
early we shall arrive at Colombo, and we have the feeling
that from the equator we are going 'down-hill' towards
home. There will be sports this afternoon, the ship being
quite steady, and a concert this evening. The wide ocean

seems to be quite lifeless; we see no fish and no bird, much as we look out for them.

September 5, 1890.

The sports on Monday afternoon were very amusing; there were potato-races, spoon-and-egg races for ladies, high jumps, slinging the monkey, tandem-driving by ladies, the first horse being blindfolded; and a tug-of-war to finish up with. In the evening we had a concert, Wilma and I playing each two little pieces, the rest being songs (two by the captain). At 2 o'clock in the night we reached Colombo, and at 8 Harry Ewart came to fetch us in the Custom House Officers' boat which they had kindly put at our disposal. He gave us the welcome news that Winzi was alive and well, and half an hour later we saw the dear little beast, whose delight was touching to witness. We drove to the Assembly Rooms to have a look at the piano which a Mr. Sivell had kindly lent for the concert. It was a boudoir-grand, by Chappell, and none of the best, but still the best in Colombo. The concert took place at 9 o'clock, and was very full, the Governor, Sir Henry Havelock, with his wife and suite being there. In spite of the climate, we did not suffer much from the heat, as the doors and the windows were all open. Harry, who had superintended the arrangements, was most busy, and his anxiety for our comfort was touching. After the concert he had a few friends to supper, among whom were Mr. Cameron, a son of our old friend Mrs. Cameron, and a former Miss Prinsep, niece of our old friend Thoby Prinsep, who had often seen me at Little Holland House, in the olden time, when she was quite young. This made the evening doubly interesting to me, and we did not go to bed before half-past two in the morning. The next day Harry and his wife brought us back to the *Arcadia*, and remained with us until the start, shortly after four. They have been uncommonly kind to us, and we parted from them very reluctantly. The weather looked very threatening, and we were afraid of a rough sea, instead of which it proved to be a very mild one, no fiddles being necessary during meals.

September 28, 1890.

On Thursday evening the first-class passengers had a fancy ball, to which the second-class were invited. It began by a grand procession, passing before and bowing to the captain and myself. Some of the costumes were very comical, and altogether it was a success, and was kept up till midnight, the ship rushing along all the while at the rate of 16 miles an hour. In the afternoon we had passed along the coast of Morea, the Ionian Islands, &c.; the view of Zante, with the setting sun upon its red rocks, being particularly fine. When we came on deck yesterday morning at 7 o'clock we found ourselves close to Brindisi and the flat shores of that part of Italy, and heard that we should arrive at 8 o'clock, for which hour breakfast was also announced. The Adriatic was as blue and glassy as the Mediterranean had been, and the weather altogether too lovely. We were at our breakfast, and had not even perceived that the ship had touched the quay, when somebody touched my shoulder; I looked up and shouted ' Ludwig.' [1] upon which Wilma gave a shriek and fell upon his shoulders, sobbing for joy. We had not expected to see him there. Shortly after we said good-bye to the captain, the officers and some of the passengers, recommended all our things and the fifteen birds to C., distributed the *pour-boires* and left the ship. At 11.30 we left Brindisi by the special train, and arrived here at Milan at 9 o'clock this morning.

And so ends this eventful voyage, which has been successful in every sense of the word. We bring home a rich store of pleasant recollections, have enjoyed perfect health, and can say with truth that nothing occurred to mar our happiness for a single moment. And for this let us be grateful ! !

---

[1] Lady Hallé's eldest son.

III

EXTRACTS FROM LETTERS WRITTEN DURING SIR CHARLES AND
LADY HALLE'S TOUR IN SOUTH AFRICA, IN 1895

Grand Hotel, Capetown,
July 30, 1895.

The mail only goes to-morrow; so I can add a few lines
to my letter, and tell you that we have safely arrived here at
half-past one in the morning, about eight hours sooner than
we expected. Our agent was with us long before breakfast,
and gave me the agreeable news that he had postponed the
concerts here one day in order to give us a day of rest; the
Tantallon Castle will actually wait for us until Friday,
instead of sailing on Thursday. More still, the ship will wait
for us three or four days longer at Port Elizabeth, in order to
take us on to Durban. So you see we are a good deal thought
of, another proof of which is that for the two concerts here
not a single ticket remains unsold, so that some of the passengers who wanted to go are disappointed. I have got one
seat for the captain in our manager's own box. This hotel is
very good, and we have capital rooms.

We have just returned from a most wonderful drive,
which alone would have been worth the trouble of coming
here. The view over the town from the height reminded me
very much of Naples and the drive along the coast of the
'Corniche.' We drove through the 'Kloof' (Dutch for
cleft) between the Table Mountain and the Lion's Head, and
back round by Sea Point; it was simply enchanting, and
took upwards of two hours. We certainly had no idea that
this was such a beautiful place—not the town, but the
situation.

I found a most nice letter from G. here, who says that the
tickets for our concerts at Johannesburg are selling most
rapidly, although it will be a full month before we get there.
They say our tour this year will be a royal triumph, and already
ask if we will not come back next year for a little longer.

Here, at the hotel, we were received with ever so many bouquets, sent by people right and left; our sitting-room is so full of flowers that it looks like a greenhouse, and such flowers! It is mid-winter here, but not a bit cold, and the air is most exhilarating. We already know that we shall return in the *Scot*, the largest and fastest ship of the Union Line, larger than the *Tantallon*. We shall leave Cape Town on September 11, and be in London on the 27th; I can therefore be in Manchester on the 28th, two days before I am wanted.

Wilma will have to go to Denmark on October 11 or 12, and not come back before about November 23, as she will have a whole series of concerts.

Now you know all about our doings, and I wish I knew as much about yours and all the other dear ones. Once more I say, give them all my love and keep writing, and tell me what news you have of Anna.

Grand Hotel, Port Elizabeth,
August 5, 1895.

I wrote to you from Cape Town, where, since then, we have given two concerts with enormous success; they took place in the Opera House, a charming theatre, and were crowded. On Friday morning we were on board again at 10 o'clock, and had the most wonderful passage round the Cape of Good Hope to this place. We were constantly about a mile or two from the coast, which is remarkably fine, and you may imagine that we looked at the Cape with more than common interest, as it is one of the places with the name of which one has been familiar all one's life. It is a very bold and striking-looking Cape indeed, and the sea, which is said to be generally wild and rough about it, behaved splendidly to us; there was no rolling and no pitching.

We arrived here on Saturday afternoon, two hours before we were expected, and were received on landing by the Deputy-Mayor and a few aldermen. The whole Corporation had meant to be there, but on account of our arriving so

much too soon the Mayor could not be found. Bouquets were
brought to Wilma on board ship, and a nice landau was
waiting to take us to this hotel, which is on the top of a hill,
and from which the view over the town, harbour, and the sea
is simply enchanting.

Saturday evening the concert took place in a very beautiful
hall, and there was such a scene of excitement as I have
seldom witnessed. The roaring of the audience outdid any
Yorkshire or Lancashire roaring sevenfold, and Wilma especially carried everything before her. Yesterday was a day
which cannot be described; it was simply heavenly. There
was not the smallest cloud to be seen in the sky, and since
we spent that happy month of August in Venice, when I
used to look out of the open window at 6 o'clock in the
morning, I have never experienced such happiness by merely
inhaling the air as here.

We have a splendid verandah before our rooms, where we
sit almost the whole day, and do nothing but exclaim over
and over again: beautiful! heavenly! splendid!

Who should call on Saturday shortly after our arrival but
a brother of Otto Goldschmidt, E. Goldschmidt, who was one
of the principal directors of the Bradford concerts when they
were first started, and whom I had known there for many
years. He has been here for the last 12 years, and has a
very large business. We dined with him yesterday, Sunday;
very pleasant it was to be able to talk of the olden times.

This is the place for ostrich feathers, and Mr. Goldschmidt
is going to make a present of a lot of them to Wilma to-day;
she is allowed to choose what she likes for a boa and a fan.
To-night is our second concert, and to-morrow we leave at
12 o'clock for Grahamstown, where we shall arrive at 6, for
the concert at 8.30. The next day we rest there, and we
have been told that the neighbourhood is one of the finest in
Africa. On Thursday we shall drive the whole day in a
landau with four horses to get to King Williamstown. We
prefer that to a very long and roundabout railway journey,
which would take much more time, especially as the country

which we shall have to pass through is said to be remarkably fine. From King Williamstown we go by rail to East London, where probably a concert will be given which is not on our list; and from East London to Durban by sea. There I shall at last get letters from you, which cannot reach us earlier on account of the enormous distances.

They call the months of July and August mid-winter here, but the warmth is just like a beautiful June day in England; I wear no top-coat, and feel very comfortable. The mail leaves here to-night, and the further East we go the sooner in the week it will leave. I shall endeavour to write by every one.

In five weeks and two days we shall be on board the *Scot*, on our return journey. Once more, fond love to all.

King Williamstown,
August 10, 1895.

I believe I wrote last from Port Elizabeth, where we had two eminently successful concerts. On Tuesday afternoon we left for Grahamstown by a train (the only one in the day), which was to arrive at 6.20 P.M., but did not do so before 6.40, and as we had a concert at 8.30, we saw with alarm the Mayor and the town clerk at the station to receive and harangue us, and some young damsels with bouquets for Wilma. They cut it short, however, and we had time to eat a little before we had to play. The room was crowded again, and the shouting something to remember. We are a bit astonished to see the halls so well filled, for the towns are remarkably small, but very pretty and full of gardens. Grahamstown being away from the coast, we there got a first glimpse of African life, and very striking it was. Carts drawn by a team of sixteen oxen are plentiful and very picturesque, but the strangest sight is that of the ostriches being brought to market. Troops of thirty or forty march solemnly, two by two, just like a regiment of soldiers, and look extremely funny. To go from Grahamstown to this place we had our choice of the railway, which takes two nights and a day, or of driving nearly six hours a day and sleeping at Breakfastoley, a halfway house. We chose the latter, as you would have done, not knowing what was in store for us. Such roads, or rather no roads, we had no idea of, and we were jolted as I hope we shall never be again. Only two-wheeled carts can traverse them, drawn by six horses, holding six persons, including the driver, upon two benches, which, however, are pretty comfortable. In spite of all drawbacks, we are not sorry to have had the experience, for we have seen many curious things; the first day we had ostriches to the right and to the left from about 12 o'clock when we left until 5, when we got to Breakfastoley, a very unpretending and very clean little inn, only one storey high, and standing quite alone. The next day we saw no ostriches, but drove past numbers of Kaffir huts and villages, which were far more interesting. The huts look like big mushrooms, having only one door and no windows whatever, and the Kaffirs themselves, draped in their brownish yellow togas, are an extraordinary sight. It was worth a good deal of discomfort to see them. Eight miles before reaching King Williamstown we saw two carriages standing in the road, and gentlemen beside them, who stopped us. They were the Mayor and the German Consul who had come out to meet us; the Consul, a Mr. Lehmann, who had his mother-in-law with him, made Wilma take a seat in his carriage, and the Mayor got hold of me, and they brought us to the house of a Mr. Dyer, a very rich man, who, being absent himself, had put his house and his German servants at our disposal, and here we have been living in clover these two days, with champagne at dinner and supper. The concert yesterday was excellent, and at 2 P.M. we leave for East London, from whence we leave to-morrow by sea for Durban.

This is midwinter here, the thermometer standing in the sun at 141 degrees! What may the summer be! And now good-bye once more, and love to everybody. We are both remarkably well, and I begin to think that we shall come back younger than when we left England.

Johannesburg: August 22, 1895.

My last letter to you was from Durban, which we left the
next morning for Pietermaritzburg. We were again received
at the station by the Mayor and his wife and lots of other
people, and driven in state to the Imperial Hotel, kept by a
widow, a Manchester woman, and frequenter of my concerts
there, who made us most comfortable. Up to the present I
have met Manchester people in every place, so that we often
say it was hardly worth while to come all this way. We had
our concert the same evening, which was crammed and very
satisfactory. I enclose one newspaper article as a specimen :
they are all very much alike. Pietermaritzburg being the
capital of Natal, the public seemed to be more *distingué*, and
included many officers, who looked very bright. During the
evening the Mayor came with the request that we should play
one piece at a concert which the Corporation would give on
Sunday afternoon at 4 o'clock. Think of that! a concert
given on a Sunday by the municipality of an English colony !
The tickets were only 2s. and 1s., but the very fine Town
Hall was crowded. We played the Kreutzer Sonata, after an
organ solo and one song had been given, and when we had
finished a member of the Corporation came forward and said
that after the impression just received it would be best to
omit the rest of the programme, upon which the public
cheered and dispersed.

The Governor, Sir Walter Hely-Hutchinson, had only
returned from Zululand on Saturday evening, but sent his
aide-de-camp early on Sunday morning to the hotel to invite
us to luncheon. We found him a very charming man, and
his wife a perfectly lovely woman, with most beautiful
children. They all went to the concert in the afternoon.
At 10.30 the same evening we left by rail, in comfortable
sleeping carriages, for Johannesburg. From daylight on
Monday morning the journey was very interesting, the
scenery unlike any we had seen before. We crossed the
battlefield of Majuba Hill, where the English were annihilated

by the Boers in 1877, and the railway climbs higher and higher until it reaches Charlestown, 5,800 feet high.

At 3.20 P.M. on Monday last we reached Standerton, and there the railway ends for the present. An enormous coach was waiting for us at the station, just the same sort of coach as the one which Buffalo Bill had in his show, drawn by ten horses and driven from the box. In this we were quite comfortable, as there was room for twelve inside, and we drove two hours more to a place called Waterfall, a single farm house, where they take passengers in. We got a good dinner, very simple, of course, excellent German beer, and bedrooms in plenty.

Tuesday morning we left at eight, got luncheon at Heidelberg, forded a number of streams in our coach, for bridges are very scarce in this country, and about half an hour before reaching Johannesburg to my great joy found Gustav waiting for us by the roadside; he is well and hearty and looks unchanged. He is very busy, but gives us as much of his time as he can, and it is a great delight to me to be once more with him, although only for so short a time.

Johannesburg: September 1, 1895.

My last letter actually, for the next mail will carry ourselves home after a wonderfully interesting, successful, and very short trip. One of my greatest pleasures has been, of course, to spend a whole fortnight with Gus.

Since last I wrote we have been twice to Pretoria, and here we give this evening, Sunday evening, our fifth concert. On our second visit to Pretoria I was introduced to President Krüger by his Prime Minister, and found him an ugly but very energetic-looking man, in manners a real Boer. I shall give details when I see you. Altogether, I need not write much to-day, because one week after you receive this I can tell you all so much better.

Yesterday we went down a gold mine, one of the best here, took luncheon with Gus, and in the evening went to the theatre to see a stupid but very laughable and well-acted farce. To-day (I write early) we shall see a Kaffir dance, got

up entirely in our honour, about which I shall add a few words
before closing my letter. The dance is fixed for 11 o'clock;
at half-past one we take luncheon with Mr. and Mrs. Rogers
(he is one of the most important men here), where there will
be a garden party in the afternoon and the concert begins at
9 o'clock to-night. The weather is always the same, the sky
intensely blue, without a single cloud, the days very warm,
and the nights somewhat fresh. Johannesburg has, however,
one great drawback: the dust, which lies at least 3 inches
deep in every street and every road. We have had one windy
day, when the clouds of dust were extraordinary to look at
and certainly not pleasant. We had quite enough with that
one day, and fortunately have not experienced a second.

We leave to-morrow at twelve, and arrive at Bloemfontein
after midnight (by rail, of course), and give a concert there
on Tuesday. On Wednesday we go to Kimberley, have
concerts there on Thursday and Friday; shall visit the biggest
diamond mine, and on Saturday leave for Cape Town, where
we give a farewell concert on Tuesday, the 10th, and on the
11th we go on board the *Scot*.

You all seem to have had very bad weather, for which we
have been sorry. We do not any longer know what bad
weather means.

We have just come back from the dance, a most extraordinary wild scene it was. There were about 1,000 Kaffirs and
Zulus, well-armed with long sticks instead of assegais, singing
their war songs, dancing and rushing about in the most be-
wildering manner, and still always orderly. They gave us
tremendous salutes, and when the performance was half over,
the chief, a most noble-looking fellow, walked up and was introduced to Wilma, and said some nice things which were translated to her. Altogether it was worth coming to Africa for;
we could never have got an idea of it elsewhere.

And now, *au revoir* very soon. We are as well as possible,
and have enjoyed ourselves thoroughly. I hope the house is
in tip-top order, and that the building at the College will be
finished in good time.

APPENDICES

I

A GERMAN CRITIC ON MR. CHARLES HALLÉ IN 1841.

(Translated from the German.)

THE celebrated critic A. Schindler thus wrote of my father in 1841:—'Shall I speak once more to German lovers of music of this young artist, whom I mentioned with praise in my "Beethoven in Paris"? I may be permitted to do so otherwise than in the usual form, as Mr. Hallé himself as a pianist is an exception to the general rule. At any rate, I wish in this way to bring this interesting artist nearer to the German musical world, to whom he is almost unknown, and to bring him into closer contact with it. Let us endeavour once again to sift the chaff from the wheat. Three days after my arrival in Paris (in January of last year) I received an invitation to a musical soirée at Erard's. In the amiable note occurred the phrase: "You will meet many artists and literary celebrities, and will also find several fellow-countrymen." The assembly must have numbered over four hundred persons, more than half of them ladies, among whom I could not find a single good-looking one, perhaps in consequence of having been spoilt by the frequentation of German *salons* and concert-rooms. It was otherwise with the male portion of the party, many of whom were handsome, and had strikingly interesting faces, amongst them some tremendous beards, and heads of hair that flowed over their shoulders. The sight carried me back to some of the synagogues I had visited in the Jewish towns of Austria, and it required some effort not to laugh aloud at this masquerade. In this pell-mell of artists, *literati*, bankers, and diplomates, I noticed a fair young man, whose figure and whole appearance bore a very striking resem-

blance to the princes of the Imperial House of Austria. In
answer to the inquiry who the young man was, my hostess
replied, "It is Mr. Hallé, a remarkable pianist, and a countryman of your own, whom I will introduce to you at once." This
was done forthwith. His appearance, coupled with a natural
modesty, the information he gave me that he was born at Hagen
in the county of Mark, and that he had studied under the old
master, Rinck, at Darmstadt before coming to this musical Babel,
made this young artist, amid the legion of his fellows, still more
attractive to me. My subsequent acquaintance with his beautiful
talent, which I often had the opportunity of admiring in the
performance of great classical works, made me rank him at once
among the most noteworthy artists of this great capital, among
those who strive after a high ideal. The readers of my aforesaid
pamphlet will remember what hopes I set upon this youth — hopes
that were being discussed in Germany at the moment of my
second visit to Paris. I had barely arrived when I heard the
news that Mr. Hallé had quite changed his original style of
playing, and had adopted the passionate and demonstrative
manner of Liszt and banged, hammered, and thumped like him.
A second and a third messenger of ill news brought the same
intelligence.

'It will be understood what a painful impression this made
upon me, and how I wished that the forerunner of these musical
fooleries were safe at Charenton, where a cell should have been
prepared for him long before his bad example had enticed young
talents to follow in his track. Meanwhile the change of Mr.
Hallé's intellectuality for Mr. Liszt's fanfaronades was accomplished, as I soon had the opportunity of being convinced.
Annoyance at having ranked this young man, according to the
best of my conviction, among the very foremost of the elect,
shame that by this classification I had done a wrong to the true
interests of art, and had over and above compromised my musical
judgment, were the feelings that for some time possessed me,
but also determined me that it was my duty to interfere, and to
attempt to deliver from the musical Beelzebub this soul, whom
some already counted among the lost. I succeeded, and before I
left Paris for the second time I had the delight to see this young
artist, in whom so many take the warmest interest, once again
upon the right road which leads to Parnassus, where there is no
chase after ribbons and orders, but after true knowledge and
worthiness.'

II

LIST OF WORKS, WITH THE NUMBER OF TIMES THEY WERE PERFORMED AT SIR CHARLES HALLÉ'S CONCERTS AT THE FREE TRADE HALL, MANCHESTER, DURING THIRTY-SEVEN YEARS, 1858–1895.

ORATORIOS.

J. S. Bach.
The Passion Music, St. Matthew   3

Beethoven.
The Mount of Olives   .   .   1

Benedict.
St. Peter   .   .   .   1

Berlioz.
The Childhood of Christ   .   3

Costa.
Eli   1
Naaman   1

Dvořák.
St. Ludmilla .   .   .   1

Gounod.
The Redemption   .   .   2
Mors et Vita .   .   .   1

Handel.
The Messiah .   .   .   55
Judas Maccabaeus .   .   16
Samson   5
Solomon   1
Jephtha   6
Israel in Egypt   .   .   4
Joshua   1
Saul   1
Belshazzar .   .   .   1
Theodora .   .   .   2

Haydn.
The Creation .   .   .   21
The Seasons .   .   .   5

Liszt.
St. Elizabeth .   .   .   1

Macfarren.
St. John the Baptist   .   2

Mackenzie.
The Rose of Sharon   .   1

Mendelssohn.
St. Paul   8
Elijah   29

Parry, Hubert.
Judith   1

Rossini.
Moses in Egypt   .   .   2

Rubinstein.
Paradise Lost   .   .   1

Spohr.
The Last Judgment   .   2

Stanford.
The Three Holy Children   .   1

Sullivan.
The Light of the World .   .   2

CHORAL WORKS, NOT ORATORIOS.

Barnett.
The Ancient Mariner   .   1

Beethoven.
Fidelio   1
Music to Egmont .   .   2

Mass in C   .   .   .   4
Mass in D   .   .   .   3
'Hallelujah' from Mount of Olives   .   .   .   2

Becker, Albert.
Geistlicher Dialog .   .   1

Flying Dutchman . . . 1
Flying Dutchman, Act II. and
  Act III. 2

SYMPHONIES, &c.

Abert.
Columbus 2

Beethoven
No. 1 in C . . . 4
No. 2 in D . . . 12
No. 3 in E flat 'Eroica' . 15
No. 4 in B flat . . 12
No. 5 in C minor . . 18
No. 6 in F Pastorale . 23
No. 7 in A . . . 17
No. 8 in F . . . 14
No. 9 in D minor, Choral . 8
Battle Symphony . . 2

Bennett, Sterndale.
In G minor . . . 1

Berlioz.
Harold in Italy . . 4
Fantastique . . . 6
Romeo and Juliet . . 3

Brahms.
Serenade in D . . 1
Adagio, Minuet and Finale,
  Serenade in A . . 1
In C minor, Op. 68 . . 1
In D, Op. 73 . . . 5
In F, Op. 90 . . . 2
In E minor, Op. 98 . . 2

Bruch, Max.
No. 3 in G . . . 1

Cowen.
No. 3, 'Scandinavian' . 2

Dvorak.
No. 1 in D . . . 2
No. 2 in D minor . . 1
No. 3 in F . . . 2
No. 4 in G . . . 2
No. 5 in E minor 'From the
  New World' . . 1

Gade.
No. 1 in C minor . . 4
No. 3 in A minor . . 1
No. 4 in B flat . . 2
No. 8 in B minor . . 1

Weber.
'Der Freischütz' . . . 1
'Preciosa' 1

Goetz.
In F 1

Goldmark.
'Ländliche Hochzeit' . . 6

Goury, Th.
Sinfonietta in D, Op. 80 . 1

German, Ed.
Symphony in A minor . 1

Haydn.
In E flat (Salomon No. 1) . 2
In D (Salomon No. 2) . 4
In E flat (Salomon No. 3) . 3
In D (Salomon No. 4) . 2
In D (Salomon No. 5) . 4
In G 'Surprise' (Salomon
  No. 6) 5
In C (Salomon No. 7) . 5
In B flat (Salomon No. 8) . 3
In C minor (Salomon No. 9) . 2
In D (Salomon No. 10) . 2
In G, Military (Salomon
  No. 11) . . . 3
In B flat (Salomon No. 12) . 5
In F sharp minor, 'Abschied'
  (Pohl No. 11) . . . 1
In E minor (Pohl No. 13) . 1
In A (Pohl No. 30) . . 2
In D 'La Chasse' (Pohl
  No. 40) . . . 1
In E flat (Pohl No. 45) . 1
In D minor (Pohl No. 49) . 5
In C 'Tours' (Pohl No. 52) . 1
In G minor 'La Poule' (Pohl
  No. 53) . . . 1
In B flat 'La Reine de
  France' (Pohl No. 55) . 1
In G (Pohl No. 58) . . 5
In C (Pohl No. 60) . . 1
In G 'Oxford' (Pohl No. 61) . 2
In E flat (Pohl No. 63) . 2
In D 3

Hecht.
In F 1

OVERTURES.

Monsigny.

Chaconne and Rigaudon from 'Aline' 1

Moszkowski.

Two Spanish Dances, G minor and D major . . . 2
Cortège 1

Mozart.

Maurerische Trauermusik . 1
Rondo alla Turca (instr. by Pascal) 1
Notturno Serenade for Four Orchestras, in D . . . 1
Chaconne and Gavotte from 'Idomeneo' . . . 1
Romanza in C from 'Eine Kleine Nachtmusik' . . 1
March in C 8

Neruda, Franz.

Aus dem Böhmerwalde, Op. 42 1

Oakeley, Sir Herbert.

Pastorale from Suite in D . 1
Gavotte and Musette from ditto 1

Raff.

First Movement from Symphony 'Im Walde' . . 1
Reverie and Scherzo from ditto 1
Evening Rhapsodie . . 1
Fest-Marsch in C, Op. 139 . 1
'The Mill' from Quartet in G minor 1
Barcarole and Pulcinella from Italian Suite . . . 1

Reinecke.

Entr'acte from 'Manfred' . 3
From the Cradle to the Grave 1

Rheinberger.

Wallenstein's Camp . . 2

Rimsky-Korsakoff, N.

Conte Féerique . . . 1

Rubinstein.

Ballet Music from 'Feramors,' Nos. 1, 2, 3 . . . 4
Ballet Music from 'Feramors,' No. 4 2

Ballet Music from 'Der Dämon' 2
Ballet Music from 'Nero' . 2
Toréador and Andalouse from 'Bal Costumé' . . . 5
Introduction, Berger and Bergère, Pélerin and Fantaisie 1
Feierlicher Marsch, 'Nero' . 1
'Bal Costumé' . . . 1

Saint-Saëns.

Le Rouet d'Omphale . . 3
Danse des Prêtresses, 'Samson et Dalila' . . . 1
Bacchanale, ditto . . . 2
Danse Macabre . . . 2
Phaëton 1
Suite Algérienne . . . 1
Ballet Music from 'Henry VIII' 1
Orchestral Suite in D . . 1
Serenade 1
La Jeunesse d'Hercule . . 1

Schubert.

March in B minor, instr. by Liszt 3
March in C minor, instr. by Liszt 3
Funeral March in E flat minor, instr. by Liszt . 1
Reitermarsch in C, instr. by Liszt 4
Entr'actes from 'Rosamunde' 9
Andante from 'Symphonie Tragique' 1

Schumann.

Bilder aus Osten, No. 4 . . 1

Smetana.

Vltava 1
Vysehrad 1

Södermann.

Swedish Peasants' Wedding March 2

Spohr.

Polacca from 'Faust' . . 4
Larghetto from Third Symphony 7
Andante from Symphony in D minor 1
Andante from 'The Power of Sound' 9

Stojowski.

Suite in E flat . . . 1

Stanford Villiers.

Prelude to Œdipus Rex . . 1

Sullivan.

Procession March . . . 2
Imperial March . . . 1

Svendsen.

Rhapsodie Norvégienne, No. 1
in B 1
Rhapsodie Norvégienne, No. 2
in A 1
Rhapsodie Norvégienne, No. 3
in C 2
Rhapsodie Norvégienne, No. 4
in D 1
Intermezzo from Symphony in
B flat 2

Taubert.

Liebeslied from the Tempest . 3

Tschaikowsky.

Marche Slave 1
Elegia 1
Ballet Music from Voivode . 1

Volkmann

Serenade in F. . . . 2
Serenade in D minor . . 2

Wagner.

March from Tannhäuser . 16
Introduction to Act III. of
Lohengrin 4
Kaiser-Marsch . . . 5
Huldigung's Marsch . . 4
Walkürenritt 4
Siegfried's Funeral March . 3
Feuer-Zauber, and Wotan's
Abschied 4
Introduction to Act III. of Die
Meistersinger . . . 3
Siegfried Idyll . . . 4
Waldweben, from 'Siegfried'. 1
Selection from 'Die Meister-
singer' 2
Charfreitags-Zauber, 'Parsifal' 1
Scene of the Rhine Daughters,
'Götterdämmerung' . . 1
Entrance of the Gods into
Walhalla, 'Rheingold' . 1
Introduction to 'Tristan und
Isolde' 1
Introduction and Liebestod
'Tristan und Isolde' . . 2
Träume 3

Weber.

Invitation à la Valse, instr. by
Berlioz 7

CONCERTOS, RONDOS. &c.—PIANO.

Bach.

In C for two Pianos . . 3
In C minor for two Pianos . 1
In C for three Pianos . . 1
In D minor for three Pianos . 2
In D for Piano, Flute, and
Violin 1

Beethoven.

No. 1 in C . . . 4
No. 2 in B flat . . . 3
No. 3 in C minor . . 11
No. 4 in G . . . 15
No. 5 in E flat . . . 18
Choral Fantasia . . . 13
Triple Concerto . . . 11
Rondo, in B Flat (Posth) . 1
Adagio and Rondo from Con-
certo No. 2 1
No. 6, in D 1

Bennett, Sterndale.

Concerto in F minor . . 1
Caprice, Allegro giojoso in E . 4

Brahms.

No. 2, in B flat . . . 1

Bronsart.

In F sharp minor . . . 1

Brüll.

No. 1, in F 1
No. 2 in C 1

Chopin.

No. 1 in E minor . . . 5
Romanza and Rondo, from
No. 1 1
No. 2 in F minor . . . 3
Andante Spianato and Polo-
naise in E flat, Op. 22 . 4

E E

Dussek.

In B flat, for two Pianos . . 2

Dvorák.

In G minor, Op. 33 . . 3

Field.

No. 7 in C minor . . . 3

Gernsheim.

In C minor . . . 1

Goetz.

In B flat . . . 1

Grieg.

In A minor . . . 3

Godard, B.

In A minor, Op. 31 . . 1

Hiller.

In F sharp minor . . 1

Hüber.

In C minor . . . 1

Hummel.

In A minor . . . 3
In B minor . . . 2
In A flat . . . 3
Rondo brillante in A . . 1
Rondo brillante in B Flat . 1

Litolff.

Concerto Symphonique in E
flat 2

Liszt.

In A 4
Fantaisie sur des Airs Hon-
grois . . . 2
In E flat . . . 2

Mendelssohn.

In G minor . . . 15
In D minor . . . 8
Serenade and Allegro giojoso . 7
Rondo brillante in B minor . 10
Ditto, ditto in E flat . . 9

Mozart.

No. 2 in A . . . 1
No. 4 in B flat . . 2
No. 5 in C . . . 1
No. 6 in E flat . . 2
No. 7 in C minor . . 1
No. 8 in D minor . . 10

No. 10 in C . . . 1
No. 11 in B flat . . 1
No. 13 in D . . . 1
No. 15 in B flat . . 2
No. 16 in C . . . 1
No. 17 in E flat, for two Pianos 3
No. 20 in D . . . 1
For three Pianos, in F . . 1

Paderewski.

Fantaisie Polonaise . . 1

Raff.

In C minor . . . 1
Suite in E flat . . 1
Menuet and Gavotte from
Suite, E flat . . 5

Rheinberger.

In A flat . . . 1

Ries.

Larghetto and Rondo, Con-
certo, E flat . . 1

Rubinstein.

No. 3 in G major . . 2
No. 4 in D minor . . 1
Fantasia in C, Op. 86 . . 1

Saint-Saëns.

No. 2 in G minor . . 5
No. 3 in E flat . . 1
No. 4 in C minor . . 1

Schubert.

Fantasia in C, instr. by Liszt . 3

Schumann.

In A minor . . . 14
Concertstück, Op. 92 . . 1

Stojowski.

In F sharp minor . . 1

Tschaikowsky.

No. 2 in G (Andante and
Finale) . . . 1
In B flat minor . . 1

Volkmann.

Concertstück in C, Op. 42 . 1

Weber.

In C 2
In E flat . . . 4
Concertstück in F minor . 16
Polacca in E, instr. by Liszt . 1

CONCERTOS, RONDOS, &c. VARIOUS INSTRUMENTS.

SOLOS.—PIANO.

Silas.

Gavotte	1

Stojowski.

Prelude, Valse, and Cosaque Fantastique . . .	1

Thalberg.

Andante in D flat, Op. 32 .	2
Study in A minor, Op. 30 .	6
Fantasia on ' Mosé in Egitto,' Op. 33	2
Finale di Lucia, Op. 43 . .	1
' Home, sweet Home ' . .	7
Funeral March in B flat minor	1

Momento Capriccioso . .	1
Adagio and Rondo from Sonata, Op. 24 . . .	1
Rondo from Op. 24	
Menuetto from Sonata, Op. 24	
Scherzo and Rondo from Op. 39	3
Sonata in D minor, Op. 42 .	3
Rondo brillante in E flat, Op. 62	1
Invitation à la Valse, Op. 65 .	5
Polacca in E, Op. 72 . .	3

Zimmermann.

Gavotte in E minor . .	1

SOLOS, VARIOUS INSTRUMENTS.

Ariosti, Attilio.

Largo and Allemande, Violoncello	1

Bach.

Chaconne, Violin . . .	7
Prelude and Fugue in G minor, ditto	1
Adagio and Allegro in C ditto .	3
Prelude in E, ditto . . .	2
Menuet and Gavotte in E, ditto	1
Bourrée and Double in B minor, ditto . .	1
Prelude and Bourrée in C, Violoncello . . .	1
Sarabande and Gavotte in D, ditto	1
Ditto, Violoncello . . .	1

Bargiel.

Adagio, Violoncello, Op. 38 .	1

Belloli.

Quartet, four Horns . .	1

Boccherini.

Sonata in A, Violoncello .	2
Largo in C, ditto . .	1

Brahms.

Hungarian Dances, Violin (Joachim) . . .	1

Hungarian Dances, Violin (Joachim) Nos. 17, 18, 20, 15	2

Fitzenhagen.

Perpetuum Mobile, Violoncello	1

Joachim.

Romanza in B flat, Violin .	3
Ditto from Hungarian Concerto, ditto . . .	1

Handel.

Sonata in A, Violin .	2
Ditto in D, ditto . .	4

Leclair.

Sarabande and Tambourin, Violin	3

Locatelli.

Sonata in D, Violoncello .	2

Marcello.

Sonata in F, Violoncello .	2

Mendelssohn.

Sonata in F minor, Organ .	1

Nardini.

Andante, Violoncello . .	1

Nessera, Josef.

Ekloge in G, Violin . . 1

Paganini.

Caprice in A minor, Violin . 1
Le Mouvement Perpétuel,
ditto 2
Le Streghe, ditto . . . 1

Piatti.

Siciliana in A minor, Violoncello 1
Ossian's Song, ditto . . 1

Popper.

Feuillet d'Album in B flat, Cello 1
Mazurka in D, ditto . . 1
Nocturne, ditto . . . 1
Minuet and Spinnlied, ditto . 1
Tarentelle, ditto . . . 1

Raff.

Cavatina, violin . . . 1

Ries, Franz.

Mouvement Perpétuel in G,
from 1st Suite, Violin. . 1

Sarasate.

Spanish Dances, Violin . . 1
Malaguena and Habanera, ditto 1

Schumann.

Abendlied, Violin . . . 4
Ditto, Violoncello . . . 1

Spohr.

Barcarole in G, Violin . . 3
Scherzo in D, ditto . . 2
Adagio and Finale, from Duet
in D, two Violins . . 1
Duet in G minor, Op. 67,
No. 3, ditto . . . 1
Duet in D for two Violins . 2

Stanford, Villiers.

Three Irish Fantasias, Lament, Hush Song, and Reel,
Violin 1

Tartini.

Le Trille du Diable, Violin . 5

Veracini.

Largo and Gigue, Violoncello . 2

Vieuxtemps.

Rêverie in E flat, Violin . 3
Tarentelle in A minor, ditto . 2
Air Bohémien, ditto . . 1
Air Varié in D, ditto . . 2
'Voix du Cœur,' ditto . . 1

CONCERTED INSTRUMENTAL WORKS.

Bach.

Sonata in A, Piano and Violin 2

Beethoven.

Quintet in E flat, Op. 16 . 1
Septet, Op. 20 . . . 2
Sonata in G, Op. 30 . . 2
Kreutzer Sonata, Op. 47 . 2
Andante con Variazioni, from
Op. 47 11
Ottetto in E flat, Op. 103, wind
instruments . . . 1

Chopin.

Grande Polonaise, Piano and
Violoncello, in C, Op. 3 . 1

Chopin and Franchomme.

Duo sur Robert le Diable,
Piano and Cello . . . 1

Dussek.

Andante and Rondo, from
Sonata B flat, Piano and
Violin 2

Dvorák.

Four Romantic Pieces, Piano
and Violin . . . 1

Grieg

Sonata, Piano and Violin . 1

Heller and Ernst.

'Pensées fugitives,' Piano and
Violin 2

Hummel.

Andante and Scherzo, from
Septet, Op. 74 . . . 1

INDEX

PRINTED BY
SPOTTISWOODE AND CO., NEW-STREET SQUARE
LONDON

www.ingramcontent.com/pod-product-compliance
Lightning Source LLC
Chambersburg PA
CBHW030942110726
47900CB00004B/1089